Kudzu!

Beyond Control

By Rosemary Coven

M. Deborah Bowden writing as Rosemary Coven

Formatted for Publication by
Pen It! Publications, LLC.

Copyright: The Harp Tree Publishing

© 2016

THE HARP TREE
PUBLISHING

Theharptreepublishing@yahoo.com

ISBN #:   0-9894331-6-1

ISBN #:   978-0-9894331-6-7

Cover Photography by: Jude Edwards

First Edition © 2016

Other Books by M. Deborah Bowden

Children's Books:

Mr. Bramble Bones Is Too Cold to Play *

Mr. Bramble Bones and Grimmy Clean Up *

Mr. Bramble Bones and Grimmy Share a Home *

The Sack Lunch *

Felicia Tales

Memoirs and Eclectica:

Daylilies and Nightshades

Dandelions and other Weeds *

Nonfiction:

Pat and Little Pat: A Slightly Unconventional Cookbook

Little Lestoil Ladies*

*Available on Amazon

All books are available signed by the author on
www.buymebooksnow.com

Also available on Amazon

M. Deborah Bowden
Writing as Rosemary Coven
rosemarycoven@yahoo.com

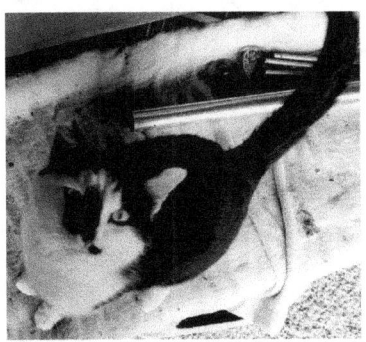

Lily

Acknowledgements

A special thank you to Jude Edwards, my photographer

Thank you to Ron Collins for editing my book line by line and for making it better.

TABLE OF CONTENTS

Tuesday

Wednesday

Kudzu! Beyond Control

Prelude

The afternoon was hot and steamy due to an earlier thunderstorm. There had been a lot of rain that summer—too much. But then, it was an unusual summer in many ways. There was more heat than normal, and Georgia in the summer is hot enough. The heat coupled with the rain turned much of the South into a lush jungle. It was hard for people to avoid the whispered worries about the greenhouse effect. The plants didn't mind; they exploded with unprecedented growth in the raised humidity. They spread faster and farther with *each* storm. Maybe it was the nitrogen raining down when the lightning split the air. Whatever it was, the vegetation loved it.

And kudzu loved it the most.

KUDZU FOUND IN INDIANA!

The plant that ate the South is now found in 150 known locations in Indiana. The Indiana Department of Natural Resources, Division of Entomology and Plant Pathology leads the ongoing effort to control kudzu with herbicide treatments. Many years of treatment and monitoring are needed as the kudzu vines (Pueraria montana) have enormous tubers weighing 300 pounds and are masters at retaining energy. Its vines can grow more than a foot a day.

The Division of Entomology has maps of infestation by counties and basic facts about the plant and treatment program.

If you believe kudzu is on your property, contact in.gov/dnr/entomolo/4538. htm.

Reprint from the
South-Central Bugler:

Newspaper Blurb from the South-Central Bugler

Prologue

The mountainous road was uncomfortably narrow with no berm and no room. Vines slithered down the stone walls like snakes, crossed the asphalt, and dived into a deep valley. Other than the bare rock, everything was a rich green. Even the thoroughfare was carpeted in several spots. The man couldn't enjoy the distant view where sky and mountains met; he had to concentrate on steering his motorcycle.

This was Highway 57, and his family had driven it almost daily. As a little boy watching from the back window in his car seat, he had become familiar with each bend or twist. He trusted his daddy's skill. So when he turned sixteen and acquired a license, he knew to be respectful of *this* road, and listened carefully to instructions. After eighteen years of driving cars, the family's fruit and flower vans, and his motorcycle, he was so familiar with its every flaw that he could navigate each nightmarish mile with his eyes closed. With that familiarity, came a confidence and lack of concern for the hairpin curves and stomach-churning drops. He wore a helmet but no leather clothing because of the heat and humidity. It wouldn't have helped anyway as flesh-ripping asphalt was the least of the worries for anyone losing control of a vehicle.

The mountains were ancient and eroding. Small landslides were common. The man knew this and drove cautiously. But sap-filled vines, slippery and as dangerous as loose gravel, criss-crossed the roadway. He drove over several, and the bike's front wheel slipped, flinging one vine into his back wheel where it caught in the spokes, then snapped like a rubber band stretched too tight. The tug angled the vehicle toward the valley and destabilized its owner. He wobbled, trying to gain control, but more of the vines wound into the spokes. The motorcycle veered toward the deep valley in spite of his frantic efforts. The long tendrils, stretched to their limit, yanked the bike off its wheels. Driver and cycle tumbled over the side.

The vehicle swung by its back wheel over the steep slope like a metronome's needle while he grabbed for vines, saplings, anything to stop his fall. Leaves and branches tore at his face and friction bloodied his hands, but he slowed, and stopped. He breathed a sigh and a prayer, thanking God that he was alive because his family desperately needed him. Twisting the vines around his wrists, he used them to climb.

The long stems holding the motorcycle split, sending the bike tumbling toward its owner below. It hit an outcrop, bounced clear, and sailed past. It slammed into the cliff below him and dangled there, caught in a web of vegetation.

He was unharmed, and continued his slow climb. Vines slid toward him as if offering hand-holds, but they were unaccustomed to a man's weight, and weren't strong enough. Tendrils holding to branches twisted and released, unintentionally jerking their victim like the end of a whip and throwing him into more interwoven stems which wrapped around his neck, arms, and legs, swaddling him like mummy wrappings. The man rolled downward like a yoyo, and like a yoyo which comes to the end of its string and snaps back, so did he. His neck broke. His body swung back and forth.

Tried.   Failed.   Sad!   Young kudzu vines waved bye-bye.

Sunday

Chapter 1

Hailey plugged in her iPhone, leaned back in the car seat, and closed her eyes. She couldn't get the smell of weed killer out of her nose. She'd been half sick all week and her mom had been worse—vomiting and unable to take many of Jen's wedding pictures. At least her mother wasn't the only professional photographer there, and Hailey still managed her bridesmaid's duties. Nice trip—her cousin's Gatlinburg wedding complete with almost daily thunder storms, oppressive heat, and people obsessing over an invasive plant. At least Indiana wasn't quite as hot, and the invasive honeysuckle was actually enjoyed for its fragrant flowers.

Hailey cast a worried glance at her mom, who was pale as flour. *She's either got to eat more or buy smaller clothes*, she thought. *Maybe Jen's wedding was too soon after the cancer. Mom won't admit it, but she's still pretty weak. We should be going home, not this stupid side trip to "reconnect with family." Why's she so afraid the cancer'll come back? She beat it, and if it comes back, she'll beat it again. She's still the same ol' iron rod she's always been.* Yet something nagged at her; something that said that wasn't entirely true. *Maybe Mom won't get it all back, but we don't need to spend ten days with some cousins named Henry and Alice Parks. Mom's not going to die and "leave her only child all alone."*

Well, strangers for family had to be better than an abusive, alcoholic, son-of-a-bitching father. She never called James her dad, not for years. Where the hell was he in all this? She hated him. She'd felt the cruel disappointment and soul-deep hurt for so long that thinking about him no longer brought stinging tears nor constricted breathing.

Still, mom's fear confused her; she seemed defeated somehow, some confidence lost. But she was healed and Hailey wanted her to be herself. Really, she should totally be herself any time now. But instead, things had changed, and Hailey knew it; maybe her mother's fear was temporary. At least she hoped so. And this trip wasn't necessary; they were fine just the way they were. They didn't have any issues really, nothing pressing anyway. Hailey shrugged and stared out the window.

She just wanted to get back home to chill with her friends before college. She loved being in the wedding and having fun with Jen's friends. But this side trip was cutting into her summer time. She wasn't ready for all the changes college might hold; she'd had enough upheaval when her mom was sick. She wanted one last normal summer before her home gang split in all directions. Maybe she wasn't ready for the big world yet; she was fearful too. Hailey knew where Marla was coming from, but she doubted her mom understood what she was feeling.

She'd offered to drive when they left Gatlinburg, but Marla was stubborn and just handed Hailey the scribbled directions.

"I'm fine. You navigate. Your GPS will only help part-way," Marla had said. "You've never driven in the mountains. There'll be fog."

"It's summer," Hailey said.

"There's always some fog higher up. It might be thick because of rain, and the roads could be slick."

Hailey didn't argue. She knew her mother needed to feel some of her old "I-can-handle-this" attitude. Maybe that was the real reason for this trip. New challenges, not stupid fear. Hailey was done with handling things; that cancer episode was enough. She was only eighteen; too young yet for tons of responsibility in her opinion. That was still mom's job.

There *was* fog. At first it was faint. Then when the rain started, it wrapped their world in a white shirt. Marla slowed to a crawl and kept going.

Near Cheryworth, the rain became a mist. Heated asphalt sent shimmering vapors up as fast as the mist came down, not quite a fog, but close. The GPS announced 57 East—left, two miles ahead. Strange....no cars.

Hailey gaze was unfocused as she looked out the window. Everything outside appeared to be covered in a green blanket. She knew there were trees under that blanket, but they were overwhelmed with vines. It was a surreal landscape of oddly bubbling shapes beneath that green mass. It reminded Hailey of a horror movie she was stuck watching with a friend where ghosts were trying to push their way through a wall. She remembered the outlined hands and screaming faces silhouetted behind wallpaper. She didn't like horror movies and that one gave her the creeps for weeks; she felt like she was reliving that scene now. Only the movement here was in slow motion. Those trees were being lulled by some sweet fragrance not unlike lavender and honeysuckle mixed with sandalwood. She sensed fear and hopelessness; the trees were dead or dying. Hailey shook her head to clear it. Inside the air-conditioned car, she sensed the fragrance more than smelled it, but she felt its affects.

Bad time to doze, she thought.

Hailey was an empath; she could "sense" people by the time she was two. By three she added animals and plants. Now rock stresses held sounds. This sensing came and went as capriciously as flitting ghosts; it wasn't something she could count on every day. The thoughts or feelings she picked up often were unconnected pictures which she had to decipher, and she wasn't always certain what it meant. Her grandma had the "talent" and so had other family members. However, as far as Hailey knew, only Marla and she were left. The others had died of old age; so there was no one to guide her as her sensing grew.

Marla claimed no such ability, but Hailey knew better. Granted, her mother didn't have a lot, but she did have some. It was always there when needed. Hailey worried whether the chemo, which had weakened Marla physically, had decreased that ability. If it had, then Hailey was alone, and she didn't want that burden. Sometimes trauma could open up the blocked senses in her family and increased such abilities, or so she had heard from Grams. She prayed it had increased rather than decreased, but only time would tell. Right now she hoped her mother wasn't sensing those trees or the fragrance. With her ear buds in and thinking, she didn't notice when the car turned onto 57.

Marla's sudden panic flooded through Hailey and jerked her out of her lethargy as if she'd been attacked by an electric eel. "Mom," she almost blurted, but stopped short, sensing that any spoken word might unnerve her already tense mother.

..........<>..........

Marla had only been down Highway 57 once seventeen years earlier, and her dad had done the driving. He had been as tight as a guitar string the entire time. She had wondered why; now she knew. She wasn't prepared for this road; no map or written directions could do it justice.

Without warning, Highway 57 twisted like a corkscrew, first clockwise, then counterclockwise. It climbed upward. It slid downward. Narrow lanes hugged the sheer mountain face to the left, then contradicted themselves, and hugged to the right like a bracket fungus circling a gigantic tree trunk. There was no berm or guard rails to help unsuspecting travelers. Rubble and boulders lay where they fell, on or off the pavement. Vertical valleys dropped into nauseating oblivion;

their true depths hidden by woven vines. And those valleys, seen only from the corners of her eyes, gave Marla vertigo. Her frail hands fought against turning the wheel toward the edge. Nausea caught in her throat and she had trouble breathing. The slippery asphalt and limited visibility were hellish. She shifted down to first. With a white-knuckled grip on the steering wheel, Marla begged for cars, humans.

"I can't see! This fucking mist!" Marla shouted. She was petrified and well aware that her life and Hailey's depended on her making no mistakes. Trailing vines, which dangled down the rock's face like long fingers reaching for the car, distracted her. They waved in the eddies created by her passing while some even snaked across the road. They felt dangerous and she didn't like that feeling at all.

A red truck came around the bend toward her. That one lone vehicle felt like someone had thrown a life preserver her way; there really were humans out here. Marla felt calmer. But another hair-pin curve immediately demanded her attention.

Eyes following that curving pavement, she didn't expect a large motor home to suddenly appear out of the mist. She hit the brakes to prevent rear-ending it. Then another one, as big as the first, appeared behind her. ...*what you wish for*, she thought.

The RV in front blocked her entire view, and she had no idea which way the road would turn next; she could only follow blindly. It made a good road break, but it went faster than she wanted to go. She couldn't slow down because the motor home behind road her bumper, and she had nowhere to pull over and let it pass. Her nails cut into her hands. She didn't even feel it.

..........<>..........

Hailey didn't understand her mother's panic. Then she looked out the window and stifled a gasp when she realized the cliff fell off into nothing only a few inches from their car's tires. She swallowed away the lump in her throat and glanced at her mom. Now she understood *why* her mom was so freaked. Marla's lips were drawn tight, and her hands were shaking. Not a good sign.

She was glad she hadn't actually cried out. She stayed as quiet and immobile as possible; the last thing she wanted was to scare her mother now. Even when the motor homes suddenly appeared and her mother threw on the brakes, Hailey didn't speak. She kept her eyes focused on the road bikes attached to the rig in front of their car to keep from looking toward the side window or her mother.

They crept around and around the mountain on the twisted road. The misty rain, rising road vapors, and water thrown back from the large wheels ahead made visibility worse. Hailey knew her mom was blindly following the tail lights in front of her, and casting her dice to fate that neither driver made mistakes. Images of the top-heavy rigs sliding out of control—brakes failing, turning over and taking the car with them flashed from mother to daughter. She knew her mother's hands were sweating.

Hailey felt her own panic as well as Marla's. It was almost too much to cope with double. The road twisted again, and *she* was next to the mountain while her *mother* faced oblivion. Back and forth, rock face, then sheer drop. Contrasts. This trip, so far, held contrasts. Hailey listed as many as she could think of, starting from home. It kept the fear contained.

"Turn signals! What the hell? Why're they using their turn signals? There's nowhere to turn!" Hailey heard her mom screech. Then they saw. The road widened and a state park sign marked the entrance which veered right. Both motor homes turned in. Marla pulled over, cut the engine, and stared at the sign.

"A state park! On this road, a state park, and RV's!" Marla chattered.

Now that they had stopped, Hailey sensed a powerful presence out there in the park, but it felt angry, hurt, and bitter. *"What gives?"* she thought and hoped her mom didn't notice. Probably too scared, she thought, and forced a smile.

She watched her mother draw a quivery breath and hold it like her Yoga instructor taught her. Both knew that park sign meant civilization and help. Marla breathed out and calmed down. It took five minutes of deep breathing before she was ready to tackled 57 again, but Hailey felt her mother's sweating palms.

"I guess if motor homes can survive this snake trail, we can too. But I can't do it again for a while; thank God I won't have to for ten days. Maybe there's another way. I don't care if it's longer. Get out Alice's directions; I hope I copied them right," Marla said.

"Mom, we have cell phones with GPS. We can call if we can't figure it out." Hailey spoke in a quiet, even tone, hoping her voice would be soothing. She didn't mention possible dead zones because she had never known her mother to be so rattled. Maybe she subconsciously felt that oddness in the park.

"I forget. Wasn't that long ago that cell phones didn't exist and neither did GPS's," her mother said. "You had to stop at a house and hope someone was home, and didn't have a mean dog or a gun and would let you make a call if you gave them some money to pay for that call, if it was long distance, and hope they wouldn't just shut the door in your face. Then you'd have to walk to another house and try again. There's no help if we go off the road. I wish I'd activated this car's Onstar. Didn't think I could afford it with all the bills." Marla chattered, tears raining down.

"We're okay," Hailey reminded her again.

She continued to keep her voice low. Her mother was her protector and shield, the strong woman who had stood up to the pedophile when Hailey was seven, that carnival owner when she was trapped and hurt on a ride, that alcoholic father with the poverty and abuse he brought, and the grandparents who rejected them both. Marla won out over all of it, and the two of them had survived and even moderately prospered.

But Hailey was just as scarred as her mother. The night Marla returned from the hospital, still weak from the surgeries and a massive infection which threatened her life, Hailey crawled into bed with her and held tight. She felt that her mother might disappear, and Mom was the only glass boat on a river of acid.

It was only last month that Hailey began sleeping in her own bed. She told herself that everything was okay, and that she needed to break free since college was only two months away. Try as she might though, she still couldn't get over her fear. Being two hours away in a dormitory with some strange roommate seemed much too far.

Eighteen months ago this road would not have fazed Marla. *Mom'll get it back*, Hailey told herself again. The more her mom talked, the better.

"Sorry." Marla shook her head, pulling back onto the highway. "What are we looking for...what road next?"

"County road 54. Alice's directions say it'll be on the left."

"On the left! Is there a tunnel in the rock or do we take a dive?"

"This road's going to straighten out, Mom. Take it easy. The notes say 54 is short and will turn to gravel about half-way, be prepared. We're looking for a horseshoe-shaped road called Seed Tick—it has two entrances off 54."

Hailey mumbled to herself, "We get to ford a stream either way. Nope, that's scratched out. The water runs over the road if we take the first entrance. It runs under the road with the other entrance. Maybe we should look for the second one because the water might be too deep. No wonder Alice said the GPS wouldn't work right."

"I can't hear what you just said. Just tell me when to turn." Marla said. Tears and sweat dripped down her face.

"We can always call if we get lost. Someone'll come get us." Hailey continued to use a soothing voice to calm her mother, but inside she wasn't calm; she was still feeling something, somewhere. It was old and carried power.

Conversation would be good to stop these feelings for both of them, Hailey decided. "So tell me about these cousins we're visiting...Alice and Henry."

"I don't remember a lot about them. Henry had a stroke a couple years ago and their son David's a florist. He has Asperger's. And they have a hired hand named Tilfort. Alice said he's a little odd." Marla said, green eyes still glued to the road."

"What's Asperger's?"

"A high-functioning form of autism. People who have it seem normal but fixate on things. David's fixation is flowers, so he's a florist. He had therapy growing up to help him with his communication and social skills. I guess he's fine now. Maybe you can learn enough from him to work in a flower shop for college money."

The conversation was working. Marla had stopped crying and shaking, although she was still gripping the wheel and her nails were still cutting her palms. Hailey could feel the pain in her own hands.

"Does he have brothers or sisters?" she asked.

"Not any longer. Ashley had cancer, and John had a motorcycle accident on this road!" Marla said, her grip tightening even more. "He's the youngest at thirty-four." She flashed her daughter a grateful smile and tried more deep breathing. "Talking helps, thanks."

The misty rain stopped as they found 54. The clouds broke up and a hint of sunshine bled through which made it hotter and more humid. Hailey concentrated on the directions, but the road refused to match them.

An hour later, with several stops and two phone calls, they reached their destination. Alice and Henry lived eight miles off the highway, but to Marla and Hailey, it was much more. Somehow they missed the stream over Seed Tick. It didn't matter, they were just glad to arrive unscathed.

Chapter 2

The car pulled into the crescent-shaped driveway in front of Alice and Henry's place. The one-story house was painted yellow, trimmed in brown and white. Hailey opened the car door and noticed that the driveway was edged with geodes. After the air conditioned car, the Georgia heat and humidity hit like a blast from a glass furnace.

She climbed out and looked around. A connected garage stood on the right. Hailey could tell that it had been remodeled into a living space because the bay door was replaced with two windows, and a lamp sat inside.

There was a veranda, complete with cushioned furniture which was perfect for lazy afternoons. Hailey wasn't sure why the house sat on concrete block pillars rather than a solid foundation, but this was the South, not Indiana.

Hailey sighed and relaxed. So far, so good, she thought to herself. She didn't notice that she had been holding her breath, perhaps expecting….she didn't know what. There did seem to be a lot of vines snaking around, near the left side of the house, and across the road. She also saw a barn, behind and to the right of the house. Over its top and up the side, where she could see, were more vines. A green tractor and a green station wagon sat just inside its wide opening. Both had vines on them too. Hailey wasn't sure if the vines made the vehicles green or if that was their paint color. A blue van sat under a huge tree nearby.

Hailey didn't like the look of those vines; they gave her an eerie feeling on the back of her neck as if she needed to whirl around and face something. For no particular reason, she wished she were back in Gatlinburg in that manicured wedding garden with Jen's boisterous friends. As pretty as the setting here was, Hailey felt uneasy. *Just nerves,* she thought. *Crazy road, new people.* She shook it off. *Bad time to let on.*

Hailey was concentrating so hard on studying the property that she jumped when Marla tapped the horn as she climbed out of the driver's side. A woman waved from a window. Hailey assumed it was Alice.

Noticing the frown on Hailey's face, she said, "Why so serious? They've had more rain here, so it looks like a jungle. No leopards though."

Hailey looked at her mother and saw behind that cheerful voice that Marla was sensing something too. *I guess I'm not alone. There is something left of normal here after all.*

………..<>………..

Alice was in the kitchen washing a cookie sheet when she heard the car horn. She looked out the large window.

"They're here," she said to her husband who was sitting at the dining table behind her. He was squeezing a rubber ball with his left hand and staring at the floor. He looked up when she spoke. Alice removed her apron and used it to wipe the sweat from her face. The fan on the counter didn't help much—not with this humidity. She walked through the wide doorway and stood in front of him, hands on hips.

"Let me he'p you up," she offered.

Henry shook his head. "I can do it, thank'ee anyway." He braced himself with his right elbow, then hand, and pushed up, balancing on his right leg. He stumbled but caught himself. Four years had made him adept in this method. He looked at his quad-cane, but decided against it.

"Smile," Alice encouraged him by smiling herself. "Let's go greet our cousins. Marla's lookin' fit, and Hailey's right pretty."

Henry smiled at his wife. "You can tell all that from the window?"

"Naturally! Now come along."

..........<>..........

Alice rushed out to greet them. Hailey appraised her approaching relative. She wasn't used to seeing a woman in a flowered shirtwaist dress, white anklets, and laced brown flats. Her own mother wore jeans of various lengths and colors. Alice had a sweet face framed in curly white hair, but her faded green eyes, thin frame, and lined forehead spoke of heartache and stress. There was something wild behind those eyes too, like a touch of insanity. *Pretty spry for seventy-something, got Mom's curly hair, wonder if it used to be blond too,* Hailey thought.

Her eyes looked past Alice toward the man emerging from the house. She figured this was Henry. He looked sucked dry from work, weather, and worry. His braced left leg slowed him down. She noted he was hesitant to leave the porch, but must have decided to keep up appearances, and braved the four shallow steps and gravel drive. His left hand gripped the handrail as he descended, but he couldn't open his fingers to let go; he used his right hand to open them. He walked towards them, concentrating as he came. Hailey noticed he tried to hide his dragging foot. *Still some pride left*, she thought, sensing his determination.

Behind Henry was an excited, barking dog, asking to be allowed out. He gave up waiting for permission and bashed into the screen door; it flew open. Tongue lolling to the side, he headed straight for Hailey. His tail was wagging his body as he wrapped himself around her legs.

Smiling, she lowered her hand for the pit bull/boxer mix

to sniff and withdrew it sopping wet from the licks. A picture of himself standing at attention flashed in Hailey's head. She assumed he was telling her he was the protector. With animals, she didn't get many words, mostly images which she had to interpret. Sometimes it wasn't easy, but this dog seemed special. Maybe he was better at communicating than the average pooch.

"Kingston, stop that," Alice said, trying to control her laughter. "He gets so excited when we have company, which isn't often. He likes you. You're Hailey. I'd recognize you as family anywhere; you look just like your mama and your Grandpa Gar. Got his red hair too and down to your waist. Just look at those big brown eyes. You were a baby the last time I saw you—Gar brought you and Marla here. Proud as he could be—thought he'd swell up nigh on to bustin'. Give me a hug, sweetie pie. You too, Marla, hugs and kisses all around. Henry, hurry up here. Give your family a big ol' hug. Kingston, get out of his way 'for you knock him down. Who you guardin', silly dog. You don't have to protect Marla and Hailey from Henry. Get!"

Hailey smiled. It looked like Kingston couldn't decide which person to rub against—Marla or herself. He wouldn't let Henry get to either woman. Alice had to grab him by the collar and hang on. He pulled her around in a circle, making her dizzy and knocking her glasses crooked. Marla caught her before she tripped. All three were laughing at the dog's antics.

"Kingston, heel!" Henry murmured. The dog returned to him and sat down.

Henry looked at Hailey and Marla with a crooked grin.

"Kingston's a mighty-good watch dog. He can tell good people from bad. Sometimes I'm sure he's got the sense because he knows when danger's sniffin'. If family's hurt, Kingston knows it ahead of time, and lets you know...like when John died." A shadow crossed his face when he said this. Then he smiled and said, "Lord he'p ye if ye get on his bad side. Wouldn't know what to do without this dog; I love him like my own self." He reached down and patted the dog's head and got licked in return. He looked up,

"David's out in the greenhouse fertilizin'. Sure does love his flowers."

"Kingston, go get David, get David." Henry waved his left arm toward the back of the house.

The dog perked up his ears. He knew a command when he heard one. His eyes followed the man's hand and he understood where to find David. Off he ran.

"Let's go back inside. He'll be here directly. Tilfort's around here somewhere. I suspect he'll come along too. Can I he'p ye carry anythin' in—can't lift much, but I'm still good for somethin'," Henry said.

"Now, Henry, we don't need to go haulin' stuff inside right now. Let the girls rest. It took them an hour to come eight miles." Her eyes sparkled with amusement as she looked sideways at Marla.

"I know how to get here now," Marla said. "Fifty-seven really unnerved me. Like Dad used to say, 'it's as crooked as a dog's hind leg' and that's my excuse. These roads may be well marked, but the signs have vines growing on them so you can't read the words or symbols. They're all over everything, even the poles and electric lines. The trees and ground look like they've been covered with a green tarp."

"I don't think Mom spotted it, but there's a truck on 54 that's covered except for part of the cab. It's sitting near something else buried in vines, maybe a garage," said Hailey.

Alice said nothing, but a crooked grimace twitched her mouth as she quickly turned toward the house. Hailey saw.

Henry led the way. The women held back as he climbed the porch steps, holding to the heavy iron railing with his good right hand and dragging his braced foot up each step. He opened the screen door and held it while the others entered.

Hailey noticed there wasn't a rug in sight. *Maybe Alice took them up so Henry wouldn't trip*, she speculated. However, the oak floors were slick with polish. *Looks like Alice is a bit compulsive*. Both women took careful steps to avoid sliding.

"That's kudzu, you saw," Henry said. "It's takin' over everywhere here-bouts. Our peach orchard out back is completely gone. We were able to hold some of it back 'til I had my stroke and John died. Then we had a talk and decided to let it go. It was too much for Tilfort. It's all he and David can do to keep it away from his flowers. We lost all that peach money, so the flower business is the only income we have outside of social security. I can't he'p anymore. Breaks m' heart, but that's that."

Henry looked defeated as if a light just winked out. His hand shook. *He's carrying a load*, Hailey thought.

"That orchard brought in some good money, it surely did. We were sorry to lose both—money and fruit," Alice said. "The trees were plumb strangled by the heavy vines; coiled around their trunks and broke off their limbs. Then covered them over and blocked the sun so they starved."

"We make do like everybody else," Henry said and smiled. "Let's sit down and get reacquainted.

He's trying to lighten it up, Hailey figured.

But Alice didn't move. Her eyes widened and she spoke directly to Marla in a conspiratorial tone.

"You're family; you'll understand what I'm saying. I could hear those trees cryin' out for us to he'p them, especially in the dark. Even Kingston tried to bite the vines off. I walked the floor many a night, couldn't sleep, knowin' those trees were dyin' and beggin' us for help. Their fearful screams gave me nightmares when I did sleep. We loved those peach trees; the children played in them, comin' in all sticky from eatin' so much fruit. They're all dead now; it only took two years to lose all thirty acres. Sometimes I still shudder rememberin' all that...murder--I guess I'd call it."

Hailey looked at Marla. *Poor Mom, she's wearing her frozen smile and stiff back look.*

Henry interrupted, still smiling, "Now Alice, it's just a vine. A bad one, but it can't murder. And you just imagined you heard the trees screamin' and cryin'. Trees don't make sounds, you know that."

He's getting embarrassed, Hailey noticed.

Alice glared at him. "You and David heard it; even Kingston. Why won't y'all admit it?" Alice said, sticking out her chin. "Marla will hear thin's, soon enough because Gar said she had the 'sense'. I figure she needs to know now that the subject's open."

So the cousins are like us; I wonder if Mom knew. Not the best timing, Alice, Hailey thought.

Alice, please. Let's not talk about it and spoil Marla's and Hailey's visit."

Alice shook herself and smiled at her cousins. "Sorry. Kudzu gets on my nerves. How about some sweet tea? I have some Muscadine jelly cookies, too. Sit right down there on the couch. No need for y'all to stand around in a heap."

"I'll help you," Marla said, rushing for the kitchen. Alice followed.

Hailey heard her say, "I'm not crazy, Marla." She didn't hear her mom say anything.

Hailey turned toward Henry, not knowing what to say after Alice's outburst; these people were strangers to her, and she had no common ground for a conversation. She looked into his eyes and smiled; they had lost that defeated look, and were bright and alert.

He sees more than he says, she thought. *I like him, at least, so far.*

"Well, we have orders to sit. That chair is right comfortable," Henry said, pointing to the chair on the left, and easing himself onto the couch.

David saved them from trying to find something to say. He swung the screen door wide to accommodate Kingston and a large flat of young plants.

Hailey looked him over. He was tall with blue eyes like Henry's and sported a mop of brown hair. *Not bad looking*, she thought.

"These are ready to be repotted," he said. "I was going to the barn, but Kingston demanded I come here first. Started dragging me by my pant leg." David sat the plants on the coffee table.

Kingston bounded toward Hailey. His nails tapped a dance rhythm on the bare oak floor as he slid into her. She patted his head, getting licked all the while.

"Yes, you're a smart dog. You should be proud of yourself," she whispered, sensing that only Henry gave him the attention and respect he deserved. *You are more than just a dog, aren't you*? He looked her right in the eyes, and a huge smile attached to his face formed in her mind. It was so silly that Hailey giggled.

Henry's talking drew her back to her cousins.

"Here now, set those plants off the table. Your mother's bringin' cookies and tea, and you're gettin' dirt and water all over where we need to put the food," Henry said good-naturedly to his son. "Hailey, this is David. We're used to dirt on all the tables, but I don't think y'are." He chuckled.

David put the plants on the floor and wiped his hands on his jeans. "Nice to see you," he said, extending his hand.

"Nice to meet you too," she said, shaking his hand. "Mom said you could teach me about flowers. It might help me get a better job than serving stir fry and burgers for college money," Hailey said.

A big smile crossed David's face. "Wow," he said. "Come

out and look at the greenhouse later. I can tell you about kudzu."

"You've made yourself a friend for life." Henry laughed. "We're so tired of listenin' about how to care for flowers or learnin' their names that we all run. Now he's got a fresh pair of ears."

Alice and Marla came bearing five teas and a huge plate of cookies.

"I heard you come in, David," Alice said. "Is Tilfort comin' too?"

"Hi, Marla, nice to see you," David said. "Sorry about the dirt."

"Nice to see you too. How's the flower business?" Marla sat the cookies on the table, ignoring the crumbs of vermiculite and potting soil, then joined Alice and Henry on the couch.

"Doing well. The kudzu keeps trying to take over the beds, but Til and I keep fighting back. Excuse me; I'm going to wash up. Mother won't want my grubby hands fingering the cookies." David smiled and walked toward the back of the living room. He stopped, remembering that he hadn't answered his mother.

"Til's not coming. He said something about family time. He'll be in for supper." David continued down the long narrow hallway, past bedrooms on either side, and disappeared into the only bath.

Alice looked at her husband. He nodded.

"Marla, I wrote in my letter that I needed to explain Tilfort," she said, taking Marla's hand.

Marla smiled, "I figured you'd tell me when the time was right."

Hailey recognized that flat smile and noncommittal voice her mother sometimes used with customers. *Mom's had enough*, she thought. *Not just the road and screaming peach trees, but Alice, in general....Now she gets Tilfort. We get Tilfort.* Hailey sighed softly.

"Tilfort's a little odd around the edges. I mean, y'all might think he's touched in the head, but he's not. He's smart. I don't think there's anything our son doesn't know about flowers, but he's not a business man. Tilfort does all the practical stuff. He's just, his thoughts are different." Alice looked at her husband for help.

"What Alice is sayin' is he rambles on somethin' fierce. He's overworked. That and the worry and the readin' too much science fiction is affectin' his brain. He reads books like *Day of the Triffids* and *The Body Snatchers*. He talks to himself all the time. I see him shakin' his fist at those kudzu vines. He's sure kudzu is thinkin' and plannin' trouble. Course, he might be right, you never know," Henry chuckled. "Y'all just be prepared."

"Be prepared for what?" David said, re-entering the room.

Alice and Henry jumped. They hadn't wanted David to hear what they had to say. Now they couldn't finish. Marla retrieved her hand.

"Talking about Tilfort's ideas? Plants do think. One witnessed a murder and solved the case." He grabbed two cookies and tea, sat down in a chair and leaned back.

Hailey's interest was piqued. "A plant was a murder witness? No way."

"It happened in Tacoma, Washington."

"Are you putting me on? This seems like science fiction."

"It happened. I saw it on a TV episode called 'The Flower Jury,' from *Beyond Belief*, and Tilfort found it in one of his books."

Hailey looked at him expecting him to say, "Gotcha," any minute now.

"I'm serious. Police found a florist murdered in his shop. Someone mentioned that the old man had a favorite flowering plant which he kept close by and talked to; he even named it. Neither the show nor the book said which plant; wish I knew because I'd grow some. It'd be a great story for selling my potted flowers. Anyway, one officer, just out of school, had studied that plants get stressed by things happening around them. He talked his partner into hooking a lie detector to that plant. Nothing happened when they questioned people until they brought in the nephew. Then the machine went nuts."

"Maybe he gave off electromagnetic energy that affected the machine. I have a girlfriend who can't wear a watch. It dies in thirty minutes," Hailey said. She still thought he was joking.

David shrugged. "They told him there was a witness, and the guy confessed."

"I've got to look this up. You better not be putting me on." Hailey pulled out her phone and Googled it. It took her a few tries, and she was about to give up. Then she found it.

"Oh My God, it's really true. You weren't trying to make an idiot out of me." She handed the phone to her mother to read.

"I just learned something new. You're cool!"

David smiled.

"Yup, a friend for life." Henry chuckled.

Alice turned back to Marla, but the moment had long passed. "Just be prepared," she whispered and touched her hand again. Marla continued reading the phone.

A loud "meow" and a bumping of the screen door startled Hailey. Kingston barked and scrambled for the door. He pushed it with his head just wide enough for a beautiful black and white cat to slide through. She pranced into the room, tail held high, and nails tapping that polished floor like fingers striking typewriter keys. She went straight to Alice and jumped into her lap.

The cat stared into Hailey's eyes. A vision of a big open eye and a talking mouth flashed in Hailey's head.

Hailey stared back, "What do you see? Who do you tell?" The cat looked around the room, then at Kingston. Then she licked her paw.

This one's special too, Hailey decided. *Maybe I can connect enough to hear words sometime.*

Alice smiled and petted her. "This is Lily, and just as spoiled as Kingston. She sooths me at night when thin's bother me. We talk. Many thin's keep me awake," her voice trailed off. Then she shook herself. "I'll be fixin' some supper directly. It's Sunday and Henry and I go to evenin' services; guess it's a habit these days, not pleasurable. Y'all are welcome to come with us. David won't be goin', and neither will Tilfort, so you won't be alone here if y'all decide not to.

"Marla, I can use your he'p; we'll take our time and talk. Henry, see if you can get any weather on television. It's been rainin' all this morning. I surely don't want it to start again tonight. Hopefully the satellite's not down again.

"David, you go get the girl's thin's and put them in the bedrooms. I'm puttin' Hailey in Ashley's old room, and Marla can have John's. There's air conditioners in each bedroom so if y'all get hot tonight, use them.

"Usually we don't mind the heat, we mostly turn on fans, but it gets real close at night. Sometimes I can't breathe. I blame it on this rain we've been havin'. It's rained more this year than I can ever remember. The plants love it; they're growin' so fast you can almost see them addin' inches a minute. They put out a lot of fragrance too. That doesn't he'p my breathing much either. It makes me light-headed.

"The creek that flows back by the orchard is overflowin'. It's turned that area into nearly a swamp. You can't tell because of all that kudzu coverin' the trees and ground. The land's lower there than here so the water stays back rather than floodin' the house and yard. That's a blessin'. The trees wouldn't have liked it, but they're dead now anyway, so I guess it doesn't matter." After her soliloquy, Alice abruptly turned and walked straight to the kitchen. Lily followed.

Marla stared after her, then looked at Henry. Her face asked a question concerning Alice.

"Later," Henry said.

Hailey turned to David. "I'll help you with our stuff. It'll get me out of kitchen duty." She looked into her mother's eyes, signaling to her, *I'll find out more*, and hooked her arm through David's. She led the way outside. He grinned at his father and allowed himself to be lead to the car.
Hailey opened the trunk and laughed when David whistled at the crammed space.

"I was in Jen's wedding" she said, "and Mom was the photographer. You should see her studio if you think this is a lot. Besides, a bridesmaid has to look good, and that means lots of stuff. I only need that one for clothes, and that little shoulder bag for the bathroom." She pointed to the smaller purple suitcase and bag. "Mom'll need that big red one with pouches on the front, and her camera equipment bag shouldn't be in the heat."

David shook his head and grabbed Hailey's bags. "After we get these things into the house, we'll move your car back by the barn. The sun's heat is intense out here with no trees. That big oak out there has plenty of shade," David said.

He led her down the hall to the first room on the left; she noticed that several floor boards squeaked when stepped on. Ashley's room was average-sized, but was unusual because of its two double-hung windows. They were mismatched and oddly placed in the wall overlooking the veranda. An antique iron bed sat lengthwise under one while the other housed an air conditioner. It wasn't perfectly fitted into the window. Hailey could see a little daylight on one side.

Then she noticed the wallpaper—pink and cream roses vining everywhere like intertwining snakes and topped with a gold painted ceiling, almost claustrophobic in its feel. Hailey assumed it hadn't been updated since Ashley was a child. A collection of antique dolls, garish clowns, and a ventriloquist dummy sat on a shelf.

Great! Lots of eyes, she thought. *Wish I could sleep with Mom and avoid the scary clowns, especially that big fat one; it's totally demonic. That dummy looks a little like Henry, so maybe I can think happy thoughts about it.*

There were no rugs in here either, and the bed was higher off the floor than more modern ones. Hailey could see underneath where a couple of pine knots had fallen through leaving holes. They resembled widely spaced eyes staring at her. She wondered if bugs or mice could crawl inside that way. A can lid was stapled to one plank under the air conditioner; Hailey assumed it covered another hole.

David said, "The bath is right behind this," David said. "And my room's behind the bath. If you want to see John's room, where your mother will be, follow me. It's right across from mine."

Hailey was curious so she took the invitation. Pine floors and no rugs. There were some covered holes in the floor too. The colors were better, tans with touches of blue.

Mom lucked out, she thought to herself. *I'm going to stuff those creepy toys in the closet whether anyone likes it or not. I'm not going to have nightmares just to be polite.*

"Mother and Daddy have the front room to the right," David said. "That room at the end there runs the length of the house. It's a sun room, or sleeping porch sometimes, with sliding glass doors and screens all around, and opens out to a back deck, but we don't use it much. Daddy sleeps there when the moon's whole. The sky is beautiful out those windows at sunset and with the windows opened, it's much cooler. My parents don't use an air conditioner, just a fan by their window. The heat doesn't seem to bother them. I guess their blood's thinner now that they're older. They used to sleep out here when it was too close in their room. Not anymore."

Hailey wasn't sure she should ask or not, but curiosity won. "Why not, I mean, if it's cooler out there. I get not using the air. Anymore, Mom only uses it when it's really humid. She used to use it all summer, but since the cancer, she'd rather listen to tree frogs or birds or bugs or wind. She bought a bunch of wind chimes, and put up ceiling fans. She says she doesn't like locking herself away from life to listen to a machine or breath "recycled air. Me, I'll take the air conditioner."

"Mother won't go back there because she can see the orchard to the left of the barn. She doesn't like to see the trees all covered with kudzu. She says she can see their dead limbs waving at her from under those vines. It does look eerie at night when the wind blows—like ghostly swaying giants. You'd never know a whole orchard was hidden underneath."

"Kudzu's leaves glow silver in the moonlight and there's a wild beauty to it under the whole moon. I really like the flowers and they're fragrant. I use them in my bouquets. You can smell them everywhere when the wind blows."

"Doesn't it bother you too? Sounds like you liked the plant," Hailey said.

"I haven't decided whether to love the plant or hate it. I guess I admire it."

"But it's taking over everything, isn't it?"

David shrugged and looked down the hall. "Yeah. The vines keep moving closer to the greenhouse and the flower gardens. It's on the barn now as well as inside. Til chops it back and sprays weed killer, but he can't keep up.

"I know you let the orchard go, but since you have less to keep clear, is it really so tough to control?"

"Very tough!" David said. "That tap root is seven inches in

diameter, goes down nine feet, and weighs 400 pounds. And if you try to dig it out, you can't leave any part of it. Even a little piece of root or vine left will start it up again. And those vines can be four inches in diameter and as woody and tough as an old tire, so they're hard to chop unless you use a sharp hatchet or ax. As many as thirty vines come out of the root crown and grow a foot each day in normal weather.

"Damn! That sounds like one heavy weight plant. Guess that's why everyone back at Jen's wedding was obsessed with killing it," Hailey said, impressed. "Weed killer everywhere. Made us sick."

"I don't believe the new herbicide the Forestry people gave us is working. Most don't and some act like fertilizer. I think that's what's happening here, but that's probably just my imagination.

"With the summer heat and all this extra rain, the stuff is growing faster than usual—two or three times. Til carries a sharp hatchet or ax with him all the time. He swears the vines follow him. I guess it's good that Mother doesn't look. She doesn't see what we see, Daddy too. But he plays it down because of Mama. So, don't think too bad on Til; he has his reasons."

David was lost in his thoughts, and just stared at the doorway to that back room. Hailey felt he was talking more to himself than her. She decided she needed to break the spell.

"Mom's bags are heavy, so I'll need your help." She touched his elbow to bring him back to the present, and felt turmoil and resentment vibrate through her fingers. She jumped. *Whoa! That's new. Am I adding touch-know to my sensing now?*

Her cousin seemed to wake up. "Sorry, I was just thinking. As soon as I get your mother's suitcase, I'll show you the kudzu flowers. Wait here." He turned and left the room.

While he was gone, she sneaked a peek into Alice and Henry's room. It was larger than the others with a bigger window. The glass was open and a breeze floated the long gauzy curtains. It had an inviting feel, all painted cool browns, creams, and greens. The pine floor was a silvery green.

I like this room the best, she thought. *I could get a good night's sleep here. Wonder why Alice can't.*

The sun room beckoned her for some reason--curiosity probably. She didn't particularly want to go back there and look through the windows at the dead orchard or the waters flooding it. Still it might give her some insight into the strange atmosphere at the house and the stranger chatter from her relatives. She dragged her feet down the hall.

The room itself was nicely decorated in a pale yellow. A brown rattan couch with matching chairs and a chaise lounge were scattered around facing outward to take full advantage of the view, or what would have been a beautiful view. Hailey had no trouble understanding why no one wanted to come in here. Looking through three sides of windows, she saw an alien invasion. The orchard dominated the land and sky, left, beyond the barn. It *was* a nightmare. Hailey gave Alice credit for that one.

More of the barn was covered than she had seen from the driveway--nearly the entire right side and part of the roof. Its twin gabled roof and opened doors was the face of a terrified victim watching itself being engulfed by a monstrous predator, and it was in shock. So was Hailey. She rushed out.

She met David dragging Marla's red case behind him. "I see why no one uses that back room any more. Why does Henry sleep there?" She followed him into John's room.

David left the big suitcase standing by the bed and sat down. He looked at the floor then up at Hailey and just stared at her chin a few seconds without answering. She could tell he'd made a decision.

"It's as good a time as any, I guess. Have a seat."

Hailey sat down next to him on the bed and deliberately bumped his shoulder as she did so. She felt turmoil rolling off him in waves, traveling from his shoulder to hers. *Here it comes*, she thought.

David didn't look at her as he spoke.

"Mother has had a rough time with Daddy's stroke, then John's death, and the orchard being strangled all in four years. Ashley went two years before that with brain cancer. We don't see her twin boys hardly as her husband Jimmy took them to North Carolina soon after she died. If Mother could see the boys more often, I think it would help ease her mind. All the misery has taken its toll on her. She started walking the floor during the day, back and forth, after Daddy's stroke. She seemed absent-minded like she was looking for something but couldn't remember what. I'd come in and find her. Since John's death, she's been sleepwalking and going outside, especially near whole-moon time.

"When kudzu took the orchard, she said she could hear the peach trees screaming. Now she hears 'whisperings'. She says kudzu is talking to itself, and she sees bodies hanging from the vines in the back yard.

"Couldn't it just be grief and depression?" Hailey said. "Or do you think she's picking up something psychically?"

"I don't know what to believe. I don't want to think her mind is going, but then, yes, she's a bit psychic. So maybe you're right. She's not like those television characters who solve crimes for the police. She's pretty weak, but sometimes she knows things a little ahead. Maybe she does hear kudzu whispering and maybe grief has taken over. If what she hears is real, it's affecting her mind because she can't shut it off."

"Have you taken her to a grief specialist, just in case it's something that can be helped?" Hailey asked. "Or maybe to another psychic who could help her learn how to control what she picks up? Mixing all that together could drive her crazy especially if it's real, and she doesn't know what to do about it. I ought to know."

David shook his head back and forth. "No, Daddy studied sleepwalking on line. Thought he could help her if he had information. He read about something called O'd energy, that's with a long O, which comes from the stars and sun. Gets stronger when the moon fills out—more reflected light then. The moon alters that light somehow. It bothers certain types of people and makes them walk in their sleep. It affects plants too.

"She always did have trouble sleeping, even back when—said the light was too bright or too hot and made her restless.

"But, now she's a danger to herself. She could break a leg or fall into the creek. With the flooded ground, we worry more. If Mother wandered into the dead trees and vines and woke up..." David shook his head. "Daddy sleeps in the sun room so he can hear when she goes out—she always goes out that back door. Kingston stays with him and lets him know.

"Daddy has a flashlight, and he tries to follow her, but with his bad leg, he has trouble. If she goes toward the water, he sends Kingston after Til and flashes the light at my window. The moon will be filled soon, so don't be surprised to see us all outside, walking around.

"Why don't you lock the door or wake her up before she gets outside?" Hailey was spooked.

"It stays locked at night; she unlocks it, and we don't want to wake her; it's bad to. At least that's what that web site said. We try to protect her until she wanders back in, and we get her into bed. She knows she sleepwalks; she sees her feet and sheets are dirty in the mornings. But she has no memory. Sometimes Mother says she dreams that she hears her name being called. That kudzu's calling her. Maybe that's the 'whisperings' but..." David shrugged.

"Sorry about this. You tell Marla; then Daddy won't have

to. Y'all need to know because it'll be hard to hide real soon."

"You really should take her to a doctor or a psychiatrist," Hailey insisted. "She needs help, and more than a web site. A doctor at least could prescribe some sleeping pills or valium. Maybe hypnosis would help. Or find a psychic trainer. What if she goes out the front door? You might never find her."

"Daddy carries a lot of worry. If we take Mother to a doctor or a psychic, word would leak out. Our church hired a new minister about a year and a half ago--Reverend Bogerty. He's driven most of the congregation away with his hellfire and brimstone, but some hang on his every word; he feeds their superstitions. If he knew about her sleepwalking, he'd put it on his pulpit.

"Worse could happen; Momma would be declared a witch if anyone knew she heard trees or kudzu whisper, and she talks about it too much already. Back in the inquisition days, that would get you burned at the stake. We would likely be burned out, and she might be killed because there's some around here who'd do that. We can't take that chance while Bogerty's here."

Hailey shook her head. "That stuff went out the window long ago. I didn't think anyone believed in witches and evil magic any more. Let alone go burn somebody's house."

"Folks here are worried about kudzu taking over their homes and farms. That's a lot of money and life to lose. Come with me when I take my flowers tomorrow. Then you can really see how kudzu's taking over and how some folks act. Fear makes people look for something or someone to blame, so they turn a willing ear to that damn pastor and his 'evil walks among us.' We'd be shunned or burned out, and we need that flower money."

Hailey didn't know what to say. She felt like she had opened a freezer door and all the cold and frozen things inside dropped at her feet. She cleared the lump in her throat, and swallowed.

"That's a lot," she said. "Thanks for the information. It clears up some of what I've been feeling since we drove this way—strangeness, like something's about to happen, negative vibes, angry presence, whatever. Makes me edgy. Let's get Mom's equipment inside and take the car around back. You said something about showing me the kudzu flowers."

David smiled at Hailey. He had trouble looking her in the eye, and he was turning pink.

"You know, I haven't talked about things here. Til knows, so there's no need, and I only talk flowers to Mother and Daddy. You listen well which makes it easy for me to talk. I sometimes have trouble doing that especially if feelings are involved. I have bad days and good ones. On bad days, I can't talk about anything except my flowers." David looked at the floor then back toward Hailey and smiled. Hailey smiled back. "Let's get the equipment," he said.

Hailey followed David to the car and stared at his strong back as he carried Marla's equipment inside. She felt shell-shocked from all the information; her knees were a little rubbery, but it was too hot to sit inside the car, and the metal was too hot to lean against. She just stood. When he came out, she finally took the plunge and got into the car, yelping when the faux leather burned her legs.

"Now you know why I want to move you to the shade, David said. "Park to the right of the tree, away from the barn. Til will be spraying and cutting the kudzu off it tomorrow."

The old oak was the biggest Hailey had ever seen. *Kudzu can't get this giant*, she thought. She took no notice of the vines on the ground.

Chapter 3

After they parked the car, David took her back into the orchard. She stepped over a large mound of what looked like tree roots as she and David walked toward the creek.

"That's a root crown you just stepped over," David said. "See how it's got the vines coming out the top."

"It looks more like a Medusa's head, or some giant brain from a sci-fi movie," Hailey replied.

David laughed. "Just watch your step around it, and be careful of the water too. The current flows faster than it looks. It's too deep to ford right now down around Seed Tick. That's why Mother told you to come in the other way. There's a culvert there now so we aren't trapped like a few years ago."

"So that's why we had so much trouble. I thought the directions were wrong because we didn't drive through any water," Hailey said.

As she walked, vines persistently caught on her feet over and over, causing her to stumble and nearly fall. Watery Georgia clay oozed between her toes and she eyed the water like it was a death trap. She was becoming more and more uncomfortable; it seemed like everything back here could trip her, bite her, or carry her away. She envisioned water moccasins."

"Why are we going so far back?" Hailey asked.

"We've got to get toward the back of the orchard to see the flowers blooming. Those near the yard are too young, but the ones out there are all older than three years. They don't really produce any until then. They're very pretty; you'll like them."

"Why are we coming back here? Isn't that kudzu across the road from your house?" Hailey asked. "It seems it would be easier to go there."

"It is and there're flowers there too, but the ground is really uneven and has holes hidden under the ground vines. It's too treacherous to try to go deep inside; it's better to walk along the road over there. Besides we don't own that land. You'll get a better impact back here where we can get deep inside and not fall in a hole. I know this ground."

David was intent on reaching the flowers and didn't seem to notice that the vines appeared to avoid his feet. None caught on the toes of his garden boots or encircled his ankles.

"Look here. See these tiny purple flowers. Kudzu doesn't produce a lot of seeds, but they can remain viable and hidden for several years before germinating. They belong to the Fabaceae or bean or pea family. Smell them. When the wind blows, it carries the fragrance everywhere. It's like a heavy perfume. I like the smell, and so do our bees."

"What bees?" Hailey said, looking around.

"We keep bees here. We had the hives near the center-edge of the orchard to pollinate the peach flowers, but we had to move the boxes because vines began growing into the hive openings and blocking the colony. It almost seemed like kudzu was encouraging the bees to leave the boxes and build closer to its flowers. Just my imagination. Silly, I know." David grinned. "Til and I moved them to the edge of my flower rows."

A ringing interrupted him.

Hailey smiled, "It's my cell phone. "Hi Mom. Okay, we're coming."

"Mom said supper's ready and that we need to come now because Alice and Henry will want to get to church soon after."

"I wasn't sure if that was my phone or not; we have the same ring tone," said David as they walked as fast as possible back out of the orchard. Getting out went quicker than going in.

"There's the garden hose," David said. "The spigot turns hard. I'll turn it if you can't. You may want to wash your feet and shoes. I just pull my boots off." He sat down on the steps and grabbed a foot. "I'll be using my boots later so they can stay here. You can leave your sandals here too if you want unless you'd rather wear them.

Hailey took his advice. She turned the spigot on to rinse off her feet and shoes. The mud trickled off like old blood when the water hit it.

"I'm not used to red dirt," she said. "It looks like my feet and sandals are bleeding. Sort of creepy."

"It's the iron in the soil." David said. "It stains things too. I have to add vermiculite and sand to it for the plants."

"Yeah? I hope it doesn't stain my shoes. I'm using a lot of water to get it off; they're soaking. No way I'm wearing them for a while, but I don't want to leave them out here either."

"Why? They'll dry better out here," David said.

"I've had enough looking at this back yard. I don't want to come back out here after dark to get my shoes. I feel like that barn is watching me now; makes my skin crawl."

"Kudzu can do that," he said and stood up.

"We can use the sun room door rather than go around to the front. It's unlocked during the day for shortcuts."

"Do you need to get Tilfort?"

"No, either Mother or Daddy has probably already called him. Like I said, he's not as odd as he's been colored—at least, not any more than the rest of us. Kudzu's on all our brains, that's all," David said, as he pointed to his head and smiled.

"You don't seem odd. You're pretty cool, and I'm glad you're my cousin. Can I ask you a personal question?"

"The Asperger's?"

"Well okay, that too. Actually you're fine, and so far you haven't dumped tons of kudzu info on me," said Hailey."

Justin, my partner at Jennifer's wedding, was in a work/study program with the Forestry Department during college; he's there full time now. I just met him the day of the rehearsal, but everyone was gagging from the weed killer so he told us a little bit about kudzu. I can see why it's on the brain."

David grinned. "I can't help it; I am locked into flowers, even kudzu flowers, but it's practical. I met one teenager who spent his time doing puzzles. I talked him into manufacturing them—wood, plastic, cardboard, different shapes, and whatever else he could invent, and selling them. He's got a nice little business going—even has a web site. He does keep one of every type for himself. Probably could start a museum, and he might. I talked to him about that too."

"That's really cool," Hailey said with admiration.

David looked at the ground and grinned to himself; he liked the praise. "You know the old saying about making lemonade with life's lemons. I try to help others like me whenever I find them—usually on Facebook. I reckon if someone's fixated on something, he can be good enough at it to make money with it. Us Asperger's folks never quit when it's our own lemons. Daddy taught me to be practical.

"People here 'bouts like my flowers, and I get questions all the time about names of plants, what to plant, and when or where to do the planting. They don't know about the Asperger's; they just think I'm the smartest person around except for Daddy and his peach trees. He gets calls even now-days, and he isn't autistic. I don't tell anyone, and please, you don't either. With all the kudzu and Bogerty's mouth, anything slightly different is suspect."

"That's what I really wanted to know. What will the people here think of us? We're from Indiana. Will our being here cause any problems?" Hailey asked.

"No, you're just visiting family, and we are a nice, normal

family to visit. Daddy invites Bogerty to Monday supper once a month so he's beholden to us. That man likes to eat. You'll get to see his stomach in action tomorrow night. Daddy says it's smart to keep enemies close. The Reverend thinks we're just the most wonderful, normal family around these parts. He has the congregation pray for our sorrows and loss every Sunday after his supper here. Funny, in a strange way."

"Why do Henry and Alice go to his church?" Hailey asked.

David seemed surprised at her question. "We're a church going family. Always have been, and Unity Baptist is *our* church. I used to go and will again when he's gone. I have personal reasons for not going now. Our congregation isn't wealthy, and Bogerty was all we could afford. Others turned us down because they wanted bigger towns and bigger congregations with deep pockets.

"Doesn't say much for some ministers, does it? Hailey snorted.

"It's pretty rural out here. The closest town is Unity, twenty miles on down 57. The only jobs around here are on small farms, or stores in Unity, and in the park; next county up. I travel some distance, but I have a regular route. We just keep finding ways to stay above water because we don't want to move. We love it here. Others don't try anymore; they go on welfare or they leave.

"Kudzu has changed the whole area. It's choked out a lot of the native plants that give food and habitat for the animals, so the animals have moved. People relied on those animals."

"You talk about making lemonade. Why don't the people find a way to use the stuff? It's got to be useful for something," Hailey said.

"Kudzu has a lot of uses, but farmers don't want to adapt. It can feed cows, and goats especially love it. The fiber is good for making paper, baskets, maybe clothing. You can cook it. I've tried to get Mother to use it in jelly and syrup. The leaves are as healthy as spinach, or any greens. She won't because of the dead peach trees. Others have their excuses too. They want kudzu dead and a return to the past. So if locals don't move, they stay here and get poorer. They complain and look for excuses, and Bogerty gives them answers, they think. He tells them kudzu is God's wrath for all the evil around here, and they believe him.

"Ours has always been the smallest church over in Unity so we were never flush with cash. But we have almost no money now. Even Bogerty works at a used car dealership in Unity. He'll be gone soon. He's only got six months left on his contract, and he won't be rehired. He's causing too much trouble, and over half of the church members left aren't attending, me included.

David's phone rang this time. "Yeah Mom, we're just rinsing off our feet. Be there in a second."

"Guess we've been talking too much," Hailey said.

"Mom's always impatient to start eating as soon as the food's on the table. Doesn't want it to get cold. It's especially true on church nights if she decides to go."

David held the door open for Hailey as she padded in carrying her shoes. She pitched them in her bedroom on the way to the dining room.

..........<>..........

"Something smells wonderful—fresh bread," Hailey said as they entered the house and rushed for the table.

Alice, Henry, and Marla were already sitting down.

"I thought y'all had got lost." Alice said. "We're fixin' to say grace as soon as y'all sit down. Just wash your hands in the kitchen sink. I'm sorry that supper's not much.

We usually eat light on Sunday night so I can get finished cleanin' up before church.

Tilfort will be here directly."

Hailey heard the front door bang.

"Oh, there he is now," Alice said.

Hearing so much about this strange man, Hailey looked him over carefully. He just seemed average: average height, average weight, average, brown hair. He could have blended into any crowd except for his muscular arms and wild, burning eyes. They were the eyes of a fanatic, nearly black in their intensity. Even so, she sensed an honest and gentle nature inside. He cared deeply for this family. He seemed the type who'd lay down his life for any one of them, even the animals.

"Tilfort, get your hands washed and hurry up. We'll wait on you," Alice said.

"Marla will be sayin' grace," Henry said to Hailey and her mother, while they waited for Tilfort. "Kingston and Lily are a'waitin' too. They'll accept any bites offered to them even though I already fed them their suppers. Just reach it down and wiggle your hand. They're polite about takin' the offerin's. Your fingers will survive."

"Sorry I'm late," mumbled Tilfort as he returned from washing his hands and sat down. "Y'all be the cousins. I'm Tilfort. Nice to see you."

Henry gave Tilfort the once over.

"Here now, Tilfort, you know better. Take that hatchet out of your belt and chuck it outside. I imagine the ax is on the porch, so put them together out of the doorway. No one needs to fall on them. Nothin' sharp allowed at the meal except the table knives. Go on, we'll wait on you."

Tilfort tucked his head and did what he was told. When he came back, he said, "I'm sorry, I plum forgot. That stuff is tryin' to climb on the tractor. It's all over the ground back there and grabbin' the poles inside the barn. I can see it growin' out the corner of ma' eye. It waits until it thinks I'm not lookin', then it stretches itself even more. I know one vine moved over a foot towards me as I was choppin' its partner off the tractor tires." Tilfort frowned as he spoke.

Alice said, "Hush up Tilfort; Marla is going to say grace. You keep talking and the food will be cold and ruin't. You can talk while we eat." She nodded to Marla to begin.

Marla said, "I don't know what you consider appropriate so I'll just improvise."

"Dear Lord, we thank You for this wholesome food to sustain our bodies, and we thank You for Your Blessings to sustain our souls. May we always find worth in Your Eyes as we try to always please You. May You fill our hearts with hope and peace and thank You for this reunion time. In Jesus' Name, Amen."

Marla looked around to see if what she said was alright. Alice had tears in her eyes and Henry's lip was quivering. *I guess that was okay*, she thought. *Been a while.*

Alice wiped her eyes on her napkin. "Thank you, Marla. That's the nicest prayer I've heard in a month o' Sundays."

"And it don't set us off our food like Bogerty's do," Tilfort mumbled. He goes for nye-on to ten minutes. All that hellfire."

"Speakin' of, he comes for supper tomorrow night," Henry reminded everyone. "Best behavior and Tilfort, watch what you say. Now, pass the sweet potatoes. Let's see if Marla knows how to microwave them proper," he said, grinning at her. Marla laughed and handed them around the table.

"Here's the biscuits you smelled, Hailey," said Alice. "They came from the bakery. I just unfroze them and heated. Don't tell Bogerty. I'm not an old fashioned, make-everythin'-from-scratch cook although our reverend thinks women should be.

"But this honey here is from our own bees. We had the hives to pollinate the peach trees, but now they pollinate David's flowers. It's a mixture of many flowers, even kudzu. I don't think there's any better. We sell some during the winter down in Unity. Sells out quick too.   Make sure you have some on the biscuits; makes a good dessert."

"Pass me both, please. I'll have my dessert with my sweet potatoes," Hailey grinned.

Pleasantries and good natured joking filled most of the meal. Hailey and David kept Kingston snacking throughout. Alice put Lily on her lap and hand fed her. Marla and Hailey kept the subject light by talking about Jennifer's wedding and the crazy antics of the bridal party. Tilfort even smiled as he listened.

Then Tilfort spoke up. The talk about Jennifer's wedding triggered him. "David's supplyin' flowers for a weddin' this Wednesday night up in Unity," he said. "It's goin' to be a big wing-dig. The bride and groom are midgets. The church'll be full of flowers—all kinds. We've got boxes full in the cooler right now. David'll do all the bouquets and boutonnières and the cake top. I'll be hepin' him, but he'll be workin' half the night and all the mornin' to get everythin' ready to take up there by noon.

"We'll be makin' ribbon bows with flowers for the church pews and the altar. David's plucked the petals off roses for the two flower girls to throw down and guests to throw at the bride and groom. Must be a 5 quart bucket full in the refrigerator right now.   The whole van'll be full to the top. We haven't done a weddin' with so many flowers in over a year. The money will be a big he'p." Tilfort wasn't mumbling now. His sudden garrulousness betrayed pride in David's work.

"I'm going to use a little of the money to buy some larger fireworks," David said. "Thursday is the Fourth of July. I've been stockpiling fireworks for some months now, but I want some really big ones to celebrate seeing Marla and Hailey. Don't look at me that way, Til. My mind's made up. I'll pick them up after I deliver the flowers."

"The closest fireworks display is in Unity, twenty miles

from here, but it doesn't start until around ten when it gets dark," said Alice. We stopped goin' after Ashley died and Jimmy took our grandsons up north. It wasn't fun anymore without the twins, so now we do our own celebration. Usually we invite some friends over, but we're goin' to keep it family this year. Thursday's the whole moon so there'll be plenty of light to see what we're doin'. Won't have to worry about anythin' catchin' fire. Too wet."

"I'm sure you ladies have driven enough today and would like to stay out of the car tonight," Henry said. "Unity is a twenty mile slow drive, so we'll be leavin' for church real soon. Y'all are welcome to come, if you want. You can get an early look at our preacher before tomorrow night. You won't be wantin' to stay with us through next Tuesday after bein' around him." He chuckled.

Marla just raised her eyebrows and shook her head. "Sounds tempting," she said, looking at her daughter. Hailey looked back; her face said she had lots to tell.

"Goodness, Henry, look at the time. I take it y'all are stayin', so I'm goin' to let you four clean up. Sit and take your time. No need for anyone but us to rush," said Alice.

"You go on to the car, Henry. I'll catch up," Alice said. She got up and walked to the bedroom. Tilfort helped Henry up and gave him his quad cane.

Henry drew a deep breath and let it out slowly. Then he said, "Well, we all have our marchin' orders. I feel the need to go to church, but I don't like Reverend Bogerty's sermons. Especially tonight because w'all have to put up with him tomorrow. Service should only be an hour, but if he gets wound up, it'll be longer. I'll be glad when he's gone; we were too hasty in pickin' him."

"He was the only choice. Nobody knew he'd be like this. There's no one to blame." Tilfort said in a soothing voice.

"Sometimes I think we would do alright with none. We took turns with the Bible studies when we didn't have a preacher before, and we could do the same now," said Henry. "He stirs up too many superstitions like when he said witches were causing the problems. He's not the voice of reason up on that pulpit. When it was just us, we could talk sense into scared folks. He just drives them wild, and turnin' good folk again' each other."

"David, would you go around and bring the car to the front?' Henry asked. "I'm feelin' tired all of a sudden, and that's a mite long walk."

"Sure, Daddy. Do you have your antacid pills? You know you'll need them before the service is over."

"I have a handful in my handkerchief. Hurry up now or you mother will fuss at us both. Can't be late."

David trotted out the door and ran to the barn.

Marla and Hailey began taking the food to the kitchen. Tilfort carried in the dirty plates and silverware. They had the left-overs stored in the refrigerator and were filling the sink with dishwater before David returned.

Alice was pacing the floor all this time. Henry just sat on the couch and watched her.

"What's takin' him so long? Five minutes would have done it. I hope he's not fiddlin' with his flowers and forgettin' us," she said.

Henry tried to calm her with a soft voice. "Now Alice, you know he won't do that. Maybe a tire is low and he has to pump it up. See, there he is now. He brought the van. Let's go; we still have plenty of time to make it. Stay Kingston!" He slowly got up and shuffled out the door. Alice followed.

David stood by the door watching his parents leave and holding Kingston to prevent the possibility of the dog's chasing the van. Then he came into the kitchen; Tilfort looked at him.

"What's wrong with the car that you lent them your van?" he asked.

All David said was, "Kudzu."

"Son of a bitch!" Tilfort said and rushed to the front door. Marla and Hailey heard a loud thump. He returned carrying the hatchet and ax. He raced down the hall and out the back door, letting it slam behind him.

David looked at Hailey and Marla. "Sorry, but I need to go help Tilfort. Why don't y'all relax on the verandah until I get back. Hailey, this might be a good time to tell Marla what all I said. It might take us a while, but I'll be back as soon as I can." The floorboards creaked as he walked down the hallway and out the back.

Marla looked questioningly at her daughter. "Okay spill what you know. Then I won't have to grill Henry. I get the feeling he won't talk when anyone's around, and I don't want to wait."

"Let's get these dishes finished first so there won't be any distractions," Hailey suggested. "I can't multitask on this; too much to tell you."

"You dry, and I'll wash. Let's see how fast we can finish this," Marla said.

Hailey was amazed how fast her mother moved. *She must really be curious*, she thought.

"All done here," Hailey said as the last pan lid was placed in the stove drawer. "I have tons to dump on you, and some of it's sort of weird. Go on ahead; I'll grab the bug spray from your make-up bag and some shoes, and meet you out there."

"I'll wait. I need some ice water and I'll get you some too. Me and da critters will be by the door," Marla grinned.

Kingston and Lily followed the women outside and settled near their new favorites—the dog leaning on Hailey and the cat lounging in Marla's lap. Having the pets' warm bodies touching them was comforting as Hailey related to Marla all that David had said. Then Hailey added the feelings that she had picked up while out back and in the sunroom. She described the barn and orchard with their coverings of vines. It was a lot for Marla to digest.

When Hailey finished, Marla raised her eyebrows and took a deep breath. She let it out slowly and rather loudly before speaking. She hadn't seen the back yard or even the house. Alice kept her too occupied.

"Wow," was her only comment. Then, "You've always been tuned into feelings, and since junior high, it's been getting stronger, way more than me. But either the cancer or the chemo changed things a little, but it only works part-time if I'm relaxed. And so far on this trip, I haven't been. So don't get your hopes up. I admit things seemed odd when we got here. Something about that park rattled me too, and it was more than the road or those RV's. I got hit by a huge wave of anger and hurt when we stopped at the entrance. I'm surprised I felt it because I sure wasn't relaxed. It was just so strong, and I know I only got a little bit of it. This whole area seems waiting for something to happen. Maybe it's all the stress floating around, and keeping Alice's behavior a secret could be the biggest stress of all. But I'm not feeling anything now; it's gone.

Hailey smiled. She was right; her mother's "talent" was stronger. That was a relief. Now she wouldn't have to hide her sensing to protect her mom; she wasn't alone.

Marla continued. "Keep working on David. I'll watch Henry and Alice, and we can compare. I'm sure Henry will open up to me if I can get him alone. The Fourth's a full moon, that's Thursday. We'll be in for more than fireworks; I guess we should plan on a long night."

"Mom, it might be more than one," Hailey quietly reminded Marla. "The moon is almost full the night before...and the night after. We could have a three night watch or longer, depending on that O'd energy. I'm just guessing. Henry'll know; that's when he'll start sleeping in the sunroom."

"With the heat and humidity, you and I'll have the air conditioners on," Marla said. "We might not hear anything, so we should crack the doors open and hope we don't fall asleep. We might see movement if we don't hear footsteps, although the floors creak when anyone steps on them. Could be our alarm system."

"Then what're we supposed to do?" asked Hailey. "I mean, everyone here's been taking care of the situation for what, four years? They act like her sleepwalking is weird, like she's going off the deep end. Maybe we should just stay out of it; we'll be gone soon anyway. We can't really make a difference. Do we just sneak around and watch 'cause we're curious, or what?"

"I don't know, Hailey. Maybe you're right. Maybe we should just wait and see if we're asked to help. Then do what they say…I don't want them to think we're watching a side show."

"Yeah, about that, and--I'm not looking forward to Reverend Bogerty tomorrow night. He sounds revolting."

Marla nodded, "We have to hear a sermon too. I hope he doesn't stay long. Maybe we can hide in the kitchen and do dishes."

"You wish. The only thing separating the kitchen from the dining room is a row of cabinets and a bar, and it's open to the living room. He can hold us captive no matter where."

"Let's just think of tomorrow as entertainment." Marla yawned. "I'm tired, and it looks like we've been abandoned. I'm going to take a shower to cool off and go to bed. I'm sticky, and the bugs have won." She got up, still holding Lily, then paused, like she was listening to something.

"Do you hear anything…like leaves rustling or something moving on the ground?" The cat hissed and jumped down; she ran for the door. "Ow, Lily just scratched me."

"No, but Kingston's got his ears up," Hailey said. "And Lily turned attack cat. Maybe it's a snake moving around, but I don't know if you can hear snakes."

"I don't hear it now." Marla shrugged, "Weird. Maybe some animal. Tell everybody good night if you're still up."

"I'm going to try to use my laptop soon, said Hailey. "I told Justin I'd contact him as soon as I had time, and I have time now. He wants a report on how badly the kudzu is 'impacting the people and the environment' out here. Those are his words, not mine. You can tell he's in the Forestry Department, can't you," she said, rolling her eyes. "It's late, but he'll get the message tomorrow if he's not on line. It's wireless here, isn't it and not dial up?"

"I don't have a clue, but you've got your Ethernet cord. Hook it up if you don't get a signal. Tell Justin he looked great in his wedding tux; everyone looked great, and I really liked all of Jen and Bill's friends. I wasn't able to hand out compliments Friday since I spent most of my time being weed-spray green. He can pass my compliments along to the others. Sweet dreams, Baby." Lily followed Marla inside.

Chapter 4

The late evening was relaxing in spite of the heat. Kingston laid his head down and began snoring. Hailey quietly moved her chair to the edge of the porch so not to disturb the dog, and sat for a while looking at the twilight sky. It was hemmed in by the foliage across the road, but unobstructed in the yard. It wasn't quite dark yet, and Alice said it got dark around ten. She'd never seen so many stars just beginning to blink on.

Her thoughts rambled, not realizing a soothing fragrance was invading her head. *No smog or traffic or city lights. Just nature. No town for twenty miles except Unity. I wonder if there're any gas stations or grocery stores or burger joints or anything closer than twenty miles. Probably not. Cell phones work so there's a tower somewhere. They do have land lines too. Out in the boonies. Awfully hot here, but no rain tonight, thank God! Much more, and I'll grow webbed feet. Damned bugs. I see a bat. There's another one.* Her mind continued to wander as her eyes followed the bats in the brightening moonlight.

A slight breeze picked up carrying the same heady fragrance, now stronger than before. Hailey breathed deeply. *Nature's aromatherapy*, she thought.

Silver leaves shimmered in that breeze; lots of beautiful shimmering kudzu leaves on the other side of the road. And there were shapes; unusual shapes covered with a beautiful silver blanket. Hailey felt herself drifting away—floating along on that silver magic. She got out of her chair and stepped down into the yard. She closed her eyes and breathed in the fragrance. She no longer felt the heat or her tired muscles. She didn't hear the mosquitoes buzzing her ears. Her feet drifted passed the center of the road. She didn't hear the crunching of her sandals on the red gravel. Her eyes opened, and she smiled. She began to hallucinate, recognizing two new friends who were also in Jen's wedding. They appeared dressed in kudzu's silver leaves. In fact, they were completely formed from leaves.

"Lucy, Eric? What are you doing here? I thought you went home after the wedding." she said. The figures beckoned. She moved towards them. "Come join me on the porch. I didn't know you lived close by."

A horn blasted, making Hailey jump. The sudden raucous noise shocked her out of her trance. She turned to see bright headlights blinding her. "*How did I get out here*? She thought. *Damn weird!* She shielded her eyes and moved to the narrow berm.

A van pulled slowly into the driveway. Kingston was suddenly alert; he trotted forward. Henry called out from its window.

"Sorry to startle you. I came around the curve and there you were in the road. I was just lettin' you know I was here."

Hailey walked back across the pavement. Her ears were still ringing from the horn, and she felt like she had just awakened from a deep sleep---one with only partly remembered dreams. It was embarrassing to be caught standing in the middle of the road like some zombie.

Henry opened the door and turned sideways. She watched him maneuver his way out using his right arm and leg. He held on to the door until Alice came around and handed him his quad cane. She gave Hailey a hard look. Henry didn't appear to notice Alice's look as he reached down to pet his dog. Hailey noticed however, and felt she was going to be quizzed. She didn't want any part of that. Too many women back home had quizzed her about James, especially when he and Mom were still married. Mostly so they could bat their eyes at him and strike up a conversation, hoping for a date.

"That's kudzu you were headin' toward," Henry said in a low voice, not wanting to let on that he was alarmed at finding Hailey in the middle of the road. He knew what kudzu's fragrance could do; he'd seen it affect Alice. He kept petting Kingston, but his shaking hand betrayed his agitation. "It's deceivin'. You think it's close to the road, but there's a dip down before you get to it. You don't want to be goin' over to examine it in the dark. The leaves are right pretty in the moonlight--sort of a silver gray. You should wait 'til daylight to examine it. Even this bright moonlight isn't enough to keep you from fallin' and sprainin' something. It does smell good; the humidity picks it up and carries it."

Henry steadied himself and swung the door shut. In a louder voice, he said, "Sorry to rush off, but I'm goin' inside. That preacher plum wore me out, and I need some more antacid tablets. I chewed all I had listenin' to his rantin' and ravin'. That man can carry on somethin' fierce, and his sermon ran over again. Is David inside?"

"No," Hailey answered. "He and Tilfort rushed out back right after you left and are still out there, I guess. David mentioned kudzu and both took off."

"Well, I better go see what they're doin'. So much for restin', but I want my antacids first. Where's Marla?"

"She was going to take a shower and go to bed. She's still weak from breathing weed killer for three days and the road trip wore her out—that and a full stomach; she's probably asleep by now," Hailey said, trying to lighten the mood, but Alice was still glaring at her.

Henry nodded and shuffled toward the house with Kingston following at his heels.

Hailey turned to Alice. "I was going to get on the internet. Do you have dial up or satellite?" *Act nonchalant. Don't let on you're weirded out,* Hailey thought.

Alice grabbed her left elbow. "Hush. Wait until Henry's inside." Alice's grip was tight, and it hurt. Hailey considered yanking her arm away, but decided against it. She didn't want to be impolite or upset Alice any more than she appeared already. Instead, they watched Henry as he limped up the walk and slowly dragged his left leg up the steps. Kingston was close by, helping to brace his beloved owner. When both went through the door, Alice jerked Hailey around to face her. She was intense; her eyes bored into Hailey's.

"Tell me quick and be honest. Were you out here alone? Did you hear anythin'? Did you see anythin'? Why were you out on the far side of the road?" Alice shook her with each question.

Damn you, Bitch! Don't shake me. Not now, not ever! Hailey thought. *James did that and you won't. I'm not little anymore and you won't scare me.* In spite of herself, Hailey was a little frightened. And she'd learned to turn that fear into anger—like the anger she felt now. And that anger flared from her eyes like flames from a bottle rocket.

I don't care if she is psychic. She's acting nuts. And rude. Hailey thought as she yanked her arm loose. She didn't give a damn right now about being polite or upsetting the woman.

"What's with you, Alice?"

"*Answer* me for Christ's sake!"

"Calm down and I will. You're acting crazy, and either you cool it, or I'm going inside *without* answering your questions," Hailey ordered.

Alice wilted. "I'm sorry. Can you sit on the veranda awhile? Answer my questions, and I'll explain why I'm askin'. It's important. You need to know to protect yourself and Marla too."

"Okay, but only for a few minutes," Hailey said. Alice grabbed her hand and pulled Hailey to the veranda. She was still squeezing Hailey's hand when they sat down. *She's making sure I don't get away.*

Rosemary Coven

"Now, you must have been out here alone if Marla went to take a shower. So how long were you alone?"

"Alice, I don't have any idea. Maybe an hour. I was relaxing. It's been a long day, and no, I didn't hear anything. Mom thought she heard something and the animals acted like they did too. Maybe it was a snake; I didn't hear it. I felt a slight breeze, and it rattled those kudzu leaves across the road. All I saw were silver leaves shaking. I thought it was pretty and went to look. That's all." Hailey didn't look her cousin in the eye.

"There's somethin' more. You're not tellin' me everythin'. Did you see faces in the leaves? Did the covered bushes look like people? Maybe someone you know? Did the leaves sound like voices callin' you?"

"I didn't hear any voices, okay? What's going on? Why all the questions?" Hailey asked.

"You didn't answer my other question. You're hidin' somethin'. You don't have to be afraid to answer me. I won't think you're crazy. I know. I've seen faces—Ashley's and John's, and they beckon to me. When I'm alone, I hear their voices callin' my name. And I hear whisperings in my peach trees; kudzu's talkin' to itself and plannin', near whole moon time like now. Like tonight." Alice said.

Alice's words shook Hailey. "Yes, I thought I saw Lucy and Eric. You remember me telling everyone at supper about their silly antics right the wedding. I was tired; the shadows in the moonlight looked like them. It's like seeing shapes in clouds." *Play it down, girl. Don't let her see you're embarrassed....and freaked. You need time to figure this out.*

"No it's not! Kudzu gets to you," Alice hissed. "It plans; it can hear what you say or maybe it's readin' your mind. And it uses that know-how to lure you. It waits until you're alone and either hypnotizes you or makes you sleepy. It tries to draw you into itself. It crushes and smothers everythin' here 'bouts like it did our orchard. You just got here and already it's startin' on you."

Alice's last words really struck a nerve. What if Kudzu's flowers did put me in a trance, Hailey thought. *No that's stupid. I'm tired, and some smells are relaxing. I probably should have gone to bed like Mom did.*

"I sleepwalk, and I see and hear things when I do. I don't tell anybody because no one believes me when I try. Tilfort's right; thin's have got so strange that his explanation is the only one that feels right. That doesn't mean I like him carryin' that hatchet and ax around or talkin' to the vines. One of us could get hurt when he goes swinin' those sharp things."

This was too much too soon, and Alice didn't show any signs of slowing down. Hailey's chair was so comfortable and the night smelled so good. *I could fall asleep right here*, she thought. Alice's words began to sound like droning bees instead of words. "Alice, can't we discuss this tomorrow?"

"No! You're goin' to hear me out now, not tomorrow." Alice's words tumbled out in a rush and were speeding up the more she talked. "I've seen what it can do; I've seen it around here. It killed my peach trees. It took two years to do that, but it's movin' faster now. The rain's he'pin' it. It's only supposed to grow a foot or two a day so the Forestry people tell everyone. But now it's growin' faster. Maybe three or four feet a day. The heat helps too. Everythin's growin' faster. David'll tell you his flowers are growin' fast. He doesn't even need to use fertilizer or special pottin' soil."

She was trying to stay awake, but it was getting harder and harder. Some of what Alice said felt true, but Hailey needed to hear this slower so she could decide how much. She was only picking up some of the words. Her cousin still held her hand, and the more she droned on, the more agitated she became and the harder she squeezed. *At least the pain is helping me stay awake.* "Alice, you're hurting my hand. Let go," Hailey slurred as she attempted to free herself.

Alice paid no attention; she just clung tighter and continued talking. "Kudzu's growin' faster than the other plants. It's been coverin' telephone and electric poles on the way to Unity. I see the changes every Sunday when we go to church. This week it's on the wires themselves, and those vines are heavy. The wires could snap if they aren't cleaned off, but road crews can't keep up. It grows even faster when the moon is whole, and it has more power to draw you in."

"Don't be alone," Alice warned. "The next few days will be bad. It's startin' even now, and it shouldn't yet. That's why you saw your friends. You were alone, and it tried to draw you in. It tries to draw me in when I sleepwalk. You'll be fine as long as you aren't outside alone at night while you visit."

The fragrance stopped, and Hailey became more aware of the surrounding heat. She felt sweaty and itchy. *Did I just doze off? I think I missed something. She was telling me about sleepwalking.*

"It killed John."

Yup, I definitely missed something here. She wasn't taking about John earlier, was she? Oh well. Hailey shrugged and focused on Alice's words.

"It's been on my mind these past three years. There was kudzu all around when they found him. His motorcycle slid on some vines across the road, and flipped; the skid marks and smashed vines proved that. He was thrown down the side. It was a long way down, and his neck was broken. A vine was wrapped around it. Police said the *fall* snapped his neck. They said he just kept rollin' and wound the vines around himself as he fell. They said *of course* there was kudzu; it was all over the place, but it didn't kill him. But somethin' inside tells me it did kill my boy. Now I hate it; it's evil."

Seems like I've heard about this before. I don't feel anything murderous out here. Weird vibes, but nothing evil. Funny I should wake up just when she starts ranting about 'evil plant kills son.' Maybe kudzu wants me to hear this part and not the other. That sent an electric spark through her brain. It felt true.

Please promise me that you won't go outside alone, not while the moon grows whole," Alice said.

Hailey felt confused. *Boy, that came out of the blue! thought she was talking about John.* She struggled to connect the parts of Alice's long speech, at least what she remembered. *Must be she thinks kudzu will put me to sleep and kill me.* That idea chilled her, but it didn't feel right. At least not right now. *Maybe in the future.* She felt another shock with that last thought.

"Does Kingston count as someone? He was with me tonight, but he was sleeping."

Hailey had no intentions of making that promise, at least not until she could sort out what she missed. Until then she'd do as she damned well pleased. She literally ripped her hand away from Alice and squeezed her fingers together to release the pain and restore circulation. *I'll be bruised there in the morning.*

"He's a good watch dog. Take him with you if you need to, but even he can't he'p if he's asleep. So make sure he's awake. Maybe the kudzu made him sleepy like it did you."

Hailey decided to ignore that last statement. It was too scary to consider. "I'm going inside now. I need to get on the internet. Do you have satellite or dial up?"

"I'm sorry to keep you. And I'm sorry I seem crazy to you. Maybe some of the thin's here are in my imagination because of the stress, but I feel thin's. And thin's aren't right. Oh yes, internet. We have dial up because satellite's gotten too expensive for us anymore. You can use my old computer in our bedroom if your laptop doesn't have a converter. But not tonight because Henry will be goin' to bed soon, I imagine.

Bogerty plum wears him out."

"No problem; I have an ethernet cord—a converter. See you in the morning, Alice." Hailey couldn't get away fast enough; she almost ran to her room. "Damn, she's a total nut case; she definitely can't handle her own abilities. I hope that never happens to me. And, let's add Tilfort and we have a *lovely* pair of psychotic bookends," Hailey mumbled under her breath.

Hailey was shaking when she entered her room. Alice's behavior was scary, but suspecting kudzu had drugged her was even scarier; she felt like she was in some horror movie.

Speaking of a horror movie, she thought, *those dolls have got to go, especially that one with the cracked head.* She grabbed all the toys and threw them in one jumbled pile on the top shelf in the closet and shut the door. *How could Ashley collect those things?* Hailey shuttered.

After a shower to get the bug repellent off, she sat down to contact Justin. She had only known him the three days of Jennifer's wedding, but at seven years older, he had become like a big brother. He worked in the Forestry Department, so if anyone knew more about kudzu than David, he did, and Hailey wanted some answers. He was the only one she could ask. She sure wasn't asking her cousins; she wanted facts not feelings right now.

It's only 11:30, she thought; *he should still be up.* Dial up seemed to take forever to get on Facebook. *Finally! Hello Justin, are you there? Yes!*

Hailey began typing as fast as she could, telling him all that had happened since she saw him. It seemed like the last eleven and a half hours were a week long. She had run through a gauntlet of emotions, and she didn't really know how to condense it all down. If this didn't tell him how kudzu was impacting people here, nothing would. She hardly gave

Justin a chance to respond.

Hold on, slow down, he typed back. You're typing so fast that your words are running together. What does 'Aliceidcrezykudzucantkellucanitt?' mean?

I'm sorry. It's just that that highway 57 was a nightmare. I've never seen Mom so scared or me either. Then the relatives. David is cool, but this guy who works for them, Tilfort, has bat shit for brains. He brought a hatchet to dinner. And had an ax on the porch. I've got bruises from where Alice grabbed me. She says the trees talked to her, and that I shouldn't be outside alone because kudzu will kill me. David says she's psychic, but it's messing with her head. I was tiret, and sitting on the porch and wishing I was back with you guys. I thought I saw Lucy and Eric across the road in some kudzu, and Alice dragged it out of me. I told everyone at dinner about Eric barking when he got the garter, so they were on my mind. I miss all you guys. Last week was so much fun and now this. She was shaking me like a dust mop. Freaked me out. I wisd I hadn't told her.

Hailey knew that she'd typed mistakes, but she didn't care as long as Justin could read it. Her hands were shaking and she was close to tears. She couldn't bring herself to tell him about her zombie state. He'd think she was crazy too or tell her she was just tired. He might be right.

Tell your mother tomorrow what happened after she went inside. Maybe you should cut your stay short if this is a one-day sample of the rest of your visit. If David is cool maybe you should tell him too. No offense, but she needs help and soon!

So Alice isn't right. Kudzu isn't a killer and it can't read your mind to get ways to kill.

No, but Alice is psycho. I worked with the stuff for three solid months during my college work/study program and never had it talk to me or try to kill me. I was by myself in some areas for hours. I felt weird a few times because of the herbicide I was spraying. I even got light headed from the heat and bending over a lot to chop it near the ground. It's no space alien. They've been finding lots of good uses for it now. Check it out on the web.

Thanks Justin, she just got to me tonight. She starts sleepwalking soon. I guess no one will get any sleep this week. We get to meet the preacher tomorrow night too; he's coming for dinner. I guess he's a real fire and brimstone type.

Can't you and Marla escape?

No, it wouldn't be polite, and it might 'cause trouble. I guess that man can be nasty with his kudzu is God's punishment and finger pointing. I get the idea we're going to be checked and judged, and we need to pass the test. No sleep tonight. I'll probably worry myself awake.

Well, I need to get some sleep—work at eight.

Thanks for listening, Justin. I guess this sort of

gives you your impact report—people are going crazy because of a plant. Don't use our names, please. Sleep well.

Thanks for the info. I'll put it in the psychological impact section. Night.

Hailey felt better now, but her thoughts still flashed wildly. She looked at the clock by the bed; it was one-thirty. *Didn't think it was that late. Sorry Justin*, she thought. *Bedtime.* She hooked her PC to the charger and grabbed her overnight bag.

I should've brushed my teeth after my shower, then I wouldn't have to leave my room. I didn't hear David come in or anybody. Wonder where Tilfort sleeps. Unity, I hope.

She looked out in the hall, but saw no lights. Hailey assumed everyone was asleep and tip-toed to the bathroom. The hall floor squeaked. *So much for silence*, she thought.

She stepped inside and closed the door before turning on the stark overhead lamp. The room was still humid from her shower and the opened window wasn't any help. Hailey didn't know which was hotter, the outside or the inside. Even the little fan on the table under the window just stirred the heat around. She was glad for the air conditioner in her room.

Hailey rummaged in her bag for toothpaste and toothbrush, found them, and glanced in the mirror over the sink. Her eyes locked on something green reflected within. She pivoted and stared at the ceiling. At the top of the pale green walls were silk ivy vines, suspended from cup hooks. For a moment, she thought it was kudzu and that frightened her. Then she realized her mistake and drew a shaky breath. Fright flipped to anger and she blamed Alice.

"Seriously? That psychotic damn bitch has vines around her bathroom ceiling." She couldn't help speaking out loud. Hailey stared into the mirror and began vigorously brushing her teeth; the bristles scrubbing against her gums removed her anger. Something had to relieve both emotions.

She started laughing and had to spit out the toothpaste and saliva before she swallowed it. She sat on the toilet seat and tried to hold the laughter in so not to wake anyone. Toothpaste trickled from the corner of her mouth, and mucus, running from her nose, joined it. Gradually the tension broke and she relaxed. *I can sleep now*, she decided and finished brushing her teeth.

Monday

Chapter 1

The gang was at the Green Man Inn, a new place decorated with kudzu. Even the tables were woven from the vines. Dan demonstrated how to make shakers balance in a pile of black salt just by psychically willing it. Everyone grabbed the little jars off surrounding tables, much to the kudzu-wrapped waitress' mild annoyance. One by one each person succeeded. Gabby's shaker was the only one not balanced, and the girls were cheering her on. "I'm the shaker king, and my wedding partner can't make it stand up," Dan grinned evilly.

"Give me some salt peter, and it really *won't* stand up," Gabby retorted. Cat calls followed.

The loud knocking at her door was a rude awakening.

"Breakfast in a half hour," David called. Hailey jolted upright from her dream, then lay back down and groaned.

Shit, day two in the weird world, she thought. *I miss the gang, and even my dreams are weird.*

"Thanks, I'm awake," she responded. She threw the covers back and forced her feet off the side of the bed. The bare floor seemed rough beneath her bed-softened soles. Her mind registered it absentmindedly. She checked her cell phone for the time.

"Seven? No way I can be ready to eat in a half hour," she squawked in a gravelly voice. Grabbing her robe, she raced for the bathroom and bumped into her mother coming out.

"Gotta go! Gotta go! Gotta talk to you too, Mom, ASAP." she said, and rushed inside, shutting the door in her mother's face.

"O....kay then," Marla chuckled, and proceeded to her

room to find some shorts and a thin top. Today promised to be a scorcher.

Hailey deliberately ignored the vines looped through cup hooks and urinated. Then she washed her face and slid back to her room. To save time, she grabbed the first thing on top in her suitcase and trotted to her mother's room to dress.

She scratched at the door--their special way of announcing each other, and rushed in, closing the door, not as softly as intended. Marla was fastening a sandal strap when Hailey flopped on the bed and began stripping off her short pajamas.

"Good morning, Sweetie. You have some urgent news for me?" Marla said in a stylized voice. Hailey thought her mother looked rested and her color was good. She took that as a sign the weed killer and stress of highway 57 had worn off.

"You have holes in your floor too; I see the can lids."

"People saved money by only putting hardwood where it could be seen. Pine was used in bedrooms. If the knots fell out, they nailed can lids over the holes, and rugs covered the repair jobs. No rugs here, so be careful you don't cut a bare foot on the metal edges. Now, what's up?"

Hailey's words tumbled out of her like boulders in an avalanche; she hardly stopped to breath. Talking to Justin wasn't enough; she needed her mom, and she'd waited all night to tell her. She couldn't slow down now until it all poured out.

"Alice is a total psycho even if she's psychic. They got home around ten-thirty. I was wandering over to look at the kudzu across the road. I was so tired that I thought I saw Lucy and Eric standing over there. I admit I was in the middle of the road when they showed up. When Henry went inside, Alice grabbed me and shook me like James used to. She said kudzu makes you see things that aren't there, and then it wraps around you and kills you like one of those big snakes from South America. I've got bruises on my arm from her holding me too tight and yanking on me. She was crushing my hand too. She insisted that I not be outside at night alone. She admitted to sleepwalking and said she hears the kudzu talking to her, and...she totally believes it killed John."

Marla stared at Hailey. Then she raised her eyebrows and said, "I guess I should have stayed up longer; sorry I missed the side-show. I was dead when my head hit the pillow, but I did hear a horn. Was that them?" Hailey nodded. "Let me see the bruises."

Marla's lips drew into a thin line when she saw the dark blue splotches on Hailey's elbow and upper arm. Her fingers appeared swollen too.

"You finish dressing while I go look for Henry." Marla reached the door, when David called them to eat. She looked at Hailey. "I'll talk to Henry later. I don't want a scene at the table. Comb your hair quickly and come on."

"Mom," Hailey said with her head down, "there's a little more. I was kinda in a fog like a zombie. I don't remember actually walking into the road. I just remember smelling kudzu's flowers. Do you think Alice might be right? I didn't let on, but it freaked me out." She looked up and encountered her mother's eyes. They just stared at each other.

All her mother said was, "Let's go eat."

When Hailey reached the kitchen, Alice was bringing a skillet of fried apples covered in sugar-froth to the table with Kingston following hopefully behind. The cinnamon smelled wonderful. She realized that she was really, really hungry. *No, no scene. I just wanna eat*, she thought. Then she saw the table.

Her mother hadn't warned her about Southern meals. Grandpa Gar took Grams and Marla away from Tennessee into Indiana when Marla was in her teens. Hailey hadn't been south since she was a baby. Now she was wide-eyed looking at all the choices. Hailey hadn't understood what Alice meant when she said they eat light on Sunday nights. She would see, come supper tonight. For now, the breakfast was an eye opener. Choices were biscuits and the Muscadine jelly or honey, fried apples, crescent-shaped pancakes, bacon, sausage, ham, fried eggs, grits, cold cereal, grape juice, orange juice, milk, and coffee.

"Sit down, Honey," said Henry. "You look like you never saw a good Southern breakfast before. Everybody sit. Tilfort, you say grace."

"I'd rather not," he mumbled. "Not much thankful after last night."

"Don't be so ill tempered, Tilfort. You can say grace this mornin' or tonight when the good reverend comes," said Alice. Looking at Marla, she continued, "Our praying always gets him goin'. Says we don't pray strong enough, and he shows us how by his example." David and Henry both groaned.

"Yes, Ma'am. Lord not tonight. We thank'e God that we have food to eat and the kudzu hain't got everythin' yet. As for the preacher, bless his heart! Amen."

Alice cleared her throat and made a face. To Hailey she said, "Blessin' is cursin' down here." Then she smiled, "Thank you, Tilfort. Now, would you please pass those apples to Hailey. Marla, you can start the eggs around. Ignore Kingston. He'll get plate scrapin's later.

Henry was watching Hailey as she took the eggs from her mother.

"Lord child, I don't remember those bruises yesterday. Did you fall outside last night? I told you the land dipped over across the road and that you could get hurt."

Hailey looked at her mother, asking silently what she

should say. Marla frowned.

She said, "Hailey and I don't want to talk about it now. After breakfast."

Alice looked at her food.

"I'm the 'cause of that," she said. "I'm sorry, Hailey, I didn't know I held you so tight, but you got to know the dangers here."

"Alice," Henry asked softly, "what did you do to her?"

"I just tried to warn her. She saw people in the kudzu. It hypnotized her. She thought she was just tired, but it was drawin' her, and she was alone. It would have killed her like John. I shook her a little to make her listen to me. I was savin' her, Henry, please understand. I was savin' her. I made my special magical moon cakes and apple froth this mornin'. I'm still tryin' to protect her. I wanted to tell y'all last night, but you were asleep and I couldn't find David or Til. Y'all wouldn't have listened to me anyhow. And I've been cookin' and spellin' all mornin', so I haven't had time."

Lily had been watching from the couch. Hearing Alice's distress, she jumped down and trotted to the table where she climbed into her owner's lap and pawed her face. Alice hugged her like a child drowning on the Titanic. For a second time, the cat looked at Hailey. But now instead of pictures, Hailey heard words in her mind: *"Can't heal. Tried. Danger."*

Hailey felt Lily's need. *I understand*, she thought back, hoping the perceptive cat heard her.

"No," she heard in return. Lily looked disgusted as if Hailey didn't understand at all.

What? But Henry was speaking and the thread was broken.

"All right, Alice, I know." He looked at Marla and Hailey. "Thin's are tense here with the kudzu and Bogerty stirrin' up people. Tends to put everyone on edge. There will be a few more problems comin' later on this week. We need to talk after breakfast on the verandah."

"It's alright, Daddy," said David. "I told Hailey yesterday, and I figure she's already told Marla."

"Yeah, Henry, we know about the sleepwalking and the voices. We'll help keep you safe, Alice, and Bogerty won't find out from us. Still we should all have a talk, maybe after Bogerty is gone tonight. The family needs to close in, and we're part of this family," said Marla.

"Thank the Lord y'all have come to us now. Y'all are sorely needed," Henry said. He looked like he was trying to hold back tears. He took Marla's hand and shook it as he held tight. "Let's eat now, then David, you and Tilfort can tell me again what kept y'all outside so long last night. I know you said, but I don't remember. Too much Bogerty nonsense was ringin' in my ears."

"Changing the subject here," said David. He was concerned for his father and didn't want to bring up last night just yet. He also knew how his mother would react to what he'd say, and he found it hard to cope with her emotional trauma. All strong emotions were hard on him. They made him feel as if he were being attacked by swooping vultures and usually the stress sent him running to his flowers if he didn't shut down first. "What are you fixing to feed old lard belly tonight, Mother?"

"David, where's your respect. What with your names for him and Tilfort's blessin' his heart, that man must have his ears ringin'." Alice was chuckling and trying hard not to. "We didn't send you to college to insult your...betters?"

That brought a laugh from everyone. Tilfort deliberately laughed the loudest. He watched everyone carefully.

Still laughing, Alice said, "Alright, here's what I'm fixin' to cook. I thought since Marla's here, she could he'p me again. Seems like I'm not lettin' you out of the kitchen while y'all are here, Marla. I won't after tonight; I'll let you rest. We'll be eatin' left overs and cold, light meals for a few days until the moon's done. I won't be cooking much 'til then.

"I'm fixin' to have corn bread, purple hulled peas, fried ochre, fried chicken, ham, corn, mashed potatoes, fried sweet potatoes, a lime Jell-O salad with cheese and pears, and a peach pie. Do you think that'll fill him up and keep him happy, Henry? I'm hopin' he'll be too full to preach much."

"Better make it two peach pies. I'd like a piece, and that man will eat two-thirds of one himself," mumbled Tilfort.

"And ask for a piece to go," added Henry. Yes, that's fine. Just make those pies big ones or maybe a third since there's six of us to share what's left. Do you have enough peaches?"

"David brought me a bushel last Wednesday when he went to his restaurants deliverin' table flowers. I need to cook or can them real soon, so I'll fix four. It's no more trouble than two or three. I'll start right after I clean up the breakfast dishes."

"Don't worry, Marla, I buy the pre-made pie crusts. We will have to peel the peaches and add sugar and spices. I'll teach you my special ingredient that keeps the men askin' for more. Maybe you can snare a new Yankee husband with my recipe."

"I'd love to have your recipe, but I'll skip the Yankee husband. Maybe a Southern one, though." Marla winked at Henry.

"Well now, I didn't know you were in the market for a new husband. Reverend Bogerty is divorced. His poor wife looked like a scared rabbit—all nervous and twistin' her hands when they came to be interviewed. She bolted soon after they moved here. Mighty quick divorce if you ask me, only a month. Never thought a preacher would be divorced, but times are changin'," Henry said. "I could put a bug in his ear if you find him agreeable."

"Lord no," said Tilfort. "I can't hardly stand him one night a month. Don't want him visitin' any more often, unless you promise to take him north with ye."

Marla shuddered and said, "No thanks; he sounds abusive. I'll stay single; my photography pays the bills pretty much. Maybe I can get some good pictures with kudzu in the background. I bet they'd sell well back home. Pass me some more apples, please. Grits and butter too."

"Better eat and slow down the talkin' or the food will get cold. I'll have to microwave everythin' and the eggs will get rubbery," Alice said.

"Or explode; did that once to eggs. Even the bowl broke," David said as he speared a hot cake.

In between bites, Henry asked, "David, what all do you have to do today since that weddin' is Wednesday?"

"I'm fixing to run the flower bouquets to the groceries and churches, and I'll take the restaurants' flowers too rather than Wednesday. They'll keep in the walk-ins until they chuck out the old ones. I won't have time then or room in the van. I thought I'd take Hailey with me, that is, if you want to come," David said, the last part directed at his cousin.

"Sound like fun. Are we going to Unity?"

"That's one place. The other is that state park y'all passed coming here. They have a lodge and restaurant. Are you ready for a return trip on 57?"

"Only if I can hunch down in the back of your van. I don't want to look out the windows, but I'd like to see the park. I can't understand how anyone would take that road to go camping. I bet no one does it twice," Hailey said.

"The views are great," David said. "And the land is flatter there thanks to heavy earth moving equipment and some dynamite. When we get to Unity, I'll introduce you to a friend of mine—Janice. She's part Cherokee and owns one of the restaurants I supply. You'll get a different view of kudzu from her than Bogerty's punishment from God."

"She learnt knowledge from her grandma and great

grandmother up in North Carolina. She knows plants think, but she doesn't know kudzu," said Tilfort. "I've learnt the hard way."

Henry said, "Looks like everyone is done eatin'. Now David, time for you and Tilfort to tell us about last night. I was too tired to take it all in, and my heartburn was kickin' up real bad; the antacid tablets weren't hep'in'. I swallowed some tablespoons of Milk of Magnesia. That finally did the trick. You said the car was covered from sittin' in the barn. That's why we had your van, and why you took so long to get us goin'. What all had to be done while we were gone? When did you come to bed?"

"It was about three, wasn't it Til?"

"Yeah," Tilfort said, looking at his empty plate. He was trying to keep his mouth shut with the new relatives here.

"I was so dirty and sweaty that I just slept on my cot in the work shed. I had to clear out some vines there too before I could go to bed. They had covered the roof and were inside on the floor and on the mattress. The vines aren't on the greenhouse yet, but getting close," David told his father.

"Did you take a shower, Til, or just go to bed?" David asked.

"No one was up; I just stripped outside and hosed myself down. Cold water felt good. Turned the water on ma' clothes and chucked them over the old clothesline. Came in ma' door; didn't use the back. Didn't want to get caught if I'd roused anyone."

"I should *say* not, Lordy, Lordy," said Alice, grinning. "If Marla sees you do that again, we might have to marry the two of you. No man or woman should see each other naked unless they're married."

Tilfort turned bright pink. "I'll make sure I have ma' swimmin' trunks with me next time. I don't want a shot gun weddin'."

Hailey was dying to crack a joke about having a new step

dad, but decided against it since poor Tilfort looked as if he were about to sink into the floor. She just giggled behind her napkin. Marla was doing the same, only Hailey saw that her mom's forehead looked suspiciously pink like Tilfort's cheeks. She just winked and Marla returned that wink.

Henry smiled, "Well, Tilfort, looks like you're missin' your chance. With our Reverend Bogerty comin' tonight, there could be a different husband for Marla. Two good choices. We'll get you married yet, Marla."

At that point, Marla threw both her hands up and just said, "Uncle, uncle, I give up. I never saw such a bunch of match makers."

"Daddy, if you and Mother are done trying to marry off my right hand man, I'll tell you about last night before I need to get going on my rounds," David said.

"We're just tryin' to ward off the soberin' facts I know we are goin' to hear, Son," Henry said, his smile disappearing. "Tell us," then I'll get my antacid pills."

Hailey saw David nod. *He doesn't want to talk about it either, but he has to—now*, she thought. *It's time.*

"The vines have been growing through the barn door and across the floor all week," David said. "I haven't been paying attention because this wedding is taking a lot of my time, and Til's been helping me. I just didn't want to chop that stuff for a few days; doesn't leave me much time for my flowers. So I didn't notice that it had also climbed the stalls and grown up to the hay loft. The whole front of the tractor up to the seat was covered yesterday. I've never seen vines grow so fast, no matter how ideal the conditions are. I'll have to see if there's anything on the web, but it will have to wait until after the wedding."

So, the tractor and car did have vines on them when we got here yesterday; that's why they looked green. It wasn't their paint color, Hailey thought, but she didn't want to interrupt David's explanation.

"When I went to get the car so y'all could leave for church last night, there was some on the hood and door where it had dropped down from the loft beams. I tried to drag it off, but some vines had got through the rubber on the driver's window and were inside. I couldn't break them, so I got my machete from the shed and cut the stuff off the outside, and opened the door and pulled the rest out.

"When I tried to start the car to bring it around front, the motor wouldn't turn over. The vines had gone underneath and up around the engine. They were wrapped around the front axle too. That's when I gave up and brought my van around. I knew I couldn't get all of the kudzu off in time for y'all to leave. I should have been paying attention. It's my fault." David had his elbows on the table with his arms up and hands clasped. He rubbed his forehead on the back of one hand.

He looks tired and not just from no sleep last night, Hailey observed, watching him. *I don't need to be an empath to figure that one out. Everybody's worn out, and I can't believe a plant is causing all this hassle. What's with this kudzu? Turned me into a zombie. Is everyone so tired that they can't see something's not right here? Maybe Alice and Tilfort aren't so bat shit after all.   And.....maybe kudzu didn't want Henry and Alice to leave. Maybe it knew how Bogerty upsets them. That would be a good thing.* Hailey shook her head. *Where'd that thought come from?* She looked down at Kingston and then at Lily. Lily just stared at her and Kingston only wagged his tail. *Kudzu?* Tilfort's words broke through her thoughts.

"No it's *not*; that's *my* job—to take care of this place!" Tilfort said.

Wow, He's not mumbling now. He's all about defending David. Hailey was impressed and getting a good idea of what Tilfort was about.

"I should have been watchin' that damn crap." Tilfort blushed. "Pardon my cursin', ladies. David's been needin' my he'p 'cause there's a lot to do for this big wing-dig Wednesday. He can't earn us money and chop that cursed vine too."

"I should have been hep'in' David myself, Tilfort," Henry said. "That would have freed you up. You aren't Superman, just because you think you are. Guess I've just been restin' up for this week to come; been so tired. And Bogerty worries me a lot. He nearly eats us out of house and home when he comes around, and I'm afraid his radar will pick up some material for his Sunday rants. It's too close to whole moon for him to be here right now. One of us is bound to mention the sleepwalkin' or voices or somethin'. Then he'll mark us as belongin' to the devil. I don't know how long we can keep up this pretense. I have to bite my tongue the way he orders Alice to go cook more food right when we're eatin'."

"I know you say havin' that bastard come here to eat keeps him at bay," Tilfort said, "but it's wearin' us all down. You sure you want to keep doin' it? Find some excuse; tell him we're too busy fightin' kudzu. Tell him we have family visitin' right now. Tell him we don't have money for extra mouths, anythin'."

"No, Til," Henry shook his head. "I'm afraid gettin' rid of him will be harder than keepin' him. He'll just suggest a different evenin' or take to droppin' in when his stomach moves him. He does that to others around here. We can't risk his comin' during a whole moon. No, I'd rather have some control over his visits."

Henry turned back to his son. "I'm sorry, David, we got off track and I know you need to finish and get workin'. We won't interrupt again."

David smiled. "It's all right, Daddy. There's not much

more to tell. Til and I spent the rest of the night cleaning vines out of the whole engine block and clearing the undercarriage. It was around the muffler too and in the trunk. Then we cleaned the tractor. That was an even harder job. We moved both vehicles near the big tree."

"I used the ax and chopped the vines apart outside the barn around the edges," Tilfort included. "We pulled down what was on the beams and stall posts and carried it behind the barn and burned it. It's only a temporary fix because the roof is almost completely covered now except on the left front. You don't notice it from the sun room; you have to go out there to see. Even the back has vines coming down from the roof to the ground. We can't keep it out of the inside much longer. Guess the vehicles will have to stay in the open if we don't want to keep cleaning them off."

"First the orchard. That took two years to cover thirty acres," Alice chimed in. "It's only taken this spring and summer to grab the barn. It's on your shed; we had to move the bee hives; it's growin' in the back yard. Now the cars. What can we do?" she asked.

Hailey heard rising panic creeping into Alice's voice.

"We could try a controlled burn," suggested Henry. "But I don't know if it'll do much good. The more we try to get rid of it, the faster it grows back. Normal plants don't do that. But kudzu's not normal; it gets more unstoppable every day whether y'all chop it, burn it, or douse it with weed killer. Reminds me of that Steve Allen movie we saw last month: *Little Shop of Horrors* with a man-eatin', talkin' plant." Henry smiled at Hailey. "Guess that tells you my tastes in shows; I like Steve Allen."

I'd compare it more to a zombie movie, Hailey thought, *if you want to think unstoppable. But it's not a bad choice; Audrey II didn't just talk and eat, she planned things. After my being a zombie last night, I don't know.*

"I keep tellin' you that plant ain't normal; it's got intent,"

Tilfort said. "I won't say no more because you keep tryin' to be logical about it, and when's that logic goin' ta break down? Folks say ghosts aren't real until one stands in front of them and attacks. Well, kudzu's attackin' right in front of you now!" Tilfort shook his head and sighed.

Henry believes in that "ghost" more than he's letting on; he's afraid. Hailey sensed a whole pan of emotional dish water. *He's tighter than a piano wire and about to break. No wonder he had a stroke. I think he's trying to be an anchor so Alice's and Tilfort's boats don't fly off to Never Never Land and take David with them.*

"Maybe the Forestry people could help or the men at the fire station although they're mostly volunteer," said David, ignoring Tilfort's outburst. "I'd like to save the barn. The orchard can go."

Damn! He's wound up too. I bet he thinks he's protecting Henry. Those two need to do some serious talking. Hailey felt she was swimming in their emotional secrets.

"Don't burn my trees, please. They've suffered enough. I don't want to see them burn," Alice begged.

"Why not, Mamma?" David said. "You don't need to see them all covered up like they are. You know they're dead. None of them could still be alive under those thick vines. If they were burned, then the ground would be free. We could find the root heads and pour herbicide right down on them and maybe they'd die. It would get any seeds too."

"My trees, burn my trees." Alice started wringing her hands. "Ashley. John. They played in there. I see them in there. If you burn my trees, they'll be gone. They won't talk to me anymore. Don't burn my trees."

"Well, let's not do anythin' just yet," Henry said. "Let's think on it this week. David, you need to get on with your work. Tilfort too. Hailey, you go on with David, and I'll he'p

the girls clean up. Alice'll be in the kitchen all day, most likely.
I'll be out directly to look the barn over." He hoped to quell
his wife's agitation, at least for this day.

David got up first and carried several empty plates into
the kitchen. Hailey followed, juggling milk, two pitchers of
juice, and a cereal box under her arm.

"Hailey, I'm fixing to make the bouquets for the grocery
stores. If you want, I'll show you how since you said you
wanted to learn," David offered. "I could use the help too.
It'll go faster."

"Sounds good to me. As soon as I help clear the table, I'll
follow you out. Will you be in your work shed or the
greenhouse?" Hailey asked.

"The work shed," David said. "All my supplies are there as
well as the cooler—runs on propane. There's another, larger
cooler in Tilfort's room. We can bring flowers in from the
greenhouse to work with. And we'll need to put some
wedding things in the big cooler later."

"Where's Tilfort's room?" Hailey asked.

"Through that door there off the dining room. It was a
garage at one time until we did all the remodeling. We made
an enclosed walkway between the two buildings. The back
part has a work room with a door. That's the one he used last
night when he was buck naked." David grinned as he said the
last two words.

As there was only a row of cabinets and a bar separating
the dining room from the kitchen, Tilfort had no trouble
hearing the "buck naked" part, especially since David said it
rather loudly.

"All right, now!" Tilfort said. "I said I'd use my trunks
next time or at least as long as the ladies are visitin'. I don't
promise after that," he said, turning pink again. "I'm fixin' to
cut more kudzu. It's less embarrassin' than bein' in here."
Hailey saw past the door into Tilfort's room as he exited
through it rather quickly.

Marla and Hailey grabbed as much off the table as they could to save their older cousins the trouble. Henry removed the butter, jelly, and syrup. He left the honey and biscuits on the table for piecing later and covered them with a cloth. Alice wiped the table clean and ran the dish water. She handed Marla a dish towel and started talking.

Hailey listened while she slowly scraped the plates into Kingston's bowl. She expected the dog to start gobbling, but he was paying more attention to Lily than to his table scraps. Hailey thought the two were talking. She sensed worry, but no visual impressions. *I wonder if I touch them I'll get more*, she thought. Both pets looked up at her when she thought that and walked off. *Apparently you don't want me to know.*

Alice said, "It was just too far for Tilfort to drive here every day. The gas was eatin' him up, and he puts in long hours. We just moved him in with us. He's family. He never takes a day off; wish he would. He doesn't have a social life, and no other family except a sister, Arlene, in South Carolina. She's married with two girls and a boy. Once in a great while, his friend Charlie calls, but that's about all. Maybe he did have a social life before he moved in here. I hope he didn't stop it for us."

"He didn't," said Henry. "He was pretty lonely in Unity with his parents dead. He's shy; doesn't make friends easily. You notice he's been mumblin' a lot around y'all. It's the shyness. He's startin' to talk more now and mumble less.

"He showed up workin' one day where we get our gas. He took to David first. When he put the two of us together, he started talkin' to me. I found he was a jack-of-all-trades; done all sorts of jobs. I said if he was lookin' to change his line of work, I could use him. Hired him that next week," Henry said.

"He's 43; same age as Ashley would be. He went to Georgia State and has a business degree. His shyness kept him from gettin' good jobs 'cause he couldn't talk to people. He helps us manage what money we have, and he has some right good ideas too. Wish the kudzu wasn't twistin' his brain. He needs some free time," Henry shook his head as he spoke.

"Well, I said I'd look at the barn." Henry turned to Alice, "Put that fan on, Alice; it's fixin' to be another hot one; news said scattered showers, but maybe we won't get any here. All that bakin' and fryin' is goin' to heat this room up fast. I need my antacid tablets before I go out." Henry stared at his quad cane, seemed to make a decision, then took it from the corner and slowly walked toward the hallway with Kingston following. The dog ignored his scraps. *Henry doesn't want to use that cane*, Hailey observed. *Or maybe he doesn't want us to see him using it.*

Alice handed Hailey a small pail. "If you would please, before you go, knock on Tilfort's door and see if he's around. Mind the steps goin' down. He's so embarrassed over the teasin' I don't dare ask Marla. Tell him to fill this bucket with peaches. If he isn't there, go on in to the left; the work room is all the way in back. He won't mind. There's a door; you'll see it and the bushel is in the cooler. I'll get the pie crusts out of the freezer and start them thawin'; Marla and I can peel and make the fillin' while we're waitin'."

Tilfort had already left. Hailey found the peaches quickly enough, but she took her time returning. She thought looking around his room might give her some additional insight into this odd man.

The room was painted off-white. Only the necessities were there, and they were neatly placed. His diploma was framed and hanging on the wall. A picture of a family, probably Arlene's, was by his twin bed. There was a lounge chair next to a table and lamp by the window. Three bookcases, filled from top to bottom, stood against the wall, and more books were piled by the chair.

Hailey mused, *Well, he likes to read a lot.*

She looked at some of the authors: Arthur C. Clark, Isaac Asimov, Heinlein, H. G. Wells, Andre Norton. But not all the books were science fiction. Technical manuals of all sorts were filed next to biographies and histories.

There were some books on birds, animals, antique cars, and the Mayan civilization. There were far more on plants and flowers. *The Secret Life of Plants, ESP with Plants and Animals, Orchids, Plants Are People Too, Perennials: The Comprehensive Guide, and Ancient Plant Myths* caught her eye. *Lost Science* and *Bizarre Phenomena* sat next to them. She saw a couple by Sitchin and Danikin. Quite a few were on parapsychology, telepathy, and spiritualism. There was one titled *Ouija: The Most Dangerous Game* and even one on Native American jewelry and its spiritual symbolism. *That's an interesting assortment*, she thought, *but I don't see a definite pattern. Maybe enough to see why he thinks kudzu is a thinking plant, maybe not. What came first: killer plant or his weird ideas; one had to influence the other. I wonder if kudzu zombified him some time or other. That would do it, living here constantly.*

When she returned to the kitchen, Alice and Marla were cutting up three fat chickens. Alice looked up and smiled as Hailey entered.

"I figured you might want to do a little sight-seein'. Did you figure Tilfort out or is he still a mystery?"

"Was I gone that long?" Hailey was embarrassed.

Alice shrugged. "There's not much to see except his books. It helps to know his mind some. Tilfort's different, but I've accepted his views on kudzu. They fit with my whisperin's."

Hailey said. "I had a psych class this past year, and learned that minds can play some weird tricks. You said Tilfort just works, cuts kudzu, and helps David. Seems his only fun is escaping into his books. Maybe with all the other weird stuff going on here, he's imaging his stories are real when he's really got battle fatigue."

"Maybe Hailey, but *I'm* not going crazy, please believe me. I fought believin' Tilfort's ideas even though I suspected it for awhile, but I just couldn't accept that a plant has intent. That's why I was so rough on you last night. I see things—just flashes, but they scare me, and they fit with Tilfort's opinions.

"Henry keeps sayin' I'm overreactin'. He's afraid my abilities are short circuitin' my mind; that I can't control it. He won't tell me what he believes, but I know he's thinkin' about kudzu too; he's worried real bad. I think he feels he has to play it down so we won't all go screamin' down the road. Like he's the only tent pole holding up the canvas."

"Maybe all of you should move out of here. Kudzu is taking over no matter if its thinking or not, and you could be reinforcing each other's fear. Just a suggestion," Hailey shrugged.

"I didn't want to because of all the memories, but I think movin' to Unity could be a blessin'. I just can't make up my mind to really leave; I keep holdin' back. I don't want to burn the trees; leave them all alone. Leave kudzu alone so it won't get mad. Let it have this place without the burnin' if that's what it wants, and I hope that's *all* it wants *from us*. Then if Bogerty moves away, Unity might be normal," Alice said. "Oh! Be wary, Hailey, I don't think Bogerty likes anyone under 21 much."

"I'll keep that in mind. Guess I'd better go find David before he figures I'd rather cook than help him." Hailey left, deciding to file everything away for now. *Although*, she thought, *kudzu could go after Unity as easily as here. That's freaky. Stop thinking!*

"Speaking of Bogerty, do we really need three chickens?" asked Marla, determined to skip the kudzu subject even for a little while. "We're having a lot as it is."

Rosemary Coven

"Yes, and I'm double batterin' everythin' too just to add filler. My peas will be swimmin' in bacon fat only because I can't bread them."

"How do you double batter chicken?" Marla asked.

Alice smiled. "It's my new Bogerty weapon. I use thick batter. I fry the chicken in it for a while, then I roll it in more batter, and fry it some more. The more breadin' I can stuff down that man, the sooner he fills up, if that's possible. Watch your figure tonight. It won't hurt my feelin's if you want to skin off the breadin' and just eat the meat—less grease too. I'm even coatin' the sweet potatoes. The more battered and fried, the better."

"I just can't imagine a man eating that much," Marla said. "How big is he anyway?"

"He's about six feet with a fifty-eight inch spread. I know because Jill Eaten works at the clothin' store in Unity, and she waited on him for pants. She told me at church several months ago. Those new pants seem a little tight now. They're blue pin-striped, and he usually wears them here and on Sundays. You decide if he needs bigger ones."

"I imagine the fried ochre will be double battered too, and there will be gravy for the mashed potatoes?"

"You're gettin' the idea. We'll make the potatoes from boxes. I'm not peelin' and boilin' and mashin' all afternoon. I learned my lesson last month. I fixed a six quart bowl of potato salad and each of us only had one hep'in'. He ate the rest."

"Oh my God! Seriously?" Marla was shocked.

"That's not all. I fixed ten big pork chops, but I didn't batter them; I wish't I had. There were five of us, and I figured two each. He took the platter first and piled five on his plate. Then he said to me, 'Alice, that's a mighty puny plate of meat to feed your men folk. You better go fix some more.'

"He sent me back into the kitchen to fry more without getting' to eat anythin' myself. I fixed seven more and while I was fryin' them, he ate two more. My family only had one apiece, and he ate mine while I was in the kitchen.

"When I brought out the last I had, Henry got up and took two off the platter and put them on my plate. Then he made sure David and Tilfort had one more before he sat the platter down and took another for himself. Reverend Bogerty, bless his *heart*, took the final two. He ate nine big pork chops—the boneless ones, a half-inch thick. The potato salad was low by then too. And that was in addition to the rest of the fixin's. Henry was so mad; I thought he'd blow a gasket. Tilfort was stabbin' his chop like he was imaginin' it was Bogerty's hide.

"Sounds like he's a real glutton or else he's got some eating disorder," Marla said while shaking her head.

"I had two chess pies; if you remember, they're made from lots of eggs, butter, and sugar, so they're real fattenin'. He put one whole one, plate and all, in front of himself. Tilfort jumped up and took it away right quick, sayin' he'd cut it for the reverend. Bogerty told him, 'Now don't be shy, Tilfort, cut me a great big ol' piece. I dearly love Alice's home-made pies.' Tilfort cut it in fourths and gave him one. Bogerty just said, 'Tilfort, give me that other piece there too.'

"And when he left he said, 'Alice, I know there's some pie left. I'd dearly love to have another big ol' piece to go with me. Nobody can bake a pie like you can. I have my mouth fixed for a piece when it's time to come over.'

"That's why Tilfort said to make extra. Mr. Stomach took three quarters all by himself. I'll be hidin' two in Tilfort's room and keepin' two in the kitchen. Bogerty will spot them before we sit down to eat."

"Now I know what Henry meant about Bogerty ordering you around," said Marla. "How can you put up with that disgusting man?"

"He's got the power of the pulpit behind him, and he uses that weapon freely which can get ugly. Some of the folks here think he's a new messiah, and the others don't go to church much or they go to the other churches. The ones he drops in on for food, detest him. The offerin' plate isn't gettin' much in it these days, and it's not all because everyone's dirt-dog poor."

"Can't your church get rid of him?"

"Bogerty's got a two-year contract which will be up in six months," Alice said. "The whole congregation has to vote secretly whether to renew it or let him go. I hope he gets voted out. But the ones who hang on his every word may want him to stay. They're desperate to find some hope or someone to blame. He gives them both—ferret out the evil, and God's Grace will cure all the problems here. Thank God it's a secret vote or he'd know who wants him out. He can be vindictive; people would be afraid to vote him out if we had to say openly."

Marla took a deep breath and shook her head. To keep from commenting, she began peeling peaches as fast and hard as she could. She hadn't even met the man, and she despised him already. Keeping her mouth shut and being convivial was going to be a hard test. She'd dealt with some difficult customers in her line of work, but this guy seemed like a real piece of work. Then she had an idea that might help everyone.

"Alice, I take this guy has a big ego," Marla said. "What if I take pictures of him tonight, outside? That would get him away from the table before he can start preaching."

"Well, he usually preaches right as he's eatin' and keeps on afterwards. But it would certainly shorten it some," she said.

"Just keep the focus on me. I know he'll start judging

Hailey and me the minute he gets here. I've had some practice steering customers off subjects they've fixated on. I'll rattle like a magpie until his eyes glaze over. I'll tell him all about my work and Indiana. Then I'll tell him I want to take pictures of everyone, but we need good daylight. What time is he coming?"

"He usually shows around five and wants to eat by five-thirty. He starts complainin' he's hungry if he has to wait until quarter to six."

"Good. Make him wait until six. I'll say it's my fault that supper's late. Then I'll be slow to pass the food. I'll just hold the dishes in my hand and talk. I'll drag the meal out until seven or seven thirty, and give him no time to preach. Then I'll say we just *have* to get outside quickly for those pictures while the lighting is still perfect. My camera's digital so I can take a hundred and erase them all if I want. Maybe I'll even get a few good ones to keep. I'll take so much time posing and reposing him that I'll wear him out. He won't have time to preach. We should be able to send him home a happy man. And we won't have our ears worn out. How's that for a plan?"

Alice's eyes sparkled, and she started giggling. Marla knew she needed that lightness. They spent the rest of the morning conspiring and laughing. When Henry and Tilfort came in for a quick lunch of leftovers, the women shared their scheme. Both men gladly offered some ideas of their own. For once, they were looking forward to entertaining the honorable Reverend Bogerty.

Chapter 2

Hailey was quickly learning how involved a florist's work can be. David was a patient teacher, but she felt sure she was more hindrance than help. It took her several tries before she could make a satisfactory bow and several more before she perfected it. She knew that if she had to make all thirty, she would need a week. She admired how fast her cousin worked. He was totally focused and his hands literally flew over the wide ribbon.

Next he taught her how to make the flower bouquets which he sold in Unity's only grocery store. The color, proportion, and amount seemed simple enough when he explained it, but hard to actually do. She thought that it might be easier if there weren't so many flowers to choose from, and if each grouping didn't have to be so very different from the others. Then each had some little extra decoration included such as gold streamers or tiny silver beads. Her cousin truly was an artist.

David explained that he wanted many varied choices to entice his customers, because they had so little money to spend. He knew folks would want some beauty and hope to brighten their somber homes, and flowers could do that. *His* flowers would do that. He had them priced so low that Hailey wondered how he made any money at all. That is unless the shoppers bought lots of his flowers each week. He sure seemed to be making a lot of bouquets. *Well, that's Tilfort's job to manage the money Henry said*, she remembered.

She was amazed when David told her that consumer psychology was part of his college training. He'd even studied marketing research. All this to be a florist. That's when she realized just how fixated he really was. A lot more than simple dedication and love of his chosen career. He even had pictures of flowers hanging in his shed. *I wonder if some of the books in Tilfort's room are really David's? "Plants Are People Too?" That sounds like David. Wish I could sneak a peek at his room. Wonder what books or collected stuff he has? Maybe even some flower puzzles from that guy he helped or a DVD of "Little Shop of Horrors." I bet the whole room has flower stuff in it. Maybe I'm glad I didn't see it. His t-shirt has a Venus Fly Trap on it. Wow! Just noticed that.*

Watching him closely, she fully understood that her cousin definitely cared about every plant which he touched. When he took her into the greenhouse to gather the various flowers from the potted plants, she could feel a heavy atmosphere, almost electric, of love and trust. Those plants loved him as much as he loved them! *Now* she could imagine how a plant would become traumatized by seeing its owner murdered. How it could help convict that murderer.

He touched and talked to each as he passed by. He even kissed one large, thriving bush near the back corner of the greenhouse. He called her Mary and hugged her. Hailey could swear that "Mary" wrapped her stalks around him and hugged back. Plants suddenly weren't just things, they were loving, living entities and no different from her own beloved Toby and Rowdy back home—like Kingston and Lily. She wondered if plants experienced jealousy like pets sometimes did. Her new understanding would take time to absorb. She had never considered the possibility. *Maybe it's because plants don't walk around or talk like animals do. You can't play with them. Well, I did make dolls from holly hock flowers when I was little so I guess you can play with them.* Then she thought about the kudzu vining around and in the work shed.

The odd thing, well it seemed odd to her, was that he incorporated a little kudzu in most of the groupings, even the ones he already had for the wedding. More than several of these groupings also had the delicate flowers woven within.

He told her the vines and leaves added greenery and interest and the flowers added additional fragrance.

He was right about the fragrance, Hailey thought. The entire work shed was filled with an almost hypnotic smell. Only the fast work and her intense concentration kept her from sitting on the floor and meditating. David didn't have to go far for his greenery; it was on the shed floor where he had pulled it off his bed, and was all over the ground outside. When he needed some, he just took his knife and cut the young vines with their smaller leaves right off the floor. Larger ones simply required a few steps further outside.

Maybe it was her imagination, but Hailey felt that the kudzu was making itself available to David. Like it wanted him to use it in his arrangements. Is that why it wrapped itself around his cot in the corner? Her cat Toby liked to lie on her bed at home even when she wasn't in it. He went there when he was nervous and wanted comfort because the covers smelled like her. He always slept with her at night. Was the kudzu needing comfort? Was Tilfort and Alice stressing it out? She shook her head to clear it.

Oh Lord no, she thought, *I'm starting to think like Alice and Tilfort. Get a grip. It's a plant, not a pet. Well, maybe it is to David, but that's because of his Asperger's. It isn't going to come running to him if he calls "Here Kudzu" and it isn't asking to be used in his bouquets. It's just growing every-which-way because of the heat and extra rain, or is it?*

She had to stop these crazy ideas. "David, why so many bouquets for just one grocery store? How big is Unity?"

"About a thousand inside the city limits, but it's the only grocery for a long way. So lots of people come to shop—even tourists from the state park in the next county come here rather than Danvers; they say Unity's 'quaint.' There's a little grocery in the park and some of these will go there. My bouquets get used for weddings and funerals too because most can't afford large arrangements.

"This wedding on Wednesday is unusual. The bride and groom aren't from around here, and they've got money to burn. Somehow they found my name; I'm lucky. The extra money will really help. I'm not overdoing it, if that's what you're thinking. Tilfort keeps me in line, and he's figured how many I should make each week. It's also the Fourth coming up, so these red, white, and blue ones will show up all over town by tomorrow. Come help me get the singles from the cooler in Tilfort's room. Those'll go in bud vases at the restaurants. Then we can load the van and get moving."

Hailey thought loading the van would be easy. She tried to help, but finally just handed David what he asked for when he asked for it. That was the first time she actually saw he was getting a little exasperated with her attempts. He hid it well, but she could still read him.

David took the same route she and her mother had. When they reached the culvert, water was rushing through like deer being chased by a pack of dogs. There was so much force that it couldn't all go through. Much splashed up over the road and around the culvert's constricting sides. Hailey wondered what the other end of Seed Tick looked like.

In truth it wasn't passable. And the water was steadily moving towards the peach orchard. It was filled with silt and chemicals washed down from higher ground. Some ingredients in that soup were good rich soil washed from farms, and some of that soil contained organic fertilizer and nitrogen, and some ingredients were herbicides used in vain hopes of killing kudzu, including some herbicides that made the vine grow better. With the configuration of Alice and Henry's land, much of that water would flow into their fields.

When they reached 57, Hailey kept her eyes closed until her curiosity got the better of her. The road itself hadn't changed, but there was more kudzu everywhere. Evidently the rain had washed the vines loose from up above. It tumbled down the rock face like an exuberant child and flowed onto the fallen boulders by the edge of the road. More arms were stretched across the pavement than the day before. Kudzu on the rocks above seemed to wave happily at the van as they passed by.

The trip to the park was much shorter today than yesterday. As David had said, the views were spectacular, and to Hailey's surprise, the park was filled. A posted sign at the entrance said, "Camping, No Vacancy," but she had thought she'd read it wrong. People were everywhere, and many either were here for two or more weeks or were repeat visitors, because several recognized David's van and either waved or came over to talk about flowers. It took some time to reach the tiny camping and bait store. A small group of people were examining the holiday bouquets with their tiny American flags before he could get them inside. Then there was the lodge and restaurant. Hailey helped carry what seemed like the contents of an entire bus inside, but barely made a dent in the inventory.

The rustic timbered lodge was beautiful, but Hailey preferred to look around outside while her cousin finished his business and talked to various people. She knew it would take him awhile, and she didn't want to stand there with a frozen smile on her face feeling as awkward as hell.

The grounds around the building were landscaped and carefully manicured like an aristocrat's garden, but further off, the vegetation seemed less domesticated, wilder. In the overlooks, she could see more kudzu blanketing trees and open areas down where no vehicles could travel, and even walking would have been difficult without ropes and harnesses. The areas reserved for tourists seemed like some sort of reverse oasis—an empty island surrounded by a vast tangled of green vegetation, its bitter and angry depth unknown. The presence she felt earlier was here.

Hailey hadn't noticed how far she had wandered from the van, but she was feeling very tired. Her steps slowed, then stopped. Five hours of sleep, early heavy breakfast, heat, no lunch, and steady work were a good recipe for legs which wanted to sit down.

Sit down she did, balancing on a short stone wall topped with an iron fence which prevented incautious tenderfoots from rolling downward into oblivion. She didn't have much room for her hips, but by leaning against the fence, she managed. The fragrance from unseen kudzu flowers wafted toward her. *Someone should market that smell for incense or candles or soap*, she reflected as she drifted into a stupor.

Her mind wandered back to when she was a little girl and Mommy and Daddy were going to take her to Spring Mill Park. Daddy had promised and she was so excited. They didn't get there until closing time because Daddy was too drunk to get up and was in a nasty mood when he did. He didn't want to go, but Mommy insisted. She said she was tired of him breaking his promises. There was an argument, and he slammed the back car door when he stumbled in. He cursed at both of them half the way there, then wouldn't speak the other half. Hailey didn't like sitting next to him because he scared her. She was glad when they arrived.

Mommy found a park ranger and begged him to take the two of them on a boat ride into a cave to see the blind fish and other animals. Then she and Mommy looked in the windows of the restored village. The doors were locked, but Mommy held her up so she could see. Then they played in the river. Mommy was fun to play with because she didn't mind getting splashed, and she splashed back. Mommy's laugh was like warm biscuits with pancake syrup. She wouldn't look at Daddy who was glaring at them the whole time.

She was asleep when David drove up and called to her.

He had to get out and shake her by the shoulder. She jolted, instantly awake, fearful that James was shaking her. She hoped that fear didn't show on her face.

"I couldn't find you, and when I did, you didn't answer. You must be really tired. Me too. Three hours sleep wasn't much. Let's get going. When we get to Unity, we'll stop at Janice's place first. She always has a free lunch waiting for me. I'll buy you whatever you want. Did well today and I'm not even a third done," he said.

They were out of the park before Hailey fully awoke. *David must be running on adrenalin alone*, she thought. Back on 57, one look downward and *her* adrenalin kicked in. *Three hours sleep and he's driving this road. I don't want to think about it.* She slumped down in her seat and stared at the sky. The clouds had gotten much darker. Then a flash of lightening seared the air, followed by a loud crack. Both jumped.

"More rain, or is nature starting an early Fourth of July," she quipped.

"I don't like driving this road when it rains, especially if I'm tired," David said. "That lightening so close by means the storm's right on top of us. It'll be a slow crawl when it hits." Another deafening crash and water spilled from the bloated clouds.

It beat down with fists, driven by strong winds and making everything invisible. Knowing the road as he did, David found a narrow widening of the berm. There was enough room to pull partly off the pavement behind a boulder. The cliff didn't provide any wind break so the gusts bounced the vehicle like a spring-actioned toy horse. Then hail danced to the rhythm of lightning and thunder while it pummeled everything, even the ancient mountain cliffs.

Kudzu vines, driven off the rock above, landed on the van's roof and windshield. Hailey had never been claustrophobic before, but now fear rose into her throat like vomit; she covered her mouth with her hands to avoid screaming. She couldn't take her eyes off that mass of vines just three feet in front of her face. It looked like a heavy tangle of green snakes trying to reach...trying to break the glass...trying to...

"Hey, it's okay. We're fine. This gully washer will burn out soon."

David's voice grounded her, and she came back to reality. Even so, she remained wary of the kudzu, like it was playing with her head. *It might be, and maybe that fragrance in the park too?* She told herself that it was this damned road from hell and the wind that had petrified her...not a glob of vines knocked off some rocks. She knew she needed to eat. She could feel that her blood sugar was low. That always made her jumpy.

"Sorry, those vines spooked me," Hailey said, trying to smile so David wouldn't think she'd gone bat shit on him. *Guess I'm playing the logical explanation game now too*, she thought.

"The rain's slowing down. It ought to stop directly, then I'll pull the kudzu off."

He didn't have to. When the rain slowed to a drizzle, David backed up. The kudzu, still attached to the top of the cliff, simply slid off. He drove around it and continued toward Unity.

Yep, we're play toys. She thought she sensed laughter.

David drove slowly as the road was slick, and he didn't want to hydroplane. They encountered more vines knocked off the rock and jumbled either on the edges of the road or in the road itself. He ran over some, and a few wrapped around his axils. They broke easily as he continued to drive; they weren't a threat.

The closer to Unity they came, the more evidence of civilization appeared. But there was something more. Several houses were being swallowed whole with only a vague outline or section of roof still trying to escape the closing jaws. Others, though overwhelmed, had uncovered doors and windows. Families still lived inside.

Alice's words rang like warning bells as Hailey saw the road signs, electrical wires, and telephone lines. Kudzu had climbed all of them and was overhead on tree limbs. It formed a canopy with tendrils dangling down and waving with the breezes or whipped by passing vehicles. Out in one field stood a tall caped figure with its draped arms outstretched from side to side. It resembled a Grim Reaper waiting for the wind to take it flying. Hailey had no idea what it really was under all the vine wrappings. The whole area looked as if a sculptor had gone completely mad.

Lines were sagging, and limbs were bending low over the road. How long could either hold the growing weight? Hailey could imagine current shooting from broken electrical wires entangled within the kudzu. It was too wet for fires to start, but any unwary traveler could drive over them and be electrocuted. Large falling limbs could effectively block all vehicles temporarily. Road crews would have to chop the kudzu off before branches could be pulled over. Wrecks could happen. There would be no electricity for houses. Communications could be cut off except for cell phones. If kudzu got the cell towers or if there were dead zones, then people wouldn't be able to get help if there were emergencies. They'd have to wait hours to contact the rest of the world.

Hailey stopped thinking. She stared at the road and willed her eyes not to see the vines.

"Look around, we're coming into Unity," David said. There's Janice's place." He turned into The Hungry Dawg.

There weren't too many parking spaces and the lot was

narrow. It backed up to a kudzu-covered rock wall and dead ended. He had to wait until a car pulled out before he could drive in. They parked next to a rusty dumpster where grease trickled out from underneath, coating a few vines. More were growing up its sides and some were gliding toward several cars' wheels.

The restaurant looked as if it had been assembled from odds and ends of logs, boards, and metal. Hailey couldn't be sure if the mélange of advertising signs were just decorations or part of the structure. A veranda ran around three sides of the shack and had numerous benches where customers were sitting. Its eves dripped water, but the seats were dry. Kudzu dangled down from its roof like Christmas tinsel and entwined the trellises sharing space with the roses.

The Dawg seemed busy. This was confirmed when they went inside. Many folk of all ages sat around the hodge-podge of tables and chairs. Metal kitchen tables, round antique pedestal tables, and square or rectangle ones with Formica tops mixed together throughout the rustic interior. It looked like the owner had shopped at yard sales and Goodwill stores to furnish the place. Paper advertisements decorated the walls. Water colored greeting cards on hand made paper and hand crafted baskets sat near the door enticing customers to buy. All in all, it had a comfortable, welcoming atmosphere.

Curious customers looked up to smile and wave at David as the two of them took a table near the door. David waved back but didn't speak. He stared at his water glass instead.

Hailey sensed that so many faces looking his way made him nervous. *He wasn't that way when he was holding flowers and talking about them at the park. Asperger's?* That was the first glitch she'd seen.

A friendly waitress came right over with water, a small plate of biscuits, and menus. Hailey noticed that every table had a vase with two or three flowers incorporating small sprigs of kudzu. This place, at least, was prosperous.

Two men stopped at their table on their way out.

"Hey David, how's the kudzu your way?" one asked.

The other spoke to Hailey. "Nice to see you."

Hailey smiled. She was glad he didn't offer his hand; she didn't want a repeat like when she touched David's elbow. David introduced Hailey to his fellow church members, Billy Purdue and Olive Hudson.

"Saw your parents in church yesterday evening. You're turning into an old heathen, Boy. You haven't been there in a month o' Sundays," Olive grinned.

"I know. Have to find some way for the family to survive," David said. "I'm working on this big wedding come Wednesday. There're a lot of flowers and details, and I want everything right. They're paying good money."

"You sure missed a good sermon," said Billy. "Bogerty said it's time to exorcise the demon and all its minions. He says God's Will protects the faithful. Several of us have been holding rituals every night for weeks in our yards and burning kudzu in front of a cross. The Ku Klux Klan's been organizing. Only a few members right now, but we'll add more from towns nearby. You should think about joining. There's a meeting this Friday night at Wit Delmore's. We'll be lighting our torches from the cross and moving in small troops to burn out the evil. Probably a few Indians and their witch doctors will be on the list, but mostly the unholy and the unfaithful. Others will be burning the demon kudzu everywhere we can get to. Bogerty's blessing us some holy water to protect ourselves. We'll need it if some of the Indian legends are true. The Reverend says the water will protect us from the walking plant spirits taking revenge. God's been letting it happen because many have strayed from His ways. If the fallen don't repent, fire will purify them. That old witch Elowese is on my list and the rest of her family. Bogerty says the devil is strong in her. We may have to beat the demons out."

"Be careful you don't burn everyone out," said David. "You don't want to set the whole county on fire or have the sheriff after you. Then who'll I sell my flowers to?"

"Same thing I told him. Bogerty's really got some of our church folk riled up. Billy here's like the others, all flying off the handle. Can't talk any sense into him,' said Olive, shaking his head.

"You should come to the prayer meeting Wednesday night and bring your Yankee relatives. You'll be done with your wedding work by then. You'll know Bogerty's speaking for God if you hear him. That Indian woman's waxing up your ears."

"Now Billy, you're being right rude to David and Hailey," chided Olive. "And it's not Christian to speak ill when you're eating under Janice's roof. Let's get out of here. Sorry David. Was nice to see you, Hailey. Don't let this jackass get to you. Most of us are real good people." Olive practically shoved Billy out the door.

Hailey was absolutely stunned. She'd seen Klansmen on TV, but this guy was a real piece of work. *God, I hope I never meet another one of those, EVER!* All she could think to do was take a big drink of water. *Billy is worse than sucking on a slimy frog that shit in my mouth. I'll never wash it out, and he's for real.*

David reached for his glass too. "Need to wash that out of my mouth," was all he said.

She nodded, slightly surprised at his identical gesture. *Guess he's picking up my feelings, even to the nasty taste. Another empath? Can't be.*

But, listening to Billy, she got a feeling for the superstitions and fear creeping like the kudzu vines through this area, and how Bogerty was feeding his church members even more of it. *Billy just gave me the whole Sunday night sermon I'm so glad I missed. I'll need a gallon of water to wash away that Bogerty crap.*

Their waitress must have told Janice that David was here, because a very striking woman, around 39 or 40, wearing a white gauze dress belted with turquoise and silver, soon joined them. More turquoise graced her wrists, ears, fingers, and neck. She had braided, waist-length black hair trailing down her back, and a round face with a friendly smile.

This must be Billy's "Indian woman," Hailey thought and knew from the confident demeanor that she was the owner. Her eyes were what grabbed Hailey. They were dark brown, and she knew they missed nothing. There was calm wisdom reflected in their depths with a no-nonsense practicality and sincerity. Hailey liked her immediately, like she was reacquainting with an old friend.

"You're early, David," Janice said quietly, sitting down. I expected you'd come Wednesday." She tilted her head and looked at Hailey. "You're Hailey, the younger cousin. Welcome. Order what you will, both meals are free." Turning back to David, she said, "I assume Wednesday's wedding is why you came today."

David nodded. "I still have way too much to do, and the van'll be stuffed to the roof with all the arrangements. I figured you wouldn't mind."

"You know I don't; there's room in the cooler. Even if there weren't, your flowers never wilt here." She turned to Hailey. "I send the old ones home with my customers. Many come in on Wednesdays to get them. They tell me that even after sitting on my tables for a week, his flowers hold for two more before they throw them out, and they enjoy the fragrance combinations. David puts love into them."

The waitress returned and took their orders. Janice remained and observed the pair. She was silent until the girl left. Then she deliberately touched Hailey's arm so that she would look up. Her eyes seemed to bore into Hailey.

"I see the same tiredness and worry in your face as I do in David's. But...perhaps not quite for the same reasons." *You're an empath, aren't you? Picking up others' feelings can be troubling and sometimes wears you down, and you never know when or if those feelings are going to hit, right? Even touching a person can trigger impressions.*

Hailey's head jerked and she stared at Janice. She wasn't used to being spoken to empathically, at least not by humans. If animals "spoke" to her, they sent mental pictures or a simple word or two. Feelings and impressions were what she usually got from people and animals, and vibrations from rocks. But this was whole sentences. *Janice is a lot more than an empath! OMG!*

Janice smiled at Hailey. *I thought so. It travels in families, some members stronger than others, so your mother must also be. David is, although he won't accept it. Feelings give him a lot of trouble because of his Asperger's, and he tries to shut them out except when he connects with his flowers. He can't help being empathic; his father is, but Henry won't admit it either. Afraid it might spook folks.*

What about Alice? Hailey asked.

She's not your blood, but she's picked up some psychic abilities, maybe from living with your family members. She doesn't have much; just enough to be manipulated by anyone or anything around her and that's not good. Kudzu.

You're not just an empath or a psychic. What are you? Hailey asked, knowing that Janice wouldn't think she was being rude.

Maybe I'm an alien, Janice teased.

Seriously? Hailey giggled quietly so not to alert David to their private conversation.

David didn't seem to notice that the two women were staring at each other but not speaking. He was fiddling with his table flowers.

Just a novice in training, as you are in your own way. We

have crossed paths in the past, and we may again later in this life when you are ready and when we might help each other. Your abilities are growing quickly. Kudzu has noticed. It called you already.

Huh? That sounds ominous. I'm only eighteen. You're trying to hint at something, but what? Hailey wasn't ready to admit that Janice's words felt true. She didn't want to think any farther ahead than college and graduation. No other ambition; four years was far enough in the future.

Janice smiled. *You recognized me when you saw me before we met. Same here. That's all you need to know for now. Futures change and possibly we won't connect in years to come. File it aside or forget it.*

Hailey decided she and Janice should start a verbal conversation before David did suspect something, and she wanted some answers around here--for this time period. She figured Janice had them and would share what she needed to know for now.

"Bogerty's coming this evening," Hailey deliberately brought up, wanting to talk about the Reverend.

"And the full moon is Thursday. That's a close fit," Janice said. "Alice might start walking tonight. Be careful, all of you. I saw Billy talking to you, and things are heating up. The sheriff knows. His deputies are on standby and he's notified the next county over too. There's talk of bringing in some real Klan members instead of Billy and his wanna-be pals."

"I thought he was a Klan member," Hailey said. "He sure fit the mold I saw on TV."

"No," Janice chuckled. "I doubt any respectable Klansman would want to associate with Billy."

"You coming for the fireworks? I'm buying extra big ones with some of my flower money. David asked, wanting to steer away from anything connected to Bogerty, Billy, and his mother."

Janice was noncommittal. "I'll try as you might want my help with Alice. However things are changing here, and it's likely I won't be able to. Some of the Elders are arriving, my grandmother and great grandmother included. There's to be a council."

David raised his eyebrows and made a sad face. "I want you to come," he said.

Janice touched his hand. "I know, but I won't miss Alice. She won't listen to any reason about kudzu, and she wears me out. Be careful or she'll win you to her side over me, and hate mixed with sorrow isn't a good way to live. It's affecting her mind. She's too wrapped up in herself and becoming selfish and demanding. She doesn't see what she's doing to the rest of you."

Nice picture of Alice, Hailey thought. *These two have something going, but Janice has lost the feelings. Age difference? Philosophies. Alice?*

Janice looked at her and smiled.

She heard that. Hailey realized that Janice probably could hear all her thoughts if she chose to. *Time for questions and stop thinking*.

"Is everyone in this town either afraid of Bogerty or worship him? What's with this guy, anyway?" asked Hailey.

"No, just a few people either way," Janice answered. "There're six churches in this little town. Bogerty's only one minister in the smallest one, but... he's ambitious, self-absorbed, and controlling. For extra money, he works at a car lot here, but no one even wants to buy a car there. He pushes the other salesmen away and tries to strong-arm customers into buying; he gets a commission if he sells.

"He's run off over half his congregation with his sermons. The rest are tolerating him until his contract's done, but he does hold some of the gullible. He's been trying to pull in a flock from the other churches, but it isn't working.

"So if he's leaving soon, what's the problem?" Hailey asked. "Won't things die down when he's gone?"

"His sermons will have a lasting effect after he's gone, I'm afraid," Janice said. "And he's not gone yet; he might not choose to leave even with no Unity Baptist's paycheck. He could still hold some of his flock. Let me give you an example of how he works.

"I heard from a customer that the Percifields threw him out of their house last Thursday. He showed up at supper time right when Doris's mother Elowese was having a seizure. Howard tried to be polite, saying his wife was busy and there'd be no meal until later, but Bogerty insisted that it was his right as their minister to be fed and ordered Doris to start serving. Their son Howie grabbed his hunting rifle and pointed it at the good Reverend because Bogerty tried to hit Howard with his Bible.

"Silva Matheson said he railed from the pulpit yesterday morning and last night about old Elowese being owned by the devil. He accused the whole family of listening to her evil voice and casting out righteousness. He called down God's Wrath on them saying the time was at hand to do God's bidding and go to war."

"Anyone with a medical problem or special gift is evil and fuel for his pulpit. He's using kudzu the same way. Billy and others like him believe Bogerty hook, line, and sinker. They won't forget those sermons because it feeds their fear and they need something or someone to blame. Also that fear makes them restless; they need to do something to end that fear. Bogerty has given them a call to action and some will follow through with it."

"Is that why Billy said he and others were bringing in some Klansmen from out of town?" Hailey said.

"Billy's trying to, but there're others who could be

dangerous either singularly or in a mob. That won't die out just because Bogerty leaves."

"What makes Bogerty act this way? Where's his head? It's like he's stuck in the Dark Ages," Hailey said.

"I feel sorry for him," Janice said. "He's a failure, trying desperately to be successful, and having no idea how. So he thinks controlling everyone with fear is the way. His wife is gone. Food is his only comfort. He goes to others to eat for companionship and, I suspect, he doesn't have much money for groceries."

"He's a jackleg," David said. Turning to Hailey, "In Yankee language, that's a jackass. I know I should pity him, but I can't. I worry about Mama."

Janice waited until the waitress left the food before she spoke; her employees had good ears. "It's getting worse, isn't it?"

David nodded. "Tilfort's not helping. Now, she thinks he's right, or maybe it's Bogerty's preaching. She's convinced that kudzu deliberately killed John, and that it's evil."

"You know better. Kudzu loves you like all your plants do. If anything, kudzu may have tried to save him when he wrecked, and couldn't," Janice said, taking his hand. He pulled it away.

Hailey saw. *Kudzu's their connection. They both see plants as having feelings. That's why Janice hooked up with my cousin even though she's got to be five or six years older. He's having trouble with her closeness. Flowers, but not people. Hard on a relationship.*

"Speaking of, this kudzu talk is messing me up. David says you have some sanity here. Help," Hailey was floundering and she knew it.

Janice shook her head and grinned. "I know things my grandmother and mother taught me as I grew up. But, I'm just a Southern gal—all apple pie and grits. Being quarter Cherokee doesn't make me special; David knows about plants too. But, I'll give you my thoughts. Bare with me; I'm on my soapbox now."

"Kudzu just wants to live like the rest of us. Back home in Asia, it's got natural enemies that keep it controlled. There aren't any here, but it doesn't know that. So it grows as fast as it can, hoping to survive. The Chinese and Japanese enjoy and respect it. They cultivate it for food, medicine, weaving, ornamentation, and for its pretty little flowers which have a relaxing fragrance.

"Some people here are beginning to see its worth, but many have fear and hatred. They poison, burn, and chop it. It doesn't understand, and it's afraid. These plants here have never been in Asia, but the memories of human love and pride are within its cells, and it wants to serve. It has feelings; all plants do; all life does."

"You sound like you believe kudzu has deeper feelings more like people or pets than just in general," Hailey said. "This is all new to me, but I'm open. I felt some of that in David's greenhouse earlier today."

"Good. So you understand," Janice said. "Plants aren't that different from animals or humans. They care for their young and battle other plants for survival. They taste, hear, feel, think, and communicate with each other with many different smells. They can detect lies, recognize people both good and bad, and they appear to have ESP abilities. They also seem to have close connections to their owners and feel sad when the owners are leaving and happy when they return. So why would kudzu be any different."

"Well, David has a plant in his greenhouse named Mary who seemed to hug him when he kissed it, and I could feel lots of love and energy in there. That was an eye opener. I'll have to look some of this stuff up sometime," Hailey said. "I've felt plants, but it never sank in how deep their feelings could go."

"Don't think this is only my spiritual blood talking. David found the information on the internet, but it fits with what my grandmother and great grandmother taught me. Native Americans have always known this about plants; science is finally starting to catch up. He stuffed me with scientific plant facts like he has his whole family. Guess I'm saving you his lecturing or else spoiling his fun." Janice grinned and winked at David. He tucked his head.

"So if kudzu's like any other plant, why's everyone so creeped out by it and letting Bogerty turn people into witch hunters? What am I missing here?" Hailey asked.

Janice grew very serious. "This is what I believe: Kudzu's older growth is bewildered; it feels anger and hurt at the injustice and may want revenge. Some of the oldest roots are in the park, and I have *felt* bitterness radiating outward from there. Maybe it did turn on some people, but the young vines are still like happy puppies, wanting to please and be loved; they trust everything. It even fights with itself on what to do about its situation. Only, kudzu is different because other plants stay put. Kudzu can go where it wants, and do what it wants. It knows it can. Because people around here are afraid of how fast kudzu can spread, they keep bringing up old tales of walking plant spirits, and say kudzu is one of them."

"So this stuff is evil and people are unconsciously picking up on that!" Hailey was concerned.

Janice shook her head. "It's no more good or evil than any of the rest of us. You kick a dog enough, it'll bite back. You love it, and it will defend you with its life. David probably told you about the plant that caught a murderer. I have no problem with kudzu. I use it in the restaurant but not many of my customers know it."

Janice stood up and pointed to the table. "That's kudzu jelly in that jar and those are kudzu chips on David's plate. My quiches, salads, and soups all have kudzu in them. I use kudzu flour in my baked goods, like my pies and pancakes. Even my mustard greens have kudzu mixed in. Try the jelly on one of those kudzu biscuits there and see what you think. I like the taste. Your menus, those greeting cards by the register and even the baskets are made from kudzu. I just go outside and cut what I need and I think the plant is happy to help me. It hasn't tried to take over my building or harm my customers, and I don't try to kill it. Enjoy your lunch. David, come around back when you're ready to unload. I'll help. Nice to see you, Hailey."

When Janice was out of ear shot, Hailey grinned at her cousin.

"What?" he said.

"I like your girlfriend."

He blushed. "Thanks. You finish eating. I'm going on out. I'll be back as soon as I'm unloaded."

Hailey grinned even bigger. "I'm sure she'll help you with that."

David's face turned deep pink and he avoided her eyes. "Thank you. Eat your pecan pie; it's good." He escaped as quickly as he could.

It was good, and Hailey savored each bite, slowly. David didn't rush to unload his flowers; she knew he was enjoying some alone-time with Janice. It'd probably be the only sane part left in his week. Maybe Janice could get back her old feelings for him if they had time and no interference.

While she waited, she played with the tiny bouquet in her vase.

He turns three flowers and some vine into art. Should be something attached to his bouquets that says "Creations by David." His bouquets probably go everywhere, even out of state. A little electric shock ran through her as it dawned on her what she was thinking. *His bouquets with kudzu go out of state! Tourists take then everywhere! Indiana too?* She pulled out the kudzu and examined it closely. The backs of its leaves were a pretty silver.

It was beautiful in the moonlight last night, she thought. *Nice here too.* Rubbing the leaves between her fingers gave her a warm feeling. *This little piece is happy. It hasn't learned about the "Billy Purdues" yet. I hope angry kudzu doesn't go everywhere.*

When David returned and they resumed the deliveries, they dropped three small baskets at the funeral home and several sprays at four churches. Then they visited the grocery and five more restaurants. Hailey was surprised there were so many eateries but...campers needed someplace to eat besides their campsites or the lodge. Even the grocery was fairly large. Unity was doing well thanks to the tourists. David was too. He seemed to know everyone, and everyone wanted his flowers, even though he ought to charge a little more, in her opinion. *Oh well*, she thought, *people buy more when the price is low. And kudzu goes with David's flowers.*

..........<>..........

David's face was bright on the way home—the lines were gone, and he looked much younger than thirty-four. He smiled a lot too. Hailey left him to his thoughts. She figured he and Janice had plans. The closer to home they got, the less he smiled. The deeply worried look returned when he pulled into the driveway. He drove to the back, parked under the oak tree, and leaned his head on the steering wheel. He closed his eyes and stayed that way for several minutes. "I'm tired," was all he said.

Hailey touched his arm in sympathy. Her skills kicked in with a vengeance. She felt more than she wanted to and it flowed in fast, short bursts.

He really needs to get out of here. Too much on his shoulders: he's carrying all the family, even John and Ashley.

Open a shop in Unity. He could be closer to Janice. They all need to go—sell out, grab the money. Get some sanity back. Worrying over a dead farm'll kill them all. Alice and Henry won't leave; Henry because of Alice, and he won't because of them and neither will Tilfort. They're misfits worrying that Bogerty will expose them. The flashes were intense as they slammed into her head. *I'm not sure I like this new touch-know thing. And I'm worried about going to college. Damn!*

David knew she'd picked up his thoughts; he felt the intense connection.

"Please don't, Hailey. I mean, thanks for the support, but I don't know if I want you to know everything or not. I guess I do; I need someone to, but slower. Even with training, feelings and communication can be hard for me."

"Sorry. I didn't know that would happen. I usually get small things, not buckets full." Hailey felt awkward. *I wonder if he picked up any of Janice's thoughts when we were linked telepathically.*

"I don't know if you figured it out or not, but I'm an empath; I know you are. So maybe it was my need that caused that strong connection right now. It helps with the flowers. Daddy's one too and it helped him with the peaches, but it's driving Mother crazy. Like I said, she's not so much empathic as psychic and she can't control what flows into her head. Nice family; don't tell anyone."

"I'm part of this family too; so's Mom. What about Tilfort? Is he empathic?

"No, he's normal."

"Seriously!" Hailey started laughing.

David joined her in laughing. "Come on," he said. "Let's see how things are going. Lard Butt'll be here soon, and I want a shower."

The house had almost a party atmosphere. The cooking

was done and the women were drinking sweet tea and relaxing. Lily was glued to Alice's lap. David and Hailey just stared. He had not seen his mother so happy in a long while. "You're planning something," was all he said.

"And I think Mom's the instigator," Hailey added.

"You bet, and the guys are in on it. No time to tell, just play along," Marla said.

"I'll go take my shower, and get out of here." David turned to run for his room.

"Make your shower a long one. We're eatin' at six. Take your time too, Hailey," Alice said.

He looked at both women for an explanation. "But Bogerty…"

Alice nodded, "Six."

Hailey pulled her dumbfounded cousin toward the hallway. "Don't argue with the mommies."

Chapter 3

A booming male voice woke Hailey from her short nap. It seemed to be preaching and complaining all at the same time. She changed into clean clothes and slipped into the living room. By not walking in the center of the hall, she avoided the floor's squeaking. The man didn't hear her enter--- Bogerty; it had to be. His back was to her as he stood in the kitchen doorway attempting to hurry the women. His upper arm was resting on the door-jam as he preached about not keeping the Lord waiting.

He was enormous—both directions. Alice was wrong; he must have been six-three, but it wasn't his height as much as his width. His striped pants couldn't have held any more of him. His round head was bald except for a Friar Tuck fringe that touched his collar. It was his voice that made him intimidating and demanding; he wasn't used to being defied. It would have been hard to do so.

Alice and Marla were pretending to cook, but in slow motion. Marla kept stopping in the middle of the room to chat with the man. She seemed at ease and social, but Hailey could tell that her mother was having a hard time sticking to her plan, whatever it was. Bogerty was getting to her. Where were the men? She turned and quietly slipped back down the hall to the back door. She didn't see them from the windows. The work shed? Hailey ran there. David was making bridal bouquets. Tilfort and Henry were helping while Kingston was supervising.

"Hey, you guys, Mom and Alice are all alone in there. Shouldn't you be distracting Bogerty or something?"

"Henry looked up. "We're fixing on comin' in at quarter to six."

"Well, it's show time. Mom's rattled and that doesn't happen when she's dealing with people."

Hailey turned and ran back to the house. The men followed.

She deliberately made noise when she reentered the living room. Bogerty turned and his impatient eyes ripped into her. His ugly face resembled a bowling ball. Hailey envisioned putting her thumb in his mouth and her fingers in his eyes and rolling that head down an alley. Only the sculptured beard belied his baby-soft skin. His eyes could be as cruel as a fish-gutting knife when he didn't get his way. She was barely able to withstand his gaze. She felt like closing up into a tiny ball and sucking her thumb.

He appraised her. "Where have you been, little girl? You should be in here helping your betters. If you were doing your part, supper would be ready by now."

Hailey knew she should act subservient, but she couldn't, and she certainly didn't want to. He was like James, her dad, all over again, but not this time, she wouldn't. Never again. She returned his gaze. "Hi, I'm Hailey, nice to meet you too." She knew she had startled him. He didn't like that tone; he walked toward her. She brushed past him and into the kitchen. "Can I help?" she asked.

She was a little afraid that he might hit her for what he perceived as insolence. Marla must have thought so too. She handed her daughter a plate of cold corn bread and pointed her toward the microwave. Then she blocked Bogerty's path and turned on her sweetest smile. "Here Reverend, would you please set this fried chicken on the table. We're almost ready."

His face relaxed for the moment. He smiled down at Marla. Hailey thought it looked more like a leer. "Why I'd be most happy to, Miss Marla." She almost curtsied as she handed him the platter, then turned her back to him and looked at Hailey. She crossed her eyes to say all's well, but there was a warning there too. "Keep your mouth shut," it said. Marla picked up the bowl of fried sweet potatoes and carried it to the table.

Henry was the first to enter the room. He had seen everything, but deliberately limped slowly toward the couch, followed by the other two men. Kingston saw Bogerty and growled softly; he remembered being kicked. He stood in front of Henry, blocking any access Bogerty might have to his beloved owner. The slightest move, and he might have attacked.

"Kingston," Henry whispered. The dog sat down, but his eyes never left his enemy.

Hailey and Marla watched the act. Tilfort made a great show of helping Henry sit down while David turned to the Reverend with a respectful voice.

"Sorry we're late, Sir, but Daddy and Til were helping me with the flowers for Wednesday's wedding. If Hailey hadn't run to say you were here, we might still be out in the work shed."

"She should have been in here working. Spare the rod, and spoil the child," he said, glaring at Hailey again.

Alice spoke up now that her husband was there. "She was sent to clean the bathroom, Reverend Bogerty. She *was* workin'. Just a minute more, and we can eat."

Hailey was surprised how easily that lie tripped off Alice's tongue. She felt that Alice would have considered it a sin to lie, especially to a preacher. *Well, she's defending family here; so maybe she's rationalized that it's not a sin to "deceive the devil's own." And this fat guy sure acts like some devil.* Alice's lying made Hailey actually like her a tiny bit now. It sort of made up for the bruises.

"I had her working for me all day. Making bows and helping with deliveries," David said.

"The child's been a Godsend to'll of us. You'd be ill to criticize her, Reverend," Henry said with more strength than his acting suggested. "I just wish we could keep her here. And Marla's hardly been out of the kitchen. She's a big he'p to Alice. Tilfort, he'p me to my chair. The Reverend will want to say grace."

Bogerty just growled and grit his teeth. The glaring eyes didn't soften one bit as he sat down to the table. Meanwhile Kingston raised his ears, bared his teeth, and began growling, but made no move toward the preacher.

Then Kingston followed Henry to the table and sat by his feet. His soft growl continued nonstop. Finally, David gently took him outside.

The women continued carrying the food to the table as Bogerty prayed. He was still at it when they finished and sat down. The prayer continued for another ten minutes and included praising the family and food, Marla, in particular, ranting about sin and kudzu's being God's punishment thereof, embellished visions of hell, and a final dig at Hailey's slothfulness. Tilfort had been right—his praying did ruin the appetite, especially the sexual tortures inflicted by devils for punishment and pleasure. He seemed especially proud of his scenario of a demon inserting a glass rod into a penis and hitting it with a large rock. He returned to that picture a second time to drive home his vision of God's hatred for sinners. Bogerty was red in the face from his exertions, while the others were decidedly green. "Amen" couldn't come fast enough for Hailey. In the same breath, he said, "Pass the food."

Hailey was so flabbergasted by his prayer that she couldn't help thinking, *Good thing we didn't served hot dogs.*

He set the chicken next to his plate, and his meaty hand grabbed four pieces before he released it. The others passed the serving dishes away from Bogerty so they had first choice. As each bowl and platter reached Marla, who was sitting next to him, she did as planned. She helped herself, then held the food and talked endlessly. Hailey almost felt sorry for the frustrated man. He was obviously enamored of her mother and trying to be patient. Finally he could stand it no longer, and took the purple-hulled peas from her hand and scooped half into his plate. Then he stood up and reached over everyone to get what he wanted. Alice excused herself and ran to the kitchen saying she forgot the lemons for the tea. Bogerty told her to bring more sugar for him. She buried her head in the refrigerator to hide her giggling.

The plan was running smoothly and Hailey watched it unfold. Marla talked and smiled, and he ate. Not one bit of preaching poured from his full mouth. Alice's double-breaded everything satisfied him to his toes.

When the pies were brought in, Alice told him that they were Marla's own recipe which was the truth; she had suggested adding sour cream to the mix as fattening filler.

Bogerty went puppy-eyed when Marla dumped two huge pieces, nearly two-thirds, on his plate and added a snow drift of whipped topping. She even wrapped him an extra piece with topping to take home and put it right by his plate before his other two were gone.

Marla said, I'm afraid you might get hungry later in the evening." He was completely under her spell.

Marla had already told him that she was a professional photographer. Now she regaled him with hilarious predicaments involving children, newlyweds, and animals— mostly false. Her act was riveting; she would have made a good stand-up comedian. Hailey was impressed. *Mom's her old self tonight, and in overdrive*.

On cue, Alice suggested everyone retire to the verandah to relax and have more tea. Hailey, at her mother's suggestion, volunteered to stay behind to clean up. She was more than happy to be out from under Bogerty's scrutiny and took a long, slow time. Still she listened carefully from the kitchen window. For the reverend's part, he began to see how useful the girl could be. He was not feeling up to a sermon just yet.

The sun had long since returned after the mid-day storm, and the early evening was pleasant although humid. The ceiling fan added a breeze. Lily was back on Alice's lap. She had not been allowed inside with Bogerty there; he hated cats as much as dogs. Kingston stayed off by himself, but kept a steady watch.

It was Henry's turn to remark on how nice the light was. This gave Marla the opportunity to suggest taking pictures of the kudzu, the house and surrounding areas, the animals, and everyone present. On cue, the family all rose and dragged Bogerty with them.   She fed his ego by taking many photos with him in the foreground. Hailey crouched down and watched everything from the slightly opened sun room windows. She could hear just fine.

Henry returned to the verandah after a short while. Hailey noticed that he was badly winded and couldn't keep up, and that Alice looked worried. She overheard him telling Alice to stay with the others and not leave Marla alone with Bogerty. He didn't tell anyone that his chest hurt, but Kingston knew and he sent a mental picture to Hailey who suddenly felt that pain; she gasped and grabbed for her chest. Her eyes followed the dog as he helped steady Henry while he limped away. She guessed Kingston would come get someone if it were serious, so her focus returned to Bogerty and a comedy act.

Bogerty was having a lot of trouble walking over the kudzu in the back yard. It threaded through his shoe laces, caught on the toes of his black and white wing tips, wrapped around his ankles, and pulled at his pants' cuffs. He looked so foolish holding up one fat leg, then the other, to pull the stuff off, that she was sure her mother had to hide her face with the camera. No one else had any problem. The vines seemed to part, giving the others clear passage.

Bogerty became so frustrated that the cords stood out in his neck. "Tilfort, go get a machete and chop these cursed vines out of my path."

Tilfort obediently trotted to the veranda and returned with his dull ax.

"I ain't chopping nothin', Reverend. It ain't safe." Tilfort said while handing the ax to the preacher.

Knowing how liberally Tilfort swung that instrument, Hailey suspected he refused to do any chopping so that the comedy could continue.

Howling like a demonic cat, the fat man swung the ax at a large root crown, severing several old vines. His mouth spewed curses as he continued to chop, beginning with, "You fucking foul penises slithering from Satan's mouth!"

Alice covered her ears and Hailey imagined that the plants were as shocked as the rest of the group. The hatred directed at those vines would have been enough to make them wither if they could hear, and Janice had said earlier that they could. More likely than withering, kudzu would want revenge if the angry presence she felt in the park was any indication. Too bad for Bogerty if it did.

David suggested that they return to the verandah, before their minister could begin a sermon. Everyone scattered leaving Bogerty to follow. Hailey slipped back into the kitchen to listen. Alice told Henry what transpired, then joined Hailey inside.

"I guess you've been listenin'," she said. "Get me a tall glass and dump two heapin' tablespoons of sugar in it please while I get the sweet tea. He needs extra sugarin' up," she said as she winked at Hailey.

The tea was waiting when he struggled in.

"More pie, Reverend?" Marla offered.

Their catering soothed him back into a mellow mood. Henry sat silently; he just petted his dog.

It was sliding toward twilight, and Bogerty showed no sign of leaving. David said that he needed to get back to work. The reverend just waved him on, not taking the hint. David had no choice but to leave; however, he signaled Tilfort to stay. Tilfort understood and so did Kingston. The dog moved next to Marla and sat in a guarding position in case he needed to protect her.

The conversation drifted to the Fourth. Bogerty was, not so skillfully, asking about their plans for celebrating. Alice should have said that they were going to Unity for fireworks, or that they hadn't decided. Instead, she mentioned shooting fireworks at home. It probably wouldn't have mattered what she said. It was plain to all that Bogerty was determined to insinuate himself into their plans. He was smitten with Marla.

"Henry, I applaud your decision to have a small family celebration. Unity will be over run. Sometimes it's even too much for me. Our lovely town can't hardly hold all the tourists who wish to help us enjoy this most patriotic of days—our independence from tyranny and oppression. I do believe that I shall join you come Thursday and escape the maddening crowds. Shall I again arrive at five?"

Now mad at Alice for divulging their plans, Henry thought to himself, *Lord, I don't want to feed that son-of-a-bitch again, not on whole-moon.* He knew he had to be careful. He mustered his strength and said, "I'm sorry, Reverend, but we're fixin' to take the ladies sightseein' most of the day. I reckon we've all been workin' them harder'n dogs and they deserve a rest. We're eatin' out. I don't want them cookin'."

"Well now, that's a lovely sentiment, lovely indeed. I myself know many remarkable locations that will certainly please a discerning eye like Miss Marla's. I offer myself, dear lady, as your personal guide. I insist that you take along your camera. Many wonderful sights will be uncovered. You may find them inspirational."

Marla blanched. She could practically see him bowing low with a medieval flourish and a sweep of his peacock festooned hat. Then a quick vision of his backside being liberated from his pants nearly sent her into hysterics. She recovered, allowing only a small giggle to escape. Bogerty took it for coy acceptance, but Henry came to her rescue. He saw her vision.

"I'm sure we'd all appreciate your he'p, but there won't be room in the car; it only sits five, and David's van has no side windows or seats," Henry said.

"Well then, may I have the honor of joining ya'll for supper downtown? There are some mighty fine eateries in Unity. If I might, I will take the liberty of suggesting one for your culinary pleasure, Miss Marla."

Henry championed her again. "I was fixin' to wind our way to Gatlinburg, not Unity. There's more to see. I know Alice wants to shop for some shoes and a purse. Somethin' about needin' pink. I have no reckon where we'll eat. So I can't he'p you unless you want to follow us for a long shoppin' day."

Bogerty was relentless. He ran his hand over his perspiration covered head, thinking. Marla noticed a large gold pinkie ring stuffed on his fat finger and turned away.

"Well, I see my services won't be required. The better part of valor says a man should never interfere with ladies and their shopping. However, I shall join you for your evening celebration. I shall come about nine. Perhaps I may be of assistance in some small way—set out the lawn chairs, help carry the fireworks, say a prayer of thanksgiving for our independence. Well, gentle folk, I must be winding my way home." He rose and took Marla's hand in his. "My dear, it has been wonderful to see you. I look forward to seeing you again Thursday next. Your peach pie recipe is definitely something to write home about. I shall endeavor to not give in to temptation, but save my spare piece, which you so graciously offered, for a morning treat. It will remind me of you." He patted her hand and waddled to his car.

Hailey came out on the veranda and stood in the shadows until Bogerty drove away. Then she sat down next to Henry. He seemed more and more like the father she wished she had. *It wouldn't take me much to love him. I feel protected like I did with Mom.*

Kingston growled softly not taking his eyes off the reverend's retreating backside. He too relaxed when the man left. He walked over to Marla and leaned against her leg. She reached out to pet him when he began licking the hand which Bogerty held. "Thanks, Kingston; it needed to be washed." "Henry, you were amazing. You countered his every move. I especially loved the shopping for pink shoes and purse," Marla said. "He's the most pompous, disgusting animal I've ever met."

"Around here we say somebody like him is a 'big dog with a brass collar'," Alice said.

"I think'ee ov'r did the actin'," Tilfort said. "He's sweet on you, and iff'n you tell 'im you got a boyfriend, he'll say you led him astray. Then the preachin' and rantin' will start. You got a fine wire to walk come Thursday."

I know, and I'm *so* sorry. I didn't expect this. What can we do?"

"I need to think on it a spell," Henry said soothingly. "We have three days. We'll send him home after the fireworks. I'll say I'm real tired or we all are, and need to sleep. He should be decent enough to leave."

Tilfort snorted. "That bastard ain't decent. He'll keep Marla up and cull her from the herd. He won't go home."

Alice agreed with Tilfort. "He hasn't got a lick of decency in his bones. You should know that, Henry. I can say I'm sick from the heat and need Marla to he'p me."

"That won't work," Tilfort said. "You saw how he acted t'ward Hailey. He'll make her he'p you and hold on to Marla. And if you say you need to he'p Hailey 'cause she's sick, he'll say she doesn't need he'p or she's tryin' for attention. *She* can't do nothin' right. He decided right off he don't like her. He might of hit her when she talked back to him. Better ya'll get sick of the givies."

"The what?" Hailey asked. That wasn't a word she'd heard before.

"It means the humidity. We should get sick because of it. The car's air conditioned, but if we all are walkin' around shoppin', we could get sick," Alice interpreted what Tilfort was saying.

"Maybe Henry could call Bogerty and cancel, saying we aren't having a celebration at all because we're sick," Marla suggested.

"He'll just come pray over us and still cull you from the herd. That one's like a pit bull when he latches onto somethin'. Ya'll have to let him come and hope to get rid of him afterwards. You can't go to sleep, Alice. Fix yourself some coffee. You don't need to go walkin' with the devil around," Tilfort said.

Henry listened to everyone. "Tilfort's right. We'll just have to put up with him. David can cut short the fireworks, but I hate to disappoint him. He's been buyin' a few here and there so we'd have a good show. He wants to go buy better ones with his weddin' money to please ya'll.

"David better tell Janice not to come, and he won't like that; her neither," Tilfort continued. "They don't get much time. But she don't need to be near Bogerty. If that suck-egg dog knows they're connected, she'll be on his pulpit list again. And he might add David, sayin' he's under her heathen spell."

I don't think Janice is coming," Hailey said. "David asked her today and she said her relatives were coming and there was going to be a counsel meeting."

"That would be a blessin' because I won't have to ask David to tell her not to come and cause hard feelin' all around. Bogerty's none too happy with Janice because she won't give him free meals," Henry told Hailey and Marla. "He raised such a ruckus when she handed him his bill that she called Garnet Easley, our police chief. He paid after Garnet told him to pay or go to jail, and she told him not to come back. That Sunday, he preached that she had no charity and didn't 'give to the Lord his due.' Remember that, Alice? David swore he won't go back 'til he's gone."

Henry looked like the world had fallen on him. He tried to get up, but fell back down in his seat. Tilfort launched himself out of his chair and grabbed the old man. Seeing how pale Henry was, he helped him up and gave him his cane.

"I'm goin' with you, Henry," he said softly. "You don't look too good. Lean on me. I'll get you outta their sight. Put you in the sleepin' porch and bring David." He looked as worn as Henry. Henry put his free arm around Tilfort's shoulder and Tilfort put one around Henry's waist but he was off balance and used the veranda wall for support. Hailey took Henry's other side to help balance Tilfort as they half carried the man inside. Kingston followed them, whining. Balanced better, they got Henry down the hall and out to the couch. Hailey opened the outside door and all the windows wider to help the night air flow through, hoping the slight breeze might help. At least it was cooler than the veranda.

Remembering some facts from high school health and Marla's doctors, Hailey ordered, "Sit him sideways and raise his legs, Tilfort." She cushioned his back with pillows, and gently took the quad cane from Henry's hand and set it close by.

"You stay with him. He must not lie down if he's having a heart attack."

"Kingston, protect," she ordered the dog. He understood. Henry started to slump down and the dog pulled at his hand until his beloved master straightened back up.

"I'll get David, and you stay with Henry, he shouldn't be alone."

She realized she was giving orders to a man over twice her age, but too bad. She knew what to do, and even if Tilfort also did, she was taking no chances. She took care of her mother and now it was time to take care of Henry. Her chest ached with emotions she hadn't felt since nursing her mom. She knew she was very attached to Henry. She needed a father and he was a good, loving person. She surprised herself in how quickly she responded.

Hailey ran to the work shed, and burst in shouting, "David, it's your Dad. Sun porch, hurry!" It was all she could get out. He dropped the arrangement he was crafting and raced ahead of her. Tilfort was checking Henry's pulse when they arrived.

"I reckon you should dial 911," he said calmly. "I don't know if it's a heart attack or tension. It's Bogerty's fault whatever."

Hailey yanked her cell phone from her back pocket and made the call. "Paramedics will be here as soon as they can with that road," she said. "David, get an aspirin and have him chew it. Also a glass of water. Have him drink all of it. It should help. And keep him awake! He already had one stroke and this might be another. I'm getting the others." She rushed to the veranda.

Her mother was coping with another crisis. Alice was crying and rocking her body back and forth as if she were attempting to head-bang at a rave. "He wants to marry Janice, but he won't leave, and we need him bad. It's my whispers. It's eatin' Henry up. It's gonna kill him, and I'm afraid. He's right about burnin'. Burn the orchard. Burn all the kudzu; I hate it. It's killin' this family. Keep the house and David's workin's. Or sell it. Move to Unity. Everythin's gone. Bogerty. Horrible!" Alice suddenly clutched the arms of her chair as if it were the only parachute on a falling plane. Marla looked up at her daughter and widened her eyes.

"Help," they said. Hailey knew her mom was at a loss how to comfort the hysterical woman. But Henry was more important. She hadn't taken crisis multitasking 101. Hailey was beginning to feel resentment toward her mother. *Why isn't she taking charge instead of me? Why do I have to do this? I'm 18! She's not that weak*, she thought.

"Henry may be having a stroke or heart attack. The guys are with him and the ambulance is coming. I don't know what you're going to do with her, but she needs to know before the paramedics arrive, or she's going to be more freaked than she is now," she whispered. "Go check her nightstand or the bathroom. Maybe there's some valium or sleeping pills for her walking. She's got chamomile tea, if nothing else." Marla left; she was glad that Hailey was in charge. She wasn't up to all the stress; not anymore. This past week proved it.

Lily appeared from under the table, rubbed at Hailey's ankles, and chirped. Hailey listened to her. "Yes, you can help," she said and put the cat in her cousin's lap. Lily rubbed against her owner's stomach several times before she lay down; her loud purr was relaxing. Alice stroked her pet. She was calmer, but her eyes were empty.

Marla found sleeping pills. They weren't prescription, but that might be better, she thought because overdosing Alice right now wouldn't help the situation with Henry. The shit had already hit the fan enough. She was to blame for Bogerty's attachment to her. None of this would have happened if she hadn't come up with such a "wonderful" plan and played her part so well. She returned to the veranda, but neither woman knew how to get Alice to respond enough to take a pill.

"She's almost a zombie, so maybe she doesn't need a pill," Marla offered.

"She will when she hears about Henry or sees the ambulance."

"Lily, make her take the pill," Hailey ordered. Lily pawed at Alice's chin and continued to purr. Alice looked at her cat and some communication passed between them.

"All right, Lily," she said. She took the forgotten glass of sweet tea from the table and swallowed the pill. Lily stood on her hind legs and put both paws on her owner's cheeks. Alice, in turn, lowered her head and looked into the cat's eyes, then she slowly looked at Hailey and Marla. Her voice sounded flat, far off in the distance. "Lily says Henry's bad stressed. It's not a stroke now, but soon. She says I should sleep. I won't walk tonight."

Lily meowed, and Alice rose from the chair holding her. The cat wrapped her paws around Alice's neck, and it looked as if she were whispering into her ear. Then the two walked inside, down the hall, and into the bedroom. Alice closed the door.

"That was spooky," Marla remarked.

"She's slightly psychic, and the pets are very tuned in. I discovered that when we got here. But we have worse issues. Bogerty's the one to watch right now. He will preach we're witches and set the locals to burn us and the property with his blessings. Especially if he doesn't get his way with you. This must stay quiet, Mom!"

Marla looked at her daughter. "*All* of us? Didn't know about Henry and David. I should have felt it. Told you I wasn't all that good, and I'm nearly useless after everything this week. So what do we do about Bogerty's coming?"

"We worry about that later. Let's go check on Henry. You can stay there, and I'll come back and wait for the ambulance."

The paramedics drove 57 most nights and were used to its faults, but they knew not to drive over 25 no matter how bad the emergency. Still they made the twenty miles from Unity in record time as the lanes were surprisingly clear of both vines and rocks.

Hailey met the men as they exited the vehicle. All she said was "sun room" when asked where. Elroy and Marvin knew their way; this wasn't their first run.

They checked Henry's vital signs carefully before bringing in a gurney to transport him to Unity's small hospital.

"Don't worry," David, "Marvin said, it's not like last couple of times; his vitals are good, and I know you're worried, but you don't need to follow us. It's your mamma that might need calming before she splits a gusset." He raised his eyebrows when he mentioned Alice, then he reached down to pet Kingston.

"I'd let you ride with Henry, Kingston, but it's not allowed. You're a mighty good dog; you sure are," he said.

Kingston licked Marvin's wrist and whined.

David smiled and shook his head. "You know Til and I are coming, Marvin. Mamma has family to help her." They took Kingston with them because he jumped into the van and refused to get out. The highway was still clear.

..........<>..........

Hailey and Marla stayed to watch over Alice. Neither wanted to go to bed until they knew something. The last time Hailey checked, Alice was sleeping peacefully with her pet nestled by her head. Lily's vigil overruled any sleepwalking tendencies.

It was almost too quiet after all the chaos, and their nervous energy wouldn't shut down. There wasn't anything except infomercials on TV, so Marla downloaded her pictures to Hailey's computer. Looking at them gave the women something to do.

Some of the pictures had unusual light spots, and the kudzu appeared to have moved positions from shot to quickly snapped shot. Hailey pointed that out, but Marla attributed the anomalies to camera angles, dust, and reflections from sun light. Hailey knew her mother was a camera expert, but she wasn't so sure of the explanations. There hadn't been any wind that late evening to move the vines, yet she thought it was following the reverend. More was on the barn too since morning and on both sides of the house near the windows. Her mother had only seen the yard that evening, so mentioning that movement wouldn't be worth it. She would have been angry if her mother laughed.

There were many pictures that Marla wanted to delete, but Hailey said to save them all for the others to enjoy. Actually she wanted to keep them for David and Tilfort to examine. Hopefully they would see what she saw even if her very sleepy mother didn't. Her dilemma was how to keep Henry and Alice from closely examining the specific photos she wanted the two men to see. It would only cause more worry for Henry and hysteria from Alice which could bring on a stroke if it hadn't already. Her college jitters were trivial compared to this reality.

David checked in sometime later to say that Henry's weakness had been caused by stress and not either stroke or heart attack. The emergency room doctor wanted to keep him overnight for observation just in case something did happen, considering his medical history.

"Daddy's sleeping peacefully, and we're fixing to come on

back. Doc Jeffries can check him out tomorrow and tell us when he can come home," he said.

Hailey relayed the information to her mother and sent her to bed. Marla protested feebly, but Hailey insisted, saying she didn't need her own mother having a set back during this crisis. She held her bedroom door open and shooed Marla out. To her relief, her mom agreed and shuffled down the hall to her bedroom, using the wall for support. Hailey watched, worrying.

She doesn't have much stamina even now and the whole past week has really been too much. She was sick enough because of the long drive from home, the weed killer, the intense heat, and trying to take pictures and help with the wedding, without adding these last two days. I'll be visiting her in the hospital soon. She used up the last of her strength with that Bogerty act. Just David, Tilfort, and me to keep things together, she mused.

Hailey felt overwhelmed right now, but strangely calm and alert. It didn't matter now if she had to be strong. She felt she could do it. *Mom can't handle it, so why resent her for it?* This mess wasn't like last year. Her mind wouldn't slow down. Memories flooded in.

Mom was always the strong one, in control. I thought I was coping pretty well with her in the hospital. I wasn't. I'd have been in a nut house or in a hospital room too. Thank God for Nancy. She promised Mom she'd take care of everything. Don't think a better neighbor exists. Seventeen days she took care of me and the cat and dog. She helped me with my homework, made me get up and go to school, made me take showers, cooked meals, gave me lunch money and did the laundry. I'd been doing my own laundry since I was sixteen, but I couldn't do it. If it had been left up to me, I'd have worn my clothes dirty, maybe not even changing them, sleeping in them. I probably wouldn't have eaten or gone to school.

I couldn't think or plan. I only stopped being a zombie

when I got to go see Mom. Nancy brought her home, cared for her, and took her for treatments. I just followed orders, functioned. I slept in mom's bed at night like I used to when I was little and had nightmares. I just wanted, needed to be held. Being next to her made me feel better. Mom was alive; she wasn't going to die; she was going to get well. I needed to touch her, feel her physically. Hailey smiled to herself. *That's when I knew. I felt her healing.*

Ugly memories rushed in, over-powering her. *My asshole, fucking drunk father. He spent the entire time attempting to insinuate his way into the house while Mom was gone. I know him. He figured once he was in, no one could force him back out. Constantly calling, begging me to help him. Never asked or cared about Mom. Weak son-of-a-bitch. Whining about his latest girlfriend problems, demanding to come stay at the house since said coke whore kicked him out of her apartment, and now he was homeless, asking for money, showing up at Nancy's and trying to live in his car in her driveway, dumping any and all sob stories or guilt trips on her, trying to intimidate us, attempting to call Mom at the hospital and screaming at both Nancy and me and the receptionist there when she refused to let his call go through.*

Faster and faster the old hurts surfaced. *Making crude jokes about the breast removals, calling Mom a Cyclops because he couldn't get it through his head that she lost both breasts, not one. Sneering that she was no longer "wife material." He should have blown a heart valve with his performance. Too bad he didn't.*

Nancy called the sheriff every day. Sheriff Benton went to school with "dear old Dad". "He's just worried about Hailey and Marla," he kept saying. He didn't want to do anything. Finally sent an officer just to get Nancy off his back. Naturally, Father was drunk when Deputy Van Oss showed up, and started screaming at him. Sheriff told Van Oss not to arrest Father. Ha, ha, the drunk went overboard and got hauled in, in hand cuffs! Finally got a restraining order. Daddy Darling stayed in jail until the court sent him to Indianapolis to a detox center.

Mom always protected me from him. She was sort of like Helga, the warrior queen. I tried to survive him, but he sucked me down like a vampire. He did that to Mom only I didn't know how abusive he was. She was the shield. Probably that's what weakened her system; why she got cancer. It was Nancy who held the shield and carried me with one arm. Nancy stepped back when Mom came home and got better. She had me take care of mom. Warrior in training? I didn't think so, but I'm handling this disaster so far. So maybe I learned something.

In the last several months, Hailey had lapsed somewhat back into the old habits, but certainly not all. Tonight, just now, it really hit home that Marla appeared well, but she wasn't, not really. And now, she was aware that her mother's obsession to connect with the only maternal family they had left was a clue to just how vulnerable she was. It wasn't adventure; it really was fear. She felt her resentment melting away, and with it, her fears that somehow, someway, she was weak like James. *I faced down Bogerty today. One for me!*

Here they were, far from home with these strange new cousins who were barely hanging on by the skin of their teeth. And two were like her, empaths, with all the craziness that entailed. Add Alice to the omelet, along with Kingston, Lily, and a sentient plant. Then there was Bogerty to contend with. How could she protect her mother or the others from him as obviously no one else could? Hailey waited for David and Tilfort to return.

Chapter 4

Bogerty drove with his left hand. His whole head beaded with sweat; it dripped into his eyes and off his fringe of hair. Some beads soaked into his collar and some escaped inside his shirt. Droplets drifted through the creases of fat and met at his backbone. Then like tributaries joining a river, it flowed to his hips and down between his buttocks. His arm pits stank with male pheromones. His right hand caressed the napkin holding the large slice of pie sitting on the car seat next to him.

His thoughts focused on Marla. He planned to get her away from the others on Thursday come hell or high water, even if he had to twist her arm behind her back and force her to walk with him into that dead orchard to hear what he had to say. She needed to know that God had chosen her to be his wife. As Mary had been God's handmaiden, Marla was to be his. Mary! Marla!

His fingers reached through the opening in the napkin and fondled the wide wedge of crust. It had a rough texture like newly waxed skin. He thrust his fingers into the soft filling. He could still taste the sour cream mixed within. He grabbed a handful of peaches and squeezed hard.

The reverend's face flushed and his breathing became ragged. He bit his upper lip and grimaced as his eyes unfocused. His foot hit the brake. His pelvic thrust toward the steering wheel's center. He crushed the pie in his hand as he shot his wad. His clothes were soaked. Bogerty withdrew his sticky filling-covered hand and licked it slowly.

He was still thinking. He'd perform the marriage that very Thursday; after all, he was an ordained minister. He chuckled with pleasure: God's Will be done. The others would be witnesses. He decided to go to the Danvers' court house and get a marriage license rather than Unity; less explaining to do.

That little bitch daughter would need attending to. *Spare the rod and spoil the child*. He liked that saying. It wouldn't be too hard to get her under control. Then, when she'd learned her manners—learned to respect her betters, to obey, she could work around the house. She'd be grateful that he allowed her a roof over her head.

Yes, that would free Marla up for God's Work. A capable woman like that would bring in a flock to fill his church. He'd send her door to door, if necessary. He could hear the choir now—fifty strong at least. She'd organize the meetings, the Wednesday and Sunday socials, be the church secretary. He'd make her take pictures of the congregation and himself, and he'd slap them everywhere—in the newspaper, the church directory, the weekly bulletins. His church would be the biggest in town, have the most money. He could affect the politics. People would listen to his opinions and agree. She'd help him get the power, money, and respect he deserved. Finally Daddy would be proud of him. *Called me weak and worthless. No more. Laughed at me, beat me. Sneered when I tried to protect Mama from you. Watch me prove you wrong. I'll be a better preacher than you ever were. Squirm in Hell, Daddy. I'll have that last laugh. Maybe Mama was weak. Effie certainly was. But not Marla, she's strong.* Daddy would see that with Marla by his side, he'd be strong, successful, and powerful.

Yes, Marla was the perfect wife for him, and she could cook. Three big meals a day. Lord, that's the way to a man's heart, to *his* heart. Of course, she couldn't do all that cooking. No. He'd need her for all those other jobs. His wife needed to be beside her man, supporting him. Maybe that little bitch could be taught to cook. Maybe she already could. Surely

Marla had taught her how to; mothers usually do. Marla could cook supper every night and let the bitch do the rest. Can't have her all worn out; wouldn't look good to the new congregation.

She's probably got a house up north. *I'll sell it—furniture too. I've got the church rectory; utilities paid, furnished. Won't need her place and the money will be handy. A better car, new clothes.* He looked at his pinkie ring. *Maybe a gold chain, nothing flashy, just something to hang a cross on. A minister should wear a cross. My congregation would expect it.*

He'd have to get Effie's things out of the basement. He should've done it months ago. Everybody believed they were divorced, and it was going to stay that way. *I'll burn what I can outside. If anyone asks what I'm burning in this heat, I'll tell them it's kudzu. The rest I'll throw out over a cliff. No one'll find anything buried in the vines.* He was afraid to before, but not now. It was an accident and God didn't blame him. He was supposed to be free to marry Marla. Effie was always crying and wringing her hands like some fucking mouse and couldn't cook worth a damn. She wasn't the proper wife. He'd have one now.

He was tired when he reached home. Sticky, drying cum pulled at his crotch hairs as he swung a beefy leg out of the car. It itched. Since he needed to change, he decided rather than sleep, to work in the basement. No one would see what he was doing as there was only one small window, and it was covered by kudzu. But kudzu saw.

He hadn't been down there during all this time so he hadn't noticed that several vines had wormed their way in through the window and were wrapped loosely around Effie's possessions. Bogerty cut them off and threw them to the floor where he stepped on them as he worked. If he had looked up, he would have seen more kudzu covering the basement ceiling under the kitchen. It filled all the shadowed places where two bulbs couldn't illuminate.

He began separating what he could burn and what he couldn't. There wasn't much clothing. Effie only owned an armful of dresses, a week's worth of lingerie, pajamas, three pairs of shoes, and a purse. He wrapped the cut vines around the clothes just in case anyone was nearby and threw them out in the trash barrel. He cut more vines to cram on top. There was plenty of kudzu if he needed additional coverage. He planned to burn it all in daylight to avoid suspicion. He could sift out what didn't turn to ash and add it to the rest to be tossed. His plan in place, he went to bed.

For the last 17 months, Eugene Bogerty had been racked with night terrors and cold sweats, thinking his wife was haunting him, accusing him. He'd wake up to screeching, or to smells and sounds of cooking, but he could've just been dreaming. Sometimes he was sure the covers were pulled off him when the alarm clock showed 3:00, the "dead of night", as it was called, but the way he rolled and turned, probably not. He'd feel cold drafts in that kitchen, day or night, where there shouldn't have been any, but the windows were old and didn't fit well anymore. He couldn't enjoy his own cooking, and he didn't like being in that kitchen because he was sure he wasn't eating alone.

Something was watching him. Maybe it was the kudzu, he laughed. After all, some was on the outside sill and the bedroom one as well. Odd that it didn't continue to cover the windows. God must be keeping it out to save him the work. He told himself it was just his nerves, and maybe it was. But nerves or ghosts could be tolerated. He'd managed all this time. He was more afraid of some local repair man being sent by a church elder when he wasn't there. What if he saw her things in the basement?

But tonight was different. Now he had a plan and a bright

future. He slept well. He wished he'd saved that piece of pie for breakfast.

Watching.   Planning.

..........<>..........

He hadn't cared for Effie Houser when he met her, but he did care about her father's money. She was a shy little thing and Bogerty was sure he could mold her into a proper minister's wife. Effie taught Sunday school where he worked as a temporary assistant minister. He hoped Reverend Hiram Jacobs would retire or, God forbid, die. After all, the man was in his fifties and battling throat cancer. Bogerty had his own ideas of how a church should be run, but Reverend Jacobs refused to listen. Sick as he was, he wrote the sermons and was there in his official robes every Sunday morning. Bogerty couldn't change one word, not with Hiram listening. As soon as the reverend was well enough, Bogerty was sent packing. That should have been his church, handed over from Jacobs. He worked hard for it. Instead, he was unceremoniously dumped like worthless trash. But he took Effie with him.

He dragged that cowering bitch from church to church over the years, but she proved worthless, and her daddy didn't leave her much when he died because of losing most during the last economic recession and medical bills. She couldn't even cook properly. He wasn't sure whether she was an incompetent fool or deliberately ruining the meals. But when they moved here, and she dropped an entire four-quart pot of spaghetti sauce when he walked into the kitchen—and he was just asking when dinner would be ready—he was sure it was deliberate. It splashed all over his new black suit pants and white shirt. He had a right to be mad and she deserved to be hit, several times. It wasn't like he hadn't hit her before, but she crouched down at his feet and held her head, screeching like some dog-mauled cat. He couldn't stand that noise. He kicked her and she screeched harder. It drove him into a frenzy. It was an unfortunate accident, but it was her fault she was dead. And his supper was ruined. He was hungry and her spaghetti wasn't all that bad. At least the sauce hid the blood. He went out to eat. It gave him time to plan what to do with the body.

Later he rolled her sauce-coated frame in an old blanket, shoved it into the trunk, and took it out on 57. He was surprised at how light she was and how easily he could roll her off the cliff and into the kudzu.

As Bogerty's car pulled away from the cliff, Effie's body, being snagged by the vines, rolled down slowly. She dangled there only a short while, then more vines gently wrapped around her until she was completely covered. Other vines formed a hammock and softly cradled her inside like an innocent babe. A soft fragrance filled the valley.

Sadness. Wrong! Anger.

Kudzu communicated with itself. Within the hour, the man and his location were known and a scent of revenge carried quickly on the wind.

Patience. Watch. Judge.

Bogerty went home to clean the kitchen. If anyone checked his trunk or house, all they might find would be traces of spaghetti sauce. She'd only gone to services that first week, and hadn't left the house since. He had told the congregation she was sick from working so hard to set up housekeeping. He even did the grocery shopping. After all, he couldn't let his new flock see her black eye. They wouldn't understand that she bumped into the edge of the kitchen door.

He waited a week and then sorrowfully told the congregation that she'd left him. That his saying she was sick was a lie and that he had been covering up that she'd left, hoping she would come back. He cried and asked his flock to forgive him as he knew it wasn't right for a minister to lie or get a divorce. It was a good act and it worked. Then the noises started.

Chapter 5

Harlem came out of his station into the sweltering heat, and surveyed his town of 986 souls. People took pride in their houses and kept them prettied up and painted. Different story out in the country where folks lived on small farms. They didn't have the energy or money to pretty-up thanks to kudzu; they sent their time chopping the plant off everything.

Heat waves shimmered off the asphalt. He wiped his face with his arm and reluctantly put on his hat.

Damn this humidity. Too hot to wear a hat, and short sleeves don't make this uniform any cooler. Don't envy my boys in the patrol cars. Air conditioning can't keep up; the engines will overheat. Most likely, Duke or Robert's got the windows down for a breeze, and I'd bet a nickel both are parked under trees or by the lake. Duke's likely sleeping and Robert's listening to his rock and roll on the radio. Harlem chuckled to himself envisioning that picture. *Imagine both of em's got their shirts unbuttoned. Couldn't blame 'em.*

At least BeBe's off 'til Wednesday, and, if I know him, probably fishing with a cold soda in his hand. Sure wish I was. Harlem smiled, thinking about the future. *Sixteen years come November; four elections. Only 42 so it'll be a while 'til retirement, but one day, I'll be doing that lazy-day fishing myself, only give me beers so cold they got ice in 'em. And no more hot uniforms.*

Harlem Gilesby usually didn't need the five deputies he had. He gave each three days off on a rotational basis. When others had questioned his decision he had said, "Don't change their pay any, poor as it is. They got to fight kudzu out of their gardens too if they want to eat."

Speaking of eating, time to meet Garnet over at Janice's. Special's black-eyed peas, pork chops, and cornbread. Hope there's some pecan pie left. Ice cream too. Best damn cooking in town. I'd spend double any day, if she'd let me pay." Harlem stretched his back. It popped twice. He turned left heading for his favorite restaurant.

From the amount of cars on the streets and tourists on the sidewalks, Harlem could tell it was a very busy day in spite of the heat.

Mountain elevation's not much help this year. Garnet's boys probably got their hands full, or at least they will soon enough. He heard some fire crackers go off. *It's July alright. I'll bet the fireworks are selling out fast over at Totem Tom's. Might be a quick lunch.* Harlem picked up his pace.

He and Police Chief Garnet Easley agreed that their jobs seemed redundant except when tourist season hit. Then directing traffic, answering questions, and handing out tickets livened up their days. A few burglaries in vacant houses, underage drinking, and a meth lab or two added spice.

Not too much of that though. Locals turned in meth labs real quick; they didn't have any respect for those types. Moonshine was more to their liking and was seldom reported. Harlem didn't mind a quart jar or two coming his way, but he'd pay for it. Didn't want anyone thinking he was taking bribes. People respected him for his honesty, and he didn't want to disappoint them. "Folks got to make a living," he always said if anyone ever did report a still. Somehow those reports usually got misplaced especially if the moonshiner contained any Cherokee blood.

Harlem waited at the stoplight; there were only two in town. But, there were six churches sitting close to one another up and down Main Street. Maybe too many for so few citizens, but people here had different opinions about religion. Six gave them a choice. People here supported their preferred church, even skimping on their own needs. All had parsonages and helped pay their preacher's utility bills as well as a salary.

Unity Baptist was the smallest and poorest. Harlem hurried by it; he didn't want to run into Reverend Eugene Bogerty. That jackleg tried to rename the church, but "Church of His Holy Feet" only got snickers, and some outright laughs. Unity Baptist stayed "Unity Baptist" on the sign out front. Harlem shook his head and grinned. That should have made some heads wonder, even then. But it didn't, he guessed.

Bogerty's a disgusting fool and a trouble maker, even down at the car lot, Harlem thought. *I'll be glad when his contract's up. Don't like how he treated Janice, and I wish Garnet had locked him up for disturbing the peace. Might of taken a little gas out of that fat wind bag even if it would of stirred up a hornet's nest among some. I bet many would of liked to see that happen. He's not much of a reverend no how; preachers don't get church members all lined up on different sides. I've got enough problems with kudzu, and everyone on edge. Folks can't keep up with it covering over their barns and houses. Damn that man's loud mouth and accusing finger. He's got some like Billy under his control and they're trying to recruit Klan members from other counties to restart an old chapter. Don't need that foolishness. Bogerty's got some so riled up they're spouting that witches and other sinful people are bringing down God's wrath. Demon kudzu is their punishment. It and the sinful needed to be burned out. His like could set the whole county ablaze."*

His mind kept running and rehashing, and Harlem felt heartburn kick in. Happened every time he thought about Bogerty.

"Thank God hardly anyone in town is listening to him." He said out loud.

His church didn't have many members, and most of them started going elsewhere to avoid his preaching, but the few Bogerty controlled were fanatical. Harlem wasn't sure he had the man power to contain the powder keg if it blew.

Easley could handle any town problems Bogerty might

instigate, like at Janice's place, but Gilesby was worried what they might do to country folk. Out of worry, Harlem had already called his buddy Clovis in Danvers; next county over. They'd gone to the academy together, and had a friendly rivalry, helping each other whenever necessary which wasn't often. Usually they just found some excuse to visit over coffee and fried chicken. This time, Sheriff Clovis Dalton might be needed, and Harlem wanted to be prepared.

Harlem shook his head to clear it. Too much to worry about. He put on a happy smile and entered The Hungry Dawg. Food smelled great, and Garnet waved him over.

He tipped his hat to Janice as he headed to Garnet's table. "Fine woman; wish she were mine," he said under his breath. *David shouldn't take her for granted or I might try to grab her up. Not even an unmarried sister. Single man can't get a break.*

Chapter 6

Udel Parks propped his stocking feet up in his lounge chair and turned the volume up in an attempt to hear his favorite Monday show, *Survivor Man*, while he ate supper. It recorded at eight, but he never got home before 10:30. It was his only enjoyment as he swallowed an always cold supper. His wife Birdie was having none of it.

"Turn that damn show off. You should be outside burning those big piles of vines. I spent most of the day cutting it out of the flowers and off the fence, and I'm tripping over it in the yard. It's coming at us from that empty acreage up the hill, and you won't even call the Brands about it."

"I did call. Nobody answered so I left a message. They don't live here so why would they care."

Birdie wasn't listening. She was on a roll and nothing was going to stop her. Too many pent-up emotions including fear, neglect, and loneliness were driving her this evening.

"Cloris and Vernell moved out Saturday, or did you notice. They went to Tifton. There's a for sale sign down by the road pointing up this way, but who'd want to buy up here. Four houses and we're the only ones left."

"I saw the sign and Vernell told me. Give me credit for not being blind or deaf. What do you want me to do? I can't be here cutting the vines off everything unless I quit my job. We could put up a sale sign and leave too," Udel offered, half hoping that suggestion might sink in. Vernell had put the idea in his head months ago, and he was seriously considering it. He was ready to pitch the game and go, but he knew his wife was as tenacious as the vines and giving up wasn't in her dictionary. Mentioning to her had only started a fight.

So suggesting moving again tonight might as well have been swallowed by a drain pipe for all the impression they made, but he hoped he could wear her down.

He saw Birdie's eyes tear up and knew she was thinking of Bella. He missed the old woman too. She'd be outside even in the heat of the day working in her flowers or cutting the kudzu away from her trees. It was the exertion that gave her the heart attack. Died right in her front yard with the cutters in her hand and kudzu wrapped around her legs.

"You can't even find Bella's log cabin," Birdie said. "It looks like a big odd lump, and it sounded like the porch collapsed yesterday. I haven't gone to see because I don't want to know. Sometimes I feel she's still there, her ghost. This whole place is being taken over and you won't do nothing." The word "nothing" ended in a high pitched squeal.

"I'm tired, Birdie, give it a rest. I'm hungry. I just put in 14 hard hours. As fast as I put out more hot dog buns or cans of pork 'n beans, they fly off. People loading up for the Fourth. Besides it's late and dark outside, so what am I supposed to do when I can't see, throw out some gasoline and strike a match?"

"Well, at least you'd be doing something to help me. You're never home, and you're useless on your day off. This stuff is starting up the trees in back and it's on the shed now. You complain about cold food, but if I have to spend any more time cutting that stuff, be prepared for TV dinners and you get to microwave them. Birdie started to cry in earnest.

"I'm sorry, okay," Udel said. "Honey, I know you're lonely. Don't you think I miss Cloris and the others too? I wanted us to climb in the car with them and go. I'm sick of my dead-end job and fighting vines."

"I'm scared, Udel. This place looks spooky even in the daytime. I'm afraid to look outside at night because it might be trying to get in the windows. It's going to get us like it has Vernell and Bella or the other houses along the roads here 'bouts. Have you even noticed that everything is covered except for one partly bare truck two places over? I hate this stuff."

"Then why won't you agree for us to leave?" asked Udel, knowing the answer but hoping to soften his wife up a bit. "Please stop being so stubborn. We could move near Sylvie and the grandkids. If we sold the house, we'd have some money to buy another, and maybe I could work less. Sometimes change is better."

"You know I won't leave. I grew up here and I plan on staying put until I die," said Birdie.

Udel sighed. He knew it was no use and even threatening to go without her wouldn't change her mind. Besides he loved her too much to go and she knew it.

"Okay, I'm done eating. I'll go do some burning. Turn on the outside lights so I can see where you left the piles. If they're too green, I'll have go use my lawn mower gas."

Udel put on his tennis shoes, always left by the door, and stuck matches in his pocket as he went out. The flood lights didn't illuminate their acre all the way out, but it was enough to see that there were eight waist-high lumps scattered around the yard, some close to Bella's and others near the fence separating their house from Cloris'. There may have been a couple more standing in the shadows, but it was hard to tell. He could see better when some piles were burning.

He was right. The vines weren't going to burn without gasoline. Udel went back in and grabbed the flashlight from the kitchen, but its weak battery only darkened the shadows to the shed. He made a mental note to get those new lithium ones. He was surprised to see so much kudzu out back. The shed except for the front was buried. He needed to call the Brands again, maybe tomorrow. He stepped carefully, assessing the coverage.

Next to the shed was Birdie's pet cemetery complete with six small concrete statues of fawns, sleeping cat angels, and rabbits. They stood sentinel over graves covered by patio blocks which had sunk in at odd angles leaving corners upended like stalagmites. Now only parts of the statues were visible because kudzu covered everything and the ground looked like undulating water. Some vines caught on his foot making him stumble, and he landed knee down on one of those hidden blocks. Pain exploded before his eyes like wildly reflecting prisms and he collapsed. Udel fell face forward onto a fawn's ear which pierced his eye.

Birdie, impatient and certain he was procrastinating, stomped back to give him some encouragement. Her angry remarks froze in her throat and screaming took their place. She ran back inside the house to call 911. Her hands shook so hard that it took several tries to punch in the numbers. The dispatcher could not understand anything Birdie said except blood and help, but her phone number located the address. Help arrived within fifteen minutes, but Udel was dead before Sheriff Gilesby and the ambulance reached him.

Harlem took Birdie inside and sat her at the kitchen table. She was calm, but he knew it wouldn't last. She could become hysterical at any minute. Unfortunately her only daughter Sylvie lived in Tennessee and the neighbors were long gone. He couldn't take her to the hospital; they wouldn't keep her, and he couldn't take her to his office. No one there to watch her except the dispatcher, and he still had two more calls he needed to check out.

"Stay here, Birdie. There's nothing you can do by going to the morgue. Wait until tomorrow morning and call Pines Mortuary. Don't you still have some of your stress medicine?"

She nodded yes and pointed to the bathroom. Harlem found the bottle and brought back two pills. He got her a glass of water and watched her swallow. He knew it wasn't the best situation, but it was too late to find any of his deputies' wives to come sit with her. He just hoped she'd fall asleep for the night. He sat her on the couch and turned on the TV. Birdie heard the ambulance drive away and stood up. She silently followed Harlem outside to his car, but refused to go back in as he turned around in the drive. That worried him. He really needed her watched. She could pull something really stupid unless her medicine kicked in; she was too calm.

He watched her from his rear view mirror as he drove away. She stood in the drive and stared aimlessly at the receding tail lights winding down the private lane.

The night was too quiet. With a sudden mindless resolve, she took the gas from the shed, poured some on each pile of kudzu, and used the grill lighter to set the fires. When the gas burned off, the flames died. Screaming hysterical obscenities, she beat at the tangled masses until her hands were scratched and bleeding. She was near Bella's cabin when she thought she saw the old woman beckoning. She smelled perfume.

Crying and shaking uncontrollably, Birdie stumbled toward the image as if tugged by green rope. "Bella, help me. This fucking shit won't burn. I have to help Udel. He fell and won't wake up. I need it to burn. I need it to burn. What do I do?"

The porch roof had indeed partly collapsed from kudzu's weight, but one vertical support post still held a section up. Birdie tugged on the vines, trying to find an opening through the tangled mass and calling for Bella. She slipped on the vines and fell face down still holding on to one mass. It tumbled off the roof and piled on top of her lower back and legs. The post could no longer hold with Birdie's frantic yanking, and certainly not with her full weight added. It gave way. One heavy roof board, already cracked and dangling, broke off and fell, ragged edge downward. Birdie's medicine had numbed her. She didn't feel it slice through her spine just below her head.

Together. Indifferent.

Chapter 7

Jebadia Flanks, or Jeb as his friends called him, was at Wit Delmore's place drinking. Billy Purdue and Thymie Qualkinbush came out later. By midnight they were burning a makeshift stick cross in the back yard and discussing the rally planned for Friday night. All except Wit were drunk. Billy wanted to start burning crosses in front yards on Thursday after Wednesday's prayer meeting, but Thymie told him to hold off.

"I'm takin' my wife and babies to the fireworks at the fairgrounds. I'm not fixin' to disappoint them and be fightin' with Norabell because you're in such a Bogerty boomalally. I'm not so sure I want to march to your tune and I'm not sure Bogerty wants you too neither. You'll be his next sermonizin' if you get too ahead of yourself."

Billy belched and laughed. "Guess I'm blessed. I got no wife nagging my ass anymore since kudzu drove her off. That's 'bout the only thing good it's done. Can't make a living on my farm unless I want to braid baskets or sell fried kudzu chips by the road. Maybe I should wear a dress while I'm doing it."

"I thought Druci Cheswick was tryin' to get you to keep goats," Thymie said. "She's got twenty eatin' their way through her fields faster than kudzu can grow, and she makes good money from the milk. She's one of the few here 'bouts that's thrivin'. Them goats don't mind the hills, like her cows do. The vines are gone off one of her fields. I was over there buyin' milk. Bought three goats after I saw that. Might work."

"Not interested. Americans ain't goat boys, they're cowboys. Maybe they keep a couple as pets for the kids, but not farming a herd. I'll take my corn fields and hogs over them goats. And I ain't feeding that kudzu crap to my hogs neither. Things will be back to normal real soon. We'll burn it back and burn out the weirdoes at the same time. I'm still going to start Thursday night whether you're with me or not. To hell with your Norabell. That nag's pussy-whipped you, Thymie. You coming to the Klan meeting here Friday?

"Them that's comin', will be here, Billy" said Wit in a quiet voice. "Don't go pressurin' nobody. And I don't take too kindly to your cursin' Norabell. You forget she's my sister-in-law and Thymie's not pussy-whipped. Neither my Beth nor Norabell's ever pussy-whipped anybody, and I don't suggest you call me that any more than Thymie here. Jeb's lookin' none too happy neither seein' how it's his sister you're cursin' and his brother-in-law you're callin' names. You wouldn't want to go kissin' your mama with them foul lips. You need to straighten up, Boy."

Wit was 6'3" and 237 pounds of pure muscle. He had been a gunner in Afghanistan, and it was generally known that he took some extreme risks to save his fellow soldiers. He had received a purple heart for his heroism, but he kept that information quiet. Bragging wasn't in his nature, and he wasn't much of a talker. Wit was talking now, and Billy knew not to rile him up. If a fight started, whatever Wit left, Thymie and Jeb would finish. It was all family here except for Billy. Diplomacy was needed and a swift get away.

"Sorry Boys, I'm drunk as a coot so pay me no mind. I'm fixing to go 'cause Oral's waiting on me to spell him. He's up in my tree blind keeping a watch on the Percifields."

"You took Bogerty's railing on Doris and Howard heavy to heart. I'd be right proud if my son took a gun and defended my family," Jeb said. "Elowese is just an old woman with fits, and not worth worrying over. They've got kudzu problems like the rest of us."

"Bogerty says she does her work while in her fits. Be back Friday," Billy said as he staggered through the vines to his old farm truck. He was beginning to wonder if Wit and his brothers-in-law were going soft. He reckoned Bogerty's Wednesday night sermon would put them back on the right path.

..........<>..........

Oral Clemet had been in the tree blind nearly four hours staring in the Percifield's windows with his binoculars. So far, there was nothing to see unless he counted the kudzu crawling everywhere across the ground, up the tree, on the ladder, and even inside the blind. He was sitting on several vines. He pulled his cell phone out of his back pocket to check the time. Eleven-thirty and from the looks of the windows going dark one by one, the Percifields were slowly going to bed. Oral was tired and stiffer than the Pine's frozen corpses. He tried to put his phone back in his hip pocket but it didn't go all the way in. Instead it slipped back out and fell to the ground below.

Oral swore and turned to climb down the vine-coated rungs when his stiffened legs buckled. He fell two stories landing on his side, pinning his right arm under his rib cage and twisting his left leg at an angle that could only mean broken. He knew there must be several more bones broken, but he needed to reach that phone if he were going to get help. Only Billy knew he was here. He tried to use his left hand since it was free, but it wouldn't move and neither would his right leg. He tried rolling, but again nothing moved. Oral panicked. He didn't know when Billy was coming, sometime near one or two, but that was a long time and he had to get help now. Nothing would move except his head.

Oral thought he had blacked out and thrashed about because there was kudzu wrapped around his ankles and shins. As he watched, the vines continued to wrap slowly around his entire torso moving upward to his neck effectively forming a body cast immobilizing his spine. If paramedics were strapping him to a gurney, Oral wouldn't have been afraid, but this was kudzu and he hated it. Bogerty had warned everyone about the Indian's walking demon-plant spirits and kudzu was one of them. He cursed and damned the vines so heatedly his face grew red from his exertions. Oral tried to bite any vines his mouth could reach attempting to pull the pieces off his neck and shoulders.

Help refused. Hurt. Anger. Hate!

Kudzu wrapped tighter around his neck and traveled over his chin toward his lips. It slid into his mouth. He bit the first exploratory tendrils off and spit them out, but more followed faster than he could bite. If he opened his mouth at all, larger pieces crowded inside. Oral coughed and ejected one small vine with leaves from his throat. He spit it out and took a deep breath. He coughed harder but couldn't dislodge any more of the small vines tickling his wind pipe as they slithered ever downward. Another deep breath and more coughing. Nothing. Spasms were now uncontrollable and intense. His diaphragm had a mind of its own. Flashes of pain and light pressured his head. Saliva dripped from the corners of his lips as his tongue would not retreat into his mouth. Lungs emptied themselves of air and he couldn't get a breath. His shaky attempts drew nothing in. Shoulder and neck muscles tightened, and he grew dizzy as his airways closed. He knew he'd lost. Oral shook his head back and forth, the only part of him that moved, to no avail. Then his eyes rolled back into his head and he lay still. The vines filled his throat, then traveled down into his lungs. Smaller tips curled back and slithered out through his nostrils, forming two thick plugs. Oral's face was blue when Billy found him.

Revenge

Tuesday

Chapter 1

It was 3:45 AM when David and Tilfort returned. Hailey heard Kingston bark and scratch at her door. She opened it to "tail wagging the dog" excitement.

"I heard, Kingston, Henry's okay for now. Yes, you can stay with me tonight," she said.

The men were sitting in the living room drinking sweet tea when she entered carrying her laptop and followed by her new attendant.

"Hi, Guys, anything new since you called?" When the answer was no, she sat at the dining table and asked them to sit next to her.

"I want to show you something. These are the pictures Mom took this evening and I want you to look at the kudzu in each one."

She said nothing as she flipped from picture to picture. She was sure both men saw the light anomalies and the vines' position changes. Then she gave them her mother's explanations.

"Sorry Hailey," David said. "I'm too tired and worried to care about this. It does look like there's a lot around Bogerty, but he kept kicking it so I'd say he stirred it up. The vines are all over the ground. You know. You walked back there and hooked some on your feet. The barn looks bad, but we've been fighting it. We worked late last night getting it out of the inside. Two late nights in a row are too much. I have to concentrate on the wedding arrangements, and only I have tomorrow to finish. Your mom's the expert on cameras and photography so I'd take her ideas. I've got to get some sleep." David looked exhausted as he shuffled down the hall to his bed. He forgot the sunroom was open.

Tilfort looked haggard too, but he put the computer in front of him and carefully examined each picture again. He looked thoughtful.

"I'm glad of these pic'ures. They're evidence if you look. You see it now too, and I'm *not* touched in the head. These vines have more ways to live than a box of cockroaches-- rhizomes, vine nodes, runners, seeds. It grows new plants just by touchin' the ground, and you can't even drop a little bit on a trash pile 'cause that'll grow too. The seeds'll hide out for years till the time is ripe, then they'll start up again.'

"Can't convince David not to put sprigs in his flowers. Tourists and folks here take his bouquets and kudzu goes too. He's hep'in' it to spread. Kudzu loves him, but I can't he'p thinkin' it's jealous of his flowers and everythin' else here. It's at the hives again, but I think it's to get its own flowers fertilized. It could be encouragin' the bees to move deep into the vines, and the bees might, but I hope they don't 'cause we need the pollinatin' and we sell the honey. It'd be harder to get to a hive all protected by kudzu."

Tilfort looked at the pictures of Bogerty again and chuckled. "Does look like it's chasin' old lard belly, bless his heart. For a reverend, he sure is creative with his cursin'. Hurt my ears. Kudzu might be spoilin' for a fight after all that and my bets on the vines."

Tilfort handed the computer back to Hailey and yawned. "I'm fixin' to go to bed. Not much sleep for any of us the next few nights. Be dog tired by Sunday and I doubt anyone will be up to hearin' the reverend. That's one blessin'. Prayer meeting Wednesday night, but don't know if Alice will go or Henry, if he's home. I'll think on those pictures and the lights, and talk to you when there's a chance."

Hailey watched as Tilfort left. She felt sorry for him. *When we leave, he'll have it all on his shoulders again. And Alice won't shut up; she's a CD stuck on replay.* She picked up her computer and headed to bed. She heard the rumbling of another storm on its way. Kingston jumped slightly and followed.

..........<>..........

The storm seemed determined to keep everyone on edge. The loud thunder and bright flashes of lightening repeatedly shocked Hailey out of deep sleep. Something kept banging against her window. The wind was roaring around the house, so it was probably throwing all sorts of loose vegetation at the roof and walls. When she slept, she dreamed of kudzu trying to break in. Then she'd lay awake wondering about the kudzu vines and worrying about Henry, Marla, and Bogerty before going out again. Just in time for more thunder.

Hailey figured everyone else was having the same trouble sleeping. The floor boards in the hall creaked several times as if someone were walking slowly up and down. A slight rustling sound caught at the back of her consciousness; she'd heard that before. Kingston was installed by her bed. Occasionally he raised his head during the night, looked around, and whined. Hailey tried to sooth his jitters by mumbling sleepily that everything was okay; she thought the storm bothered him. It didn't, but the rustling did—kudzu was on the move.

Tuesday morning came too early. Marla scratched on her door and then entered before Hailey could respond. Kingston bounded out. Marla laughed. "I guess he has to go bad. Thought I'd fix breakfast and you can help," she said. "Alice's still sleeping and I don't know where David or Tilfort are, but they probably haven't eaten."

Hailey envisioned the both of them cooking plateful on plateful of food like Alice had yesterday. "Not happening if it's a ten course snack. I'll fix scrambled eggs and microwave some instant grits. Anything else is on your head."

"Deal! I found some bacon and tubes of biscuits. That and orange juice should do it. I'd better go open the door so Kingston can do his business. See you in the kitchen." Marla left.

"She's perky this morning, wonder why." Hailey crawled out of bed, still half asleep. Her toes caught on something, and she fell back on the mattress. That woke her up. She looked down. She had tripped on a little kudzu vine sticking out from under her bed. Hailey dropped down on her knees and followed the vine with her eyes. Sure enough, it had come up through one of the knotholes not covered with a can lid. Several more stems had slipped through other holes, but were out of reach further under the bed. A few sprigs had slipped between the air conditioner and the window frame and were dangling down the wall and under the bed too.

She reached out to break off the piece that had tripped her. Her fingers barely touched it when an electric shock made of pure emotion constricted her entire arm to the elbow. She snatched her hand away. *It's a messenger! That vine deliberately tripped me to get my attention. Kudzu has made a decision and it's telling me. Why me? Why not David?*

An image of Janice flashed inside her mind. Then another image of herself with large ears and an eye in the middle of her forehead superimposed itself over Janice's image. Then a third appeared; it showed David with no ears or eyes. That image was disturbing. Hailey dropped off her knees onto her butt and sat there thinking.

Kudzu wasn't like any other plant she had ever sensed before; it was self-aware and very intelligent, possibly dangerous. Janice said kudzu could hear and that plants were psychic. This one definitely was. She just had to understand what those images meant because they had answered her question.

"Okay, you're telling me and not David because of Janice, because I accepted what she said about you, and I'm here. And that extra eye and big ears on my face must mean I can or will hear you with my ears and mind's eye, and David can't or won't listen to you. Am I right?" She knew that was a jumbled mess but figured kudzu was able to sort it out.

An image of a yellow smiley face appeared. "A Walmart smiley face, seriously? Do you watch TV too?!!" Hailey shook her head back and forth. She didn't know whether to be afraid that kudzu watched TV or amazed that kudzu watched TV and had a sense of humor.

Hailey reached out her hand and held the tiny vine. "I'm ready. What's the message?"

The little piece itself was innocent and happy, but it carried a message of deep anger from an older plant, the Elder Kudzu, and a decision or finality. That decision hit Hailey hard; she saw images of kudzu being attacked and killing the attacker. She felt kudzu judging people, and if it found them guilty, enjoying the kill. Even so, she felt love flowing outward from that little piece and a yearning to be loved and accepted.

That emotional stew still has love in it. Janice was right. Totally amazing! She sensed no danger for David, Henry, or Janice. The little vine was sending a friendly warning. *But who's the warning for,* Hailey wondered. *Mom, me, Tilfort, Alice?*

She received no further communication. *I guess you only talk when you want to.*

Hailey decided to tuck the little vine under the bed so no one entering the room would see it and cut it away. She didn't want kudzu to think its messenger was being attacked.

At least I know what Kingston was whining about. He must have picked up on the message or messenger too. I don't want to be on kudzu's bad side. She was in a daze when she stood up. She didn't notice that kudzu was camouflaged within the vine-patterned wallpaper.

"Mom's waiting," Hailey said and hurried to the bathroom to wash up. She grabbed a cloth to clean her face. As she washed her neck, she looked up toward the ceiling where the decorative ivy hung on cup hooks. She stared with her mouth open. Her eyes followed the ivy as she slowly turned around in a circle. The fake vines were thickly interlaced with real ones...kudzu. It had come in through the slightly opened upper casement by tearing a hole near the top corner of the screen and traveling along the wooden frame. It was nearly invisible. *I guess that warning is imminent.*

Her stomach lurched as a sudden thought raced through her head. She left the bathroom and rushed down the hall to her mother's room, not caring that the floor creaked with every step. She slipped in and shut the door. She was right. Kudzu was under the bed and gentle perfume permeated the air. *That's why Mom's so perky. She's not at all worried about Bogerty or anything else, apparently.* She touched the kudzu and felt peace flowing through her fingers. *That's a good thing, maybe?* But she wasn't sure.

She quickly dressed and joined Marla in the kitchen. Her mother was actually humming as she prepared the biscuits for the oven. Hailey considered the best way to approach the questions tumbling in her head. *Best is a frontal attack*, she thought. *Here goes.*

"Mom, you sure are upbeat this morning. What's up, get some magical revelation?"

Marla smiled, "Mom showed up, in a dream, I guess, and told me not to worry, that she'd take care of everything. She was standing right by my bed. I'm assuming my little bit of ability kicked in during the night and she was able to get through. I'm accepting it at face value, and am not going to analyze it."

Hailey turned away to get the eggs out of the refrigerator.

She busied herself with finding a skillet, spatula, and oil so she could think. Holding the items kept her hands from shaking. She doubted it was Grams who visited her mom. She remembered Alice saying that kudzu made you see faces. She saw Lucy and Eric Sunday night, and no amount of rationalization now could change her mind that it was kudzu's perfume that did it. She was lulled into that dreamlike state, not trip tiredness. Maybe kudzu was testing her; hopefully it found her acceptable. *It's talking to me, so I guess so.*

"Mom, let's slow down on the cooking for a few minutes. The ovens got to warm up anyway before you cook the biscuits. I have a few things to tell you."

When she finished, Marla was silent. She put the biscuits in the oven and used the skillet for the bacon. Hailey thought her mother moved like a robot. She took a deep breath and grabbed the grits off the pantry shelf.

"Talk to me, Mom. I need you now. Don't leave me all alone in this."

Marla started shaking her head. Then tears started. "I was so sure it was Mama. I was so sure she would help me. No, it had to be that damn plant; why couldn't it be Mama? I guess Alice and Tilfort are right. And I guess you were right about my pictures; it wasn't camera angles and lighting. I've been so busy cooking, helping Alice, and screwing up what I thought were good plans that I've been oblivious to the weird feelings around me....been rationalizing it all away. I don't have it anymore, Hailey; I need help. I'm so sorry, I'm so sorry. Marla covered her face with shaky hands and sobbed. "Mama, I wish you were here. I'm tired and scared."

Hailey stared helplessly at her mother. She'd never seen this side of her. Maybe it was Gram's memory that kept her strong, gave her resolve. Now she understood how alone Marla must have felt during all those bad times. She sure felt all alone right now. *Time to be a big girl*, she told herself.

She rubbed her mother's shoulders. Hailey tried to infuse some strength into her. "It's okay, we've got each other; neither of us is alone. I've got the same genetics as you and Grams, and we can handle this together. I think kudzu is telling us that it will help as long as we don't turn on it. You know, not chop it up and hate it. It has feelings too. Janice told me and I believe her. And I trust my gift. Are you on board?"

Marla stood up slowly. She grabbed the dish towel, used it to wipe her face, and blew her nose on it. Let's get breakfast fixed. Maybe we should talk to Tilfort if he has any time."

Working as a team, they had breakfast ready and waiting when the biscuits came out. Hailey knocked on Tilfort's door. He opened it quickly and smiled. "I thought someone was cookin'; I could smell it. Woke me up."

Marla told him to start eating while she and Hailey went to get the others. They figured David and Alice could eat in their pajamas. Marla entered Alice's room and quickly called Hailey before she could get to David's door. Hailey tiptoed in and saw kudzu vines around the edge of the silvery green floor and around the bed. The plant's leaves blended perfectly with the paint color. Lily was on the foot of the bed meowing plaintively. Her fearful eyes stared into Hailey's eyes. "*Help Alice. Danger coming*," those eyes said.

Guess I can talk to animals now too. A psychic, touch-know empath. What next? What's opening up my head? Kudzu? Janice? Genetics? Hailey wasn't sure she could handle all the new "talents" and she wasn't sure she wanted to, given a choice. *Oh well.*

It's ok, Lily. Kudzu is going to help, Hailey sent her thoughts to the cat.

"*No, kudzu angry*," Lily insisted. "*She hates. It hates.*"

Lily launched herself off the bed and over the vines, and nearly fell as she landed. She sprinted out the door, but seemed a little out of kilter. Hailey watched the cat's unusual behavior, wondering why. Then she caught movement from the corner of her eye; the vines were retreating under the bed. A tiny whiff of perfume accompanied the withdrawal.

Hailey didn't say anything as she didn't want to alarm her mother. To her relief, Marla didn't notice the movement as she leaned over to gently shake Alice awake. Hailey thought her cousin still seemed drugged, more than the sleeping pill would have warranted. That probably was a good thing since she wouldn't focus on the vines. Hailey dismissed her thoughts for now and opted for action.

"Find Alice a bath robe and get her to the table. I'll call David."

Alice couldn't help herself, but she managed to push her cousin away when Marla tried to put a robe on her.

"I don't want that robe; get my blue one," she demanded, slurring her words, "and my matching slippers." Marla complied and half-carried her into the kitchen because her legs wouldn't cooperate. Tilfort helped get Alice into a chair before Marla dropped her.

When Marla fixed Alice a plate of food and put it in front of her, the woman seemed to snap her out of her lethargy. "I don't feel like eggs this morning; I'd rather have oatmeal." However, she smiled after drinking her coffee.

"Goodness, I should have been doin' the breakfast, Marla. You'll run out on us if you keep gettin' stuck in the kitchen."

David showed up before Marla could respond. Everyone was tired from the late hours and the storm; they ate in silence, then Tilfort turned to Hailey.

"I thought on those pictures you showed me. It did look like kudzu was followin' the reverend and trippin' him up. I think it was havin' fun. Sure was funny to look at. Now those lights. Just speculatin', but maybe kudzu was talkin' to itself. Cameras see what people don't. Don't know how much animals get, but they feel ghosts. Plants aren't ghosts, but Kingston and Lily feel somethin'. I've been readin' and not just fiction; I've got reference books. Fiction is made from facts. Plants aren't different from animals except they don't walk, and they don't talk where we can hear 'em. They use smells. You know that smell when the grass is mowed? Grass is tellin' other plants, that it's been cut up and it's bleedin'. Maybe it's cryin' in pain or wantin' help or sending a warnin'. Maybe those lights were sun rays bouncin' off perfume in Marla's pictures, and no one smelled it what with Bogerty's bellyachin'."

Hailey was amused. She hadn't heard Tilfort talk that much without mumbling until last night. He was more at ease now. He definitely had Bogerty figured out. He was smart and obviously well read. She was pleasantly surprised to discover this for herself although everyone said so. She had her white knight now; maybe David would be another.

"I believe Tilfort," Alice said, "and those vines are killers. They killed John, and they killed my peach trees. They want this whole farm. If they don't kill us outright, they'll drive us out. I think I'm almost ready to leave, but no one will buy here. I want Henry home. Then we can burn everythin'."

David sat there listening. "Mother, I don't want to listen to your crap right now. Kudzu doesn't want this farm, and it doesn't want to kill us. People didn't do their homework when they imported it, that's all. It's not evil; it's helpful. Try loving it instead of hating. You hate it, it'll hate you back. Maybe that's why you get nightmares and see things. I'm going out to work on my wedding. Thanks for breakfast, Hailey, Marla. I hear Kingston barking out back. I'll let him in."

David left. He pounded his fists to the rhythm of his thoughts on the hallway walls as he stomped out. The creaking hall floor added its own rhythm.

Her whisperings, her hot moonlight, her spells, her hysterics, her screaming trees, her seeing faces, her accusing kudzu, her complaining about money, her whining I'm their only support, her hand wringing over Bogerty. Her demanding attention. Me, me, me, me, me. Henry cook. David clean. Tilfort do clothes. Fucking bitch only got off her dead ass because Marla and Hailey came, and she's kept Marla in the kitchen. We can't leave 'cause she won't go—peach trees. Fucking goddamn peach trees. She's killing Daddy. Hate and misery. I want it to END! He punched open the sunroom door.

That room had been left open all night. Kingston was barking at the back door and Lily was right beside him. David stopped in the doorway. The walls and floor were covered in vines. Kudzu had pushed through the screens. Some crawled across the ceiling. It draped lightly across the couch where Henry lay last night. David reached up and tenderly touched the leaves.

"Only you and Janice make sense anymore. Why are people so complicated? Plants aren't. You aren't. You just love. You never intentionally harmed anything and certainly not anyone. Let's go make wedding pretties." The vines parted before his feet. He opened the door for Kingston and Lily, then stepped out and walked toward his work shed. He was sobbing before he reached it.

David. Love. Help. Alicesssss!

Kingston and Lily bolted through the kudzu and straight for the kitchen to Hailey and Alice, vocalizing as they ran.

"Hey now, Kingston, what's got you so riled up?" Alice said as the two pets bounded into the kitchen. Lily launched herself into Alice's lap, mewing like a deranged kitten. Kingston grabbed Hailey's left wrist in his mouth and tried to pull her toward the hall.

"He wants you to follow him," Tilfort said

Hailey giggled nervously. "I kinda figured that out. Okay Kingston, I'm coming. What is it? She tried to touch him with her right hand to try out her new touch-know skill, but he was pulling too hard. She heard his words instead.

Bad! Bad! Kudzu! The dog led her to the sunroom. Tilfort followed.

Both stood in the door way and gapped. "Did it really grow that fast," Hailey asked, "or did the storm blow it in here?" A chill ran down her spine. *Kudzu meant what it said.*

Tilfort felt the couch cushions. "They're not wet so nothing blew in."

"Look at the barn, Til," Hailey said. It was completely covered with kudzu except parts of the roof. Inside the doorway, Hailey could see some vines lying across the tractor. The van and Marla's car were free as if they were deliberately left untouched.

Tilfort just stared. Hailey saw the tiredness and defeat alter his facial muscles. "I can't, I can't," was all he could say.

"Then don't try," she said. "There's not much kept in the barn anyway, is there? Just the tractor and Henry's car? Leave them out. That oak can shade all the vehicles from the heat. I think as long as those are kept clear, it'll be okay. That's all you can do anymore, Til. Stick to the flowers, house, and David's buildings. Let everything else go. The bees will be fine, so don't worry about them either. Kudzu needs them for pollinating its flowers as well as David's. It never went for the honey, so David said."

Tilfort nodded. "You're right. I can't do it all anymore."

Hailey didn't think this was the time to discuss the message she'd received earlier. Instead, she said, "You guys should really consider selling and moving soon. At least take Alice away, like maybe today; she's losing it. This place, these vines everywhere will be the death of her. She can't keep hating kudzu or calling it a murderer."

"She's got a sister in Middle Tennessee; Nora's a nurse, but Alice won't leave this place because of her peach trees. She won't listen to nothin'; we've tried," Tilfort said.

"She sounded like she's changing her mind."

"Right now, but when y'all leave, she'll be back at refusin'," Tilfort sighed.

"Well, keep at it. It's not good here for her. What if she tried to cut or burn the vines in her sleep? She could kill herself." *Or kudzu could help her die if she tries,* Hailey thought to herself. "For now though, don't bother with this room. You need to help David with those arrangements because he's way behind schedule. I can sense he's totally stressed. I'll go back to the kitchen and keep Alice from seeing the barn and this. She doesn't come through here unless she's sleepwalking." She left him standing there, shoulders slumped in defeat. Kingston stayed with him.

Hailey closed the sunroom door behind Tilfort. There was always the chance that Alice might enter the room, but Tilfort couldn't spend his time cleaning the vines out now on a chance. David needed him.

Hailey checked Alice's bedroom to see if she could push the vines covering the floor under the bed. Anything to keep her cousin calm. They weren't there anymore. That worried Hailey. *Lily's right. Alice's in danger. I think the vines were a warning, this time. But, Lily and I are the only ones to know that. Mom didn't put it together even though I told her the message. She only honed in on it not being Grams. We need to get home so she can rest, or she'll get sick again. Maybe not cancer, but something.*

She checked the bathroom next. She didn't figure Alice would be looking up near the ceiling much. *She probably won't even notice, at least I hope not. I'm not going to spend an hour separating the real stuff from the fake. Looks okay to me,* she thought as she returned to the kitchen.

Marla and Alice were happily chatting about places to visit Thursday when Hailey returned. From the quick look her mom shot her, Hailey knew it was all contrived. Marla was waiting for a report. The cat was sitting in Alice's lap, kneading her robe and purring loudly. Lily wouldn't look at her. "*Danger, Alice; you saw,*" was all she would say.

Cat's talking. Dog's talking. Kudzu's talking. Huh, I feel like a talk show host. If the rocks start, I'm checking into a nut house. Hailey sighed. *Yes, Lily. You're right. You have to help keep Alice calm so kudzu won't kill her. Draw off her hate, maybe toward Bogerty instead. And don't let her hurt any part of that plant, not even a leaf.*

Alice kept petting Lily. "Isn't she just the sweetest," she said. "Goodness, I need to get some clothes on and he'p clean the dishes," but she made no effort to get up. She seemed too exhausted to move.

"I'll take some clothes into the bathroom for you, if you don't mind what I pick out," Hailey said. "Maybe a cool shower will help perk you up. It's going to be scorching again today. I recommend lounging on the veranda. There's plenty of leftovers in the fridge. Not from supper, obviously, but we can make do. Enough cooking for today."

"Gracious me, no Honey. I can take care of myself. I'll get some clothes." Alice got up, still clutching her cat like she was the only anchor on a sinking ship, and wandered back down the hall.

Marla looked at Alice, and then at Hailey. "Don't worry, Mom," Hailey said, "the vines left on their own and she won't see it in the bath. Kudzu was only sending a warning this time. I closed the sunroom door because it's all back there. That's why Kingston and Lily were so freaked. Keep her occupied out on the veranda, and maybe Tilfort can cut it out of the rooms soon, although he doesn't look up to the job today. The barn's covered too; the wind must have blown it everywhere last night."

Hailey knew kudzu might have used the storm's wind to move faster; why not fly instead of crawl, but no sense in alarming her mother any extra. *Mom already had one melt down this morning. Got to keep it together*, she thought, *or I might crawl back into bed and suck my thumb. I just wanted to chill this summer because I was afraid of going to college and being on my own. Shit!*

Marla seemed shocked. "I don't want to go look in the sunroom; I'll gladly stay out of the way and keep Alice occupied. I'll make more ice tea and point her toward the veranda and maybe play some cards. She likes Canasta. I guess we should leave the vines in our rooms and not tell Tilfort when he starts getting it out of the house. Kudzu might consider that as an attack from us. Let's do the dishes quickly while Alice's changing. There aren't many."

Hailey was glad for the distraction. She didn't want to think right now, but she knew she had to. When would Henry be ready to come home? Who was going to go get him? She considered the choices. She doubted that David could; he was really stressed with finishing for that wedding. He'd had so many interruptions already that he was behind. She didn't figure he'd want her filling in so he could go; she only slowed him down yesterday. He wouldn't be so patient today. Tilfort seemed the only choice, but he needed to get rid of the kudzu before Alice saw it and went off the deep end. Alice didn't drive so she couldn't be sent. Too bad. That would solve the problem and get her out of the house. Mom wasn't in good shape to go; she couldn't handle that road again yet. That left Hailey herself unless there was some transportation service she could call. Hailey knew she'd drive that road if she had to, but she was afraid. She didn't know the road, and killing both Henry and herself could happen. She was thinking so hard that she didn't realize she'd finished shelving the last dish until Alice interrupted.

"Goodness, y'all already finished the dishes. I was fixin' to he'p you. I just can't seem to get movin' this mornin'," Alice said as she reentered, still carrying Lily.

"There weren't many, Alice, and we didn't mind. I've fixed more tea. Let's go out on the veranda and play some cards. I still remember how to play Canasta," Marla said. She quickly filled two glasses and lead Alice outside.

Hailey decided this was a good time to do some research. She didn't know if she should look up sentient plants, psychic plants, killer plants or what, so it would just be random. Back in her room, the little kudzu vine had wrapped itself around her computer. She carefully unwound it and laid it on the floor. She didn't want to accidentally damage it or she might be included in kudzu's threat. It seemed excited as if it knew she was going to look up information about it. She Googled kudzu/ thinking plants and one link was a documentary called *Talking Plants*. She decided to watch it.

Maybe this is the internet info. Janice mentioned. Couldn't hurt to watch, she thought. *Might mention some plant legends that fit this situation. At least, it'll kill some time.*

Chapter 2

Jebadia Flanks was over at Miter Lewis's. He fished a cold beer out of the cooler and plopped down on a metal chair next to Mite, indifferent to the vines carpeting the patio and side of the house. He had considered kicking the kudzu away so he'd have a cleared space for his chair, but decided he'd have enough work to do soon. Why make extra. Jeb shrugged and tipped the can to drink.

He'd promised to help Mite cut down some dying trees behind his cabin, thanks to kudzu, and Mite had promised Jeb half the wood for payment. There would be enough cords to keep both of them warm next winter, maybe some to share with relatives. Jeb brought along his log splitter. With two chain saws and Mite's huge industrial-grade wood chipper, the men figured they could have everything cut by evening. They'd stack as they went, and Jeb could take some home tonight and the rest Wednesday. Then they'd load and sell the mulch to the hardware store for gardeners.

It was a good idea, but the heavy storm last night had made the ground spongy, and it was hard to walk without tripping on new growing vines. The wind had blown some of the kudzu off the trees which now dangled down from branches forming a rag-like curtain. More lay in clumps everywhere. All this made it difficult to maneuver the trucks and equipment where they needed them without miring up or wrapping the kudzu around the wheels.

There would be more leg work than planned. Maybe a three day job if it didn't rain again, and the day's humidity and heat were slowing their resolve. Four beers each and the men reluctantly moved toward two old oaks closest to the splitter.

Kudzu cloaked the trees. The toes of their boots kept tangling in it as they walked. Both were experienced loggers, but the kudzu vines had laced most of the trees' branches together like one big log jam. They quickly saw that felling the dead trees was going to be harder than they thought. Cut one trunk and kudzu held it to its standing neighbor. It couldn't fall unless the vines were cut.

After another beer apiece, Mite came up with an idea. He got his repelling equipment out of the shed and climbed up one trunk. Jeb sent up a chainsaw so his partner could cut through the vines holding the branches together. Even then, the kudzu wouldn't let go; limbs and heavy vines either fell in unpredicted ways or stayed attached, bounced, and swung wildly. Jeb had to stand well clear and still be ready to run if necessary. Hard to do after five beers and griddle cakes for breakfast.

Back down on the ground, they cut the vines off the trunk so the kudzu wouldn't hamper the tree's fall. If it bounced or snagged, it could kill one or both men.

Cutting down the two oaks this way took hours. They stopped to eat. Fried corned beef hash with onions and more beers later, they were bent over the trunks cutting off the rest of the limbs. They'd do the sectioning and splitting when more trees were down.

By now, the heat was oppressive, and the beer only made the men hotter. Their sweat bands were soaked and couldn't keep the salty water out of their eyes.

"Bless your damn *heart*, Mite," Jeb said. "This is gonna need a week for your fifteen trees. We can't cut separately, so we might only get two more down today and not all of that split. We have ta shred the small branches first, or we won't have room ta section the big stuff for the splitter. We gotta get this in stages; I can't be here all week."

"We can work after dark tonight; I've got flood lights. You can sleep here on the couch so we can start early tomorrow.

You'll be out for church tomorrow night, and we can start again Saturday," said Mite. "That good?"

"Good. But I gotta go near 4:30 ta meet up with Wit and Thymie. So, we start early, by seven." Jeb was tired and feeling a little queasy. He forgot about the supper invite from his sister. Likewise, he forgot to call about the plan change.

Mite nodded and climbed the next tree. Jeb sent up the chainsaw when he got Mite's signal, but he wasn't careful of the knot he tied on its handle. He was distracted because his stomach was acting up. Mite's cooking was heavy on the grease, and the beers and heat weren't helping. He bent over and vomited as the knot came loose and the saw fell. It bounced off some vines and stuck, swinging back and forth.

Mite cursed heavily, and then repelled down and tried to kick it loose. "Heads up," he yelled as it broke free and landed three feet from his friend.

"Okay here," Jeb shouted up, and retied the saw. Mite pulled it up carefully, afraid it might fall again. Then he began the slow process of cutting the branches apart.

When the third tree lay on the ground, Jeb was feeling even worse. He figured that corned beef might have tainted from the heat; it sure felt like food poisoning. Mite didn't look sick yet, just tired, Jeb thought. "He's use 'ta his own cookin', and I'm not."

"No more trees today; I'm done in. I think that meat might of spoiled from the heat or else it spoiled in my gut," Jeb said.

Mite worked on the trimming because Jeb turned white as a lye-bleached sheet, and was too shaky to hold his chainsaw steady. He took Mite's suggestion and drank more alcohol.

"Beer ought to kill any rot," Mite had told him.

Jeb felt some better after vomiting twice more and holding down his next beer. But, he wasn't up to helping his buddy cut off the large limbs. He just trimmed the small ones and tossed them to the side. Even that was slow going because the kudzu was not letting go.

Mite was struggling too. Sweat rolled down through his eyes and dripped off his chin. His sweatband was soaked and useless. He kept stopping his saw to wipe his eyes clear. Finally he took his muscle shirt off and tied it around his head. The saw was not cutting very fast, and he had to exert more force. He was nearly spent.

"Let's get that chipper over here and start grindin' up all these branches and vines," Jeb said. "We can't section or split 'til we do; it's all too tangled. And I can't see climbin' over it with a spinnin' chainsaw. Trippin's too easy. We can blow much of it into my truck bed. Then I'm done 'til tomorrow."

"You get started with the branches. My blade's getting dull, but maybe I can get a little more done before I have to change it out," Mite said.

Jeb began feeding the chipper when he noticed his friend looked sick now too. "You need to quit, bro," he said, "before you make a mistake. These aren't toys we're playin' with. That dull blade could fly off real easy like. You don't look too good neither. It's either the givies or food poisoning."

Mite didn't argue. He turned off his saw and helped Jeb push the branches into the whirling blades. The exhausted men moved slower than two stalled trucks. The massive chipper literally yanked the wood out of their hands, quickly shredding all it was fed. The mulch sprayed out behind into the truck bed. The ground around them was thickly matted with kudzu, much of it still tangled. They kept tripping on the vines as they hefted the wood.

"Damn, Mite. Why'd you buy such a monster machine? It nearly yanks my arms out of socket just feeding it."

"Logging company bought a new one. I got it cheap," Mite answered. "Makes the work go faster."

They should have cut the kudzu holding the branches together instead of shoving large bundles into the machine.

But, heat, long hours, alcohol, and food poisoning had impaired their judgment. They just wanted to get done as fast as possible so they could rest.

One particularly large vine-matted clump required both sets of hands to lift it into the machine. The many dangling vines wrapped tightly around their wrists and legs as the chipper grabbed hold. It yanked Jeb off his feet first and sucked him through the blades. Mite followed next. Red mulch sprayed out the back.

The chipper ran out of gas several hours later. No one missed Jeb until he didn't show up for dinner at Thymie and Norabell's. Wit and Thymie found the mulched remains around eleven.

Chapter 3

Mildred Udine was laughing. She'd been trying to train her husband's dog to kill cats, in particular, her neighbor's cats, but he'd been a stubborn mutt. *He don't want to kill anything, unless licking the damn vermin will do it*. But all her hard work was paying off. Odin had finally learned to chase Shadow, Alma's daughter's kitten up a tree. He'd even bowled it over before it could reach safety. It was hiding among the kudzu vines, crying. She gave Odin the command to guard and was pleased that he sat down by the tree and stared right at the kitten.

Lord, she hated cats, but maybe she hated Alma O'Neal more. Alma was divorced, in her 30's, and pretty. Her house was paid off, thanks to a small inheritance. And thanks to an ex-husband who paid lots of child support, she and her brat Katie always had nice clothes and their utilities never got shut off. She had money in the bank for Katie's college. She wasn't even working, supposedly disabled and got paid for that. How do you get disabled teaching school? Alma didn't look disabled; she looked like bait. Bait Mildred suspected her husband was eyeing.

Millie hated kids because she couldn't have any, so she hated Katie. Alma was always taking Katie to dance, choir practice, piano lessons, or the theater. She and that kid had money for six cats; they didn't even have a dog. Prissy bitches.

She'd kill every one of those cats just to spite those bitches even if Odin wouldn't, even if she had to do it herself. Maybe rat poison or antifreeze hidden in a can of tuna or slit their throats when she called them over to eat. Then put the dead cats by Alma's front door; maybe Katie would find them first. That thought made her grin.

Millie, as her husband called her, knew her good looks were fading—thinning hair, skinny, pouches under her eyes, coarse hands. *At least I'm working; Gabe's not.* She guessed she shouldn't blame him. She did love him, but everything was so hard these days. She couldn't keep her depression at bay anymore. She needed someone to blame or she'd go crazy; so she blamed and hated everyone.

Gabe tore up his back at the mill. He was loading a large roll of carpet when a car backfired outside, and he lunged under a stand supporting several carpet spools to hide, thinking it was artillery fire. His actions caused a spool to roll off its support arms and land on his back. The VA wasn't helping his PTSD much, and now his boss fired him, saying he was too jumpy.

At least he ain't drinking no more, Millie reminded herself daily, but she was sure he was addicted to the Xanax and Hydrocodone. *They dole that shit out like candy, and maybe the medication's free, but not the gas to drive two hours there and back. There goes my house cleaning money every month, and he stays so drugged up he doesn't do nothing to help; he just lays in that lounge chair outside, stoned out of his head. He says the meds kill the pain and stress. I say he's faking it 'cause he don't want me no more.*

Several years ago when he and Millie were doing better financially, he had built a wide, deep hole in the ground a distance from their house and lined it with fire bricks. They hosted a hog or deer roast during the summer for some of his army buddies and their families. Gabe would prepare the animal and start cooking it Friday night. The parties would start Saturday morning and last all weekend. They'd had fun then. However, since he had hurt his back and lost his job, there was no money for parties, and he couldn't prepare the hog or wrestle it in or out of the hole.

Millie admitted he still made use of the roasting pit when his back would let him. As a boy, his uncle had taught him to line a pit with pointed stakes and cover it over with brush. If an unsuspecting deer or other animal fell through the thin branches covering the hole, it would be impaled below. Usually Millie had to do much of the work after the animal was killed, but it provided meat for the table.

She knew Gabe needed to feel he could contribute something to keep them going and save his pride. He had little self-respect left, thanks to her constant barrage of belittling insults and daily doses of guilt. Millie couldn't help herself and her guilt from doing it was tearing her up inside. *He won't even fight me over it; he don't care, just goes out and sleeps.*

And he don't care the water's been shut off for three weeks. He says don't worry about it 'cause the outhouse and grey well water's just fine. Done had worse when he was fighting. Well, I haven't. I hate lugging water home in milk jugs. Least my customers don't notice it's their water yet, and they don't know I do my clothes there. Been smart about it. Little laundry here, little laundry there. Nobody's bill goes up. They don't know I take my showers there too. If I'm good enough to clean their bathrooms, I'm good enough to wash myself there.

Millie smiled at Odin; he was still guarding the cat like she told him to. Odin was Gabe's service dog supplied by an agency in Atlanta, and Millie knew her husband might have killed himself several times over if it hadn't been for the dog's companionship. Odin could reach Gabe when she couldn't, and as much as she loved that dog too, she was a little jealous of that connection. Maybe that's why she was always trying to corrupt his training. That wasn't working out so well, as Odin would play ball with her as he did with Gabe, but couldn't be taught to kill cats, much to her husband's constant amusement.

Mildred told Odin to stay as she walked back on to her property. She watched Gabe sleeping in the lawn chair, one foot hooked under some kudzu vines and a can of soda tilted in his hand. *Wouldn't be hard to claim he took too many pain pills when he's all doped up. It's been two years since we've had sex; claims it hurts his back. I know he's thinking about Alma. He don't ever want me and I've tried.* She turned away, tears burning her eyes.

Jealousy, poverty, neglect, and sexual frustration caused her hate, but she didn't know that; she just hated. Kudzu fell under that category too. No one helped her cut it off the house or car. No one helped her burn the piles. Her vegetable garden was covered and mostly dead. Nothing to augment her grocery budget. Her shoulders slumped; her depression was overwhelming.

Odin showed up wagging his tail. He was proud of himself and wanted attention. He was the only thing she couldn't hate. Mildred hugged him hard and started crying. "Come boy, I'll get you a treat," she said, and walked into the house.

Chapter 4

Hailey was surprised by what she learned about plants. Til was right about them using smells or chemicals. But there was so much more! It all tumbled through her head like a pile-up of cars on an icy freeway. She felt shell-shocked. Plants communicate with each other; they cooperate, wage war, get stressed, have emotions like anger or fear, nurture their young, move, make decisions, call for help, feel pain, fight over territory, help family members like a tribe, have a sense of self, have four senses and maybe the equivalent of sight, and if a plant can't perceive itself--it will go crazy.

They were like people or animals only with their feet stuck in the ground—80% underground like an iceberg, and doing more down there than above; even using toxins to kill other plants at their roots.

The documentary said that plants have intelligence, but it was so different from humans that it seemed entirely alien. That part was scary if she thought about kudzu. She never gave plants a thought except for their flowers or food. She'd think twice the next time she hammered a nail into a tree or pulled up a plant for the fun of it. She knew she'd have to be more careful around kudzu. It could do more than the average celery or radish. That emotion-feeling and decision-making really worried her. It was happening right in Henry's house.

She also discovered kudzu was in Indiana and not far from her house. Only the cold winters held it at bay, but winters hadn't been all that cold at home. Good old global warming. That sent chills up her back, especially when she read that over 7 million acres had been taken over in the South. Could 7 million acres of plants all talk to each other maybe like one single mind? Could there be one leader?

Janice and Tilfort are right. What if the kudzu here told the kudzu back home to attack Mom and me because we had done something to anger it here? It could be waiting in ambush when we thought we'd escaped. She looked down at the kudzu peeking out from under her bed. *"Can you read everyone's thoughts if you want to? Are you psychic or empathic? Or is it just empaths and psychics who can hear you?*

Kudzu's possibilities were beginning to chill her to her soul. A sense of helplessness set in. As if the universe knew she needed to feel some control, the phone rang in the kitchen. Hailey ran to answer it.

She nearly collided with Marla also rushing to the phone. Hailey let her mother answer it. After the usual uh-huh, yes, and other worthless words, Marla hung up.

"Was it the hospital? How's Henry? When's he coming home?" Hailey chattered.

"Let's go out on the veranda and include Alice," Marla said. "Grab some tea for yourself." She wasn't in any hurry to tell, so Hailey did as she was told, and joined the two women outside.

When Hailey was settled, Marla began. "That was Dr. Jeffries. He ran several tests this morning, but the results won't be in for a day or two. Henry didn't have a mini stroke or a heart attack, but his blood pressure is extremely elevated--higher than any other readings listed in his chart. Those were his words."

"All this is your fault Marla, Bogerty wouldn't be coming back for a month if you hadn't flirted with him. Now we're stuck with him again this week. At least we won't have to feed him again," Alice said. "Henry took care of that."

"Excuse me Alice," Hailey said, defending her mother, "You were the one who told Bogerty we would be celebrating the Fourth here. If you'd said we hadn't decided where we'd be or that we were going somewhere else, we wouldn't have had him forcing his way here. So don't go dumping your slip-up on Mom. She did stop his preaching and you were in on it too."

Marla raised her voice to continue before Alice could start up again. "He wondered if Henry was experiencing more than the usual stress at home. He cautioned that unless that stress is relieved, Henry could easily have a massive stroke or heart attack at any time. Dr. Jeffries didn't want to send him home, but Henry insisted. He can walk okay, but he's shaky. He'll be here when the hospital can arrange transport. The paramedics will be monitoring his vitals on the way here, and if he spikes, the ambulance will turn around and go back.

"More than usual stress?" squawked Alice. "Of course he's got more than usual stress, Marla. Bogerty's coming Thursday night, and that's whole moon night. My spells will be comin', and Bogerty'll demand snacks to help him celebrate along with the fireworks. He'll want me to have pie and cookies or a cheese plate and meats for sandwiches, and I won't be up to all that. I get too weak before my spells, so you'll have to do all that cookin' yourself and get Hailey to he'p you. It's expensive enough to feed the two of you, let alone more food for his stomach again this week. And Henry's got to fend that man off of you because of you. And Janice can't come be with David because of you. I'd say my Henry's got more than usual stress."

Alice's words stung Marla. Hailey could feel that hurt. She doubled up her fist and started hitting the arm of her chair. It took a lot of will power not to get in that bitch's face right now and tell her all about Henry's unusual stress and how it was a lot more than kudzu or Bogerty. "Alice, be quiet and let Mom finish telling us what the doctor said."

Marla smiled gratefully at her daughter and took a deep breath before continuing. "The doctor cautioned me that Henry must have bed rest for the next several days and a calm environment. He's given Henry a prescription for some stress pills—Xanax, and he's sending a few home until David or Til can get it filled tomorrow. Henry's to take them religiously, and he's got another appointment with Dr. Jeffries next Tuesday at 1:00. His office will call with these test results if anything unusual shows up. That's all he told me. He might tell David or you, Alice, more since you're immediate family. You can call now if you want."

Alice just sat there, staring at the kudzu across the road. "I hate that stuff. David and Tilfort need to cut it down over there. I don't care if it isn't our property. I don't want to look at it anymore."

Marla and Hailey looked at Alice like they'd seen an alien disguised as their cousin. Instead of worrying about Henry, she was looking for more work for the men to do. Marla rolled her eyes at Hailey, and Hailey exaggerated her own expression of keeping her mouth shut.

"Hey Mom, let's get some more tea. I gulped mine, and the two of you are all out." She signaled for Marla to follow her inside as she grabbed Alice's glass.

Once inside out of Alice's ear shot, she said, "Is Alice for real? Shouldn't she be asking questions, calling the doctor, making plans to keep Henry calm, or something? Who gives a damn about someone else's kudzu? It wouldn't be a smart move anyway, considering that message! Those vines in her room were definitely a threat. Kudzu hates her."

"She doesn't know about that warning, and only we saw her room. She was too out of it to notice. Also, she might not really want the men to start cutting that kudzu across the road. Maybe that's how she handles some things," Marla said, "along with blaming others. Everybody deals with problems differently, and we already know she's a bit out there."

"Well, maybe, but that bit about keeping things calm isn't going to happen unless we drug her, murder Bogerty, and make kudzu disappear," Hailey said. "She reminds me of James. We've been here two days, and already I don't like her. She's selfish, self-centered, and a real drama queen. Do we have to stay the whole ten days? Couldn't we leave tomorrow? How about one last normal summer, us having fun? We'd miss Bogerty and all that stress that YOU caused, and they wouldn't have to feed us."

"I'm ready after Alice's remarks; they were uncalled for and hurtful," Marla said. "But Henry needs some kind of buffer right now, and I don't want to disappoint David since he's spending extra money for some flashy fireworks. Let's shoot for Saturday. It would be very impolite to rush off, and possibly lose the only family you have. Grab the tea and let's go back out before Alice figures we're talking about her."

"Which we are," Hailey snickered as she carried Alice's glass and a full pitcher outside.

As soon as Hailey sat Alice's glass down beside her, Alice covered her face and began moaning. "My spells will be comin' on soon. Maybe tonight, and that's always hard on the men. I can't control my walkin' or my feelin's with the whole moon. My poor peach trees will be callin' me. Henry always takes care of me. Kudzu's doin' this, and now Bogerty's showin' up again because of you. All this will kill him. You've got to help me, Marla. I need you. You've got to take care of me."

Hailey saw her mother go stiff as concrete setting up. She knew what that meant, and before her mother could explode or, possibly, implode, she cut in.

Her voice held quiet authority. "Alice, you can't go complaining around Henry; he's too weak right now."

"I don't complain. How dare you even suggest such a thing. I know how to care for my own husband," Alice said.

"I mean, you can't talk about your peach trees or kudzu, or your spells, whatever they are, or money, anything else that might stress him out. Okay?"

Alice set her jaw and lifted her head. "I don't complain," she said, as she gripped her tea glass. "You are rude!"

"Whatever! All that talk just upsets him. Also, David and Til have to get those decorations done, and you can't go interfering with them. Don't expect them to take care of you or do extra projects for you. They don't have the time."

"What about Bogerty, Miss Know-it-all?" Alice demanded.

Hailey could have strangled her cousin at this point. Instead, she said, "Mom and I will deal with Bogerty. Don't dump that guilt trip on her. You just smile as if you don't have a care in the world. Drink tea out here and stay away from Henry. Read a magazine, do laundry, mend something, cook without using Mom; just be calm and quiet. Lily will keep you company."

"Don't try to tell me what to do, little gal. I'll not mend or read. If clothes need mendin' or cleanin', Tilfort does that and he reads enough for all of us. And since y'all are causing me extra work, Marla can he'p me cook; Henry can't right now because of y'all."

Hailey ignored Alice's remarks and spoke over her, "Tonight, if the moon feels too hot, take a cold shower before bed. Then, take a sleeping pill. That should knock you out so you won't go walking. I can sleep with Mom, and you sleep in my room. That way you won't bother Dad, uh, Henry."

"I don't bother Henry. But I know he's too weak to walk the grounds, so you and Marla will have to care for me when my spells come."

Hailey seldom cursed in front of her mom, although her friends knew she was very adept. But right now, she'd reached the end of her rope. Her expression turned cold and rigid like an ice shard, and her voice came out low and slow.

"Mom needs a rest too. She's not that well, and she's not going to be your *god-damned* nursemaid, and neither am I. It's not all about you, Alice. Stop moaning, and pull your own wagon. Or, I'll get a hasp and lock off the barn and confine your hysterical ass to my bedroom. Do you understand?"

Alice was shocked. "Well, I never..." was as far as she got.

"You have now," Hailey responded. "Go cook something for lunch, and leave my mother alone."

Alice got up woodenly and marched inside. Lily hissed at Hailey and followed her owner.

"Tough," Hailey said to the retreating cat.

Marla stared at her daughter, mouth open. It shocked her and made her proud at the same time. She blinked. "Wow," was all she said.

"Like mother, like daughter," she shrugged. "I learned from the best."

Marla actually laughed. "I guess my gal can take care of herself now."

Hailey hadn't expected her mom to laugh; she was relieved. And she liked the approval. "You're not mad at me? Sorry about the cussing."

Marla shook her head, "Not a problem. Alice needed to be told that, and you were the one to do it. Good for you, Sweetie! How about gin rummy until lunch is ready? You deal."

Lunch never arrived. Hailey and Marla fixed ham sandwiches and took some to David and Til. Alice was in her room, either crying or sulking. They hoped she had spared the men. She hadn't.

"Good for you, Hailey," David said when she delivered the sandwiches. "She came right here after you straightened her tail. I said I was too busy to think about it. I've wanted to tell her the same thing for two years. Janice gets an ear full the few times she comes, but she's stoic about it." He smiled. "None of us can tell her, or we'd never hear the end of it."

Tilfort added, "Guilt trips for breakfast, lunch, and supper. Your scoldin' her makes these the best sandwiches I ever ate.

Thank'ee."

"So you're not tossing us out the door just yet?" Hailey said. "We're thinking about leaving Saturday."

"Y'all will be sorely missed. Y'all have taken a load off us for a few days. When you go, it'll all close back in." Tilfort seemed sad.

"You could pack up and move to town. Get out of here. Even Alice seems ready to consider it," Hailey said.

"Daddy, Til, and I've talked about it. I think we will. Alice's peach trees have been holding her back and all the memories. But we need a new life and maybe Momma can heal," David said as he handed the empty plates back to Hailey. "Back to work."

Til grinned. "I'll get ye a hasp and a lock out of the barn along with a screwdriver. I hear you might be needin' them." He was as good as his word.

With the men occupied and Alice still sulking in her room, there wasn't much to do but play cards and wait for Henry's arrival. Marla took a nap, but Hailey walked across the road to get a good look at the kudzu that entrapped her the night they came. Maybe she could "talk" to it. She jumped over the ditch, now spongy with water, and stepped into the densely packed vines. It was dark and surprisingly cool inside compared to the heat and humidity just across the gravel. Hailey sensed a cautious watchfulness coming from all directions. Kudzu knew she was there.

She touched several leaves. "Why," she asked, "the other night? You wanted me here then. I'm here now. You sent a message today."

Strong. You hear.

"We're empaths; we can all hear," she said.

No. Not hear. You hear.

"Alice hears you. Don't you talk to her?"

Alicessss hates. Not hear. John accident.

Hailey got nothing else; kudzu was silent. *Now I get to convince Alice that kudzu didn't kill John. She won't hear.* She shrugged and walked back to the house.

..........<>..........

Henry arrived home around four. Kingston's happy barking alerted everyone. Elroy and Marvin made him stay on the gurney while they wheeled him right into the bedroom and put him in bed. Henry protested that he had been down long enough and was getting up. Kingston jumped on the bed and lay on him. He started laughing when Hailey threatened to duct tape him to the bed rails

"All right you two, I'm outnumbered," he said. "I'll behave for a little while. At least until supper."

Marla, on Hailey's orders, kept Alice in the kitchen. She was determined to tell Henry her version of the morning. Henry didn't need to hear that; it would only raise his blood pressure. Instead, Marla convinced her that they should start supper early.

The paramedics gave Alice the doctor's instructions and medication. Included was his new diet. That occupied her with finding foods in the pantry which Henry could eat. She hadn't followed the last one Dr. Jefferies sent home, but Marla made sure she did for this evening. It wasn't what everyone was used to, and Henry howled as loudly as the other men.

After supper, Henry sat outside listening to the insects. He didn't mind the sultry night; he felt cold in spite of the closeness. Kingston leaned into his leg, and Henry absently stroked the dog's warm fur. Hailey sat nearly as close. He seemed relaxed and happy, and so did she.

Hailey admired him, maybe because he'd championed the whole family against Bogerty and didn't assign blame to the family's blunders which earned them all another visit from the preacher. He was strong and supportive, not like her weak, whining father. James would talk behind anyone's back who didn't cater to him, then lie when caught. She felt she didn't have to watch her back or fend off demands; Henry could be trusted. He was honest, and he didn't complain.

They even talked like she supposed a father and daughter should talk—him reminiscing about the past and her telling him about her future plans, and asking his advice. Henry listened to her as her father never had.

James only wanted to talk about himself; my feelings and dreams weren't important. I really loved *hearing about his girlfriends, and sneaking around on Mom, and sex with his "soul mates of the month." And you wonder why I despise you, Daddy Darling!*

Hailey wondered if Ashley and he had sat like this, talking. She knew little about Henry and Alice's daughter except for that pink and gold, viney room and its weird toys.

"You never talk about Ashley; you and Alice have mentioned John but not her. Why?" Hailey asked.

"I guess the memories are too painful," Henry said. "Ashley danced to a different drummer and she and Alice fought a lot. Even when she was a little girl she didn't conform to what Alice thought she should. You see her room. It doesn't look like any other in the house. I put up that ugly wallpaper and painted that ceilin' gold because Ashley loved it, even after she grew up. Alice had decided Ashley's room should be grey with turquoise and no wallpaper, and my wife's accustomed to gettin' her way."

Hailey giggled. "I think the paper and gold are ugly too, but maybe not if I were little. I guess I have to admire her guts for standing up to Alice. My mom didn't care what I did to my room because it was mine. When we pulled up the nasty orange and brown shag carpet, she let me finger paint the sub-floor. I put hand prints, foot prints, and drawings everywhere and sprinkled glitter in the wet paint. Mom just said I was a good artist and congratulated me on my skills. She must have gagged when I wasn't around, but she never let on. Later I painted it lavender-blue with white trim. I picked the paint I wanted, both times, no arguments."

"It was war around here," Henry said. "My little-six-year old faced off against her mamma and wouldn't back down. Alice tried tears and guilt trips on Ashley when shouting didn't work. Finally I just bought the paper and paint and fixed the room. Then Alice started in on me because I took Ashley's side over hers, all on account of a little girl wantin' pink and gold for her bedroom. And I didn't let Alice tear off that paper when Ashley moved out; I knew she'd want it there when she visited. Alice would have finally won if it came off."

"I saw some weird toys in there. Were those Ashley's choices too?" Hailey was intrigued now. She enjoyed listening to Henry, and comparing him to James. Henry was winning "father of the year" in her eyes. She even felt a twinge of jealousy because he was Ashley's dad and not hers. *Maybe I can adopt him.*

Henry laughed. "Ashley got it into her head that she wanted to be a ventriloquist. Saw one on the Ed Sullivan Show and nothin' would do but she had to have a dummy. I fought Alice on that one too. Got my little girl that dummy for her birthday. Ashley wouldn't talk to Alice for months; the dummy talked for her. Alice had fits over that one. Ashley told me she left it here to remind Alice."

"She must have liked clowns too. I never liked real clowns much. One freaked me out at a circus once. I was watching the elephants and one wearing a big green wig came up behind me. He was making me a balloon hat, but the balloon burst right by my ear and I turned around to see his big painted red mouth right by my head. I totally lost it. Mom had to take me home and I had nightmares for weeks." Hailey shuttered remembering it.

"Sorry you had that experience. Ashley wanted to collect clowns because she loved Red Skelton's clown character, and John and I got her several over the years. She took the others with her, but left the ones you saw. She said the fat one looked evil, but she still wanted it here when she came visitin'. That's the only one Alice got her. Funny in a way. I guess there was somethin' symbolic about that toy too."

"Did she collect antique dolls too? One has a cracked head," Hailey said.

"Ashley loved antiques, possibly because Alice can't stand anythin' old," Henry said. "Alice bought her a fashion Revlon doll, Barbie doll, a Honey Walker, ballerina. All sorts of modern dolls so she could keep up with her girlfriends; Alice wanted her to be popular. Ashley loved those, but she loved the antique ones more. I'd take her into an antique shop and she'd head right for the dolls. Got her that iron bed in one shop too."

"How did that one doll's head get cracked? Did you buy it that way or was it a family heirloom that had an accident?" Hailey asked. "What's the story there?"

"That was another Alice thin'. She gave Ashley that Barbie doll for Christmas, and I bought her that porcelain doll. Ashley played with my present and neglected Barbie, so Alice grabbed it out of her arms and bounced it off the floor, right on Christmas mornin'. That's how it got broke. I did the best I could mendin' it. Ashley left a couple dolls along with the clowns. I reckon it was a reminder for both of them. Ashley was good with her symbolism; it was her way of gougin' Alice."

Wow! Bet that was a bad head trip for Ashley, Hailey thought. *Nothing like having your mom blow a gasket over a Christmas present. Not my mom. James never got me anything. Mom would buy stuff and put his name on it. Half the time he'd take off to give some girlfriend a gift that he either bought or stole from Mom—like those wind chimes she was so proud of. Never got Mom anything either. Not even a wedding ring. Gave me a harmonica once that some musician guy gave him. He took it back Christmas Day when he and his new girlfriend stopped over to get what I bought him. Fucking bastard wouldn't come over until I dangled a present. Jackass want a carrot?* Hailey shook herself to stop the memories and come back to the present.

"So Ashley really liked antiques. How'd that happen since you don't have any here?" she asked. Hailey liked antiques too, and Marla bought her several antique boxes when she was little. Even a vintage Midge doll with original outfits.

Alice would hate Mom's antique jewelry and enamelware. She bought antique furniture for our whole house because she said things were cheaper than new pieces back then. Alice would have fits there if she hates antiques. Hailey chuckled at that idea.

"I don't know exactly. She just came borned that way," Henry said. "Ashley's house was full of antique things. She met Jimmy in an antique store up in Jackson, Tennessee. They even made a business out of buyin' and sellin' them up in Nashville. Jimmy had a store called Anythin' Denim and she used her antiques to display the clothes. The combination worked real well up in the city. Her twin boys remind me a lot of her. John collects old advertisin' premiums, and Robert goes for old iron banks. I miss my little girl and her family, real bad sometimes."

"How come Jimmy never brings your grandsons to visit?" Hailey asked. She wished James missed her sometimes, but then she wouldn't have believed him if he said he did.

He only used me for chick bait--parade me in front of a potential girlfriend. "See, I am a good father, you should fuck me." Kinda like using a dog to get the girl; I was his dog."

"Jimmy did for a while, but Alice either argued with him or dumped guilt in big spoonfuls on all three. Jimmy couldn't do anything right when Ashley was alive and that never changed. Alice thought he was a poor choice for a husband and was embarrassed that he owned a blue jean store. The boys couldn't stand their grandma, so I can't blame Jimmy for movin' to North Carolina."

"Why did they move there? Don't you ever hear from them?" Hailey felt sad for Henry.

Henry gave her a sly smile. "Jimmy keeps up with me on Facebook and by email. Janice got Skype at her apartment over the Dawg so I go there to talk to the boys. We used to meet in Ashville before my stroke. Now Jimmy slips into town sometimes. Alice and David don't know all that; my wife would drag it out of David if he knew. When I was gone, she thought I was up learnin' about peaches. And Jimmy had two stores, but he wore out. Sold the Nashville one and kept Asheville."

"I figure you don't want Alice to know any of this. Did Janice get Skype just for you? I don't think she'd be the type to use it herself," Hailey said.

"Well she did it for me, but Janice would surprise you. She's pretty savvy on electronics. She uses Skype to stay in contact with her relatives. Her mother, grandmother, and great grandmother are Elders and they keep up on tribal thin's," Henry said. "She doesn't tell me anythin' connected with all that, but she he'ps me sneak with the family."

At that moment in time, Hailey wished more than anything that she had a father like Henry. *Maybe he'd take me for an Ashley substitute*, she thought. *I'd have no trouble calling him Dad if he'd let me*. Henry was quickly filling that hole in her heart.

The sun went down and the air got cooler. A slight breeze

stirred the air as gathering clouds drifted across the stars. They made a contest of who could spot the most spectacular display of heat lightening.

The two women stayed in the kitchen to wash dishes and put away food. They sat talking for a long while afterwards as Marla deliberately kept Alice engaged so Henry could rest. They even giggled over the little outfits Alice made for Lily. They played dolly-dress up-with the stoic cat.

Only when Lily had had enough and escaped to the living room did they join Henry and Hailey on the veranda. With Hailey glaring at her, Alice kept her peace, for now. She wanted to get Henry alone, not have an audience. She'd wait.

Later when Henry was banished to bed, David and Til took a break from their work and slipped back into the kitchen for what they called "real food." Hailey and Marla were already there making sandwiches for the three of them. Kingston was underfoot, begging snacks. They thought Alice was waiting on the veranda for hers, but she slipped around back going through the sunroom to complain to Henry. She saw the kudzu and the screaming began.

"O Lordy!" Tilfort said. All four ran toward the sound. When they opened the door, Alice was in the middle of the sunroom turning in circles and screaming so loudly that Marla covered her ears. Lily ran in and howled in unison.

"Get Henry," she screamed at Tilfort. "You let this happen. You're supposed to take care of this." Then she turned on David, "Your damn weddin'. You're usin' it as an excuse not to he'p. You're takin' Tilfort away from his job. Y'all against me. I want Henry!" The screaming continued.

Henry made his way slowly into the room, leaning on the wall to steady himself. Hailey thought he looked utterly defeated. He barely had the strength to speak.

"Calm down, Alice," he said. He tried to walk towards her, but without the wall to lean on, he started to fall. Tilfort and David reached him at the same time. They carried him to the couch and sat him down on top of the vines. Alice ran to him, sat on his lap, and put her arms around his neck.

"Hold me, Henry," she said. "I'm scared. You've got to do somethin'. I can't take any more. The peach trees, the whisperin's. Burn it, Henry, burn it. It's evil. It wants to take our house. They're against me."

Henry patted her back and looked at his son.

"Come on, Mama; let me get you out of here. Til and I will clear out the vines tomorrow when we get back from the church. It's late. Daddy needs rest, and I have to load the van tonight. He tried to pull her off Henry, but she clutched him like a buoy in an open sea and mewed.

"Here now, David. Let me handle her," Henry said.

"Get up, Alice, so I can stand, and I'll take you to bed. You can hold tight then."

She allowed David to lift her off while Tilfort helped Henry up. Alice clung to Henry and Henry leaned on his son. Tilfort and Lily led the way. David tenderly put them on the bed, removed their shoes, and covered them. Neither parent seemed capable of helping themselves.

As David walked toward the hall, he heard Alice murmur, "The moon's so hot. Clouds don't cool it none." Lily moved to Alice's pillow and purred in her ear.

He gripped the handle. "Oh, God, not tonight. Please," he said and closed the door. Kingston lay down in the hallway. "*I guard.*"

Chapter 5

Oriel Weaver leaned against his car and smoked his third cigarette in a row. He had a bottle of holy water stuffed into his pocket and a rope wound around his waist. His conference with Reverend Bogerty left him feeling like electric eels were swimming through his intestines.

He'd gone to the reverend for advice about his wife's odd behavior. Ruby was hanging stick dolls, crosses, and dead chipmunks from the kudzu vines on their property.

"She loves horror movies about demons and ghosts. Eats them up like peach pudding," Oriel said. "She told me she'd seen the stick dolls and small dead rodents used to ward off evil spirits on one of her shows. Says she's trying to make kudzu walk away from our property. She says the crosses are there to purify."

"She's lying," Bogerty said. "She's a witch, and she's using those filthy things to help kudzu possess the land. She defiled those crosses by putting them by Satan's filth; they're not protecting anything. There's only a couple ways to cure her of her evil," Reverend Bogerty said as he pulled a rope and a bottle from his closet. "Here's holy water, and a blessed rope. I blessed it myself and sprinkled it with that holy water, so it's doubly purified. Tie your witch wife to a chair with this rope, force silver into her mouth, and tape her mouth shut so she can't spit the silver out. Put her feet on a pure iron skillet. Throw the holy water in her face and recite the Lord's Prayer seven times. If she relaxes and smiles, she's cured.

"Be warned though, if she mumbles strange sounds or thrashes about, she's deeply possessed by the plant spirits. You'll have to keep reciting the Lord's Prayer and beat the demons out of her. I recommend using some barbed wire attached to a heavy cord to scourge her like Jesus was."

"Reverend Bogerty, I don't have the stomach for that. I'm a

peaceful man. I love my Ruby too much. I've never raised my voice or my hand to her. And we don't have any silver excepting a necklace I gave her for Christmas four years ago. She might swallow it and choke. That whipping might kill her. And how do I know if the demon's let her go?

"You'll know when she stops fighting. Take off the tape and have her repeat the Lord's prayer. If she can, she's cured. If not, start over. You have to do this to save her soul. Her possession will only get worse if the devil's deep in her. Ruby might kill you while you sleep. The walking plant spirit has you blinded to your danger, Oriel. It's your only chance to save her and you. Those things in your trees will possess you before long. You haven't much time to save Ruby's immortal soul and yours too, son. It'll go for your kids too. Trust me, I know about these things. I was trained for this," Bogerty said. "It won't kill her. It will save her. Even if she does die, her soul will be clasped to Jesus' loving bosom. She'll thank you when you meet again in heaven."

When Oriel walked out of the side door leading to Bogerty's office, he didn't notice that the kudzu wrapped around the foundation of the Unity Baptist Church had climbed up the wall. It was now draping the door and window. It was as if it had moved closer to hear the conversation. Oriel simple brushed it out of his way as he left; he was too shaken to notice anything. Not even the tug when a little vine hooked onto one of his belt loops and broke off, leaving a dangling little tail as he walked away.

Reverend Bogerty watched Oriel out the window. He suspected this member of his flock was too weak to follow his orders. He tried calling Billy Purdue, but he wasn't answering. Hobart Dill would do, especially if Bentley Bishop helped him. It would probably take two men anyway.

Finishing his cigarette, Oriel crushed the butt under his

shoe, entered his car and drove to The Hungry Dawg. He desperately needed to talk to Janice about the walking plant spirits. He figured she'd know or one of her relatives would.

Janice was on the veranda enjoying a short break when Oriel found her.

"Oriel, you're shaking," she said. "Here, sit down next to me and spill your troubles."

He sat but promptly stood back up and paced.

"Janice, is kudzu the walking plant spirit I hear folks talk about? Is it evil? Bogerty says it is and says it's possessed my wife. That she's a witch helping it. I need to know. He says I should beat it out of her with barbed wire."

"The Reverend must watch a lot of television." Janice smiled. "A couple of months ago, one of my cousins was laughing about a movie she'd seen on Chiller. An evil walking tree destroyed a crew and machinery digging in a Native American burial ground. She said the monster reminded her of the Wamping Tree from Harry Potter; not very scary. I guess that movie found itself into Bogerty's sermons."

Oriel laughed at her words. He remembered watching that Wamping Tree part. It was kinda funny the way it did a number on Ron's flying car. That made him feel better.

"Spirit protectors can be found everywhere," Janice continued, noticing Oriel visibly relax. "What about your guardian angels? We also have a spirit which protects the land; it uses the plants and animals as sentries, and as warriors, if needed. Kudzu has become a protector, with the spirit's blessing. If you don't have an evil heart, it will care for you. Listen to your intuition; that's kudzu talking to your heart."

"I love Ruby," Oriel said. "She's a good person. Even takes moths back outside saying they're nature's messengers. But I'm not the smartest worm in the can. Bogerty's educated."

"That doesn't mean much. Bogerty is trying to turn a useful bean plant into a God's wrath scenario. I sense he was a fearful, abused child. His fear makes him controlling and cruel. I pity him, but this land is old and has its ways. Bogerty should tread lightly.

"Look around the veranda, Oriel; there's kudzu all over. Can you smell its flowers? I come out here if it's too hectic inside. Five minutes of kudzu's aroma therapy and I'm back working."

Janice patted the seat next to her. "Sit back down and breathe. It'll settle your brain so you can think. Then, listen to your heart. Only you and kudzu know if Ruby is a witch or possessed."

Janice chuckled. "By the way, witches and possessions are two different things. How can Ruby be both? Cherokees embrace kudzu's bounty as a blessing. We don't fight against it as you white men do. Why do you think the Dawg is so popular? Kudzu keeps everyone relaxed and happy. You never hear of an argument going on. Well, I'll leave you to your thoughts." She touched his shoulder as she left.

Oriel respected Janice so he sat and breathed. The sweet smell encircled him like a silken cocoon. He felt peaceful and let his mind float back in time. He saw Ruby standing on the restaurant's steps licking a Muscadine slushy and giggling. He remembered buying her that at Great Grape Works when they were both teens.

They'd been best friends since toddlers when he accidentally broke her birthday balloon and she just laughed. She was a cheerleader when he played football; she always cheered the loudest when he had the ball. He remembered her running onto the field when he scored a touchdown. She did four cartwheels, landed in the splits, then jumped up and gave him a kiss. Referee looked the other way.

Kudzu spoke to him.

"No, you're right," Oriel said out loud to the vines around him. "Ruby's just frightened like I am; times is hard; no jobs.

She means well. Yes, I'll take down the dead chipmunks. They stink. She can keep her dolls and crosses. I'll get her a little goat."

Oriel walked to the dumpster and threw in the rope and holy water. It couldn't be holy if Bogerty blessed it. He climbed in his car and went home. The little piece of kudzu was still attached.

Happy.

Chapter 6

Time. Now!

If anyone were out on Highway 57 Tuesday night, he would have heard a rustling of leaves not caused by any wind. Kudzu slowly and gently lifted Effie's cocooned body up to the edge of the highway. The vines fell away from her face. More vines covered the road, effectively blocking any oncoming vehicle from passing. It waited.

Ebon Arrowsong was driving home from his girlfriend's place when he caught the mass of vines in his headlights. He stopped and pulled his machete from behind his seat to chop an opening when he saw the cigar-shaped object. Advancing on it, machete held ready, he saw the decomposed head sticking out of a cocoon.

"Great One," he said and ran back to his truck for his cell phone. His hands were shaking as he punched 911.

Dixie Pumpkintown was dispatcher that evening and thought it was a prank call. Cocooned bodies lying in the road reminded her of The Invasion of the Body Snatchers. Finally she told Ebon to stay put while she agreed to send someone to investigate.

Harlem was home heating a TV dinner and watching a movie when he got the call. He ordered Dixie to contact Unity's hospital for an ambulance.

Most likely the paramedics will be Marvin and Elroy, he thought, and while Elroy didn't talk much, Marvin was a gossip. Harlem didn't need that tonight.

"Shit," was all he said when he hung up. He put the cold beer he was about to open back in the refrigerator, turned off the oven on his TV dinner, and donned his sweaty uniform. *Fourth of July, stacks of tourists, and a full moon coming. Now a cocoon. How much excitement can a man handle?* he thought, turning on the "cherries and berries" as the local teens called his lights, and drove.

Ebon was sitting in his truck when Harlem arrived.

"Where is it, Ebon?"

"Over to the left just before the drop off. I'm not going over there. I'll be having nightmares already," Ebon said.

Harlem walked over to the body and shined his flashlight over the entire form before resting on the face. It was decomposed beyond recognition, but the hair suggested a woman.

"The ambulance'll be here shortly. The coroner'll have to identify this if he can," he said. "Maybe you can give me a statement while we wait."

"Not much to tell. Kudzu had the road blocked. I got out to chop a path; the vines separated, and there was this wrapped body. When I went to Gloria's, there was nothing on the road. Is now."

"Must have fallen down from somewhere," Harlem said. He flashed his light in all directions, looking for a logical explanation. "BeBe or Robert can check things out tomorrow to look for evidence. It's too dark to see through the foliage now."

"Chop those vines off the road. That'll take your mind off this," Harlem said.

"A lot slid off already. Back down over the side under its own weight. I watched them. Kudzu put that body there; it wanted it to be found."

"Now, Ebon." Harlem started to say, but changed his mind. Ebon was three-quarter Cherokee, so he must know. He remembered Janice talking about the plant and spirits. "See if you can push the rest off the road; don't cut none."

Both men heard a rustling, sliding sound. They turned in time to see kudzu slide off the road and down the sheer drop to the valley below. Only the stems attached to the cocoon remained.

Harlem looked at Ebon. "I'm going to have trouble explaining this in my report," he said.

It was Marvin and Elroy in the ambulance. Their arrival saved Harlem from thinking about possibilities, but now he needed to fend off Marvin's curiosity. Asking questions was a necessity for a paramedic, but sometimes Marvin asked too many.

So before he could start, Harlem raised his hand and said, "Don't ask, Marvin. I don't know nothing more than you do right now. Just load it up."

Marvin let out a low whistle and looked at his partner. They loaded the body, cocoon and all, and left as quickly as they came. Harlem sent Ebon home.

He walked over to the edge of the road and shined his flashlight on the sheer drop to the valley. Next he checked the cliff on the other side where the rocks had been blasted to create a ledge for the road. He knew he couldn't tell anything in the dark, but he couldn't help himself. He had too many questions right now. Knowing what Ebon said and what he'd seen, he agreed with Ebon's logic that kudzu wanted the body found. Harlem respected Cherokee beliefs because his own grandfather taught him bits and pieces that Great Grandpa taught him, and he knew kudzu was powerful. It was just hard to accept a sentient plant; sheriffs had to be strictly logical. But that wasn't how he was thinking right now. *Wish I could think like Janice, but that can't be in a report.*

Harlem knew Dr. Alvis Moten wouldn't be at the morgue until morning. He had a head full of questions, but couldn't get any answers now. So there wasn't anything more to do except go home; his report could wait. He'd lost his appetite by now, but he really wanted that cold beer and a hot shower. He knew he'd be awake most of the night over this one.

Chapter 7

Hobart Dill got Bogerty's call. After work, he stopped off at the parsonage for the holy water and rope. He met his buddy Bentley Bishop at the Crooked Nail outside of town to make plans and swallow some encouragement.

"The reverend said we might need some barbed wire," said Hobie, "but I don't have none. You got some?"

"Nope, but I got wire cutters and Druci Cheswick's got barbed wire on the top of her fences to keep her cows in. She's got more goats than cows now, so she won't be needin' a few feet, and she's got money to replace it what with her goats' milk. You pull up close by, and I can slip over and cut a couple sections. Better wait til's it's dark. Then we can go on over to Oriel's."

"Man alive, I don't want to drive twelve miles to her place and eight more to Oriel's," said Hobie. "Don't you know of some close by?"

"Yeah, I do," said Bent, "but it's all covered with kudzu. At least her fences is cleared off thanks to her goats. It'll be easier to get the wire."

"Okay, okay. How about some pool 'til it gets dark? I got five dollars says I can beat you for three games. You got your downers with you? Gimmie three."

"Three?"

"We got heavenly business tonight, so yea, one for now and two for when we leave," said Hobie.

About ten o'clock, the men slipped out the Nail's back exit hiding beers under their vests. Hobie pulled the pills from his pocket, tossed them into his mouth, and chugged his beer. Tossing the bottle, he climbed into his truck and waited. Bent staggered to his station wagon for the cutters. When he returned, the truck's right door, mirror, and running board

Rosemary Coven

were laced with vines.

"Fuckin' kudzu, it's crawlin' all over," said Bent.

"Well, pull it off and get in. It won't bite."

Bentley tried, but the stems were too strong. He stretched the door and squeezed in.

"It'll break when you drive off," he said.

The vine broke, but a section remained wrapped around the handle and the rear view mirror.

Hobie was quiet for a while. "Hey Bent, Gimmie a couple more pills, will ya man. I need the courage; I dated Ruby in school and this isn't gonna be fun even if Reverend Bogerty says it has to be done."

"You still sweet on her? I thought you hated her for picking Oriel," Bent said, handing over the pills.

"He was better'n me in football, and I couldn't compete. More jealous of him, I guess; never hated her even though I said I did. Kicked myself for awhile. My DeDe's ok; she wants to get married, but, I donno. I can't figure Ruby for a witch. She loved her horror movies, especially ghosts. Most people do, so what's the harm? The Reverend must see more in it than I do. Skip it. Stick in some music."

The pills stuck in Hobie's throat, making him cough and swerve in the road. Several vines lay in their path. The worn shocks made the truck bounce as the tires rolled over them.

"Damn it! Watch what you're doing before you wreck us," Bent yelled. "Why the hell did you have to do those shots of tequila? Roll down your fuckin' window and sober up."

Hobie nodded and complied. A sweet fragrance rushed in with the hot breeze.

When Hobie stopped at Druci's farm, it looked different. The ground and fences were covered with thick vines.

"I thought you told me there weren't no kudzu on her fences. I don't have nothing in the truck that'll cut through that stuff," Hobie said.

"Drive a little bit. There's got to be some free places."

"Hell, no! You climb out and walk the line till you find a bare spot. I ain't going nowhere.

"Fuck you." said Bent.

"Get moving."

"Fuckin' doped up bastard." Bent grabbed Hobie's flashlight, and slammed the door behind him. He waded through vines waist high. He had to climb over many which were too thick to push aside. The fragrance was stronger now and the way seemed easier. The vines were thinner, almost as if they were moving out of his way. He shined his light forward. He discovered he had angled to his left. There was a section with no kudzu on it. Hobie was standing there.

"Thought you were staying in the truck," he said. "Wait a minute. How'd you beat me here?" He looked toward the truck, but he couldn't see over the vines. Bent looked at Hobie who was still pointing toward the barbed wire.

"I'm coming. Don't bunch up your panties." Bent cut a twenty foot piece, curled into a circle, and turned to go back to the truck. He didn't see it. "Hobie, where's the truck? You move it?" Hobie beckoned and pointed further on. Bent followed. The ground was bare of vines. "So this is how you got ahead of me; you found a path. Got to hand it to you buddy." Then Hobie beckoned again and Bent followed. "Where's the truck? Don't be playing games with me." Bent knew the truck was on the road, but he didn't know where the road was by now. He had completely lost his bearings. He blindly followed Hobie. And, Hobie wasn't answering his questions. In fact, he wasn't saying anything at all.

The kudzu was thicker now. The more he followed Hobie, the thicker the vines became. His circle of stolen barbed wire kept snagging on vines and tearing into his hand and arm. He laid it down on a pile of vines, and tucked the flashlight into his belt to use both hands to climb over the twisted

vegetation; he forgot the wire. Kudzu was chest high now. The flashlight fell out of his belt and lodged within one tangled mass. It wasn't easy to pull free. When he succeeded, he aimed the beam towards his friend. Hobie was gone.
Bent flashed the light in all directions.

"Nice joke, Fucker, now stand up and show me where you are." There was no response. Bent was beginning to panic. No matter which way he turned, there was only kudzu. His flashlight caught on another vine and flipped a distance away, shining brightly and illuminating long thick stems whipping like tentacles toward him. They grabbed his legs and pulled him down to the ground where more wrapped tightly around his torso. His screams echoed only a short way through the thick greenery. One vine looped around his neck and yanked tight. Bent heard a cracking sound. His screams stopped.

Hobie was bored and sleepy. The pills, the fragrance, and the booze were wearing on him. "Maybe we should save Ruby's soul tomorrow night," he thought. Suddenly a flashlight flared in the rear view mirror.

Shit, where'd that come from, he thought. *Don't need a DWI tonight. Bogerty will preach me to death.* Hobart released the latch and nearly fell out. He slowly slide his feet to the ground, holding onto the door and the back of his seat. He hoped he didn't look as stoned as he felt. Those pills were kicking him worse than a barroom fight. He couldn't focus and his head was spinning. Where was the sheriff's car? He could barely make out the outline of a man; the light was too bright for his dilated eyes.

"Sheriff Gilesby, that you?" Hobie mumbled. "I'm just waiting for Bent; he's taking a piss out there somewhere.

The sheriff didn't answer. All Hobie saw was the long barrel of a shotgun as it fired. He collapsed on the ground, pain running from his chest down his arm.

"Sheriff, why?" he whispered.

Hobie didn't see the sheriff anymore, just a flashlight beam aimed under his truck. Then a rustling sound. From between the tires, he saw kudzu drag Bent's body onto the pavement. He vomited and sucked it into his lungs before he blanked out.

Wednesday

Chapter 1

Harlem slept fitfully all Tuesday night; he saw kudzu in every one of his dreams: some good, some nightmares. He shut off the alarm before it rang and dragged himself into the kitchen to grab some instant coffee. It would tide him over until he could get dressed and drive to the Dawg for breakfast and a decent cup. He'd have enough to keep himself busy with the tourists until lunchtime. Then he'd go to the morgue. Hopefully Doc would have a preliminary report by then.

He put two teaspoons of the granulated stuff in his cup when the phone rang. "Damn!" It was Dixie.

"Sorry to bother you so early, Sheriff, but there's four more bodies been hauled in. Well, two bodies and a chopped up mess."

"Jesus Christ!"

"They came in last night. I called BeBe and Duke so's to let you alone seein' as how you already got your own stiff. But they say you need to come take a look."

"Who are the bodies?"

"Bent Bishop and Hobie Dill were the ones we can tell for sure. Duke says he thinks its Jeb Flanks and Mite Lewis who done kissed a wood chipper. Also, Sylvie Parks got in last night to help with her daddy's funeral, but Birdie's missing. Robert said it don't look like foul play, but he couldn't see much outside, it bein' dark and all. He's goin' back out there around ten, and she's comin' in to file a missin' person's report."

Harlem swallowed and said nothing for a long moment.

"Sheriff, did you hear me?" asked Dixie.

"I heard. Thanks Dixie. 'Fore you clock out, get a holt of Garnet Easley, would you please. Tell him what's going on here and have him call if he can't drop by. Might need him or a couple of his officers. Better tell Geb and Pete that they're on call too. Hate to ruin their days off, but I might need 'em."

"We got a serial killer in with the tourists, you reckon, Sheriff?" Dixie asked.

Harlem bit his lip. He didn't need a lot of conjecturing going on right now.

"I need to talk to Doc first and get his coroner's report. Maybe just a bunch of accidents. You keep quiet for now, and advise the boys to do the same. Only report to me and not each other."

Harlem thought about the others. Ebon most likely told some friends and possibly the Elders about last night. That would be okay as the Cherokee could be closed mouthed. The problem might be Marvin if he talked to the other paramedics.

"Shit," Harlem said. He dumped the instant coffee back into the jar and put on his last clean uniform. He hauled the bag of dirty uniforms to his car, hoping he'd have time to drop them at the cleaners, and drove into town. He nearly stopped for a fast egg on a biscuit, but changed his mind and parked at the Dawg. There was kudzu in the lot, but it moved away from his feet. Its fragrance was especially strong as Harlem walked to the door.

I'm having a decent breakfast, dammit, before I start all this. Janice will know something, seeing how her grandmother's an Elder. Sure wish I was psychic like her family, but one-sixteenth means nothing. Just a white man, he told himself.

Harlem was feeling helpless and lonely until he saw Janice smile and wave as he came in. He'd been in love with her for years. Right now, he could have dropped to his knees and begged her to marry him. She'd been his anchor and support many a time. Probably most every plant, animal, kid, and adult around felt the same way. *I'm a fool*, he thought, *and definitely bad timing. Don't even know why I'm thinking this way right now. Mind's not on my work.*

He sat down heavily on his chair; it swayed in protest. Janice came right over.

"You retracted your landing gear on that descent, Harlem," she said. He looked up to see soft eyes watching him, and smiled. She sat down. "The body count is mounting, isn't it? I heard that Birdie Parks is missing, and Oral Clemet's funeral is Friday."

Harlem nodded. "At least Oral's death is normal. He fell out of a tree blind."

"Was it? He didn't have a gun, just binoculars."

"Marvin's been talking, hasn't he?" Harlem chuckled. "I need to duck tape that man's mouth."

"You know I have my own sources," Janice said. "Anyway, the only house nearby is the Percifield's. I'd say he was spying on them. Al's report said Oral must have been hungry because kudzu was found in his throat. Probably stuck there when he fell."

"You don't believe that?" Harlem asked.

"He's another of Billy's pack and worships Bogerty. He also hates kudzu, so why would he be eating it? Bogerty railed against the Percifield's from his pulpit. I'd say more than likely something unpleasant was being planned, and kudzu stopped it. I'm sure Al will have a logical explanation for the others too. You already know my thoughts on kudzu, and after last night, I think you agree with me. Enough said. Now, turn off that walkie-talkie thing of yours for a few minutes. I'm ordering your favorite breakfast and you're going to sit, eat, and relax." She lit a small candle on the table and walked to the kitchen.

He liked the fragrance coming from the candle—like that in the parking lot. He wasn't much on things like scented candles, but this one took the knot out of his stomach. *Guess food won't give me heartburn today like it does must tourist seasons.* Janice returned with a glass of orange juice and some freshly brewed coffee with four creams.

"You get half decaf and half regular, Mister. No arguments. The extra cream is compensation. Did you have your usual instant this morning?" she asked, sitting back down.

"You already know the answer to that. Dixie beat me to it. I like your candle; it stinks good."

Janice threw back her head and laughed. "I'll have to remember that compliment. There's kudzu oil extracted from its flowers in the wax. My aunt made them and asked me to try them out. I think I'll have her sell them here and in some of the gift shops. They're more relaxing than lavender oil in my opinion."

"Don't tell any of Bogerty's wolves. They'd be howling and you'd be pulpit fodder again. Everything in here has kudzu in it somewhere. Wish more people would be as inventive as you rather than hating or fearing it. Wouldn't be enough kudzu to go around if they did; high demand and all that."

Harlem drank his coffee and breathed in kudzu's fragrance. It helped him make a decision. Maybe bad timing, but he was only three years older and he knew she was phasing David out. Hell, her late husband was seven years older. Maybe he'd have a chance.

"Janice, I don't know if you know how I feel about you, but," He was interrupted by a waitress bringing his breakfast. Janice got up and returned with two coffee pots, one decaf and one regular. Harlem gave up and ate. She kept his cup filled and said nothing.

He couldn't look her in the eye even when finished. He reached in his pocket for his billfold and stood up to leave. She touched his hand.

"Harlem, only you and David always eat here for free," she said. "Even Garnet pays; I tell him I keep a tab for you."

"You know I'm more than willing to pay. That's why I leave

five or ten dollars on the table. I'm not a mooch."

"That's not what I mean; think about it on your way to the hospital. Tell Al I said 'howdy'. And Harlem, you're still blood. David isn't. We fit well."

He stared at her for a moment, not knowing what to say. "Imagine that," he smiled. Harlem put on his hat and left.

Outside, he touched the kudzu vines draping off the veranda roof. "Think I'll buy some of your candles, and you make a damn good omelet too. I owe you one, and seeing what you're doing, I might be useful sometime. Janice and me; I never thought. Thanks for the courage." He swore he heard giggling as he walked away. *I'm picking up stuff. Huh!*

Chapter 2

Doctor Alvis Moten, coroner, was in the morgue. Usually he was in his office reading some vintage comic book as super heroes were his passion. Harlem figured they compensated for something missing in the Doc's psyche. He was the only sixty-year-old Harlem knew who lived and breathed antique comics.

"Beats watching soap operas," Harlem always said when one of his deputies raised an eyebrow.

The morgue was cold! Al had his back to the door when Sheriff Gilesby shivered in. He had the cocoon cut off and was examining the dress on the corpse.

"Any information for me yet, Al?" he said.

Al glanced over his shoulder as Harlem joined him by the examination table.

"Pretty cut and dried, pardon the pun. I could smell beer a yard thick when I rolled Hobie and Bent out. Bent had some prescription Oxycontin in his pocket. Hobie strangled on his own vomit, but he had a heart attack first."

"Heart attack!" Harlem said. "He was in his early thirties."

Al shrugged. "Probably had Bent's pills in him. I sent some blood to the lab to be sure. I'm betting alcohol and drugs nailed him. Bent, I don't know, he's the odd one. Can't figure a reason for the broken neck."

"Maybe he and Hobie got into a fight."

"I donno. There's no bruising except around the neck."

"Hobie strangle him?"

Al shook his head. "The marks on his neck don't suggest that. You're the detective here, Sherlock. You tell me."

"I heard my deputies found barbed wire and cutters beside him. That's odd too," Harlem said.

Al didn't say anything.

"What about Jeb and Mite?"

"Real ugly," Al said with a noticeable shiver that had nothing to do with the chilled room. "Wit and Thymie found them around eleven. Said they were cutting trees. Looks like they mulched themselves."

"Accident?"

"Nothing suspicious that I can see. Wit said Mite liked his supersized toys, and his wood chipper was professional grade. I imagine it had no trouble pulling them in. Sent blood to the lab too, of course. I'll let you know if anything crops up."

"Thanks, keep me informed," the sheriff said as he turned to go.

"Harlem," the coroner said.

"What?"

"That Jane Doe's the strangest one of 'em all."

Harlem sighed when he saw the confused look in Al's eyes. That always meant more work. "I'm listening."

"Her dress has some red stain on it. Not blood; it's too bright. The body's badly decomposed, but there are some areas that look like massive bruising as if she were beaten to death. I'll finish the external exam, and then start the internal. I suspect I'll find broken bones. Whoever wrapped her in that kudzu cocoon did it carefully; it took some time to wrap those small stems so closely together, and there's a blanket inside too."

..........<>..........

Late in the afternoon, Harlem was on the phone discussing the situation with Clovis when Dr. Moten called on another line.

"I've got something interesting for you, Harlem," he said. "That red stuff on the dress was tomato. I had a piece of the material in my hand while I was talking to an orderly when Devi Eaten, she's one of the nurses, walked by. She saw the material and said it looked like some of the dresses her mother Jill carried down at Great Digs. I cut a better piece and took it over there.

"Jill didn't have any more left since it was too long ago, but she remembered the material because she thought it was an ugly plaid for a dress. And apparently customers thought so too. They only had five to start with and three were sent to the historical village in the park. They shred all donated material to weave into rag rugs or table clothes for the tourists."

"So what happened to the others? Did Jill remember?"

"She said the other two were marked down to five dollars. Reverend Bogerty bought one for his wife. They were in town at the time for his job interview, and he said she needed a new dress. She thought Doris Percifield bought the other one for Elowese because she loved plaids."

"I guess I should call Doris."

"I already did. Saved you the trouble. Elowese still has that dress, about to wear it out."

"Well, that narrows it down, but it still don't mean that's Bogerty's wife in that dress. She could of given it away," Harlem said. "Any dental records or anything you could use for a match?"

"No dental records, but I found that Effie had a broken wrist that hadn't healed properly. It was suspected at the time that her husband may have been the cause. Our Jane Doe has that same wrist."

"Oh boy! Bogerty claimed his wife left and got a quick divorce." Harlem tapped his pen on his desk top. He did that when he was putting pieces together.

"Sheriff, I think you have a murder on your hands. There were some old healed bones. But, there were several broken ones. In my opinion, she may have been beaten or kicked to death. I'll get you my final report by tomorrow."

"Thanks, Al."

Harlem sat in silence for a short while, still tapping his pen. Then he punched the intercom.

"Dixie, tell the boys to bring Bogerty in for questioning. Suspicion of murder," he said. He called Sheriff Dalton back again.

Chapter 3

Millie Udine walked in the screen door, put her jugs of water and a small bag of leaves on the kitchen table, and sat down. Odin came in too bringing his ball to her, but Millie wasn't in a playful mood. She'd been fired and she needed the money. She didn't have many clients any more who could afford to hire their cleaning done; they were moving out. Now she was down to only three. Oribel Dardy caught her washing clothes and taking a bath at her house.

"That bitch wants me to clean her house, but thinks I'm too dirty to use her shower or washer. Threw money on the counter, told me to finish cleaning, and get out. Made me take my wet clothes out of her washer," she said to the dog as she reached down to pet him.

"I fixed her real good, Odin. Hope she likes the oleander I stirred up in her meat loaf paste. She'll get a nice surprise tonight when she cooks it. So thoughtful of her to be growing it in her back yard along with her kudzu, all mixed together and she don't know it. She's always bragging that kudzu makes the best salads. I put some kudzu in too. It'll look like she accidentally picked the one with the other. Should we wish her bon appétit, Odin? Brought some home; thought it might come in handy." Mildred smiled at Odin. She knew he didn't understand a word she said, but that was okay. "Okay, baby, let's go outside and play."

Katie's kitten scampered across the O'Neal's yard next door. Millie tried to get Odin to chase it, but he was too interested in playing fetch. She threw his ball next door hoping he'd spot the cat and, hopefully, play with it hard enough to kill it. He ignored the kitten, and proudly brought back the ball.

"Guess I need to mix some leaves in a batch of tuna. Hell, why don't I give some to Gabe as well as the neighbor's cats.

What do you think, Odin, does Mommy have a good idea? Yes, she does," she played with her dog's ears and kissed his face. "Go fetch," Millie ordered and threw the ball next door again.

As she watched her dog chase his ball, she planned. *No, the pills would be better in case that sheriff wants an autopsy. Put a bunch in his chili and that coroner will say it was an overdose. Get him cremated, real quick. Then maybe I won't need to kill Alma.*

While Millie and Odin were playing in the front yard, Gabe was sleeping out in the back. His pills had fallen out of his pocket and lay in the kudzu by his chair. One vine snaked over and wrapped around the container. If he hadn't been so deeply asleep, Gabe would have heard his pills rattling inside the plastic bottle as it was dragged away.

After Odin wore down her anger, Millie sat on her porch to wipe the sweat off her face and rest. She debated whether to turn her plots into reality today or push them into the future.

"Hell, I laced Oribel's meatloaf. No time like the present." She went inside to fix a batch of chili. Gabe loved anything spicy since he had come back from fighting, and chili with lots of Habanera peppers was his favorite. She grew them in her garden for that purpose. Not that it was much of a garden anymore with kudzu taking over. She went outside to grab a few for the soup, but vines were twined around all her peppers, the only plants still alive. Her anger flared again.

"Goddamn, mother-fucking vines," she screamed and grabbed her hatchet off its hook on the back wall of the house. She unleashed all the rage she felt toward everything wrong in her life on kudzu and her pepper plants. Only after she crushed most of the peppers to pulp did she stop and throw her hatchet down. She picked several from the dirt, covering her hands with the spicy liquid as she did so. She wiped the sweat off her face and inadvertently transferred the pepper juice to her eyes.

The pain was maddening and tears streamed down. She needed to get to the cream in her refrigerator to splash on her face. It would stop the pain. She couldn't see, so she called Odin to her. She ordered him take her to the house, but he took her further back toward Gabe as he had been trained to do. She pushed him aside and tried to find the way herself.

There was so much kudzu in her way that she couldn't walk in a straight line. She kept bumping into tangled vines and changing direction. She didn't remember having to skirt so much of it earlier. Finally she was out of the tangle and on clear ground where she could walk faster. To her relief, it wasn't much farther to the house although she had taken the long way around.

Her eyes were on fire, and only getting worse. She was so desperate to get to the kitchen that she increased her speed even more. There was a small area in front of her covered with vines; it wasn't as thick as what she had encountered. She confidently stepped through it. The ground beneath her gave way.

She pitched forward catching her chin on the side of the pit which snapped her neck backwards. She heard a cracking sound as she tumbled down onto the sharpened posts below. She went down knee first, hitting the tallest stake which bounced off her knee cap, inserted itself to the side of the joint, and slid under the muscle to her groin. Another ripped into her abdomen and out her back while a third entered through her lower jaw and tongue before emerging from her mouth. She dangled there impaled like meat on a spit and bled out. The interior of the pit darkened as vines covered the opening.

Murderer Guilty

Chapter 4

Wit had seen a lot of bad deaths in Afghanistan, but never anything like Jeb and Mite's. It only brought back the old memories and tangled them up with last night's horror. He had never spoken much about his tour of duty to anyone, least of all his family members, but after last night, Thymie wouldn't ask again. He'd seen his fair share of action too, but was glad he hadn't been assigned there.

Both men sat up all night trying to drink the sight from their brains. Thymie had never seen Wit drunk, but he was seeing it now. Wit had even been crying like a baby. To get their minds clear, they cut some of the kudzu off the patio, poured on kerosene, and burned it. It gave the men an aggressive outlet for their pain. It was now early afternoon, and they were getting hungry.

Thymie figured grilling something might help, but he sure as hell didn't want any hamburgers. He was trying to hook up the new container of propane to the gas grill, but his hands were shaking so badly that he was having trouble tightening the fittings. *Good enough*, he thought. He tripped over kudzu while walking toward the back door.

"Damn, Wit, I thought we cut all those vines off last night. The son-o'-bitchin' shit is back. I'm fixing to fry up a pork chop to tide me over 'til the girls get back with the groceries. I'll bring back the bourbon."

The sight of raw bloody meat made him vomit in the sink. Thymie put the chop back in the refrigerator; they could eat when the girls returned from Unity. They'd have to do the grilling.

Beth and Norabell had dropped the kids at Grandma's, and then made funeral arrangements for Jeb, and Mite too. They considered Mite family, and there was no one else to take care of him. They were loading groceries into the car when they ran into Billy Purdue and two strangers named Claude and Mink, Klan members he was showing around town. They appeared bored. Billy sensed that they were going to nix his idea of forming a chapter around Unity, and he was looking for some chance to impress them.

When Beth tried to convince Billy that there wasn't going to be any Klan rally at the house Friday night out of respect for the dead, Billy, thinking that this was his chance, became abusive. He punched Beth in the mouth, telling both women that the Klan didn't take orders from women. Norabell rushed Beth to the hospital and called Thymie while her sister-in-law was getting stitches.

Billy tried to swagger in front of the two men to show how tough he was. Claude and Mink were not impressed and told him so. They declined the invitation to visit Wit when his family was grieving; they called Billy a "wack job" over his weird ideas about witches, walking tree spirits, and demon kudzu; and they were sick of hearing about some preacher named Bogerty. Nor were they interested in being around when Billy had to face an angry husband. They left in their cars, telling Billy to forget about recruiting Klan members elsewhere. He would get no help.

Billy was humiliated and headed to the Bent Nail to bolster his ego. No one there was interested in listening to him. Instead, two men told Billy that he'd better go apologize before Wit came looking for him. He stormed out, saying he'd not apologize for hitting a mouthy woman. When he got in his car, he decided maybe he should at least explain himself to Wit before Beth and Norabell returned. "Best defense is an offense," he said to himself.

Billy realized his mistake when he walked up to Wit and Thymie. Norabell and Beth were already back, and both husbands were waiting. Billy didn't get one word out before

Wit's fist hit his solar plexus. When he awoke, he was hanging from his bound wrists to a limb by the patio. The four were calmly eating, but Beth was doing more drinking as every bite was painful. If her glares were any indication, she was mentally skinning Billy alive to slow roast him, rotisserie style.

"Potato salad, baked beans, and peanut butter-tomato sandwiches, what the hell!" Billy yelled to them. "What kind of meal is that? I've paid my dues, boys, now cut me down, and I'll grill us some meat."

Wit looked at Billy with disgust. "Next time you want to impress some Adam's off-ox, don't use my Beth," he said. "Cut him down, Thymie, and let that suck-egg dog serve us hand and foot." Thymie threw a well aimed hatchet at the rawhide strap holding Billy in the air. He crashed hard on the concrete pavers.

"Wit, those were Klan, and we need more recruits for power. We'll be laughed out of the county if there's only a cup of us K'ers."

"We can still do what needs to be done next week, after the funeral," said Thymie. "Twenty men is fine and the girls will help too. You don't need many to burn crosses and kudzu; just give everyone gasoline and matches and the work will go fast. Norabell's got her 38 special; I put hollow heads in it and my rifle has deer slugs. But we shouldn't need to go firing on anyone unless it's self-defense. So, quit your whining, and keep yourself under control; we don't need outsiders."

"Burning crosses in yards ain't enough," Billy yelled. "You going soft on me, ass- wipe?" We should burn down houses and kill those in league with the devil. Reverend Bogerty said we haf'ta exorcize the demon and all its minions, the unholy and unfaithful. God will protect us; I've even got my holy water, and I got special orders to get Elowese and her family and beat out their demons. We gotta get the Indian witch doctors too because it's their walking plant spirit. They conjured it, and that Janice Singing Grass and her family is heading it up around here. We need to burn her out. Reverend said fire will purify."

"You're off the deep end, Billy," said Wit. "This isn't a war no matter what the reverend says. I've seen enough killing, and people here aren't unholy or unfaithful; they're just desperate because there's no money.

"And why's there no money? Kudzu's wrecked the farms so no one's got crops to sell. You got no money, you can't buy nothing. Then stores fail and those workers got no money either. Kudzu started the stones rolling. It's God's punishment for the unfaithful. If people were doing right by the church, they'd be working and that demon plant would die away," Billy said. "So we have to get God's enemies and burn them. Then God will help us destroy kudzu instead of cursing us with it. And those unholy Cherokees conjured it up because they hate the white man; it's their walking tree spirit. You missed Bogerty's sermon. He explained it real clear," Billy said.

"The only enemy is kudzu and maybe we can't win against it. Maybe it *is* a walking plant spirit, but I'm not taking on the whole Cherokee nation. Screw Bogerty. There's folks that need taking care of, and we will, in time. We can drop their bodies down in the vines and likely they'll never be found. You want to go after someone? Take on Millie Udine; that bitch is pure evil."

"Fuck you. You've lost your nerve. Gone soft since you've been back. Rather fuck Beth than fight. It is a war whether you see it or not."

Billy, my son, shut your mouth. Bogerty's got you all messed up, and he ain't God," said Thymie. "There's fresh steaks in the Frigidaire; go fix them, and make them well done. None of us want rare today."

"I'll be blowed. So your family members got a little messed up, and now you want over-cooked steaks. I'm a man, and I want mine dripping blood, and I'll eat it right in front of all of you," Billy sneered.

Wit pulled his hunting knife out of its sheath and threw it into Billy's shoe, barely missing his toes. All he said was, "That's enough," but the look he gave Billy suggested he might be the first body to be tossed into the kudzu. Billy slunk into the house.

The stilled heat surrounding the back yard made everybody listless, and Billy's ranting sucked the last of their energy. No one noticed vines snaking up the propane tank to the fittings. Soon gas was leaking slowly around the line feeding the grill above.

When Billy used his cigarette lighter to start cooking, the spark ignited both the grill and the leaking gas. The pressurized tank exploded, throwing the grill into the air as shards of metal hurled in all directions, piercing soft flesh. Billy's face and legs splattered on vines and trees alike. One shard drove through Beth's throat slicing her carotid artery. Norabell was unlucky enough to be sitting right where the grill landed; it crushed her skull. Wit, in his lounge chair, took the expanding air pressure full force. It carried the long grill fork with it straight into his chest. Burning vines wrapped around Thymie and turned him into a human torch. More flaming vines snaked onto the house walls, setting them ablaze.

Kudzu snapped off its burning stems and retreated far enough away to remain unscathed. It watched impassively. When the flames died much later, kudzu covered everything over as if nothing ever existed there.

Janice Love Protect

Chapter 5

Alice didn't walk outside Tuesday night, due to the pets' efforts. Lily continuously purred in Alice's ear, and licked or pawed her face when she became restless. Kingston blocked her at the doorway, the one time she escaped her cat. Most of the night she either walked in circles within the room, or, when she did go back to bed, she woke up moaning and clasping her elbows while throwing off the covers.

Her constant activity took its toll on Henry. He couldn't sleep and spent most of the night trying to calm her or get her back into bed.

It was a restless night for Hailey too. Maybe it was her worry for Henry knowing that Alice would not let him rest. Maybe it was the barely audible footsteps that she attributed to Alice's walking around and around the room, and Henry's muffled attempts to calm her. Maybe it was the constant creaking floorboards in the hall, and Kingston's small whimpers. She got the feeling that kudzu was prowling around under the house, but wasn't sure if the dog was whimpering over the floorboards or Henry. And, Hailey suspected the moon's energy was affecting her too, or she was picking up Alice's emotional restlessness.

She attempted four times to connect to the internet just to have something to do, but there was no service. She found herself pacing the room between tries. Finally Hailey gave up and climbed into bed.

She got up several times to check on Kingston. He wouldn't leave his post outside Henry's door, but something was agitating him. Hailey tried to sooth the dog by sitting down next to him and petting his head. She asked him several times what he sensed, but he wouldn't answer; he seemed in turmoil. Twice he got up and scratched on the door, asking to go inside to Henry. Hailey took pity on him and quietly opened the door just enough for him to enter.

Finally deciding she wasn't going to get any sleep, she got dressed and walked out the sunroom to the back yard. She was glad she had on rubber flip-flops because the ground was wet. Even walking on a thick blanket of kudzu, the water seeped through, soaking her feet. The moon wouldn't be full until Thursday, but it looked bright enough to her. David's van reflected some of the light.

Hailey eyes were drawn to the peach trees. They resembled misshapen silver giants as the kudzu covering them glowed in the bright moonlight. In fact, everything seemed silver. The barn was completely covered, even the doorway. She imagined everything still inside was too. She was surprised that the tree which shaded the two cars and tractor was sporting some kudzu.

I thought that huge oak was safe. I'll have to make sure Mom's car is free for Saturday. Then Hailey had a chilling flash, *What if kudzu won't let us leave!*

Chapter 6

Everyone was worn out by Wednesday morning and slept in. Even David and Tilfort had overslept and were in foul moods because of it. They loaded the van in slow motion and left with empty stomachs. Neither Alice nor Marla cared whether any food was prepared when they did make an appearance. Both sat silently in the kitchen drinking coffee. Lily was nowhere in sight.

Hailey knew Henry needed to eat something, so she took it upon herself to do the cooking. She wasn't sure what he could have, so she figured oatmeal and a steamed egg would be ok. She added a piece of toast with Muscadine jelly and some milk. Even her mother didn't offer to help as she worked, saying she'd have toast with her coffee shortly.

Alice whined, "That smells good. Where's mine." Hailey told her to fix whatever she wanted, but this was for Henry. Alice went back to her coffee, and Hailey took the tray to down the hall to his room.

Kingston was on the bed as close to Henry as he could get. He whimpered softly as Hailey came in; his look said he was grieving. Hailey didn't like that look, but ignored it for the present. She smiled as she woke Henry and sat the tray on his lap. He gave her a weak smile in return.

"Thank'ee Hailey. I don't feel much like eatin', but since I guess you fixed it your own self, I'll gladly try."

Hailey sat down on the bed with him. "You had a pretty bad night. I heard you trying to calm Alice. I should have put her in my room and moved in with Mom rather than let you handle her alone. I'm sorry. Maybe, staying in the hospital would have been better. You could have got some rest; I doubt you will here."

"No, there's no rest here until I'm in my grave, but I'm hopin' for one or two more years. And you wouldn't have been able to pull Alice off me anyhow. She'd have clambered somethin' fierce to get at me. She can be nonstop like a piece o' mountain rollin' downhill when she gets her mind at it." Henry chuckled.

"I know you love Alice, but can't someone make her understand what she's doing to everyone here," Hailey asked.

"It was easier when John was alive. She'd sometimes listen to him because he was her favorite. He buffered us all against her; even I couldn't cope sometimes, and that gal would clin' on me like a tick. She's a good woman, but she's got her demons and none of us can really he'p her."

"Maybe she does need to be in a nursing home," Hailey suggested. "Her psychic abilities might calm down if she's away from here and kudzu's not affecting her. If she can't control it, she might go totally off the deep end. Maybe Janice or her family can help. I'm just throwing off ideas; don't know if any are useful."

"I don't like to think of her in some rest home, but it could come to that. Janice tried talkin' to her many times, but she won't listen. Now Janice is fed up; I doubt she'll try agai', and if she won't, none of her kin will. David's tired of bein' the tent pole; I see his resentment eatin' at him be times, and Til is loyal to us, but he might suggest Alice be put away so David can have a life. He may have Asperger's, but it's still autism. He needs to focus on his flowers; he can't do that and everythin' else. He's frail some ways." Henry took a bite of his egg. "Good, but I wish I could have some salt. Did you brin' me any?" Henry asked, knowing the answer.

"Nice try. I'm not sure you should have that brown sugar in your oatmeal. I just winged it, so enjoy what you have. Cooking's not my top talent."

"And I bet you haven't had a bite. You go fix your own self some food; it's nearly lunch time so's you got to be hungry, and take Kingston out to do his business. He needs fed too, please. It's hard to eat with him almost sittin' on me," Henry chuckled and petted his dog's head.

"I love this dog so much, Hailey, he's been my only comfort. But I need to ask you this. Will you take him when y'all leave? He's taken a shine to you more'n anyone else except me, and he'll pine away all alone here if I die. You understand him; he's special and no one else sees it. Us all bein' empaths, even so. They ignore him like he was only a dog."

That shocked her, and she sputtered, "But, but, you two are totally connected. There's no way you can be separated; it'll kill you both. Besides you said you have some years left. Why send him away now?" She hardly noticed that he said, 'us all being empaths.'

Henry looked Hailey in the eyes so she'd catch it the second time. "There I said it. 'All of us bein' empaths.' It's in our blood. None of us seems to own up to it, at least out loud. You're the strongest since your grandfather. Your energy floats a ways out from your body.

Hailey tucked her head. She liked the praise, but it was still embarrassing. She didn't think she was that strong, or was she?

"I suspect kudzu sensed your strength when you got here. I hear it sometimes, but I don't often understand what it's sayin'. I just feel thin's about it. It has its ways. Shook me a bit when I saw you in the road. I didn't think you were old enough to be so strong, but kudzu did. It called you, I know. I blew the horn to wake you up.'

"Kudzu told me it didn't kill John. I saw a flash of it trying to save him. It knows Alice blames it. It hates her in return because she won't listen." Hailey was glad to get that out in the open, and she knew Henry would believe her."

"I know'd that," Henry acknowledged, "and I know'd it tried its best, but it didn't have the know-how at the time. It's learned things since then, and maybe what it's learned ain't all that good. It's hurt and angry, and I think it can really do harm if it decides to go bad. Alice hates it over the peach trees, and she won't be changed on her idea that it murdered her favorite boy. I've give up tryin' to talk sense into her; she's locked into her hatin'. I don't doubt kudzu hates her back."

"Henry," Hailey said, "kudzu already gave me a warning that it's not taking any more. It'll start getting even with those who hate it or harm it. I'm worried for all of us. Kingston and Lily knew before I got the warning. They've tried to tell me, but I didn't get specifics."

Henry pursed his lips. "I suspectioned it might come to that. It's child-like, I think, and like a child havin' a tantrum, it could lash out at everybody, innocent or guilty, if it feels betrayed by somebody it cares for. Anybody in its path could be a victim then, even if it regrets hurtin' them later, the damage would be done. Like innocent bystanders in the wrong place at the wrong time if a shootin' goes down. Everybody dies."

"Janice was saying similar things."

Henry nodded. "She and I have talked a bit. She's fed up with Alice and David both. He, of anyone, should know about kudzu, but he's blind to it, and I don't know why. I know it's deliberate though.

"Maybe it's just one more thing he doesn't want to deal with, or can't. I don't know much about Asperger's, but he's really stressed. He could shut down sometime or go the other way—ballistic. Maybe he needs help like Alice. If his empathic skills are dumping extra emotions on him from everywhere around, and he's dealing with Alice's emotional mess, and that's hard for people with this problem to handle lots of emotions..." she raised one shoulder. "You know what I'm trying to say."

"Yes I do, and I know it's after Alice. Maybe he senses that, and it might be hard knowin' his beloved plant is stirrin' up trouble. It's messin' with her head, and I hope that's all it does. I feel it filled up the sunroom and barn to spite her. Unfortunately we're all sufferin' from it. We have to get her out of here for her safety, but again I don't like the idea of a rest home. I'd send her with you, but you might toss her down a deep holler before you leave Georgia. And kudzu thinks everywhere, so where could you take her that kudzu wouldn't follow if it wanted to?"

"You're like a dad to me, really special, so I'm worried about your health," Hailey said. You're tired and I don't mean just this morning. I wish you didn't feel so defeated, and I wish Mom and I could help. We plan on leaving Saturday rather than next week, but if you need us to stay for a little while longer, or maybe I can stay and Mom go back. She hates 57, but she could make it. David could take me to a bus station later. I just have to be back in time to pack for college in August. Say the word, and you know I'll stay for you."

Henry patted her wrist. "Thank'ee Sugar, but I've only got awhile; like I said, I'm hopin' for a year, maybe two. You go on back to Indiana and take my dog with you. Maybe even to college if you can. He won't do no good unless'n he's with me or you." He was silent a moment as if thinking about something. Hailey waited, knowing he was making a decision.

He resumed, "If you could, take Lily too; she's Alice's knee baby. If you can't take her now, come get her or have her sent to you when Alice is gone or in a rest home. They don't allow pets there and neither David nor Til pay any attention to her. She'd be fed, but nothin' more and given away when they leave, and I reckon they'll go soon as I'm gone if I can't get us moved anytime soon. If you can't maybe Janice would want her."

"Kingston will have to make his own decision, Henry, so will Lily," Hailey said. "I'm not sure he'll want to leave as long as you're alive, and Lily's just as attached to Alice. She probably won't leave, and she'd run away to try to get back here if we kidnapped her. She looked at the dog. Kingston couldn't cry; no animals can, but if he could, she felt he would be crying now. He whimpered instead.

"You leave us now, Hailey, so we can work this out. You can take him out later. Hope you don't mind, but I've started to care for you like I did my Ashley. It's been good havin' you here."

"I could use a dad, and if you're volunteering, I'll accept." Hailey gave him a kiss and left; she felt like she was leaving half of herself in his room. *Well, a short term dad is better than James. Hope he does live a couple more years, but I don't think Kingston thinks so. Damn!* She sighed and it came out shaky. When she returned to the kitchen, her face betrayed that something heavy had come down.

Marla noticed. She pushed her coffee mug aside and scrambled some eggs for all three of them. Alice wanted fried, but wasn't given a choice. Marla told her she could fix fried if she wanted, but scrambled was the only type she was fixing. Alice made oatmeal instead. Hailey ignored both women; she more played with her food than ate any.

Chapter 7

Bogerty was out of town for most of Wednesday. Not wanting anyone in Unity to know he was planning to wed Marla, he went to Danvers to buy a cheap wedding band and marriage license. He also treated himself to a new dark brown suit with brass buttons. It was a bit more than he could afford, but he decided he needed something elegant for his wedding.

Clovis Dalton was the sheriff in the county, and he had Harlem's order in his office.

Clovis knew what Bogerty looked like, but didn't expect to see him in his territory. He had finished some business and was flirting with a meter maid outside the courthouse that Wednesday afternoon, when he was surprised to see the reverend come down the steps and open his car door.

Town wasn't his jurisdiction, but there was no time for debating the issue when he had a murder suspect so close at hand. He accosted the reverend and attempted to bring him in for questioning. It was a mistake to do anything solo concerning this Unity Baptist minister. He had no idea how powerfully intimidating the preacher could be. Bogerty was half again as big as Clovis and not about to put up with such "foolishness." He fixed his "eye of the righteous," as he liked to call it, on the unsuspecting sheriff and gave him a short sermon. Clovis pulled out his gun.

"Make way for the servant of the Lord," Bogerty said in a booming voice, shouldered past the sheriff, climbed into his car, backed out quickly, and sped off. Clovis lowered his gun; he didn't want to shoot at Bogerty or his car on a crowded street as a stray bullet could hit a pedestrian.

Clovis ran for his car and grabbed his radio. He ordered two back up units and an advisory to Harlem. Traffic slowed him down as an older man with a cane jaywalked in front of him. He reached the intersection just when the light turned red.

He crossed over into the oncoming lane to get around and flipped on his lights. Just then a car turning right on green blocked his route. Other cars to hit their brakes and turned sideways to avoid hitting each other and the sheriff. Bogerty had had no such trouble. Timing was with him.

Mine

Chapter 8

Bogerty was in a quandary; his mind raced while he drove slowly back to Unity on 57. He stopped in the area where he thought he'd dumped her although he couldn't be sure as it was nighttime then. Falling rock and crawling vines had changed the landscape some too. He walked over and stared straight down into the tumble of kudzu.

There's no way her body could be seen from the road, he thought, *but maybe she didn't roll as far down as I thought and someone standing up here spotted her. Maybe she rolled all the way down and someone found her at the bottom.*

He climbed back into his car and continued home. He knew Harlem would be looking for him just like that Danvers sheriff. Surprising that there was no car following him although it seemed like the guy was going to. Maybe Dalton changed his mind, and radioed back to Unity instead; it wasn't his county anyway. He was glad for the reprieve; he needed time to think.

Effie would be badly decomposed by now especially with the extra rain and heat. No fingerprints on that blanket, and no one could identify it at his.

He could still be as surprised as anyone. He told everyone that she left to get a divorce. That was his story and he could stick to that. Had he told anyone about receiving divorce papers? He didn't think he had. He hadn't even said where she went. Just said she took a bag and said she was going to the bus station. That she refused his offer to drive her.

Harlem would want to know why he left Danvers instead of going in for questioning. *I'll say ministers are above reproach. That I thought the sheriff was ridiculous; it couldn't have been Effie.*

Bogerty needed to make plans. He decided to go by the parsonage and grab some clothing if no police were there.

Then he'd calmly get Marla and marry her. He didn't have time to sweet talk her; he'd have to make it a quick marriage, and both of them leave the state. That brat of hers could find her own way back home. He and Marla would go, maybe to Texas. He'd work it out as he went, and God would help him. After all, he was God's loyal representative.

..........<>..........

While Bogerty was relieved for the time, Sheriff Dalton and his deputies were frustrated in their attempts to give chase. There was only one narrow highway so they couldn't fan out on separate trails. They simply followed one behind the other. Six miles out of town, a blockade prevented any further travel. Kudzu covered the road forming a wall two feet high and just as deep. The men tried to push it to the side both by hand and with a patrol car. It couldn't be moved; it was as if the vines were growing through the asphalt. No one had any saw or machete which could be used to cut a pathway. There was nothing they could do but turn around and leave. When a large motor home rounded the turn later, the road was clear.

Harlem received the message that Bogerty was returning to Unity. He contacted Garnet Easley to get an unmarked police car to tail the preacher at a reasonable distance around town.

BeBe had the sheriff's department's unmarked car today so Harlem stationed his deputy outside the city limits to report when Bogerty showed up. Gilesby wanted as much evidence as he could muster because, as yet, he didn't have enough to book Bogerty on murder without his fanatical followers working themselves into a frenzy. He knew some were capable of violence, and his county full of tourists didn't need that.

Police Chief Easley and three officers did a quick check of

Bogerty's office and parsonage. Kudzu surrounded the house and was in the basement. It framed the outside door to the church office. The men found all those vines spooky and couldn't get out fast enough. They missed several of Effie's belongings in the basement which Bogerty had separated out as not burnable. They did find what looked like parts of shoes and a melted plastic purse in a trash barrel out back. They took those items.

Bogerty hadn't noticed either unmarked car as he came into town and stopped at his bank to withdraw $600, all he had. Marla would have more, he told himself, and she'd willingly hand it over as a good wife should. He used the ATM so the tellers wouldn't ask questions.

He also hadn't noticed he was being followed as he drove home and parked behind the house. He systematically went through each room deciding what he should pack. He put his choices in a trash bag rather than a suitcase because he reasoned it would not do to have any of his flock suspect he was leaving town. They'd slow him down with questions. He was so preoccupied that he didn't see that there was more kudzu around than there had been that morning.

Then he remembered he hadn't disposed of some of Effie's belongings in the basement—the ones he couldn't burn. He shouldn't leave them there, should he? He could say she left them, and he put them there because he couldn't bear to get rid of them. No, that wouldn't work as some of those things she wouldn't have left behind. Cursing himself for not dumping that stuff earlier, he crammed everything into a second trash bag. He'd figure out something later. Checking carefully out the windows first, he slipped out back to examine the trash barrel. He used a shovel to sift through the ashes, but was relieved to see everything had burned. "God has blessed me," he said.

He went back into the house, grabbed both bags, and put them in his trunk. Then still seeing no police or sheriff's car, he went back into the house. He was hungry and figured he had time to fix something to eat before going to get Marla. *A man's got to eat*, he chuckled to himself.

Officer Bishop Cardew parked down the street under a shade tree where he wouldn't be seen, but where he would have a good view of the front of Bogerty's house. He couldn't see much toward the back where the reverend parked, but there was no way he could drive down the alley without being spotted. He would know if Bogerty left. So until then, he'd have to be content where he was, at least as content as he could be while sweltering in the humid late afternoon heat. It was getting on and he was hungry. He'd missed lunch long ago, and his blood sugar levels had dropped. He felt weak and his brain was so fuzzy that he forgot he had several protein bars in the glove compartment for just such an emergency. He wasn't aware he was falling asleep.

Chapter 9

After brunch and dishes, Hailey went back to Henry's room to pick up his tray. He was asleep, so she carefully whispered to Kingston to come out for his breakfast and to go outside to do "his business" like Henry had asked earlier. She took his bowl of dog food mixed with breakfast scraps out on the porch and waited in a chair until he returned.

When he did, he wouldn't touch his food. Instead, he sat down and leaned into Hailey's leg. She knew he was miserable. She just sat and petted his back and head gently and waited.

I go, he said. *Smell death. Soon.*

"I'll take good care of you, Kingston," Hailey promised. "Henry's the dad I wish I'd had, so I know how much he means to you. What do I do about Lily?"

Not know, he sighed and lay down.

Hailey continued to rub his back unconsciously while staring at the kudzu across the road. She hoped she would sense something from it or hear something, but it was silent; there wasn't even a fragrance blowing over. She gave Kingston a final pet, and walked over to touch some of the vines.

"Talk to me," she asked one long section covered with flowers. All she could sense was that kudzu was listening to itself as if some fellow plant was communicating with the one she was holding. She shrugged and decided to explore the barn to see how thick the vines were inside.

As she walked around the left side of the house, she noticed a lot of kudzu growing under the foundation columns.

Good reason not to build up on columns, she thought. Just on a hunch, she got on her knees and looked under the house; vines were thickly massed as far under as she could see.

That explains why the hall boards were creaking. No one

was walking on them, just crawling under them. She stood back up and walked by her bedroom. Kudzu was draped over the top of the window frame above the air conditioner where it couldn't be seen if she looked out the glass. It had come up between the veranda floor boards and climbed the wall. David's window was draped also. Hailey walked behind the house to the other side. Her mother's room, the bathroom, and Henry's room were similarly clad. She continued around were Tilfort's room jutted out from the rest of the house. There wasn't any on the back wall where the work room was, but on the right side, kudzu framed the outside door and windows. Again, nothing could be seen from the inside.

I guess everyone has been too busy to walk around outside, but why have you positioned yourself this way? Other than the windows, you're not covering any side of the veranda. She reached up to touch a dangling leaf. Again, she sensed nothing.

Hailey walked back to Henry's window. Since there was no air conditioner, she could peek inside to check on Henry. He was still asleep.

Good, he needs his rest. All hell could break loose tonight because Alice will definitely be sleepwalking. Then tomorrow we have to deal with Bogerty and more sleepwalking. Happy Fourth!

Since she had already walked around the house, Hailey decided to inspect the barn. She had to fight her way through the vines blocking the doorway to squeeze inside. It had grown up all the upright support posts and was in the hayloft, but very little was on the floor as yet. She wondered if Tilfort could cut the vines off the opening, then maybe the van and car could still be parked inside. Maybe kudzu didn't want the barn; maybe it was simply messing with Alice's head like Henry thought. Then she shrugged. It wasn't her problem as she and Marla would be gone by Saturday. The barn could be the incentive to sell out and move to town.

Remembering her fear that Kudzu wouldn't let her mother or her leave, Hailey inspected their car. So far no vines were anywhere near either vehicle, but it was on the tree trunk and by looking up, she could see it was entwined within the branches; that wasn't visible from the house. Kudzu could easily drop down and cover the car whenever a heavy breeze or storm dislodged it, and this had been a summer for heavy storms in Georgia.

Moving out from the shade of the oak tree, Hailey could feel the heat and humidity inching up by the minute. That meant another storm was brewing even though few clouds were evident yet.

She went back to the front of the veranda to check on Kingston. He hadn't moved, but his food was gone. She sat awhile longer before the heat drove her inside to her air conditioned room. The dog wouldn't come in with her which she thought was odd. She had thought he'd want back in to be with Henry.

Lily was on the couch when Hailey entered. The cat raised her head and glared at Hailey. *Not go!* she said.

Hailey walked on passed the angry cat. No one was in the kitchen which meant Alice and Marla were in the bedrooms. She needed to tell her mother all that Henry had said, and to inform her that Kingston was going with them. The extra dog part might be a surprise; getting Lily would be a whole other issue. Alice wouldn't willingly let her go and all hell would break out if they just grabbed her and took off. It was possible that Lily couldn't be helped unless David was willing to ship her up to them somehow.

Marla was in bed but not asleep yet.

"You have a bad night too?"

Her mom nodded. "I heard Alice up 'til all hours. She's tired and went back to bed in David's room. I told her to leave

Henry alone since she had him up all night. Thankfully, she listened. I hope tonight won't be like last night."

Hailey figured she could save her talk with Henry until later, and closed the door. She decided a nap was a good idea, so she went into her room.

The closet door was open where she could see the ventriloquist dummy sitting upright on the shelf. It was leaning over perilously close to falling out and its mouth was open. It hadn't been either when she threw it in there with the other toys. She walked over to shove it back in when she noticed the kudzu. The fat clown, sitting next to the dummy, slid off the shelf, hit her on the head, and landed face-up on the floor. Its black vacant eyes stared upward, and combined with its blood red mouth, looked manically evil. Hailey kicked it into the back of the closet and slammed the door; the whole scenario unnerved her.

"Is this some warning or are you playing with my mind too?" Hailey said to the vines. Since she didn't hear any answer, she shrugged and climbed in for a nap.

Even though she was tired, Hailey didn't sleep. She couldn't forget that clown and dummy, and was sure kudzu was telling her something, but what? She got out of bed and opened the closet. The clown, now propped against the inside of the door, flopped out on its back, and again she looked into that face. Now that old cracked doll was there too. The dummy was back leaning over with its mouth open; this time it fell, and Hailey caught it before it hit the floor. Its open mouth and limp arms and legs made her think she was holding a corpse. It still looked a little like Henry.

Hailey shook with imagined horror, and dropped the dummy.

"Talk to me dammit; what are you telling me?" she shouted at the vines which were now trailing down from the shelf. She was so shaken that she wasn't certain she actually heard 'warn' flash in her head, but that was all.

"So I get to figure out what these things mean," she said. "You said I can hear you, so why aren't you talking to me." She hadn't noticed vines on the closet floor. They slithered out, shoving the clown and doll onto her feet.

Kudzu was angry; Hailey guessed that much, but at what or who. She knew she needed to tread carefully. She sat down on the floor, and the vines slid from the closet and surrounded her. She laid several across her lap. She hoped that gesture would ease any anger kudzu might want to direct towards her. She picked up the fat clown and touched a leaf. "Is this Bogerty?"

Again she received no answer. She sat on the floor holding the leaf for several minutes waiting for some communication, but there wasn't any. Then the vines slid off her lap and retreated into the closet. She knew that was all she was going to get and stood up. It was her puzzle to solve, and she thought sitting on the porch breathing kudzu's fragrance might help. She left the toys on the floor.

Hailey checked on Henry first. He was asleep, but something didn't seem right although she couldn't figure out what. She grabbed some sweet tea and went to her chair where Kingston hadn't moved from his earlier position.

"Lily won't go," she told Kingston. He looked up at her with sad eyes, sighed, and put his head on his paws.

She couldn't worry about the cat at the moment; she felt whatever kudzu was telling her was more important. Alice and Janice said kudzu could read minds, so was kudzu using the toys as a warning? Hailey was sure the clown was Bogerty, but what about the dummy or that damaged doll? Her thoughts were hindered by her feelings of fear and revulsion. She never could stand clowns because they reminded her of vampires; those big red mouths looked coated in blood. The doll and dummy were no better; she knew there was evil behind those staring eyes. She couldn't sit still, and needed something to do to get her mind off those toys.

"Face your fears," she said and returned to her room to examine the dolls again. She couldn't; instead she shoved them back into the closet, and tried the internet again, but there was still no service. She suspected kudzu was the cause and that worried her. She glanced around the room, not really thinking for the moment. It was then that Hailey saw the vines attached to the wallpaper. Her stomach muscles knotted and suddenly she felt like screaming maniacally and ripping the vines off the walls, but she knew that would be a mistake. "Stay calm," she told herself; she didn't feel any threat so she ignored the kudzu and went back outside.

It was late afternoon, and Hailey was deep in thought and lazily scratching Kingston's ears when David's van startled her; he gunned the wheels, sending gravel flying as he sped to the back, and that wasn't normal for him. She assumed he was angry about something and followed him around to where he parked. Kingston perked up his ears, but stayed behind.

She heard him shouting at Tilfort, but David didn't seem to be directing his anger at him. So something had happened in town, hopefully not problems with the wedding. Hailey stood back and tried to hear what her cousin was saying. All she caught was, "How could she? I thought she cared for me."

Sounds like trouble with Janice, Hailey thought and slipped back around the corner, hoping she hadn't been seen.

She made it back to the front and sat down as if nothing had happened. Apparently Tilfort had seen her because, not long after, he came through the sun room straight for her. He dropped his ax and hatchet in the corner, and took the chair next to her.

"I saw you comin' back to us," he said. "Thank'ee for leavin'."

"How'd the wedding decorations work out? Was everyone happy?" Hailey asked, trying not to let on what she heard.

Them weddin' decorations took awhile to set up, and we had to rush 'cause we left here late. We were runnin' to put everythin' where the bride wanted it. That little gal sure could bark orders. Moved some of those decorations around to two or three places 'fore she was satisfied. I did most of the runnin' 'cause David couldn't cope with all. He partly shut down. I put him in the car and finished up. I reckon she was a nervous wreck, it bein' the weddin' day and all, but she was finally happy, and the groom even gave David a bonus. I think that poor man was relieved too 'cause he was real tense until she smiled and said it were all perfect. Don't think I want to go through my own weddin' iff'n it turns nice ladies into rabid werewolves." Tilfort laughed and slapped his knee.

"You should watch a couple of those wedding reality shows on TV," Hailey grinned. "Everything from picking a dress, to bridesmaids, you name it, is stressful. I've watched mothers screaming at daughters, daughters screaming at bridesmaids. Seems like every step in the planning causes tantrums. There was even an episode where the groom broke it off and left. I don't usually watch that stuff; I like the shows where mediums talk to dead people or Sherlock Holmes type shows. But my girlfriend Anne loves them so when she's over that's what we watch."

"No thank'ee. Them shows wouldn't be my choice; I want something calmer. I got enough trauma to cope with around here without watchin' screamin' women on TV. I like those Bigfoot chasin' or UFO shows. They're more thought provokin'."

"I heard David shouting something that I guess is about Janice," Hailey said. "That must have been another trauma today. Can I ask, or is it none of my business?"

"Janice broke up with David," Tilfort said. "Henry and I figured it was goin' to happen sooner or later. The only thin' they had in common was plants, especially kudzu. I think she imagined something spiritual in him since he's an empath and fixates on flowers. They mostly talked about those thin's 'cause she don't have many outside of family she can talk to. Just us as far as I know'd."

"I didn't think Janice was lonely. She seems so with it."

"She was married before, but he ran out on her, and then got killed in a bar fight over in Alabama. Shootin' pool and some drunk accused him of cheatin'. Whole bunch jumped him sayin' the only good Indian was a dead one. Beat him up bad and threw him in a dumpster back in the alley. Died before the ambulance got him to the hospital."

"When did this happen?" Hailey asked. She couldn't imagine all that pain, nor did she sense anything like that when she talked to Janice. *She must hide it well or she's found a way to let it go.* Does she have kids?"

"Been about fourteen years ago; she was 'round twenty-five," Tilfort said. "Husband had an insurance policy she used to open the Dawg. That restaurant and her family's what got her through all that mess. Her Great Grandmother Ivy's a shaman and taught her many thin's. One being how to use kudzu and honor it. Maybe that had something to do with her takin' up with David. She don't have kids, and he's five years younger. Not had much of a mother of his own 'cause he ain't Alice's favorite boy."

Hailey didn't know what to say. This was a picture of Janice she would never have suspected. "I imagine she had a lot of hurt and bitterness inside. Must be David does too."

"She hated all white men for a while. I think Ivy used kudzu's flowers to calm her and he'p her get over all that. She's right mellow anymore, but she don't like puttin' up with constant upsets from anyone. She's real connected to that plant nowadays. Maybe the feelin's mutual. That's where her strong feelin's at."

Hailey snickered. "Dealing with Alice must be a real headache. That's nothing but trauma. And kudzu's in the middle of it."

"Her hatin', and Janice lovin' it. Yup. And, I think she saw another wounded person in David. That and his condition; he has trouble with givin' and takin' feelings. I think she's tired of givin' and not gettin' much back."

"Maybe they helped each other some way, like comfort. How long have they gone together?" Hailey asked.

Tilfort sat thinking. "I don't rightly know when it went from him selling flowers to the Dawg and them hookin'up. She always insisted he put kudzu in the vases. That got them to talkin' and they became buddies. She's had the Dawg about ten years, and he's been doin' her flowers from the start. I think they just grew into it the last three or four years."

"They never actually dated?"

"No, usually Janice comes here, but not hardly anymore 'cause of Alice. You know how Alice is since y'all been here. Imagine all that every time Janice comes; it never ends." Tilfort shook his head. "Don't think I'd want to be around Alice iff'n I didn't haf to."

"Do you think the relationship was more in David's head than reality? Or was she really into him?"

Tilfort shrugged. "Everybody gets somethin' when they pair up. I don't know all on the list. Sometimes it's even and sometimes it's side heavy. Not had a lot of experience that way. I did have two girlfriends, one in high school and one in college. But I know there's always reasons. I figure the same's true with them two."

"Woo hoo, way to go Tilfort. Alice said you never dated." Hailey teased him.

Alice don't think I ever did; I don't bother to educate her. David and Henry know, but I asked them not to let on. I don't need her pokin' her nose into my business, 'cause it'd just give her fuel to start another fire."

"That sounds like you're holding secrets too. Not into telling me?" Hailey asked.

"I can tell you the first one. She didn't want me to go to college. Said it would make me think I was better'n her. We fought a lot, then she went out with another guy to spite me and make me jealous. Sayin' if I didn't stay to keep an eye on her, I wouldn't know what all she'd be doin'. Dumped her; didn't need all that," Tilfort said. "And after that bride today, I'm glad I didn't take Kellie up on marryin'." He chuckled. "Damn, she could be a hellcat! Pardon my cursin'."

Won't tell me about the second girl?" Hailey smiled. "Must have been something heavy."

"It was, and no, I don't want to talk about it." Tilfort stood up to go. "That one hurt real bad. That's why I know David's hurtin' and don't know how to handle it; he could go wild screaming out the door or shut down like a light bulb going out. He hates the world and blames Janice; says she took kudzu over him. Just leave him be 'til he calms down. I'm goin' back now, but I reckoned you'd want to know."

Hailey sensed a deep pain in Tilfort that he'd hidden away. He didn't notice that she touched his arm when he turned to pick up his hatchet. She got flashes of a baby and an abortion. Aimee. She had brown hair and hazel eyes.

Tilfort looked at her strangely for a second, then that look disappeared. "How much did you pick up there, Missy? Guess keepin' secrets ain't possible with you around."

"Not much, Tilfort. Really. You have it buried pretty deep," she lied.

It's a pain that won't never go away, and talkin' about it only brings that pain back sharp. Never dated after her. Couldn't take anymore. Let it be. I think I'll leave my ax here for safe keeping as David's ready to chop and burn every kudzu plant he can get at. He might cut himself while he's at it." He tucked his hatchet into his belt as he left.

Tilfort's got more surprises than a candy box, Hailey thought, still amazed by all she'd put together about him.

However, Tilfort's saying that David blamed kudzu sent chills down her spine. She remembered Henry's words about what the plant might do if it felt betrayed. Hailey wasn't sure she wanted to wait until Saturday to leave, but running out the door today wasn't possible.

She heard David stomp into the house from the back and go toward his room. He cursed and muttered as he went, and slammed his door open. He must have startled Alice out of her nap because she squealed.

"Oh God, Alice's in his bedroom, and they'll feed off each other," Hailey realized and hurried to Henry's room to act as some sort of buffer. Kingston went with her.

Henry was awake when she slipped in as quietly as she could. Kingston jumped on the bed and put his head in Henry's lap.

"I heard all David's commotion comin' in. What's he upset for?" Henry asked.

"Janice broke up with him and now he's in talking to Alice. He probably woke her up when he went in because he didn't know she was sleeping in there. I thought I should warn you in case it lands in here," Hailey said. "Tilfort said some of it was because of Alice and her hating kudzu."

"Oh Lordy, there'll be nothin' but anger, misery, and blamin' for months. Janice is a good woman, and I'm sorry David lost her, but figured it was comin'. Felt it. I'll have to bite my tongue until the tailspin slows down 'cause there'll be no talkin' sense into either one 'til then. If I lose my temper, I'll have both of them bitin' on me sayin' I'm takin' sides."

"Can I do anything at all? I know we're leaving soon, but….," Hailey felt helpless and she didn't like that feeling, not at all.

"No Honey. I wish't you could, but only John could have

done anythin'; they both would of listened to him. I'm so tired of all this turmoil. You were right, I should of stayed in the hospital," Henry said with a bleak smile. "I'm goin' to get up now and put my clothes on. Do you think you could find me somethin' sweet to eat somewhere in the kitchen? You can do that for me. Sugar helps me feel better, betimes."

Hailey started to protest, but Henry waved it aside. "Never mind my diet right now. How about sweet tea if I can't talk you into somethin' else. I'll meet you on the veranda. I want to be up when it all hits my way."

She was waiting with a tiny sliver of peach pie and the tea when he joined her, Kingston in tow. She held the chair steady as he sat down; Henry looked even frailer now that he was upright. His leg dragged so much that she was afraid he would fall before he could get to his chair. He was even using his quad cane which he had spurned most of the time she and Marla were visiting. He smiled gratefully as he ate his pie tiny bite by tiny bite as if it were the last time he'd ever taste any. Kingston lay at his feet.

Shortly thereafter, Marla joined them.

"There's a lot of commotion going on with Alice and David. He stormed out the back, slamming doors as he went; she's arguing with someone on the phone rather loudly back there."

"Dear God," Henry said, "Alice must be givin' Janice the what-for. That poor gal has had enough of Alice's moods without a tongue lashing today. Alice calls her all the time to complain about something, and she don't like bein' Alice's counselor."

"Maybe Janice should change her number. That would stop things," Marla suggested.

"Alice don't have her cell number; it's the restaurant phone and Janice can't change that." Henry said. "Mostly her employees answer instead and say she's busy. David must have given her his phone what has Janice's private number. She'll have ta change that real soon, 'cause Alice will be using it day and night now that she's got it."

"So what's Alice's problem now?" Marla asked. "I imagine David told her something that upset her. She's screaming loud enough to break ear drums, and it's definitely about David. The air's vibrating with her emotions. I had to leave."

"David and Janice broke up. Alice is most likely defendin' David over her. She won't stay out of anybody's business; slin's a lot of guilt around. It's goin' to be hard here for a while." Henry gulped the last of his pie as if the sugar would save him; he heard family coming.

"Damn it, Til, I said I want everything burned. The peach trees, the barn, everything, And I want to start now. " Tilfort was trying to calm David down as they rounded the corner of the house.

"Now don't get all fixated. We can do the burnin', but we need to do it carefully. You can't go runnin' around like a chicken with its head cut off, settin' everythin' on fire," Tilfort said. "You'll set us on fire; the house too. And thin's are wet right now. You don't want to go throwin' kerosene or gasoline everywhere just so's it'll burn."

"David," Henry said. "Come over here, boy. Why in hell are you so determined to start burning the property down for?"

"Janice dumped me, Daddy. She says she won't put up with Mamma's hatred of kudzu any more or our problems; she's not a counselor. She picked kudzu over me; I'm going to burn the damn stuff to the ground, and take a burned pile and dump it on her veranda. I'll show her it's not a gift from her Great Spirit bullshit."

"I know you're hurtin' right now, son, but don't go off half-cocked. I own this land, not you, and you ain't goin' to do nothin' without my say so. You listen to Tilfort. He's got a good head on his shoulders, and right now, you don't. There'll be no burnin' today. We've discussed all this before, and I'll decide what we do or don't do and when. You hear me, boy?"

Alice chose this time to storm onto the porch, carrying Lily, and David's cell phone. Angry words poured out of her mouth.

"Henry, that Indian broke up with David. I called her and gave her a piece of my mind. She's got no right hurtin' him, and she don't even feel guilty doin' it. After all we've done for her. All those flowers. And do you know what she did? She hung up on me! Do you hear, she *hung* up on me!" Alice's voice would do a banshee proud.

Henry gripped the arms of his chair, and while his voice stayed calm, his eyes blazed.

"Alice, enough! Sit down and be quiet, and if you won't, go in the house where I don't have to listen. She's done for us; not the other way around."

Henry's voice was forceful and authoritative. Alice stared at him, and, for once, she obeyed. She sat down, but she was by no means done with her tirade. She'd continue later. She petted Lily so roughly that the cat growled and jumped down.

Hailey wondered how much of his waning strength Henry just used up, and she was afraid. He was like a father now, and she didn't want to lose him. Didn't these people see what they were doing to him, or were they so wrapped up in their own crap they didn't care?

Marla felt her daughter's turmoil. She cleared her throat and stood up. "Henry, why don't I get you some more sweet tea, and I think there's still cookies. You look like some extra sugar would do you good. I'll bring everyone glasses and a full pitcher." Hailey saw him wink at her.

Marla was trying to defuse the situation, Hailey understood, but for how long. She could feel the maelstrom all around her, and only Henry could keep these people from exploding. When he died, all hell would break loose. Hailey only hoped she and her mother weren't casualties. Another thought struck her. *Mom picked up on that sugar!*

Before Marla could return with tea and cookies, Bogerty drove up.

"Damn, don't this take the rag off the bush," Henry muttered. "What's that jackleg doing here? He's not due round 'til tomorrow night." Everyone held their breath and stared. Kingston growled low in his throat and crouched ready to spring if needed. Lily took her cue from him and bristled; she stayed close to Alice, claws ready.

"Howdy to y'all on this fine late afternoon. Where might I find that lovely lady, Miss Marla?" Reverend Bogerty said as he climbed the veranda steps. Hailey could see beads of sweat on his forehead.

He's in a hurry about something, she thought, then it hit her. *The fat clown! Kudzu was warning me that Bogerty was coming today*!

Marla stepped out the door carrying the tray of cookies, tea, and an extra glass. She had heard his disgusting voice from the kitchen and considered running into Tilfort's room to hide, but knew that wouldn't work; she would have to play it by ear and hope for the best.

"We didn't expect to see you until tomorrow, Reverend," she said. "To what do we owe this unexpected pleasure?"

"Marriage, my dear lady. I'm fixing to do you the honor of making you my wife. Your charms have enthralled me, and I can think of no one else but you. Please accept this wedding ring as my token of esteem. I have taken the liberty of procuring a marriage license this very day and my heart could not wait until tomorrow night. So I have come here today to perform the sacrament so that our hearts can be joined in harmony and bliss. All you folks can be witness to this blessed event."

Bogerty took out his book. It appeared that he was going to start the ceremony immediately. Marla's eyes nearly bugged out of her head. Hailey could hear her mom's internal scream.

Everyone else should have too; it was that loud!

"Now, hold on, Reverend," Henry said. "This is not at all appropriate. You haven't properly asked me if you could court my cousin, let alone asked her if she wanted to be courted *or* to marry you. This isn't done in Georgia. I know that other places where you have preached have different customs, but surely you know the South has always demanded certain proprieties. This suddenness is not acceptable."

"I do understand that this might appear unseemly, but I have accepted an offer for another ministry and will be leaving this evening. I simply could not leave without taking my beloved with me. Now, Miss Marla, let us begin."

Taking her cue from Henry and adopting his "Southern" style, Marla said, "Reverend Bogerty, this is unacceptable. I won't be treated as if I were a cow to be purchased; your intentions are very insulting. I'll never marry you. Leave, now!"

"Now Miss Marla, I am so sorry to offend your sensibilities or your family's customs, but I must make haste and my mind is made up. You will marry me now. Perhaps I can make it up to you at a later time. Now we will begin: Dearly beloved, we are gathered here in the eyes of God..."

"Ain't no God in this," Tilfort said. He grabbed his hatchet and pointed it at Bogerty. "Now you leave this woman alone or I'll sample a piece of your hide."

"You dare threaten one of God's chosen! He will send you to everlasting hell fire and utter damnation. He will cut off your engorged penis and cram it down your throat so that you choke on your own cum as it spews out." Bogerty moved menacingly toward Tilfort.

"Reverend Bogerty!" Alice spoke up. "There are ladies present and we will not permit such filth to flood your mouth. You've been given your answer, now leave. I'm callin' 911."

She grabbed Lily, afraid the man might kick her cat if she attacked, picked up the phone, and ran into the house. She stood by the screen and called. Dixie heard the commotion as she took down the facts and contacted Harlem.

David seized the ax and stood next to Tilfort. Hailey moved beside her mother. They formed a united front blocking Bogerty. Kingston snarled as he protected Henry.

"Attack me and you'll all suffer the righteous fires of hell," Bogerty bellowed. "God punishes those who wrong his prophets." He did not believe they would dare attack him. Screaming, "God will prevail," he barreled into Hailey and shoved her into Tilfort. Tilfort threw his weapon wildly at Bogerty's feet and caught her. The hatchet glanced off the side of his shoe-boot, slicing the leather, and spun in the grass. Tilfort and Hailey landed in a heap on top of Alice's chair; it overturned dumping them on the floor.

Bogerty felt a sharp pain where his little toe had been as he lunged for Marla. He was off balance when he grabbed her arm and tried to pull her off the veranda. He would have fallen if she hadn't pulled back. That steadied him and his momentum propelled her off the veranda and onto her knees. He grabbed her hair and forced her to stand. She dug her feet into the gravel and clawed at any available flesh.

She was no match for his bulk, but she wasn't about to give up without fighting tooth and nail. In exasperation, he wrapped one beefy arm around her waist and tried to drag her toward his car. He wasn't having an easy time of it, and that surprised him. He forgot that Effie was five-foot one and weighed less than a hundred pounds. Marla was seven inches taller, forty pounds heavier, and fought like a hellcat; Effie hadn't. She kicked as hard as she could, attempting to hit his kneecaps, shins, anything available. Her nails couldn't penetrate his suit coat, so she aimed for his face and eyes. He was too fat and out of shape for such exertion.

Tilfort extracted himself from Hailey, dived off the veranda and reclaimed his hatchet, but Hailey was right behind him and was in front of him when he stood back up. She was in his way; he watched for a chance to attack. She linked to her mother and smelled what Marla smelled—Bogerty's body odor. She heard his labored breathing wheezing in Marla's ear, and she felt her mother's disgust and fear.

"Not <u>my</u> mother, you fat ass," she shouted, and picked up a baseball-sized geode from the driveway, aimed for his face, and threw as hard as she could. She thanked her years as a pitcher in little league at that moment. It hit him on his cheekbone, splitting the skin. Blood flowed. She grabbed another and ran forward twisting her body to gain more momentum as she threw. This one hit Bogerty in the mouth, breaking teeth and causing more bleeding. She got too close to him when she grabbed the next geode. He freed one arm, swung, and knocked her to the ground. She heard a crunch as her forehead smacked into the gravel.

Blood ran from the cut down into her eye, blinding her on the left side. She staggered up and grabbed another geode, but her throw went wild, hitting his shoulder rather than his head. Then dizziness forced her to flop down on the driveway where she unknowingly grabbed a fist-full of kudzu; it soothed her.

Kingston launched himself at Bogerty the minute the hated man hit Hailey. He couldn't go for the throat as he badly wanted to because of Marla; instead, he attacked the left ankle and held on. Bogerty couldn't pull loose from those massive jaws, and he couldn't kick the dog off, not at over ninety pounds of long pent-up fury. Kingston's four canines slashed in, but the ankle was protected somewhat by the shoe-boot. Still, he ripped the flesh above it and slowed his enemy down as well as shredded his pants. Bogerty dragged his bloodied leg with the dog attached as he maneuvered his prize toward the car. He felt his pulse throbbing in his neck and was getting light headed.

David followed, carrying the ax, but just stood there afraid he'd hit the wrong person or Kingston. He threw his weapon down and jumped at the man's back, but couldn't clasp his arms around Bogerty's fat shoulders to hold tight. The reverend spread his elbows outward and reared back; David lost his grip and fell to the ground.

Bogerty tried to force Marla into the passenger's side but her outstretched arms and legs prevented it. He was panting harder now and didn't have enough strength left to push her in. Instead, he grabbed her by her hair and punched her in the face, knocking her out. Then he shoved her limp body into the back and slammed the door.

That was more than Tilfort could stand. He tossed the hatchet and grabbed the ax off the ground. He ran forward, raised it above his head, and sank it into the center of the windshield with every pound of force he could muster. He hoped having no windshield would stop the man. The safety glass disintegrated into hundreds of small pieces covering the front seat and dashboard. Kingston let go when Tilfort shattered the glass, more startled by the sound than any fear. Bogerty, suddenly freed of that 90 pound ballast, rounded the back of the car and climbed into the front.

Kingston aimed again for a piece of the minister, but the man was too quick. He only managed to sink his upper canines into Bogerty's left calf and rip the flesh a few inches before the hated man pulled in his leg loose and slammed the door. Tilfort backed up when Kingston nailed Bogerty, but swung again when the dog was out of the way. He smashed the driver's side window and sliced into the steering wheel. Bogerty covered his face to prevent the flying glass from entering his eyes, and started the car. He aimed next for the front tire, but Kingston lunged at the opened window, and Tilfort couldn't get a good angle to swing his ax without hitting the dog. Kingston caught Bogerty's shoulder and ripped the suit coat. His canines planted deep bruises before he dropped to the ground.

While Kingston and Tilfort slowed Bogerty down, David ran to the back door and grabbed Marla out as their minister slammed the car in gear. She was dead weight as he pulled her off the seat by her feet. He tried to cushion her fall with his body by wrapping his arms around her, and rolling away from the moving car. Bogerty sped off throwing gravel as his tires lost traction.

Tilfort threw down his ax and helped Hailey up. She staggered as she attempted to walk. He pulled off his t-shirt and pressed it to her head to stanch the bleeding and half carried her up the veranda steps to a chair. She needed to sit upright.

David had Marla sitting up also, but she was not quite lucid. He didn't try to get her to her feet until she felt ready. Both her eyes were turning purple.

..........<>..........

Alice slipped back to the veranda when the fighting moved to the yard and flopped down next to Henry. He asked her to bring his house revolver so he could shoot into the air to stop the chaos. She refused, so there was little they could do except wait for the sheriff or deputies to arrive. However that fact didn't stop Alice from returning to her ranting against "that Indian witch" for "misleading David. When that fell on deaf ears, she turned her complaining to Marla. She attempted to dump all the blame for the fiasco occurring in front of them on her cousin, and kept up a non-stop tirade until Henry lost all patience with her.

"Alice, I never hit a woman in my life, but right now I could knock your teeth down your throat, and God forgive me for thinkin' so. With all this goin's on, you sit here blamin' others. You've worn me to the bone. You alienated your daughter, and pushed David away all 'cause of his Asperger's. You use him like a cur dog. Now it's Janice and Marla. Right now I can't stand the sight of you," Henry said.

"I've spent my life worrin' over y'all and workin' all the time and this is the thanks I get!" Alice's screeching hurt Henry's ears.

"Lord, I should of left you failin' on that stage. You never turned your princess hands around here. You love nothin' but yourself and maybe Lily. That little guardian angel's been patient, and you don't even know she's an empath and more psychic than you'll ever be. Turn your eyes outward, not inward for once in your selfish life."

Alice began howling, "You don't love me; I've done everything for y'all, and no one cares. I was a good actress, but I gave it up to marry you and live on this farm. You never think of *my* needs or *my* wants. It's all about *you* and the *family*. I never wanted kids, but I endured, and what did I get---a genetic misfit and a defiant little bitch. And every last one of you's weird empaths. Even turned me that way. It's your fault; I hate y'all."

"Janice has been mighty patient with you, and so has kudzu. I don't know how, for the life of me. We've talked many a time, and she's right; you're all eat up with hate. Just shut up; I'm done tired of listenin' to you." Henry stood up, took his quad cane and carefully stepped over to Hailey and Tilfort just as three cars rushed toward the house.

Harlem and two deputies whirled into the circular drive swerving to Miss Marla and David. Bogerty had given Officer Bishop the slip when his blood sugar bottomed out, but the reverend could only go east or west on 57 if he left Unity. Harlem was just leaving to travel east and his two deputies west when Dixie radioed in. An ambulance was on its way too.

Harlem made a quick assessment of the situation and told Alice to get ice for Marla's swollen face, and a clean towel to press to Hailey's head. She sat there with a stubborn look on her face and did not move. He shrugged and sent in BeBe.

He returned with two handfuls of ice. "I couldn't find any towels, Sheriff," he said, "just this little wash rag. Will it do?"

Harlem nodded and turned his attention to Hailey. Tilfort's wadded up shirt was working okay. They just had to wait for the ambulance now.

Oddly, Hailey's forehead didn't hurt too much. It was tender to the touch, and she was getting a mild headache, but she expected more pain. She smiled at Tilfort. "Thanks Dr. Tilfort," she said. "I wonder how many stitches I'll need. That ass hole."

"Don't talk, Missy; sit quietly. Your Mamma's better'n you right now," he said smiling back, but his eyes registered his concern. "You got good aim. Remind me not to git you mad at me."

Suddenly she jerked. "What's wrong? You ain't convulsin' on me, are ye?" Tilfort gasped.

"No, just thought of something. Sorry, I'm fine," she said. Kudzu's warning had jerked through her mind like an old comic strip light bulb. *The doll with the cracked head! That's me, and the fat clown hit me in the head when it fell!*

Knowing that kudzu would hear her, she sent a silent thank-you to the plant and an apology for being so blunt earlier. She was barely acknowledged.

When she heard the word "murder" her focus shifted to Harlem. He was explaining that Bogerty was wanted on suspicion of murdering his wife.

"That's why he was in such an all-fired hurry." Tilfort grinned at Marla and said, "I guess he was real taken with you to get hitched before fleein'. I can't see it, not with those raccoon eyes of yours."

His teasing made Marla smile. *He's a good man*, she thought as the ambulance turned into the drive.

Marvin and Elroy pushed everyone out of the way and examined both women. They insisted on transporting them to the hospital even though Marla insisted that she didn't need to go—only Hailey. Tilfort overruled her and promised to follow in his car.

"Y'all can't hitchhike home so I'm forced to follow you like a trained dog." He grinned even more as Hailey flipped him the bird.

"Not a trained dog; a knight," she said, as Marvin helped her onto the gurney. With both women in the ambulance and Elroy attending them, Marvin drove off.

Tilfort tucked the hatchet underneath the car seat just in case Bogerty followed them and left too.

Harlem seemed in no hurry to pursue Bogerty. He and his deputies sat on the porch to talk to Henry and David. They helped themselves to the tea and cookies. Alice went inside as she was still nursing her anger and was in no mood for pleasantries. Lily refused to follow her or be carried; it seemed her loyalties were shifting.

When David told Harlem that Janice had broken up with him, Harlem inadvertently sucked in his breath. He covered his surprise by finishing his tea and pouring more. He felt sorry for David, but couldn't help the happy glow that filled his chest. He kept his mind on business, fearful that his hopefulness would be suspected.

Henry was speaking to him, but he didn't hear.

"I'm sorry, Henry," he said, "what were you asking?"

"I was wondering why you ain't tearin' after Bogerty right now," Henry repeated. "Not that I'm tossin' you out. You must have something planned."

"You know 57, Henry; there're no side roads. Bogerty can only go straight and slowly to boot. I radioed ahead and

Sheriff Clovis Dalton will be waiting right past the county line. Bogerty won't get through *that* roadblock. Clovis spotted him earlier in Danvers and the altercation that followed is sticking in Clovis' maw. You know the old saying, 'pay backs are hell.' It's Clovis' time to payback, and I don't feel sorry for that bastard one bit. Bogerty beat his wife to death, so if he picks up a few bruises swinging at the deputies, then he's resisting arrest. It'll be his second resisting today because he shoved Clovis around earlier.

"I do need to be heading back to Unity. I'll station my boys a piece down the road in case Bogerty doubles back. You wouldn't want him again today as an unexpected house guest, and if he's sweet on Marla, he might if he gets away from Clovis."

Harlem gave instructions to his deputies, thanked Henry and David for their hospitality, and left. His thoughts were on Janice the whole trip back.

It was past the supper rush hour when Harlem parked at the Dawg. He saw Janice sitting outside on the veranda, her face framed in profile by the late afternoon light. He stood to the side not ready to climb the steps yet; he just wanted to look at her. He figured she knew he was there, but showed no sign of it. Her long hair was braided and draped over one shoulder. She was wearing a turquoise dress belted with silver. Harlem thought she was the most beautiful woman he'd ever seen.

She turned and smiled at him. "If you're done staring at me," she said, "come sit."
He did as he was told, but was unable to talk.

"This is a fine way to begin. You've never been silent around me before, and there's no need to start now, although a strong silent man is attractive."

Harlem realized she was teasing him. A dozen questions filled his head, but he couldn't form a sentence if his life depended on it.

She did the talking for him. "I've always admired David's ability with flowers, but his mind is closed and full of turmoil. I had hoped he could embrace some spirituality, unfortunately, he would not accept anything because of his mother's corruption. I've wanted to break away for some time; it was simply finding a calm moment in his life. I decided he wasn't going to have a calm moment, and a confrontation was inevitable. You gave me the incentive to get it over with."

"How did I do that?" Harlem asked.

"I've known your feelings for a long time, but until you spoke, I didn't feel I could either because I didn't want to scare you away," Janice said. "I want us to work. I cared for you but was afraid, and reasoned David would be a safe choice."

"Did you love him? It isn't really important. I'm just curious," Harlem said.

"No, but I thought we could work spiritually together," Janice said. "Because he is younger, I assumed he could learn. You know my past. That wound never healed, and I've been afraid to love; didn't want to. I was being logical with David. But, feelings count, not logic."

"And here I didn't think I had a chance. You've been in my heart for so long. It's why I never dated much, let alone married. I wish I'd had some hint. You hide things well," Harlem said.

"We were both hiding—from each other. Kudzu knew. It told me to use its flowers to scent candles and light one by you. That it would help us."

Harlem grinned and nodded, "Kudzu's smell was really strong when I got here, and the vines moved away from my feet. It was leading me down a different path than food and deaths. Kudzu's why I couldn't focus on my job, just you. It was already softening me up even before you lit that candle."

"You're Cherokee, Harlem, and your blood is growing stronger; kudzu is helping you. Ebon saw it that night you found Effie's body. You told him not to cut the vines; just push them off the road, and you accepted his explanation that kudzu wanted the body found. You heard kudzu's voice today without knowing. It was directing you east to look for Bogerty and that's the direction you decided to go. Dixie's call confirmed your decision."

"I never figured I had enough in me to call myself Cherokee, and I wished I had some of the abilities my great great grandfather did. He was a shaman, and my family told stories. My father taught me some things, but he didn't remember much. Everyone back then tried to hide it. I just let it go," he said.

"You're opening up faster than you know. We'll work together. Great Grandmother Ivy has been teaching me for years and she will teach you too. All my family will help, but it's already strong within you." Janice smiled. "Here's your first lesson. You don't need notes, you'll feel it inside. The Great One has given us Kudzu, and it will protect us and provide for our needs. And yes, it's a walking plant spirit, only it isn't evil. But it'll judge and punish those that hold evil in their hearts. Even we aren't immune if we're evil or turn our backs on it, but it belongs to us, and we to it. There's great power in its love, and it decided it needed to play matchmaker between us."

"Then since it's playing matchmaker, does that mean we could marry?" Harlem asked, hoping for a 'yes.'

Janice laughed. "Shouldn't there be a long courtship?"

"Nope. I think we've waited long enough. Do you want a formal white man's proposal? How about...Janice Singing Grass, will you marry me? Do I need to offer horses to your father or something?"

Janice nearly doubled over laughing. "You don't own any horses. How about a couple goats? We could have a mixed up Cherokee/white man wedding."

"Whatever you want, Love. Guess we need to go look for rings; that is, if you want one."

"Of course I want one, but maybe not a diamond," she said.

Harlem reached up and touched a leaf. "Thanks for giving me the courage to almost get the words out," he said and laughed. He felt kudzu laughing with him. Then he felt something else—a warning. He turned to Janice, "Kudzu will take care of Bogerty, and we're *not* to interfere." That thought left him ambivalent as he drove to the station.

Chapter 10

One mile inside of Green County, Sheriff Dalton set up his road block. Three cars perched in the road with five men, each armed with Tasers as well as guns. Clovis had a rifle loaded with deer slugs leaning upright in his front seat; it wasn't regulation, but none of his deputies would ever admit to seeing Clovis carrying it.

Bogerty might be unarmed or he might have picked up one of his fanatical parishioners with a connection to the Klan. Either way he was a mountain of a man, exceedingly strong, and monumentally intimidating, therefore very dangerous. None of the deputies alone could hold him as Clovis discovered earlier to his embarrassment. That wouldn't happen again; he only hoped the handcuffs would fit the reverend's fat wrists; it didn't matter how tight they were.

Their location was carefully picked. It was just out of Harlem's jurisdiction, and hidden around a curve so Bogerty wouldn't see the trap. Once he spotted the road block, there would be no room to turn around. On the right, a high cliff littered the three-foot berm with rubble and boulders, and a sheer drop to oblivion waited patiently on the left. The road itself was narrow, necessitated from building in a mountainous area. Still, there was always the possibility that Bogerty might escape Clovis and head back west toward Unity.

It was an inconvenience to tourists and locals alike; however Clovis told them a rock slide had caused the temporary closure, and that the road would be clear within two hours. He didn't want anyone in the way; Bogerty was dangerous. As boulders lying by the road's edge were a common sight, no one suspected. They simply turned back to wait.

Harlem's two squad cars were positioned near the entrance to County Road 54. Their job was two-fold; they were to prevent Bogerty from getting to Seed Tick and Marla, and they were to block 57 if Bogerty did escape Clovis; in either case, they were to call Dixie for reinforcements. Clovis would be in pursuit, and Bogerty would be sandwiched in.

Clovis had more vehicles, men, and equipment, so Harlem hoped his friend would have everything well in hand; BeBe and Robert would merely be back up. It was a good plan and should have run like a new clock battery.

Kudzu had other plans. A large wall of tangled vines slithered across 57 East at the county line and out of sight of Clovis. A second tangle crawled across 57 West past county road 54 and out of sight of BeBe and Robert.

Those coming from Unity saw the tangled wall, returned to town and complained to Dixie. Harlem instructed her to tell those who called that the department was aware of the problem, and it was being addressed. He sat at his desk with the door closed, trying not to think. It was giving him both a headache and a stomachache.

Bogerty was alone, in between.

..........<>..........

Air funneled through the broken windshield simultaneously drying Bogerty's eyes and making them water. Driving slowly, he pulled down the sun visor to deflect the currents and noticed that his shoulder hurt when he raised his arm. His left ankle and calf were swollen and dripping blood on the floorboard; that pain only added to his rage.

"How dare those ingrates treat him so ill," he thought. He had graced their table many a time and had the congregation pray for their good health and prosperity. He was doing them a great honor in choosing to marry Marla. And Marla, that bitch attacked him like some hell spawn. Come Sunday, that family would feel his wrath from the pulpit. That made him stop for a moment. No pulpit. God will provide.

Marla was rightfully his; God had chosen her, but she needed to be taught who was master. He was sure she would become compliant soon enough. She was all he could think about. He remembered her nails clawing at his face: her spunk excited him.

When they were married, he would fuck her rough--force her over his knees and whip her ass with his belt. He would hold that bruised ass and ram his fingers up her cunt and ass hole. He would suck her hardened nipples and bite her engorged clit. He would hold her by her hair and slap her face over and over, then force her to her knees to suck him off. She would beg for his mercy as she sucked harder and harder. He would ram his hard cock down her throat and unload a huge wad of cum, enough to choke her. Yes, she would submit, and he would enjoy forcing her. A wife must always submit to her husband. By God, that witch excited him.

He needed to shoot his load now, but didn't want to soil his new suit. He stopped the car, got out, and unzipped his pants. He pulled out his cock and softly stroked it. As his need grew more demanding, he squeezed it hard and yanked it up and down, even slapping it against his leg. He grabbed his balls and pulled them around the stump of his cock. He could feel the hot cum working its way up. It shot onto the pavement speckling the tips of his shoes. He yanked harder and faster, forcing more cum out. He didn't know he had that much in him. He laughed as his knees buckled, and he fell back against the car groaning. Damnation, she made him hot.

He wiped the sweat streaming down his cheeks, and felt the salt sting his face. Then he remembered that little horror of a daughter; she threw rocks at him. He looked in the side mirror and saw that his eye had turned purple. There was a cut surrounded by a large welt on his cheek bone, and his mouth was bloody. He felt his front teeth with his tongue; two were broken off. He would make her pay someday, but it was more important to get Marla right now. He touched his bruised shoulder, remembering Hailey's last rock. It hurt. Then that damn hell hound too. He was surprised to find his jacket shoulder torn.

It hurt to shift weight on his left leg to climb into the car; instead, he sat down on the seat first and swung in his legs. His new suit pants were torn too, and his foot felt slippery inside his boot; it was filling with blood from his missing toe. The loss of his expensive new suit saddened him, but he didn't have time to worry about that now as there were more important considerations. With considerable maneuvering on the narrow road, he made a u-turn and headed back toward his beloved.

He decided to retrieve Marla late when everyone was in bed. He'd park his car at the entrance to Seed Tick and slip back to hide in the vegetation near the house until all the windows went dark, and then he could sneak through the sun room and find her. He would bind and gag her with her own clothing, then drag her to the car.

God had provided a full moon for tonight so there would be enough light; a flashlight wouldn't be necessary. It might alarm the others and he didn't want to face that madman with an ax.

Still busily planning, he wasn't watching the road. Old kudzu vines blanketed the highway ahead of him, but the reverend bumped over the thick layer unconcerned. Some thinner stems wound around his left rear wheel and snapped off as he drove, but others followed, each thicker than before until the wheel stopped rotating. More twisted around the axel and bumper. Bogerty smelled burning rubber as the bald tire dragged along the pavement, seeping air.

More kudzu entwined the front wheels making steering

difficult. Bogerty stomped the accelerator to the floor; the motor raced, but the car didn't move. He shifted to park, left the engine running, and limped out. Vines snaked outward from the undercarriage and encircled his damaged leg, tripping him. He grabbed the door as he stumbled from the pain, and scraped his left temple and hand on the pieces of glass still framing the broken window. He landed back on his car seat.

Extracting himself, he carefully stepped over the blanketed road, and leaning on the bumper for support, bent down to examine the front tires and axel. The vines were tightly woven, but he had a tire iron in the trunk. He hoped he could use the one end to break the stems and pull them off.

He wasn't concerned about the time needed; he had several hours to kill, and he felt sure God would send a helpful soul to do the work for him. After all, God helped those who helped themselves.

Shifting vines made getting to the trunk difficult. At every painful step, he removed kudzu crawling inside his pant legs; he found it erotic but aggravating. Some of his confidence vanished when he saw the back bumper; a clump of kudzu the size of an overstuffed recliner was attached. The tire was ruined, but he did have a spare, so he opened the trunk to remove the "doughnut" and tire iron. The trash bag containing Effie's belongings lay on top.

Damnation, he thought, *I forgot to dump that.*

He lifted the bag out and limped his way to the edge of the steep valley where he flung it as far out as he could. He watched with satisfaction as it tumbled through the vegetation, and nothing was visible when he heard it finally land far below. However he left a trickle of blood from the car to the road's edge marking where the bag went over.

Back at the trunk, he fumbled for his jack. Bogerty had

never changed a tire before. His contracts always stated that members of his various congregations were to provide free labor and parts for his car; therefore, he didn't know to turn off the engine or set the parking brake.

He maneuvered the jack under the axle with the tire iron, but as soon as he began ratcheting, the car shifted and the jack bent, rendering it useless.

Reminding himself that God would provide, and that he could drive on the flat, he fought the kudzu still attaching itself to his legs and returned to the front of the car. He got on his knees to see which vines he could pry or break with the tire iron. To his delight, there weren't as many coiled around the axel as he thought. The few there pulled off easily.

Bogerty leaned on the bumper to get to his feet, but as he turned around, he saw the trash bag sitting on the road. He looked in all directions to see who set it there. Seeing no one, he carefully made his way to the bag, not certain if it was the same one or not, and opened it; Effie's possessions were inside. He felt panic rising in his throat. He grabbed the bag and threw it back into the valley, then stumbled towards his car.

The engine was no longer running, and would not start when he turned the key. When he opened the hood, kudzu was everywhere—even inside the air intake, entangled in the alternator, and curled around the fan belt. The cables were off the battery terminals and all were wrapped with tiny stems. Now he knew why there was so little around his front axle; that accursed plant had uncoiled and crawled inside through the engine mount. He pulled out all the vines he saw and pushed the cables back on the battery.

The engine started, but the kudzu mass still held the car as effectively as an anchor holds a ship. Exhaust fumes flooded the interior and wafted out the broken windows. He turned off the ignition, got back out, and stepped over the vines to examine his tail pipe; it was full of dried tree leaves. He pulled out the smoldering plug and tossed it to the side of the car.

Tripping his way back along the car's side, kudzu thrust out from the undercarriage, hit the man behind his knees and dropped him on the burning leaves. Sparks leaped to his jacket. He rolled away, putting out the small flame as he did so, and sat up. The trash bag perched next to him.

He shoved it away with his hands, but kudzu thrust it back, this time into his lap. Bogerty beat it off, jumped up, and, mindless of his damaged leg, flung the bag far to the road's edge before stumbling toward the opened car door. More kudzu lashed around his ankles and coiled tightly. It dragged him face down to the edge of the road and dangled him over the side.

Bogerty screamed obscenities at the plant and cursed it in God's name. In response, kudzu pulled the fat man back from oblivion and dragged him snake-style across the pavement. That little pile of burning leaves had grown far larger, and Bogerty's eyes widened as he was dragged into the fire. The vines released their captive and moved away. He frantically yanked off his flaming jacket and swatted at the leaves, scattering them. He staggered up and shook his fist at the plant.

"You hell-spawned Cherokee demon, do you think you can defeat the Lord? Your flames scattered before me. I am stronger than you, and I have prevailed."

He left his jacket on the asphalt, and returned to the driver's seat. Several vines carrying flowers lay across the back floorboard. Their scent encircled the man's head. He believed it was kudzu's way of acknowledging his superiority and breathed deeply with satisfaction.

The trash bag still sat at the road's edge where he threw it, but someone dressed in black was standing next to it looking out over the valley. The stranger picked up that infernal bag, turned, and walked partway toward Bogerty's car before throwing it down and pointing his finger at the now terrified man behind the wheel. A sneering look of disdain poured from his face as he mouthed, "Weak, worthless!" He picked up the bag and threw it towards the car, then proceeded to remove his belt.

Bogerty cowered. "Daddy, no, please. I'm a good preacher. People look up to me. I've found a strong wife, not like Effie. I got rid of her, and I'll get rid of that bag too, I promise," he sniveled not knowing what he said, just trying to keep his father from beating him with the buckle end of his belt. He covered his head with his arms and wept; in his fear, he wasn't aware that he pissed his pants.

When nothing happened, the Reverend peeked around his arms and saw his mother standing a few feet from his father. She was smiling at her son.

"Mamma, help me, *please*! Daddy's so mad. I'm sorry I couldn't save you. I'm afraid; he's so *mean*."

Bogerty was still begging when his father grabbed his mother and began beating her to her knees. She lay in a bloody pool, her face turned toward her son.

"Mamma, Mamma," Bogerty screamed as he ran from the car toward the limp body. When he reached her, the face changed. It was Effie, not his mother lying at his feet.

He shook with realization: like father, like son. He sank to his knees and gathered the broken body of his wife to his chest. He kissed her hair with his broken teeth and torn lips as he rocked back and forth sobbing, "Mamma, Effie."

Bright blood pooled from his leg onto the dark asphalt.

Play time over.

Tiny tendrils inched forward while Bogerty sobbed, unaware of anything around him. They crawled up his shirt and encircled his neck, many times. More snaked across his hunched body, coiled around arms and legs, and pulled tight.

Effie disappeared from Bogerty's embrace. He looked down

in bewilderment and kudzu attacked.

Now!

The tendrils pierced his eyes and ear drums. When he screamed, they filled his mouth. Some slithered to the edge of his throat, curled back and threaded out his nostrils while more writhed down his throat causing him to gag and cough. He tried to breathe, but both his throat and nose were filled, allowing only trickles of air through.

Now blind and deaf, he could not see his fate coming; he could only feel rough stems scratching his neck and hauling him across the asphalt. Kudzu threw him headlong into the valley, while the vines around his wrists and ankles lashed out to grasp kindred plants and pulled tight. He hung, spread eagle, upside down, barely able to breathe, but only if he relaxed. A blanket of green enveloped him. No one except kudzu had watched him fall; now he was hidden. There would be no rescue, and death came slowly.

The vines walling both areas of Highway 57 slid back off the road. Any traffic on the road would no longer be blocked by kudzu.

……….<>……….

Sheriff Dalton looked at his watch and frowned; Bogerty was past due which meant he'd doubled back. When Clovis radioed Harlem, he was advised about the vine wall on Unity's side and the possibility of one his way. He radioed back all clear, and Harlem left to join BeBe and Robert; both squads traveled towards each other hoping to snare their man in the middle.

They located Bogerty's car. The driver's side door was open and a trash bag containing Effie Bogerty's belongings sat in the front seat. A scorched suit coat lay crumpled on the pavement near a pile of leaves and ash. Clovis easily identified the jacket; the arm wearing it had elbowed him aside earlier in Danvers, but the man had vanished.

Clovis turned to his men. "Head on back to Danvers, boys; it's Harlem's mess now."

Gilesby radioed for a tow truck, and sent his deputies back to Unity with the jacket and trash bag, and with orders to inventory everything for evidence and fingerprints.

Harlem and Clovis remained behind to wait for the truck.

"What do you think happened? Maybe kudzu did this?" Clovis asked.

Harlem spoke softly to his friend, "My report will have to read 'Missing, presumed dead.' We won't find him, and I don't relish his way of dying. Kudzu blocked the road on purpose, and then judged, tried, and executed him."

Clovis put his hands on Harlem's shoulders and spoke one word, "Brother."

"May the Great One protect us," Harlem returned.

Concern showed on both their faces, but they said nothing, as kudzu would hear. They parted when the tow truck hauled the car back to Unity.

Chapter 11

After Harlem left, both men sat for a while buried in their own thoughts. Kingston leaned against Henry, trying to offer some comfort. He felt not only his owner's turmoil, but his own too. Henry absently stroked his head and got licked in return. Finally David spoke.

"Daddy, you want me to go check on Mamma? I think she's real upset about Bogerty."

"No, Son, Leave her be. We had an argument. She's nursin' a grudge again' me, and one over Janice and another over Marla. And she's not goin' let go; not by a long shot."

"She won't keep mad at you, Daddy, she needs you more than us to take care of her."

"Alice will this time. I've never told her to shut up before when she gets goin', but I've had enough. I can't hold my peace anymore; it's eatin' me up inside."

"I've wanted to do that many times, but she's my mamma, and she'd like me even less if I did. I'm glad you finally spoke up; you've got more patience than Jobe."

"I'm tired to the bone with everythin' here, Henry said. "That woman will kill me as good as if she used a gun. I've tried my best, but maybe she belongs in a hospital ward.

"And, I'm real sorry about you and Janice, but I suspected it was comin' for a while. Your mamma ran her off. And it's your own fault too for not takin' Janice's side. No woman wants to play second fiddle to her man's mamma, especially *your* mamma."

"It's kudzu, Daddy, that she dropped me for. She says it's a gift, but it's not. It's a useful plant, and Janice's done a lot with it. I use it in my bouquets, and it smells wonderful, but it's taking over our home and our life--everyone's life. I hate it too, now."

"Son, hate does nothing but eat you up inside. It's done that to Alice. She only has her hate and misery anymore. We don't count except to do her bidding. If she's not crazy now, she soon will be. Don't you go down her path," Henry said, but he doubted David was listening.

"We needed those peach trees; we made good money. Til can't cut the vines back fast enough, and I can't keep us going with my flowers. I try hard for you and Mamma, but I can't do it. John was better, but I'm not John. I've failed you, Daddy, and now I failed Janice. I shouldn't have argued with Mamma about it; she's right to hate it. Hate and anger is all I've got now."

Henry's sad eyes looked at his son. "Maybe we've all failed each other, David. I know I've depended on you too much, my own self, and, Lordy, you've tried to be everybody's tent pole. I should've put Alice away; instead I catered to her, and she's done been spoiled rotten. It was fear that owned me. I worried more what others might say, than I did about supportin' you; now we're all sufferin'. I should be askin' your forgiveness."

"No, Daddy. You've always been here to protect us. You've done your best. Things have just gone against us."

"I've made up my mind," Henry said. "There's government he'p for us poor folks. Soon as Hailey and Marla leave, I'm goin' lookin' to rent a little place in town; maybe get moved in a couple weeks. There's those that'll move us. Maybe Alice can heal some if she's away and around our church friends."

"You know Til and I will help you move, and I can go look at places with you," David said. "But you know Momma won't go. She'll fight us all tooth and nail. She'll try to stay even if we move out all the furniture. Her fighting could put you back in the hospital or kill you."

"It's possible. I don't have a lot of time left anyway; I'm

hoping for a year or two. If I don't make it, you put Alice in a place that can care for her, and don't feel bad about doin' it. You got Til; he needs a life too. Sell this place, if anybody'll buy it, and start your flower business somewheres else. You won't get back Janice, but there's more out there. Hell, maybe you can find one that'll stick to Til too." Henry smiled and gripped his son's shoulder.

David had his head down and his elbows on his knees when he felt his father's hand. He started crying. "Thank you, Daddy," was all he could get out.

"Well, now boy, instead of cryin, let's go fix some supper, or we won't get any tonight. Your mamma's hold up in the bedroom, and not in a mood to he'p us fix something. When Til gets the girls back, they'll be ready to eat a whole hog. I know I can right now. Damn diet. He'p me up."

Using their imagination to create a meal, the two men enjoyed each other's company more than they had in years. It seemed a special time, and they were glad to be alone together. When the food was ready, they took their plates to the veranda to escape the heat. They told Alice supper was fixed; if she chose not to come out, that was her loss. David didn't take her a tray.

They were finishing some peach pie when Tilfort drove up with the girls.

He called out, "Eatin' without us, are ye. Hope you saved us some."

"Course not," David responded. He set his tray on the floor, and went to help Marla and Hailey get out of the car and into chairs.

"They put six stitches in Hailey's head, and there's a nasty bump,' Tilfort said, "But she don't have no concussion. Marla's bunged up everywhere, but nothin' broken. She'll just look like a raccoon for a while. I picked them up some pain pills the doctor prescribed, so they may be more loopy than usual if I can get them to take any. Too damn stubborn right now, both of them. I reckon they'll want them later. Where's the food and who made it? I'm bettin' it weren't Alice."

"We cooked it, so no complaining. Come help me fix three more trays," David said.

With Tilfort and David occupied, Marla looked at Henry. "I know you men are worried, but I'm more stiff, than in pain. It's Hailey who concerns me; I can't get her to take the medicine, and I know she's hurting."

"Leave her be; when she hurts enough, she'll take 'em," Henry winked at Hailey, and was pleased when she winked back.

He was well aware of Hailey's strong attachment to him. Since Ashley died, there'd been a hurting place in his heart. Not that he didn't love his sons, but she had been his little girl; he supposed every father had a special love for a daughter.

Hailey was quickly filling that hurt place, not as a substitute, but as an individual in her own right, and he hoped he could be a part of her life for a little while. She was as perceptive and gifted as he was, even more so, since she didn't try to hide it, at least not around him. He wanted to watch those abilities grow.

Seeing her bandaged forehead, he wanted to hug her because she was hurt, and because he was proud of her strong will. She sure stood up to Bogerty and Alice.

Til told him about Hailey's threatening to padlock his wife in the bedroom, and Alice certainly informed him her version of how badly she was treated. That still made him chuckle.

Ashley hadn't had that spunk; Alice had sucked her spirit more than the rest of the family, and she tried to do the same with Janice.

Hailey's words brought him out of his reverie.

"Yeah, I'm hurting, Dad, but Alice will probably sleepwalk tonight, and you'll need everyone to keep an eye on her. I'll be no help if I'm gaga," she said.

"Not goin' to keep watch tonight, and I know she'll walk. But none of us is up to it, not after these couple of days. Tilfort's in better shape than all of us, but he's needin' sleep and food, 'cause he took the brunt of everybody's else's mess. We don't consider him enough, and it's time we do. I'm not meanin' you two, so don't go thinkin' I am."

"So what do we do about her?" Hailey asked, a little surprised. "I know you worry that she might get hurt."

'We're all goin' to get some sleep tonight, and Alice can walk to Unity and back if she takes a notion; no one's goin' to corral her. I'm fixin' to sleep on the living room couch because it's comfortable, and I won't have her walkin' around in there keepin' me awake as she always heads out the sunroom. And there won't be no wet, dirty sheets for me to sleep on when she comes back in. It always does bother me, and I think when we move to town, I'll get us twin beds for that reason." Henry actually laughed when he said that.

The food arrived shortly thereafter. Hailey was starving, and from how fast Tilfort and Marla inhaled theirs, they were too. The five spent the rest of the evening discussing the day's events and laughing.

David hurt deeply over losing Janice, but Hailey's being here had opened his eyes to his family problems. He realized that Janice had given him more emotional support than he had ever given her. Showing his love was hard, given his autism, but because she was older, he figured she knew. He understood that many things needed to change, soon.

The five formed a tight, spiritual bond that evening, and kudzu listened. It sent a subtle fragrance their way to show its approval. Alice, however, was a different story.

No one was pleased when she joined them; certainly not kudzu.

"I see y'all been eatin'. Why didn't anybody come bring me somethin'? Good to know y'all so wrapped up in your own selves. It's been a bad day, and my spell's comin' on; I can *feel* that hot moon even when it's not up yet. The whisperin's are startin' too, and I don't know how y'all goin' to manage tonight, Henry. Marla and Hailey most likely won't be he'pin' much, sayin' they're too bunged up."

"No one's goin' watch you tonight, Alice," Henry said, "we're all wore out. You always managed before when we did, so I figure you can manage tonight. And it's not Marla's or Hailey's responsibility to watch you, never was."

"Well, they're family, and family takes care of its own. Besides, they said they'd he'p, and they owe me. If Marla hadn't played the hussy with Reverend Bogerty, we wouldn't a had all that ruckus today. It's *her* fault, and it's *her* fault you went to the hospital from worrin' over Bogerty comin' back. They shouldn't have come here, but since they did, they can work."

Henry's good hand gripped the chair arm, and because of his fury, he managed to rise with no help. Where he found his inner strength, Hailey didn't know, but she was awed.

"I'm done listenin' to your dumpin' guilt where it don't belong, and expectin' us to treat you special, Alice. Your talent ain't any better than the rest of us, only we keep quiet and don't beat each other with it like you go on. You suck the life out of us, you damn vampire," Henry shouted.

David and Tilfort stared at Henry. This was the second time today they'd watched him lose his patience with Alice, and now he was shouting *and* standing.

"Mamma, don't fight with Daddy, please," David begged. "He's not well enough for this, and Bogerty would have caused some ruckus here in time anyway. He has everywhere else, so don't blame Marla for his behavior."

"You shut up, boy, I didn't raise you to be mouthy to me; I suckled you, but it must not of been milk. And while I'm in the mind, I'm glad that Indian witch is gone. She was tryin' to fill everyone here's head about how wonderful kudzu is. I tried to talk sense into her, but she wouldn't listen.

"That worthless weed should be dug up by its unholy roots and burned like the Satan it is. My peach trees are dead, and that filth sends the whisperin's, and makes me walk at whole moon time. I *hate* it! I *hate* it! Do you *hear* me? It murdered John; it gave your daddy a stroke; it's taken our land. I curse it to hell and back again!"

"Do you hear me, you filthy son of Satan? I know you do, and God will strike you down. I'll burn you to ashes my own self," Alice's voice rose in crescendo as she screamed at the vines across the road, and shook her fist in the air.

Alice turned back to her family. "Y'all *will* take care of me tonight. I don't give a *damn* if you're tired, sick, or bunged up. It's my time. I'm not askin'; I'm orderin'." With that, she stomped back into the house.

"Come on, Lily," she said over her shoulder and held the door.

The cat looked at Alice then turned her back and sat down facing Hailey.

"Fine then," Alice said, "you go to hell too." She slammed the screen door as she left.

Hailey looked at Henry, "I guess she's going back into the bedroom again."

Henry chuckled; he knew she was trying to lighten things up. Hailey helped him sit back down before he collapsed.

"She'll get a mite lonely in there," said Tilfort. "Neither Henry or David should try to mollify that hell cat right now. Y'all better wait 'til she turns human again."

Alice's last tirade drained everyone's good humor. They sat quietly and listened to the evening's insects. The stars were coming out and the moon would soon fill the sky. Kingston picked up a small geode and brought it to Henry. It was his attempt to change the mood.

"No need for a rock, Kingston, it'll hurt your teeth," he said. "David, where's his old Frisbee? He and I haven't played in a month of Sundays. Might be my last chance."

"It's in my room, Henry," said Tilfort as he rose to get it. "It's a mite dusty."

When Tilfort returned and handed the old toy to Henry, Hailey saw it was well chewed.

They must have played a lot in the past, she thought, and watching how excited Kingston was when he chased it, she understood how much that playtime must have meant to the pair. Henry was laughing out loud. Then David and Tilfort got into the act. All three were tossing the Frisbee to Kingston, and he was retrieving each throw and returning it to Henry for him to toss.

He only really wants to play with Henry, Hailey observed. *Kingston knows it's his last time. I hate to think of separating those two when we leave.*

"I go too. Alice bad," Lily said to her. Hailey looked at the cat. "Won't you miss her?"

"Yes, I miss. Kingston need me. I go. Can't help Alice. I afraid. Kudzu." The cat jumped onto Hailey's lap and pushed her head under the girl's hand. She wanted to be petted.

Hailey felt the sadness in this pet too, and she was surprised that Lily would show so much feeling; she was more guarded than Kingston.

"Mom and I'll take good care of you and Kingston. I don't know if you can stay with me at college, but I'll try for an apartment, and Mom can hear too sometimes. She just needs practice; try her."

Lily looked up at her with trust and said nothing.

Marla was nodding in her chair when the men stopped playing. David dug into the linen closet for sheets and pillows to make Henry's bed, and then everyone trickled away except for Henry, Hailey, and Kingston. Lily followed Marla and joined her on the bed.

"It's been a good evenin', Hailey, and I'm glad to know you. It'll be lonesome here when y'all leave, but I'd be proud if you want to call me 'Dad'. If you want to get a hold of me from college, I'll get that Skype thing here instead of sneaking to Janice's so I can see your face."

Hailey slipped her hand into Henry's and said, "I wish you were my dad, I need you badly."

"All right then, I'll be your daddy and you be my daughter. It's a pact."

Hailey scooted close and hugged Henry hard. She couldn't stop the tears from falling.

He just held her and let her cry. Kingston leaned against both of them as if to say, *"Me too."*

Later Hailey went to bed, and Henry sent Kingston with her although he whined about it. The dog didn't need to have any bad memories.

He stayed outside watching the heat lightening play across the sky. Kudzu leaves quaked in the slight breeze revealing their silvery underside to the bright moonlight.

"It's a beautiful night," he thought to himself, and a good life. He smelled kudzu's fragrance.

Henry sleep. Rest. Heart.

"I know it's comin', but I hope I have a little more time. I'd like two more years. Time to get us moved, and time for Hailey," he said. "I promised her."

Much later, he shuffled into the bathroom when the attack came. He stumbled backwards and sat on the only thing available--the closed lid of the toilet. The pain was unbearable for only a few seconds before he stopped breathing. He fell forward and would have landed face down on the floor except Kudzu slid from the silk ivy where it was entwined and grabbed him quickly around the neck and shoulders. It held him in that leaning position, still sitting on the toilet. His mouth slacked open like the ventriloquist dummy.

Sad.   Henry good. No more time.

Chapter 12

Everyone slept while Alice paced in her room. She continually rubbed her hands on her upper arms and turned her head back and forth.

"Hot, so hot," she said over and over.

Exhausted, she went to bed and fell into a fitful sleep. Within minutes, she threw off the covers and sat up. Her eyes opened, but she saw nothing. Then, barefoot, and in her night gown, she slipped out of the room. The floors creaked as she wandered down the hall and opened the sunroom door. Kudzu moved aside as she stepped out into the yard and the moonlight. Her full moon walk began and kudzu watched. Grief held the plant at bay, for now.

Alice stumbled through the marshy ground back into the peach trees where the creek overflowed its banks. There was still a strong undertow and vines interlaced underneath. Water rose above her ankles and calves the further she walked while her gown soaked up the liquefied mud and clung to her legs. Vines curtained down from tree branches to block her advance, but Alice forced her way through.

She hummed to herself as she walked further and further back. She started down the creek bank when saw John and Ashley peeking out from the vines and calling to her. Alice changed direction away from the creek.

When she reached the spot where her children were, they disappeared. Alice turned around and around searching. They were off on her right, waving to her. Alice followed and they again disappeared. This cat-and-mouse game continued until she left the orchard and moved toward firmer ground near the barn.

The moon came into full view as she crossed the yard. She

stopped and stared upward while the bright moonlight washed over her. Alice whispered gibberish, giggled, and swayed in tempo to some unknown beat. The swaying became dancing as she whirled and gyrated her head and arms and moved closer to the barn.

"Dance with me, Henry, it's Esbat," she said. She stopped dancing when she reached the doorway and began shaking her head from side to side.

"Not here, not here," she said, and turned toward the oak tree where the vehicles were all parked. She looked inside the windows. "Not here, not here," Alice said again.

She climbed onto the tractor and tried to start it, but Til never left the key in the ignition. Over and over, Alice's hand went through the motions of starting the tractor. Finally she sat still and let her arms dangle freely while she tilted her head as if listening to some inaudible voice.

"Yes," she said, and nodded. "Dead."

Presently she climbed down and slowly circled the veranda, stopping to look through each dark window as she passed and knocking on the glass. When she reached the bathroom, a light was on. Henry was sitting inside. Alice called his name over and over, but he didn't respond. She knocked loudly several times before circling the house again, and again looking in the windows and knocking. She exited the veranda, got on her knees, and looked under the house.

"Not buried here." She stood up and meandered away.

Her wanderings took her to the front yard and across the road where her orchard now stood. She breathed in the aroma of fresh peaches, yet they smelled slightly different somehow. It didn't matter. What mattered was her trees were alive again. She picked several peaches and sat down in the middle of the gravel to eat them. John and Ashley were sitting on the veranda waving to her.

"Hi, Babies. Want some peaches? Momma will get you some," Alice said. She returned to the orchard, and gathered as many as her arms could carry. She fell in the ditch while returning to the road, but John picked her up and carried the peaches to the veranda. The three sat there quietly eating, and Alice was content. Fragrance filled the air.

"Your Daddy can't come eat some with us," she said. "He's dead. These sure are sweet, aren't they? They make me sleepy. Do they make you sleepy? Let's all go to sleep now, okay? Night, night." Alice folded her hands in her lap, and slept.

..........<>..........

The first time Alice knocked, Marla jumped in her sleep. She looked out the window and saw Alice appearing as wild as any ghost. Stifling a scream, and thinking it was a nightmare, she turned over and drifted back to sleep. Lily jumped up on the air conditioner and looked outside. *"Alice real,"* she said, but Marla didn't hear.

Kingston barked when Alice rapped on Hailey's window. The combination shook her so badly, she fell out of bed. Kingston crawled toward her as if he had done something wrong. Hailey held him tight.

"It's okay," she reassured him. It scared me too."

She was still sitting on the floor when another set of knockings came. Hailey wasn't in a position to see over the air conditioner. All she saw was a fist hitting the glass.

She heard Kingston say, *"Alice,"* and she groaned.

By now, everyone was awake. Tilfort had seen Alice the second time and was not happy about it. Hailey, David, and Marla stumbled out of their rooms and met in the hallway. Tilfort joined them, wearing only pajama bottoms.

"I reckon Alice found a way to get us all up to look after her," he said.

"Daddy told us to leave her to her spells, and I'm not going out to chase her through peach trees or high water anymore," David said. "Mamma can bang on my window until it breaks, and I still won't."

Marla was holding Lily and grinning; she couldn't help herself.

"Looks like you're running around half naked again, Tilfort," she said.

He turned bright red and tried to cover his chest. He practically ran back into his bedroom. That broke the tension. After some good natured teasing through his door, he reemerged in jeans and t-shirt.

In all the commotion, only Hailey remembered that Henry wasn't with them. He had planned on using the couch rather than the bedroom. She walked over, hoping that Henry was still asleep or at least sitting there. He wasn't.

"Where's Henry?" Hailey asked. "I hope he didn't go outside after her."

"I'll check the sunroom and out back," David said, rushing down the hall, stopping to glance in the bedroom first. He thought maybe his father had gone in there.

Tilfort went out the front door and saw Alice sleeping in a chair.

When he returned, he said, "I found Alice and at least she's gettin' her beauty rest on the veranda. Didn't see Henry and it's bright enough out there to spot him. I'll go he'p David look outside."

Marla decided to sit with Alice in case she started sleepwalking again. Lily jumped out of her arms and refused to go with her. She joined Kingston instead.

Hailey noticed some communication pass between the pets. Kingston walked to the bathroom door; he scratched at it with his paw and whined. *"Henry here,"* he said.

A fearful shiver crawled up Hailey's spine as she knocked and called, "Henry, you in here?" There was no response even though she could see light shining off the doorsill.

She knocked again a little louder, but again received no reply. She slowly opened the door and peeped around, not wanting to disturb him in case he hadn't heard. No, he *hadn't* heard.

Hailey shook and hyperventilated as she broke into sobs and sank to the floor. She couldn't breathe; it felt like an iron band was constricting her rib cage. Her jaw locked open and muscles pulled the corners of her mouth into a grimace; only groaning sounds escaped as she grabbed Henry around his knees.

"Daddy! Daddy! Daddy!" she moaned incoherently over and over as she leaned her head against his thigh. "Why?" Her sobbing only intensified as tears rained down her face and mucus poured from her nostrils, both dripping onto the floor.

How long Hailey stayed that way only the pets knew as they slid inside next to her. Kingston licked his beloved master's dangling hand, and then rested his head on Hailey's ankle; Lily stood on her hind legs and nuzzled Hailey's sodden cheek. The girl was oblivious to any comfort they offered.

When the sobbing abated somewhat, Lily left the room and went to the front door. There, she called and clawed the screen until Marla opened it, thinking the cat wanted out. Lily backed up, still calling.

"Hailey needs," Marla heard her say. It was the first time she had ever heard any animal speak, and it surprised her. She also wasn't sure she heard right or if the cat could hear her. It was a new experience, but one Marla had little time to savor as her 'mother instincts' kicked in.

"What does she need, Lily?" Marla asked.

"Come," the cat demanded and turned toward the hallway. When she saw Marla following, Lily lead her to the bathroom.

"Oh my *God*!" Marla exclaimed as she rushed to gather her daughter in her arms. Kingston moved aside so she could reach Hailey.

"Daddy's dead," Hailey panted against her mother's chest. By now her nostrils had swollen shut, and she was breathing from her open mouth. Saliva dripped onto Marla's pajama top as her panting got louder and faster.

"Oh, Baby, I'm so sorry," Marla said as she rocked her inconsolable daughter back and forth. "Let me get you out of here. I have to tell the others, and they will need to move Henry; there's not enough room for us all in here. Let me take you to your bedroom. You don't want them to see you like this because it's not your father. It could cause animosity."

"No!" Hailey shouted and pushed her mother away. "I *won't* get out of their way. I *won't* leave my daddy! I *won't*!" She grabbed Henry's legs again and shook so hard that she nearly pulled Henry down on top of her. Only kudzu held him tight; its leaves drooped as if dehydrated. It too felt her pain, but it had no fragrance left right now to send her way. It would be a few hours before its flowers could replenish any quantity.

Helpless. Sorry.

"Kingston," Marla said, "go get David or Tilfort."

Kingston whined and sat down. He wasn't leaving Henry or Hailey; he knew what it felt like to be pushed aside. "*No*," he said.

"Fine then, I guess I have to be the practical one." Marla left.

"Thank you, Kingston," Hailey said and hugged the dog so tightly she almost shut off his windpipe. He had to slide his paw between her arms and push her loose.

"*David coming*," Lily warned.

The door swung hard and bounced off Hailey as David entered. Kingston and Lily fled.

"Get out of my way," he said.

Tilfort was second in the door. He stepped around David, reached down, and picked Hailey off the floor. He ignored her protests and carried her to the couch. Then he sat down next to her and held her hands.

"I know'd your feelin's for Henry 'cause I watched you," he said, "but David's all ate-up right now, and Alice'll be hysterical soon as I wake her up. You don't want them stampedin' over you.

"Can you call the sheriff or an ambulance for me? Doin' somethin' will get your head back straight. It's goin' to be all about them, but I can't care for both 'cause they'll split me in two. Y'all I've got, and I asked Marla to stay with the pets in her room; I don't trust David or Alice not to hurt them right now. Please he'p me."

Hailey nodded then sniffed. He handed her his bandana and told her to blow real hard.

"There's paper towels in the kitchen," he said. "You're gonna need more than a hanky to clean up. When you're ready, you call. I got ta wake Alice now." He made a silly grin at her and walked out on the veranda.

Hailey slowly cleaned her face in the kitchen while the front screen door banged open and Alice ran screaming through the house; Tilfort followed. She ignored the cacophony and continued to splash cool water on her flushed skin; it felt good and sobered her for the tasks ahead. Then she dressed in her room and combed her hair. By the time she finished, she felt in control of herself. At least enough to call the sheriff's department and request an ambulance.

Poor Tilfort, she thought. The noise was incredible even through her closed door. She knew she couldn't hear anything on her cell so she slipped out to get the kitchen phone. She saw Alice suctioned to her autistic son and screaming, "Hold me, David, hold me, he'p me." David was shouting, "Get off me, Mamma. Tilfort get her off."

Dixie had the night shift. She could hear the voices in the background while Hailey carefully explained the situation.

"Lordy, I'm glad you're calm," she said. "Usually I have to decipher all the screaming there when things go si-gogglin. At least your call is normal; been a lot of crazy stuff tonight. I'll tell Sheriff Gilesby, but I don't imagine he needs to come; just the ambulance. Everyone knows Henry was living on borrowed time. Tell the family I'm so sorry."

"Nice lady," Hailey thought. "I wonder what she meant about 'crazy stuff'." She shrugged and went to help Tilfort.

Henry was lying on the hall floor when she reached everyone. She wasn't sure they should have moved him, but maybe it was more respectful. David stood pressed against the wall, eyes glazed and saying nothing; he looked incapable of functioning. At least Alice left *him* alone for the moment while she vented all her hysteria on Tilfort.

"You see that damned vine around his neck. It was chokin' him. That's what caused his attack. He came in to use the toilet and that vine grabbed him around the shoulders and held him so he couldn't get away while it wrapped around his neck. It's as plain as the nose on your face, Tilfort. Don't be so damn dumb. It sneaked in there and hid in my ivy decorations and waited for the chance." Then Alice spotted Hailey standing there.

"You found him. You know that hellish plant killed him, don't you? You saw it do it, didn't you? You straighten him out. He doesn't have enough sense to bell a buzzard."

Hailey believed that kudzu simply kept Henry from falling, but she knew that Alice wasn't about to listen to anyone except herself.

"No Alice, I didn't see anything like that. The ambulance will be here soon to take Henry to the hospital where the coroner can decide. Let me get you a sedative and some water. This is too much for you right now, and I don't want you to have nightmares."

Hailey turned on the loving concern. Too bad she didn't feel it; she simply wanted to shut the bitch up. She put her arm around Alice and steered her toward the bedroom. It was almost pathetic how easily her cousin took directions as long as she was coddled.

Hailey found the sleeping pills in the bathroom. She refused to look toward the toilet even in the cabinet mirror for fear that she might break down again. She grabbed the pills and retreated quickly. Then remembering that sugar or chocolate always helps women, Hailey searched the kitchen for something sugary along with sweet tea. She found two cookies.

Alice was sweeter than the tea when Hailey handed her the cookies and pills. "Take two, Alice," she said. "You've had a terrible shock and you don't want to start sleepwalking on top of all this. Let me get you a clean nightgown and a towel and wash cloth to get the mud off you."

"Mission accomplished," Hailey thought to herself as she tucked the drugged woman into bed. Alice asked for Lily as she fell asleep, but Hailey didn't think the cat would join her, and she was right. Lily switched her loyalties earlier after Alice told her to "go to hell." The pet felt deeply hurt and betrayed that her owner turned on her. Now she took her cue from Kingston who thought Hailey had no faults.

Elroy and Marvin finally arrived, and Hailey pointed down the hall when they came through the door. David was still pressed against the wall and as unresponsive as the paint.

"Sorry we took so long," Marvin said. "Kudzu is all over all the roads; I think it found its own stash of fertilizer. It's even downed some power lines and cut internet service to a few people. We knew it wasn't an emergency since Henry's already dead so we drove slower."

Hailey thought the paramedic was especially talkative tonight. She stayed in the living room out of their way but within earshot.

Tilfort explained how Henry was found and helped them slide the body bag underneath his corpse. Elroy zipped it shut from feet to face and the three lifted Henry onto the gurney. David watched every move. The sound of the zipper closing over his father echoed over and over again in his ears.

After some condolences, Elroy and Marvin pushed the gurney toward the front door. Tilfort followed and Hailey held the screen open for them, but nearly slammed it in their faces when she heard what Marvin said next.

He turned back toward David, "Sorry about your losing Janice to Harlem. I thought you two were a good pair, but she's more Harlem's age. I guess that might be part of it; that and they're both Cherokee and like kudzu. Tough break, guy. I've got a couple of single cousins if you're interested. Good looking too. Let me know and I'll fix you up." Marvin whistled as they wheeled Henry away.

David was still unresponsive while the paramedics loaded his father into the ambulance for transport; he'd had too little sleep and too much emotional turmoil, and his Asperger's prevented him from expressing much of it. But after Marvin dropped that bombshell on him, the pressure was too much. Adrenalin kicked in and as it flowed through his body, he exploded.

He ran past Hailey and Tilfort and down the drive to catch the ambulance, but the men were already on the road. He tried to chase them while screaming, "Stop, stop, I want my daddy! Give him back!"

Marvin had the radio on and neither he nor Elroy heard. The lights receded into the darkness as David tripped and fell down in the gravel, still crying, "Daddy, come back."

Tilfort and Hailey were watching from the veranda. He waved Hailey to stay back as he walked to David to comfort him, but the distraught man simply shoved his friend away with abnormal strength.

"Come on back inside, David. I got some bourbon in my

room. It might take the edge off your hurtin'."

"Get the fuck away from me," he shouted as he pulled himself off the road. "Where's your ax? That goddamn kudzu took my girl and my daddy. I'm going to destroy it all tonight, right now, and you're not stopping me. I'm going to burn down this whole damn place and I don't care who burns with it, even you. I'll gladly cook my witch mamma to hell. Now get me that ax!"

Hailey quickly grabbed the ax from the corner where it usually leaned and slipped back into the house. She ran to the sunroom and shoved it under the sleeping couch.

"David, it's late and no time to go choppin' nothin' nor burnin' nothin' neither. Please let me he'p you."

David pushed past him and dashed to the veranda. The ax wasn't there. He charged through the house and into Tilfort's room. The work room in the back held an extra ax. He grabbed it and went out the side door where Tilfort stored a five gallon container of gasoline. Carrying both, he ran toward his work shed.

Tilfort bolted through the sunroom. Hailey stopped him long enough to give him his ax.

"Thank'ee, but he's got my extra, and I suspicion he got the gas too. You hold on to this one," he said. "Follow me, but don't get too close. I might need ya."

"No more flowers for your tables, Janice," David said while pouring the liquid everywhere and tossing down matches. He backed out quickly as the gas ignited and flames flew everywhere.

When Tilfort reached him, David punched him in the face.

"Leave me alone," he yelled and ran off. Tilfort looked at the flames shooting from the shed and decided he couldn't save it. Then he saw David advancing on the barn.

"Hailey, he's goin' after the barn. We got to get the cars

away," Tilfort bellowed.

Hailey hit the ground with the ax, leaving the handle sticking up so she could find it if needed, and ran for the house. When she burst into her mother's room and scooped the keys off the dresser, Kingston slid backwards getting out of her way. Marla was sleeping, but sat bolt upright when Hailey charged in. Lily jumped off the bed and hid underneath.

"What's going on?" Marla demanded.

"Moving the cars. Go back to sleep," Hailey yelled over her shoulder as she raced out leaving the door ajar. Kingston followed. Making a quick decision, Hailey grabbed her purse containing her cell phone from her room. "No extra keys, in case David circles back," she thought.

Tilfort was already backing Henry's car away when Hailey ran for Marla's. Kudzu slid out of her path. She jumped in, turned the ignition, slapped it into reverse, and spun gravel and grass as she raced the car to safety. She passed Tilfort running back on foot.

"I'll start the van. You get it out whilst I get the tractor."

Hailey took both set of keys with her, threw her purse in the trunk, and checked Henry's car.

"No key, good; Tilfort kept it," she thought and ran. The flower van was idling when she reached it and Tilfort was driving the tractor away.

Back out front, Hailey said, "Here's your keys; I've got mine. Now what?"

"He's chopping the kudzu off the barn doorway. I think he's goin' ta burn it from the inside out. I've got ta get that ax away before he hurts hisself, but I don't know how. He's gone crazy."

Hailey said, "I'll try to get the gas can while you distract him."

"I help," Kingston said as he ran toward David.

Tilfort and Hailey followed, but Kingston ran faster; she knew *he*, at least, had a plan while they didn't. They would have to follow the dog's lead. Somehow it seemed natural, if funny.

The dog ran in circles around the man as if he wanted to play. He jumped and yipped and wagged his tail. David turned round and round, attempting to keep the dog in front of him. He dropped the can and gripped the ax with both hands. Kingston's actions seemed like any average dogs, but he knew to stay out of reach.

"Get away, you damn dog. I don't want to play anymore," David shouted, flailing the ax in all directions. Kingston kept circling and blocking. While the dog distracted him, more vines trailed down forming an impassable barrier to the barn. Tilfort tried to talk to him, but David wasn't listening.

Hailey waited behind the huge oak. As soon as she saw her chance, she darted out, and grabbed the gas. She heard David yell and start after her, but he never came. She figured Kingston stopped him.

She intended to pour it on the grass far away from the barn, but changed her mind.

"We might need this to get out of here fast, the tank's low," she thought and half carried, half dragged the cumbersome container to the car. She got the funnel out of the trunk and emptied the contents into the tank. She threw the now empty can under the tractor and ran back.

No one was there, not even Kingston.

Strange, she thought. Not knowing what else to do, she picked up the hose, turned on the spigot, and walked to the burning work shed. She figured the gas was burned up and the watery grass wouldn't catch fire, but it was something useful. She sprayed water into the building until the flames were gone and only steam rose. The kudzu vines had retreated and weren't burning, but she sprayed them too, just in case.

"There," she said. "Don't say I never did anything for you."

Kudzu said nothing. It was occupied elsewhere.

"You're welcome," she said and carried the hose back to the house.

By now she was completely exhausted and dirty. She didn't want to go in the bathroom, but it was a necessity. She took a quick shower, wrapped a towel around her, and slipped into her room. She cracked the door in case Kingston returned, but then the keys poised a problem. She decided to put both sets in her pajama pocket instead of on the dresser. *Lumpy but safer*, she thought. She collapsed into bed and was asleep within minutes.

Chapter 13

When Hailey ran with the gas can, David charged after her. He didn't know whether he wanted to burn the barn or to take the van and kill Janice. Kingston herded him back by jumping and barking, first one side, then another. Tilfort figured out the dog's method and tried it himself.

"There's no keys in the cars, David," he said. He waited until the dog moved to a new spot, then he moved opposite and called out again. "Hailey's poured out the gas, David. I have the keys here, David. Let's talk, David."

David couldn't focus: Kingston's barking, Tilfort's yelling, and both circling was too much to handle. He roared and escaped to the orchard. The man and dog followed.

Tilfort found Hailey's ax sticking up from the ground and took it with him. He had no idea if he would need it, but figured it would be better than leaving it.

It was dark under the canopy of thick vines; only a little moonlight dusted through. David stumbled and bounced off trees, low branches, and other obstacles. His eyes adjusted to the low light, but only enough to make out black shapes silhouetted against deep gray. He randomly chopped any vine near him as he maneuvered his way deeper among the trees.

"Murderer! Daddy never hurt you. Janice's wrong; you're no gift. You took her away. Now she's with Harlem. You going to kill her like Daddy? You like killing, monster? Is it fun? I'll spend the rest of my life killing every bit of you I can find." With every bellowed sentence, he swung the ax, hitting more tree trunks than vines and working himself into a maniacal frenzy.

He was obsessed with hacking the thick vines off one particular tree where Henry had hung a tire swing for Ashley and him years ago. The chains were rusted nearly through and kudzu had claimed the tire, but it was still recognizable.

Kingston reached David before Tilfort did and tried his tactic again. This time, however, he had little maneuvering room and David grabbed him by the collar."

"You damn dog," he said, "I ought to kill you, but Daddy loved you, so I can't. But you won't be in my way again. David grabbed a vine hanging down from a tree branch and yanked Kingston up on his hind legs. He looped the limber stem through the dog's collar several times, tied it, and left the dog dangling. If Kingston's lost his balance, he would strangle.

"Hang, you son of a bitch," he said.

Tilfort picked this particular moment to find his friend. When he called out, David whirled and cursed.

"I told you to leave me alone. Now go to hell." David swung his ax. Tilfort dodged. He swung again, and this time he hit Tilfort in the calf. Even though the ax was dulling, it still sank deeply enough to cut an artery. David grabbed Tilfort's ax, threw it, and pushed further into the orchard. He ignored his friend's plea for help.

Tilfort knew he was in trouble. He pulled his belt off and made a make-shift tourniquet. He tried to crawl out of the orchard, but it was a futile attempt with all the thick vines, and any exertion would only make him bleed out quicker.

Kingston tried to jerk loose, but he only managed to turn in circles. He couldn't help himself, let alone Tilfort. He whined piteously. *"Can't,"* he said.

Tilfort yelled, "Hailey, he'p," over and over, but the blanketed trees muffled his calls, and Hailey was deeply asleep. He tried one last idea; he figured it was crazy, but he had nothing to lose. He talked to kudzu.

"I know'd we ain't on the best of terms, but I could sure use some he'p right now. You talk to Hailey and she talks back. Could you tell her I'm bleedin' to death, and to call for he'p. Tell her where I am, please. I'd be right grateful," he said.

He didn't know if kudzu would help or even if it could hear him since he wasn't empathic or psychic, but he was all out of ideas. He turned onto his stomach and used his elbows to propel himself over the vines while trying not to flex his leg. He was surprised to hear dragging sounds as the plant moved out of his way. Some vines wrapped tightly around his bleeding calf, making a better tourniquet than his belt. Tilfort resumed his crawling through the cleared path. Kudzu would do no more; it had other interests. The rest was up to him.

David. Betrayed. Hurt. Kill.

Kudzu waited as David ran deeper and deeper into the orchard and neared the creek before it struck. One vine lashed at his face, slicing his cheek open. Another coiled around his ankle and yanked him to the ground where more encircled his legs. He leaned over to chop at his shackles in an attempt to sever them, but another stem whipped around the ax, and jerked it away.

Next, it towed him by his legs down into the water and held him under. Before he could drown, kudzu pulled him back out and dragged him like an old sock all around the sodden landscape. It threw him over its vines and against tree trunks, and lifted him into the air only to throw him head first like a yoyo toward the ground, and to barely stop his fall before he could crush his neck or head. In a final burst of hurt and bitterness, kudzu slammed the ax into David's chest while he dangled feet first high up in the twining vines.

Alicessss. Revenge.

Now it concentrated it's hatred on Alice as it regrouped by her side of the house. Kudzu tore a corner of the screen and snaked from the window down onto her coverlet and waited, writhing like tentacles in anticipation. Its vines, still lying under the bed from earlier, crawled up both sides of the mattress and interlaced over her body, holding her down as effectively as six interns controlling one patient in a mental ward. Camouflaged stems around the perimeter of the floor now crisscrossed in the center of the room. More entered through the pine boards wherever there were holes.

It filled the room, blocked the door, and covered every piece of furniture. Eager stems spilled from the closet. Alice was unaware of the danger she was in, thanks to the sleeping pills. Even her empathic abilities couldn't fathom Kudzu's intent or hatred.

. The waiting vines on the coverlet waited no longer. They rammed into her mouth and up her nostrils. Her body twitched and flailed as the stems slithered down her windpipe and gullet. Other pieces penetrated her ear drums and inched into her brain.

More wrapped around her neck and squeezed. Her eyes flew open in horror as she gasped for breath. No air was available no matter how hard she coughed to clear her airways or how hard she tried to draw in oxygen. She flung her head left to right and up and down attempting to loosen the vines. The twitching continued as her eyes opened wider and bugged out. Then the flailing stopped and her body relaxed. The look of horror remained on her face.

All die. Hate.

Chapter 14

Lily awoke with a muffled yelp. Her nightmarish visions were true, and she knew she couldn't help Alice or David, but Kingston, she could. She meowed in Marla's ear and gently butted her head. Marla was dead to the world and emotionally drained from sleepless nights, traumatic days, and Bogerty's attack. She couldn't help, but Hailey would.

She slipped out of Marla's room and pushed through Hailey's door. Lily saw kudzu camouflaged against the vines in the wallpaper. It was sliding out from under her bed and down from the closet. It scared her.

"No time. Hurry," she told herself.

She bounced on the bed, walked on Hailey's sore head, smacked her eyes, and screeched in her ear as loudly as any cat ready to attack a rival. It took two such screeches, but it worked. Hailey sat up, shaking her head.

"Damn, Lily, did you have to be so loud?" Hailey said as she rubbed her ringing ear. "What's wrong?"

"Kingston, Tilfort, help, NOW," Lily threw her thoughts at Hailey.

"Okay, let me grab some clothes."

"No, NOW, the impatient cat demanded.

"Pajamas, it is then," Hailey said as she slipped on her sandals.

Lily flew down the hall through the sunroom, calling to Hailey.

"Slow down some, Lily, I can't run as fast as you can. At least not until I wake up."

Lily didn't slow down; she charged into the yard, yowling. The white of her fur shimmered in the moonlight, giving Hailey's eyes a bright spot to focus on. By now, she was fully awake and able to quickly follow Lily through the marshy grass into the flooded orchard. When the light dimmed to deep gray, she followed Lily's constant howls. Kinston heard them coming and helped Hailey find him by barking as best he could.

"Oh my God, Kingston!" Hailey cried as she rushed toward the dog. She tried to unfasten the collar, but the stem was tightly wrapped around the buckle. She couldn't untie the knot David made or break the stem, nor could she pull the collar over his head. She was effectively making things worse; he was gagging from the pressure on his neck.

"I don't know what to do. I don't have a saw or knife," she said. "I'll have to go back and get something."

"*Lift. Bite,*" Kingston said.

"Huh, I can't bite that stem," she said in confusion.

Lily understood. "*Lift Kingston.*"

Hailey still didn't understand, but she lifted the heavy dog up somewhat so that the pressure was off his neck. The taut vine slackened and looped downward slightly. Now Hailey understood. She strained to lift Kingston higher until he could get it in his mouth. His powerful jaws, inherited from his pit bull father, made short work of the wood. It wasn't the first kudzu he'd chewed in pieces. He was free just in time as Hailey's muscles couldn't lift him any longer.

She unwrapped the chewed end through his collar and pulled it off, giving him room to breathe.

"I guess David did this. Where's Tilfort?" She asked. Kingston bolted from her arms.

"*Tilfort help,*" Kingston said and ran. Lily and Hailey followed his barking.

They found Tilfort lying in the grass at the edge of the orchard. Lily and Hailey had gone right by him when they ran to Kingston. He was covered in mud and blood and looked nearly dead. Hailey rushed to him and knelt down.

"I'll get help," she said, but he grabbed her wrist.

"David's got an ax. He's dangerous. Be careful," he said.

Lily disagreed, "*David dead. Kudzu.*"

Fear set in; she remembered what Henry told her. If kudzu killed David, it might try to kill everyone. "Mom. Alice," she said, and was on her feet and racing for the house. Kingston followed while Lily stayed with Tilfort.

Hailey ran to her room to get her cell phone from her purse, forgetting it was in the trunk; she could call 911 and check the others at the same time. She grabbed the door handle expecting to rush in. The door barely moved and she slammed into it. Not understanding, she stared at the wood, then tried again. The door moved slightly. She pushed harder, and it opened enough to show vines covering everything. She sucked in her breath and ran to Alice's room. This time the door opened easily showcasing the horror inside.

"Mom," Hailey screamed and flew through Marla's door. Kudzu was already on the bed and curling around her mother's face. She rushed in and yanked the vines off, screaming, "Mom, Mom, wake up, get up," and literally pulled her mother off the bed.

Marla woke quickly when she hit the floor.

She looked up at her daughter and said, "What did I miss?"

Kudzu's on a rampage, killing everyone, and now it's after you. Hailey began throwing her mother's clothes into the hall. Get your stuff to the car; it's out front. Take Kingston with you. Here's your keys."

She jerked Marla's cell phone off the side table and punched 911 with one hand and continued pitching things into the hall with the other. Marla crammed the suitcase, grabbed her equipment case, and ran while Hailey attempted to explain the situation to Dixie.

This time the dispatcher strained to hear Hailey's jumbled message. She did catch:

"Kudzu killed Alice and David. Tilfort bleeding, maybe dead."

Dixie had heard enough over the last couple of days to know how lethal kudzu was. She didn't doubt what she heard.

"Run, Hailey," Dixie yelled. "Come here to Unity if y'all can. If not, go the other way to Danvers. Clovis is sheriff there, and I'll let him know. I'm sending Harlem and the ambulance."

Hailey rushed for the car. Her mother was sitting on the ground whimpering. She had a choke hold on Kingston's neck. The ax that David had taken from Tilfort was embedded in the trunk with vines attached.

"Where's your stuff?" was all Marla said.

"I can't get it. Put Kingston in the car, and let's go. I'll drive. Hailey jumped into the driver's side and started the engine while Marla opened the back door, but Kingston refused to enter.

"Oh my God, I forgot Lily. Get in, Mom!" Hailey said. She climbed out but stayed by the car ready to leave if the cat didn't come.

"Lily! Lily," she screamed in desperation.

"*Lily comes*," Kingston said and climbed in the back.

Hailey slammed Kingston's door as soon as she saw the cat running towards her. Lily jumped into her arms and clung with all her claws. Hailey raced to the driver's side, tossed the cat to Marla, and jumped in.

"The ambulance is coming. How's Tilfort?" she asked as she gunned the car and sped down Seed Tick.

"*Not Dead*," was all Lily said.

When Hailey reached 57 to turn toward Unity, the road was blocked by a two-foot wall of twisted vines. She got out and screamed at kudzu.

"We've never hurt you. Let us go."

One vine slapped the car hood and Hailey grabbed it. She felt the plant's hurt and fury. It warned her not to go to Unity or anywhere else in Georgia.

Go home or die. Watching.

"Whatever you say," she agreed and turned the car toward Danvers.

Vines shaped a one lane tunnel on Highway 57, arching over and enclosing the car. Kudzu was escorting and protecting them during the night drive, maybe. Hailey was able to drive faster that way since she knew she couldn't run off the road, but her hands still shook. She had the eerie feeling that kudzu might change its mind at any moment and shove them into a valley, especially if there was any deviation from its orders. It didn't, and as soon as Hailey turned off 57, the tunnel slid off the road.

Lily had been clinging to Marla since they left Seed Tick. Now she relaxed and lay down. Marla relaxed also, especially now that the cat's claws no longer gouged her neck and shoulders. Kingston, who had been sitting upright and staring out the window, turned around twice in the back seat and lay down with a long, drawn out sigh. Hailey stopped in Cheryworth to get gas. Then she drove on throughout the night.

It watched.

.

Epilogue

The following winter was bad in the Midwest as well as in the South. In Indiana, the first snow fell in early November, followed by a blizzard on the fourth of December. Heavy snow with drift-causing winds didn't let up until late March, then storms added layers of ice until the end of April. Subzero temperatures prevailed all winter, rendering salt and other melting chemicals worthless. Only sand cut the slippery surfaces until another round of snow fell. Alternating layers of sand and ice built up four inches on some roadways over the winter.

Snow plows slid off roads and wreckers had to be lashed to trees when attempting to extract the heavy trucks. Even then, they danced around on their tethers making the extraction dangerous; chains broke. Indiana's public schools closed for a total of four weeks that winter. Hailey's college even shut down three times when authorities ordered drivers to stay off the roads.

Several weather records were broken that year. Deer and other hungry animals were reduced to eating tree bark as no amount of digging through the hard layers unearthed any vegetation. People were asked to put out all their food scraps for the starving creatures. Birds clinging to branches literally dropped dead both from starvation and the cold; when their feet relaxed, their bodies fell, littering the ground beneath the trees.

The same weather system that blanketed Indiana also struck Kentucky, Tennessee, and northern Georgia, but Georgia was not prepared for the amount of snow and ice that assaulted it as temperatures were normally above freezing. Houses weren't insulated against such harsh conditions. Ice coated lines, already draped in kudzu and strained to their limit, broke, causing power outages. People were freezing in their houses. Shelters were set up in schools and churches to accommodate those who could get there.

Georgia basically screeched to a standstill. The state owned no snow plows or stores of salt. People had no idea how to drive on the snow-covered or ice-laden roads. School buses and public transit couldn't run and people couldn't get to work.

Kudzu loved warm weather. That's why it grew so prolifically in the South. It had a toe-hold in southern Indiana, but vines and leaves froze out during the winter. The shorter growing season prevented the roots from stockpiling huge quantities of food, so kudzu lay dormant, using its stored nutrients until the warm sunshine and rains of late spring provided the nourishment needed for growth. Therefore, it was possible to control the invasive plants most cold years; it got the upper hand when winters were mild.

In northern Georgia, the winter this particular year was a minor setback for kudzu. Leaves and vines were coated in multiple layers of ice. Even the tops of a few massive roots froze, shutting down its outward flow of nutrients, effectively starving its many vines until a thaw. To conserve stored food, all kudzu plants halted their growth temporarily and sacrificed their blighted leaves.

Kudzu wasn't worried because its collective genetic memories recalled cold in China and Japan. It knew this extreme Georgian weather was abnormal and milder temperatures would soon return; it simply waited. It had fed well for decades and had enough food stored within its massive roots to wait seven years if necessary. Many vines on the ground lay under an insulating blanket made from its own discarded leaves.

The kudzu which draped across trees and topped man's technology felt the cold more as they were devoid of any covering. These bare entangled vines revealed all they had engulfed with startling reality; its green blanket no longer softened the effects. Dead trees, shrouded homes, and buried trucks were now uncovered and stood testament to kudzu's encroachment, and families' lost hopes.

Another secret was revealed when the leaves fell. Entangled within the vines throughout the South were human remains in various states of decomposition; however, most were not over three years old as best the coroners could ascertain. Georgia had over one hundred such dangling bodies, many concentrated in the northern part. Some were undoubtedly murder victims thrown into kudzu by their killers in hopes that the missing persons would never be found. The rest were not so easy to classify. Many theorized that kudzu had killed them while skeptics announced that they were suicides or accidents. All wondered how many more bodies might be found in Georgia's kudzu if the frigid weather had traveled further south.

With the state not equipped to handle the icy road conditions, and not having proper winter gear, it was difficult for the authorities to remove the bodies. Many gruesome tales abounded of corpses landing on men who were cutting them down, or of men slipping off ladders or ropes and dangling next to the rotted, frozen bodies until coworkers rescued them.

Reporters snapped pictures for television, newspapers, and the internet. Whatever the media, the story went "viral." No one would ever again look at kudzu without wondering if hanging corpses hid within. Such was the making of horror tales for Halloween, novels, and cinema. The mystery of what happened would be speculated for generations.

Only a small group truly knew the answer. The Cherokee lived with the knowledge on a daily basis. Their Elders wondered if any ceremony they might perform could free their spirit guardian from its judgmental and lethal ways. They have considered asking Mother Earth and their ancestors' spirits for help, but they know if they fail, kudzu will slaughter many within their nation in retaliation. Janice's Great Grandmother and Grandfather are conferring with other elders via email concerning the possibility. They don't dare speak out loud for fear kudzu will hear them. They protect their thoughts with spiritual energy.

Hailey and Marla live in kudzu's shadow even in Indiana. They saw the viral photographs everywhere and realized that no one would believe them if they told their story, and Hailey sensed that kudzu still watched them. She often contacts Janice via email or texts just to talk, and because of their talks, Hailey sent her father James a birthday card.

She and her mother are moving to upper Michigan next summer when Hailey finishes her freshman year. Hopefully kudzu won't grow there since Michigan winters are colder and longer than Indiana's. Kingston and Lily are in full agreement.

The End

Author Rosemary Coven

Rosemary Coven aka Mary Deborah Bowden first developed a love of story-telling and writing from her father, Bradley Garrison Patrick, when she was very young. In the early 1970's, Deborah began creating her own tales. She enjoys writing about animals and authoring books for children.

Deborah taught English and Creative Writing in public schools and college for twenty-five years. After retiring, to raise her daughter, Erin Bradleigh Bowden, Deborah honed her story-telling skills by telling her stories to Erin. Now that she is retired and Erin is grown, Deborah enjoys spending much of her time writing.

Deborah lives in Nashville, Indiana. She has been in love with Brown County since her college friends enticed her there in the early 1970's. She visited once and knew she had found her home. Brown County is a quaint little community full of unique shops, artist's workshops, craft works, and much, much more. Deborah was born in Owensboro, Kentucky and lived in Hartford, Kentucky for a time. She returned there annually for many years to visit her grandfather before he passed on.

She is a member of the Writers, Readers and Poets Society of Brown County, where she serves as Treasurer. Deborah is also a member of the Bartholomew County Writers Group in Columbus, Indiana.

Photo credit: Jude Edwards

www.ingramcontent.com/pod-product-compliance
Lightning Source LLC
Chambersburg PA
CBHW070221260626
47160CB00002B/626